Do Virgins Taste Better?
and
Other Strange Tales

Deborah Millitello

Word Posse

Dedication

To my children: Tricia, Dan, and Ben

Acknowledgments

I want to thank my writing group: Laurell K. Hamilton, Mark Sumner, Martha Kneib, Sharon Shinn, Lauretta Allen, and Tom Drennan, for all their help and insight. I also want to thank Barb Young and Marion Zimmer Bradley for the guidance and suggestions they gave me. Thanks to my family, Mom, Dad, Dennis, Diane, Donna, and Lonna for understanding my writing obsession. And for Carl, you're still the love of my life.

From Word Posse

The Naturalist, Mark Sumner
Sleeping the Churchyard Sleep, Rett MacPherson
Pandora's Mirror, Marella Sands
The Water Girl, Deborah Millitello
Thor McGraw & the Ice Man, Tom Drennan
Restless Bones, Marella Sands
Do Virgins Taste Better? and Other Strange Tales, Deborah Millitello

Visit us at www.wordposse.com
Like us on Facebook: facebook.com/WordPosse
Follow us on Twitter: @WordPosse

This book has been typeset in Fanwood. Titles and headers are in Alien League. Cover design by Word Posse. Cover art by Dana Newman

ISBN-10: 0-9861511-8-1
ISBN-13: 978-0-9861511-8-7

Table of Contents

Murder Most Fowl

When I was young, I loved to watch a program called "Fractured Fairy Tales" that took traditional tales and gave them a delightful twist. I like to do the same.

The Goose was dead. Anyone could see that. And the murderer had been caught plucking feathers. It all seemed a simple case of theft with intent to feast. At least, that was how it appeared, but something told me there was more to this situation than just a hungry peasant stealing poultry.

First, the Goose wasn't an ordinary goose. It was the mainstay of Basilopolis' economy because it laid golden eggs. Yes, I said golden. You know, that yellowish metal that's used for the standard coinage of most countries. Instead of mining and refining gold as other countries did, Basilopolis' Keeper of the Treasury went to the Goose's nest twice a day and gathered eggs of solid pure gold. Sometimes one, sometimes two, no one could predict which.

A young beggar named Thom stood before me, bound so tightly his chest barely moved when he breathed. His patched, oversized clothes were as dirty as his gaunt face, and he stank worse than the filthiest stable I'd ever smelled. Dozens of guards surrounded him, some keeping back the crowd that filled the judgment hall, some intent on saving Thom for themselves. Lovely way to start a morning.

"Do you have anything to say in your defense?" I asked.

Thom crumpled to his knees and started to cry. When he spoke, his voice was higher than I'd expected. "Please, Your Highness, I didn't do it!"

"Your Honor," I corrected him. "I'm the King's Magistrate, not King Cannard the Fifth himself."

"Your Honor, I just found it layin' there by the wall," he sniffed and rubbed his cheek on his grimy shoulder, "an' its neck all twisted an' I just picked it up an' took it back to my house an' started pluckin' it 'cause I was hungry an' I didn't do anything! I didn't, I didn't!" He started blubbering.

"Silence," I said, frowning. He sniffed back several sobs and gazed at me, trembling. "That's better. Now, what is the evidence against him?"

One of the king's guards opened a burlap sack and dumped the contents on the stone floor before the dais where I sat. A few feathers—long, white, and marked with a swirl of black—floated down beside a crude knife. "These were beside the prisoner when we found him, Your Honor. I saw him plucking the Goose myself. He's guilty, no doubt."

I looked at the feathers, then at the dead Goose, its neck broken. Only one goose in the kingdom, or in the world, had those black swirls on white wings. It was the royal golden egg-laying Goose.

"Where was he found?" I asked.

"Just beyond the north wall, close to Fern Wood. Bunch of thieves." The guard kicked Thom.

I glared at the guard. "Don't touch him, soldier, unless I tell you to."

The guard paled and swallowed visibly. Being half-brother to the king does have its advantages. Makes people very polite and civil.

I studied Thom. He looked as if he belonged in that nest of hovels huddled between the castle and Fern Wood. "How did he get in?" I asked.

The guard looked puzzled. "Well, he, uh, must've snuck in the gate."

"Have you checked with the gate wards?"

"Then I suggest you check with them."

The guard spoke to another soldier, who almost ran from the room, then turned back to me. "Even if he didn't come in the gate, he could've climbed the walls."

"How? With what? Did you find any grappling hooks and rope in his house? Any ladders tall enough to reach the top?"

"Well...no. But we didn't search everywhere. Besides," he drew his foot back to kick Thom again, then stopped dead still, glanced at me, and put his foot on the floor, "he's guilty. The King knows it, the people know it, I know it. That gutter rat's a traitor! I say hang him and be done with it!" The rest of the crowd cheered him.

I sighed, blinked my aching eyes, and ran my fingers through my short, greying hair. An hour's sleep wasn't enough for anyone, especially after an all-night feast. And I'd slipped away early. "Who discovered the Goose was missing??

"I did, Your Honor." A buxom woman with masses of red curls stepped from the early morning shadows that darkened the hall. Her mouth was a little too narrow, her eyes a little too wide to be called beautiful, but she was attractive in a rough sort of way. And she was vaguely familiar.

"Who are you?" I asked, trying to remember where I'd seen her before.

She bowed low. "Marnie Sieler, Keeper of the Royal Goose, Your Honor."

Ah, yes, the original owner of the Goose. "Were you with the Goose when it was stolen?"

She hesitated for a moment, then said, "No, Your Honor."

"Where were you?"

"I went to speak with the husbandman about some new straw for the Goose's nest."

"Straw?" I closed my eyes and rubbed the lids. "At night?"

"He's busy during the day, watching after the royal herds and flocks."

I stared at her silently, just stared, letting the time pass. She looked away, back at me, at the ceiling, at me, at her hands, at me, shifted her weight from one foot to the other. I knew she was lying, and she knew I knew. "Is there anything else you have to say, Mistress Marnie?"

She scrunched her lips, glanced left and right, then shook her head. She knew more than she was saying. I'd have to talk to her again—after I'd talked with the husbandman.

I glanced across the soldiers in the room. "Are the Royal Goose Guards who were on duty tonight present?"

Two soldiers stepped forward, wearing red tabbards with golden eggs embroidered in the center of each. One man had an eye swollen shut, scratches on his face, and held his side. The other man's head was wrapped with white cloth, his nose was bent and twice the size it should be, and he walked with a limp. They tried to salute and grimaced.

"Tell me exactly what happened," I said.

The one-eyed soldier spoke first. "We was standing duty like always, when I heard a noise. Herman and me, we knew Mistress Marnie wasn't there, so we crept into the Goose's room and looked around, but it was dark, see? I mean we couldn't see too good, but the garden door was open, and we hurried quiet as a mouse to the door and looked out."

"An' we don't sees nobody at first, does we, George?" Herman broke in.

"Shut up, Herman," George growled, then continued. "We didn't see anyone at first, then I saw a shadow running for the wall. We ran after it, and suddenly we was attacked by two or three men..."

"Or five or six," Herman said.

George glared at his comrade. "Three or four, counting the first one we spotted. We fought and kicked and tried to stop them."

I shook my head slightly, disgusted. "Which was it: two, three, four, five, or six?"

"Four," said George.

"Six," said Herman.

Wonderful, the guards were as honest as Mistress Marnie. "Why didn't you call for help?"

"I started to," George said, glaring at Herman again, "but one of them grabbed me around the neck and cut off my breathing. I passed out not long after."

"An' I tries to stop them," Herman said, bobbing his head, "but they hits me on the head and knocks me out. I woked up when Mistress Marnie was shaking me and screaming the Goose was gone."

I glanced around the hall until I spotted Marnie standing beside the court wizard, Arcus Magnus. "Mistress Marnie, where did you find the guards?"

"On the porch leading from the Goose Chamber to the garden."

"And how long were you absent," I paused, a half smile threatening to escape my practiced detachment, "talking to the husbandman about...straw?" I think her face reddened, but I wasn't certain.

"An hour, maybe two," she said as she glanced at the wizard next to her. "Three at the most."

"Hah!" Herman said with a sly grin. "She'd been gone at least four or five hours before the fight."

Mistress Marnie started to reply, but glanced at Arcus first. Interesting. "I...may've been gone that long," she said.

I didn't speak for several minutes, merely looked across the crowd. The people shuffled, jostled, grumbled to each other until at last I said, "So the Goose could have been stolen anytime during the night."

She nodded slowly. "I suppose that's so."

There were too many secrets, too many 'hows' and 'whys' to settle the case right then. I needed to check several things before I was satisfied I knew who had killed the Goose. "I must think on this for a time," I said as impassively as I could. "Take the prisoner away until I render my verdict."

The guards fairly grinned at that.

"And..." I said snowflake soft, "he will be unharmed until I determine his guilt or innocence. Do you understand?"

The guards muttered something, but saluted me and dragged Thom from the hall. A servant stuffed the dead Goose, feathers, and knife in the burlap sack, and carried it to the guarded chamber where I keep evidence during trials. The crowd wavered a few moments, then drifted out of the judgment hall.

I stood, stretched, and wished I'd had more sleep. My stomach churned, reminding me I'd eaten very little at the banquet and that it was past sunrise.

Maybe after I'd checked out a few things, I'd go to the kitchen and see what Wild Bill could find for my breakfast.

I shuffled from the hall and headed toward the Goose Chamber. I wanted to see where the murder took place, and maybe find something, anything, to confirm my suspicions. If Thom had crept inside and killed the Goose, there would be some sign of his presence. My stomach growled insistently, and I decided to visit the kitchen first.

I'd left the main corridor and turned toward the kitchen when suddenly Arcus Magnus stepped from a doorway. He was nearly a head shorter than I and stringy as a winter-starved deer. He moved like shadows, silently, as if he had no true substance.

"Your Honor," he said in his low, oily voice, "if I could speak to you on a matter of importance?"

"What—" my voice cracked slightly as I swallowed my surprise, "what matter?"

"What is to be done with the Goose? I mean, what will happen to its body? Surely, it will not be roasted and eaten, not the Royal Goose. It was unique, a treasure lost for all time. If only I had been allowed to study it while it was alive, if I could have discovered what forces had combined to create such a marvelous bird...but no, I was never allowed to examine it, and now it is gone! Such foolishness, such waste!" His hands twitched like jumping spiders, and his sallow face was taut.

It was several moments before he looked at me again, his greying brows furrowed. "I am sorry for my outburst, Your Honor. I am distraught at the loss of so great a treasure to our city and our king. I know that I am being bold, but I request the Goose's body for study." He paused, then bowed a bit too quickly, as if he were nervous. "That is, if you would grant me this most extraordinary privilege. I should be exceedingly grateful." He gave me half a smile as his fingers played with a small but bulging leather pouch tied to his woven belt. The man had all the subtlety of a hammer.

"I will inform you of the King's wishes in this matter," I said, giving him my most daunting stare.

He cringed, shrank back, bobbed a bow, and hurried away. I don't think he wanted the King to know about the request. Hmm. Arcus, a suspect? Possible. I'd keep him in mind.

I walked toward the kitchen and paused at the doorway, hoping to spot something for breakfast. Wild Bill was propped on his sturdy stool, gulping a mug of something. Greenish-gold mead trickled from the sides of his wide mouth and added another layer of stains to his broad apron. It always surprised me that the man could drink half a barrel by himself and still turn out a meal fit for a king. And Bill had been doing it for years, since the campaign against the Wildmen of the Western Steppes. That was when he'd earned his nickname, fighting with a sword in one hand, an iron skillet in the other, and howling like a Wildman.

"I'm hungry," I said.

Bill choked, dropped the nearly empty mug, then turned pale when he saw me. "What?" he croaked. His breath forced me back a step.

"I'm hungry," I repeated. "Is breakfast ready yet?"

He glanced around the kitchen slowly, his eyes wide as if he'd just that moment realized where he was. "Breakfast? No. I mean, yes. There's some honeyed bread in the oven, should be done by now."

He staggered to the brick oven in the wall beside the great hearth and opened the iron door. Heat flooded the room, and with it came the fragrance of yeast and honey and spice. Using a wooden paddle, Bill removed two flattened rounds of golden bread, slid them onto a table top, went back, and kept taking out rounds until a dozen lay cooling on the wooden table. He broke one of the first rounds in half and gave it to me.

I took a bite and smiled. Delicious as always. I'd never been dissatisfied with his cooking. Except last night at the banquet. The beef had been roasted to tender perfection, but the stuffing he'd served with it was, well, inappropriate. Made with apples, raisins, and no sage. I'm very partial to sage. And no poultry had been served, although the venison had been excellent. I suppose one disappointment in twenty years wasn't bad.

I left, nibbling on the bread, and instead of heading for the Goose Chamber, went up to my room on the second floor. I needed to talk to my servant, Dale. The fifth son of a minor noble, Dale was more intelligent than all his brothers together. I depended on him for information and insight. Sometimes, he heard things, gossip whispered among servants that I'd never hear otherwise.

Dale was waiting for me with a cup of wine. Maybe not the best thing to have with the honey bread, but my throat was so dry, I wouldn't have turned down anything wet.

"What's the latest gossip among the servants?" I asked, then stuffed another chunk of bread in my mouth.

"What kind of gossip, Master?" he asked as he cocked his head. His hair and eyes were chestnut brown, and he was scarecrow lean.

"Anything recent—surprising, unusual," I mumbled around my breakfast. "Anything about anyone connected with the Goose."

"Ah." Dale nodded. "Rumor has it that one of the Royal Goose guards recently married and bought property just outside the city."

I halted in mid-bite and stared at Dale. "A guard? When? Who?"

"One named Herman. He married about a month ago, a few days after buying Squire Plantus' land."

"But that estate is worth more than a guard makes in several years!"

Dale smiled and nodded.

I'd better check into Herman's sudden wealth. "Anything else?"

"Of course, Emperor Genyoofar has made no secret he wanted the Goose or one like it. He envies our wealth."

Yes, I thought. Genyoofar hap Igdon of the Seventh Dynasty of the Divinely Blessed Empire of Kolbindi—a grand title for the puny ruler of an even punier realm—had tried to wheedle information about the Goose for a long time. At that moment, Genyoofar was in Basilopolis for a meeting to discuss the mutual threat posed by the Wildmen. Last night's banquet had been in his honor.

"Anything else?" I asked.

Dale grinned. "Master Magnus is bedding Marnie Sieler. I heard she's having a wedding dress made, which she expects to use soon."

The Wizard and the Keeper of the Royal Goose. Another link between the Goose and Arcus.

"One more thing," Dale said. "One of the servants at the banquet told me that Morganstern Gleb laughed and drank a toast when he heard the Goose was dead. His hands have dozens of scars; the Goose nipped him every time he collected the eggs."

Morganstern Gleb, Keeper of the Royal Treasury. I hadn't considered him a suspect before. I'd heard him grumble because he'd had to collect eggs like some farm boy. Maybe he'd been bitten once too often, his pride damaged by his menial task. Add him to my list.

"All right," I said as I washed my sticky hands and dried them, "I want you to talk to the husbandman. Find out if Mistress Marnie talked to him during the night, and if so, how long she was with him. Also, bring the sergeant of the night watch and the Captain of the Guard when you return."

"Yes, Master." Dale bowed and left.

I looked at my reflection in the polished mirror and winced. A middle-aged man who'd been up most of the night wasn't a pleasing sight. Mirrors should be covered until midday at least.

The Goose Chamber was my next destination. I went downstairs, past the kitchen, and turned the corner. No guards bracketing the door. No reason for them, now. I pushed the door open and went inside.

Mistress Marnie was there, sparring with another goose, the companion of the dead Goose. Geese need to be with their own kind or they die of loneliness—at least, that's what Marnie had told the King. So a second goose had been purchased at the same time the Goose had been declared Royal Property and moved from Marnie's farm to the castle.

The companion—a sleek, grey female—was nipping at Marnie, flapping wildly, and squawking and hissing while the Keeper tried to loop a rope around the bird's neck. Marnie swore at the goose and kicked at it, and the goose flew out to the garden.

"A most gentle technique," I said, trying not to grin.

Marnie jumped, cursed again, then turned as red as her hair when she saw me. "Your Honor, I was trying to remove that...beast from the castle, since it's not needed anymore."

"Noisy bird." I massaged the back of my neck. "Does it always act like this?"

"No," Marnie said as she threw the rope to the floor, "I've never seen it act like this before. It's usually good-tempered. Except when strangers are present."

"Why didn't anyone hear the companion when the Goose was stolen?"

Marnie started. "I...don't know." I wondered if her surprise was genuine.

I scanned the room. The pale grey walls and floor were all smooth stone. There were three doors: one to the corridor; one to the garden; and one to Marnie's own bedchamber. Two large boxes, filled with straw, sat in the center of the room. Nearby was a feed bin and a tub of water. Straw was scattered across the floor, probably from the deadly struggle.

I searched the floor, lifting large clumps of straw, moving smaller ones aside with my foot. There were no eggs in the nest, golden or otherwise, but I found some crushed and nearly dried leaves in one. I rubbed them between my fingers and sniffed. Herbs of some kind.

I walked out to the square, walled grassy garden. A dark purplish-red stained the stone porch, probably where Herman hit his head. The grass looked trampled, but that could've been from the geese. A small pond took up the southwestern corner, still shaded by the castle. The smooth, stone walls were high and kept clear of vines. Any thief would've had to climb over the outer wall, cross the surrounding courtyard without being spotted by patrols, climbed the inner wall to this garden, kill the goose, and get out the same way. No, I decided, not likely, especially for several men, if the guards were telling the truth—which I was certain they weren't.

To the right there was a door in the garden wall I tugged on the iron ring handle, then pushed on the door, which didn't budge. Looking over my shoulder at Marnie, I asked, "This leads to the kitchen garden, doesn't it?"

She nodded. "Sometimes I let the geese go in there. The King insisted they get to eat what they want from the garden."

"Is it usually unlocked?"

"No. Only when the geese were feeding. It was left open so they could come and go when they wanted."

"Who besides you has a key?"

Marnie slid her forefinger back and forth across her lower lip as she gazed at the door. "One for the kitchen and one for the Goose Guards."

Three keys. That cut down the possibilities. "You had yours with you all night?"

"Well," she stared at the grass, "no. I left it on a peg in my room except when I was using it."

"Get it."

She hurried back inside the Goose Chamber while I examined the door for evidence of force. There was none, no splintered wood, no pry marks, nothing. If anyone had come through this way, they hadn't broken in. Marnie returned moments later with an iron key. I took it from her, unlocked the door, and pushed it open.

The kitchen garden was the largest open area inside the castle walls, except for the courtyard. Several gardeners were hoeing and watering rows of beans, cabbages, greens, and herbs. At the far end a pair of boys picked plums and peaches from the small orchard. And two women carried baskets of vegetables to the open kitchen door. I shook my head and sighed. I wouldn't find signs of any intruders here. Even if there had been footprints, they were probably lost in the passing of all the servants.

I walked to the kitchen and found Wild Bill growling orders to the other cooks and scraping leftover stuffing into the compost barrel. "Where do you keep the key to the Goose garden?" I asked.

Bill nearly dropped the bowl he was holding. "Don't creep up on me like that! If I'd been holding a knife, you'd be dead now!"

"I'm sorry," I said, stepping back a bit. Bill looked as if he'd been drinking ever since I'd left him. He was formidable sober. I didn't want to know how dangerous he was when drunk. "Where do you keep the key to the Goose garden?"

He pointed to a peg beside the door.

"Anyone could take it from there," I said.

He kept scraping. "Only if I didn't see 'em do it."

"But anyone could, if you weren't here."

"I suppose."

"How many had the opportunity?"

He was silent a moment. "Let's see—six undercooks, four gardeners, two boys, seven serving women, four drudges, and me."

Twenty-four people. Wonderful. That narrowed the possibilities. "How many of those were in the kitchen last night?"

"All of 'em," he said as the last scrap of stuffing fell into the barrel. "Because of the banquet. We were working all yesterday."

"Did you see anyone come through who shouldn't have been here?"

He paused, then shook his head.

"Did anyone here go to the Goose garden regularly?"

Bill dropped the wooden spoon he held, then cursed as he had to fish it out of the barrel. "Oh, uh, yeah, I took greens and stuff to the geese sometimes, or I sent one of the boys in my place. Other than that, no one."

I sighed and went back through the gardens to the Goose Chamber. I wanted to see the Goose Guards and ask about their key. The companion goose was wandering about the garden, honking and flapping. Noisy creature. Just as I reached the door, I heard arguing.

"He'll be back any moment! Now leave!" Marnie hissed.

"But the Goose—I must have its body! I may be able breed a new one, and then we will be wealthy beyond even your dreams." I recognized the man's voice: Arcus Magnus.

"What good would another golden goose be if the King takes that one, too? I'm almost glad the thing's dead. It'd serve the King right, thief that he is! He stole it from me! It was mine; he had no right to take it!"

"Kings have the right to do as they wish, my dear," Arcus replied. "However, if I can retrieve the Goose's body, I may be able to create another, perhaps breed an entire race of golden egg-laying geese. Every ruler in the world would pay to own one. And we would be richer than any of them."

I stepped into the room. Marnie and Arcus started, glanced at each other.

"So," I said as I watched them shift nervously. "Marnie, you resented that the Goose was taken from you by royal decree."

Marnie didn't say anything.

"The King shouldn't have taken the Goose, should he? It was your Goose, your property. You would've been rich, a queen yourself. He had no right to take what belonged to you."

"No, he didn't!" Marnie shouted, then clapped her hand over her mouth. "I mean, yes. Yes, he did. He's the King."

I didn't stop. "It wasn't fair, was it? The King stole the Goose from you. And then he made you its keeper, a servant to a goose! But you found a way to pay him back, didn't you? Kill the goose, take away what he'd taken from you. You killed the goose and threw it over the wall, didn't you? Didn't you?"

"No!" Marnie shouted. "I didn't! But I wish I had! It might be worth seeing the King's face when I admitted it! But I didn't!"

"Where were you all night?" I held up a hand. "And don't tell me you were with the husbandman. I didn't believe you the first."

"She was with me," Arcus broke in. I don't think I'd ever seen so much color in his face. He almost looked healthy.

"All night?"

"Yes!"

"Did anyone else see you?"

"I doubt that anyone espied her entering my chambers. We were most discreet."

I almost smiled. So discreet that every servant in the castle knew about the affair. "You were together all night?"

"Yes."

I turned to Marnie. "And when you returned, you found the Goose gone and the guards unconscious on the porch?"

She glared at me. "Yes."

She might be telling the truth, but I'd keep her—and Arcus—on my list. "You are both under arrest for dereliction of duty. Don't try to leave the castle."

I'm not certain what Marnie mumbled under her breath as I left the room, but I'm sure it wasn't complimentary.

I headed back to my room, hoping Dale had returned. I climbed the stairs to my floor when I saw the shadow of someone tiptoeing up the spiral stair to the next floor, the guest floor. I followed; I couldn't help being curious.

As I reached the dimly lit top, I flattened against the cool stone and peeked around the corner. George, the Goose guard was just entering a guarded room—Emperor Genyoofar's room. I stepped out into the corridor, walked past the door guards, and entered the room next to the Emperor's.

Being Minister of Justice and half-brother to the King, I knew all the secret passages in the castle. One was in the room next to the guest quarters occupied by Genyoofar. I opened a wardrobe door, entered, and eavesdropped through a disguised opening. "You fool! Now the Goose is dead, and I have nothing!" Genyoofar's voice was as puny as his stature, almost a whine. "I should expose your stupidity to King Cannard!"

"That wouldn't be smart, Emperor," George said as soft as snow. "You'd have t' tell how you know. And you couldn't do that without exposing your part. Do you really want to tell the King you paid me to steal the Goose? While you're still here in the castle? I don't think you'd leave here alive."

Genyoofar didn't reply immediately. "Very well, but if you ever reveal any of this, I'll have Delmairin take care of you."

I shivered. Delmairin was Genyoofar's wizard-assassin and the only force keeping the emperor in power. Black Del he was called. Even Arcus was wary of him.

"And you remember, Emperor," George said, "I've hidden evidence of our deal in a safe place. If anything happens to me, everyone'll know what you've done."

"Then we will keep our secret."

"Yes, we will."

I heard footsteps, then Genyoofar's door opening and closing. So, George and Genyoofar had conspired to steal the Goose. Had Herman found out? Was that why the two guards had fought? Possible, but not likely. George would've killed Herman to silence him. Or maybe Herman had blackmailed George with the knowledge. Herman's sudden wealth had to come from somewhere.

I'd have to talk to George and Herman separately. And I'd have to tell the King that it was time for Genyoofar's visit to end. I didn't trust that imperial snake any farther than I could throw him.

I headed back to my room and found that Dale had returned. Beside him the Captain of the Guard stood spear- straight. Dale bowed. "As you requested, Master. The sergeant of the night watch has been sent for. He left the castle grounds for his home in the town."

The captain saluted. "You wished to question me?"

I nodded. "You have the key to the door between the kitchen garden and the Goose garden?"

"Yes, Your Honor."

"Do you keep it with you always?"

"Yes, Your Honor."

"Have you ever noticed it missing?"

"No, Your Honor. I even sleep with it around my neck. It never left my possession."

Third key accounted for. "Has there been anything unusual among the ranks lately?" I tried to sound careless, as if making idle conversation.

"Unusual?"

I poured myself a cup of wine, offered it to the captain—who refused it—then I took a sip. "Rumors," I smiled, "gossip, anything strange."

He thought for a few moments. "No, not that might have anything to do with the Goose...except one of the Goose guards is leaving. Married about a month ago and decided to try his luck at farming. I heard he won a lot of money gambling and bought Squire Plantus' estate."

Gambling. I should have such luck. "Thank you, Captain. Please see that no one leaves the castle without my permission. I need to speak to the sergeant as soon as possible. Also, I want to see Herman and George, but separately at first, then together. Can you arrange it?"

"Yes, Your Honor." He bowed and left.

I turned to Dale and took another sip. "Who do you think killed the Goose?"

"Who had the most to gain from its death?" he asked.

"Everyone," I said. "Everyone but you, me, and the King."

"Why not the King?"

I gazed at Dale, puzzled. "Why would the King want to kill the Goose? It brought him more wealth than he'd ever had."

"True, but I've heard he's unhappy with his new wealth." Dale leaned closer and whispered, "I've heard Treasurer Gleb has shown the King evidence that Basilopolis' treasury was being depleted almost as fast as the Goose laid eggs, what with all the extra guards needed to protect the kingdom from invasion. And goods from other realms are becoming so inexpensive, merchants and craftsmen of our country are being driven out of business. Gold is too common here, and its value is dropping."

I considered what he'd said. Economics had never been my strong point. I'd been relieved when I'd been appointed Minister of Justice instead of Keeper of the Treasury. "So you think the King could've been behind a plot to destroy the Goose?"

Dale shook his head. "I'm saying he had reason to want the Goose dead. But so did many others. Every ruler in the world wanted the Goose or wanted it dead."

More suspects. Just what I needed.

"Oh, the husbandman said Mistress Marnie did come to talk to him about straw, but it was just after sunset and only for a few minutes."

I smiled to myself. A knock at the door startled me. Dale opened it, and George strode in.

He saluted. "You sent for me?"

"Yes," I stammered. "I'm surprised to see you so quickly."

"I met the Captain downstairs. He said you wanted to see me, so I came straight here."

"Ah." I nodded at Dale, who bowed and retreated to the inner chamber. "Now...how long has Herman been blackmailing you?"

George jerked. "Blackmailing me? Why would he do that?"

"He found out you were working for the Emperor of Kolbindi."

The guard turned milk-white. He started to say something, but no sound came.

"Herman found out, didn't he? And he threatened to turn you in if you didn't pay him. You've been giving him money to keep quiet. That's how he had the money to buy the land and marry. What happened? Did you stop paying? Is that why you fought?"

"No—I—no." George started to sweat. "It wasn't like that. He wasn't blackmailing me. He didn't know about the Emperor."

"Then where did the money come from?"

He hesitated, then his shoulders sagged and he hung his head. "From the Goose."

"What?"

"We took eggs from the Goose," he mumbled. "Not often, only when it laid two and when Marnie wasn't there. We'd agreed not to spend the money until we retired in a few more months. But Herman wanted some girl from the town." George cursed under his breath. "She wouldn't marry him if he didn't have a house and land and enough money to keep her. So he used his part to buy Plantus' land, then married the girl. I told him he was a fool.

"Last night, he said he needed more money. I told him he'd have to wait 'til the Goose laid another egg. He said he couldn't wait that long. He needed the money now. I said he couldn't make the Goose lay another egg, and he said that I could give him some money. I told him no. He said if I didn't, he'd tell the Captain I'd been stealing eggs an' I'd be hanged as a traitor."

"And that's when you fought."

George nodded slowly. "I told him he'd hang, too, but that didn't make any difference to him. He wanted the money, that was all that mattered. But we didn't kill the Goose. We fought in the garden, he knocked me out, and I don't know what happened after that. Marnie said she found Herman on the porch, his head bleeding. He said he fell and hit his head, and I guess it's true. I don't know who killed the Goose."

I looked at George silently. I didn't believe he or Herman had killed the Goose either. But I didn't know who had. "About what time was it you fought?"

"Sometime after sunset. It was dark."

"You may go now." I paused as he saluted and turned to leave. "And I think you and Herman should resign from the Guard today. I don't want you here in the morning...or the King will hear the whole story."

George faltered for a moment, then proceeded out the door.

Dale came back. "So, if it wasn't Herman or George, who was it?"

I rubbed a cramp from my shoulder. "I still don't know. I have to talk to the sergeant first, then I'll talk to a few more people. I'd love a few hours of sleep."

The corner of Dale's mouth twitched. "Perhaps later, after you've solved life's great mystery."

I gulped the rest of my wine and immediately regretted it. Wine on a nearly empty stomach is a recipe for nausea.

I was feeling better by the time the sergeant of the night watch arrived. He looked as if he felt as good as I did.

He bowed awkwardly, as if stiff or sore. "You sent for me, Your Honor?"

"Yes. Did you notice anyone on the walls last night who wasn't supposed to be there, anyone not usually present?"

He thought for a moment. "No...no one I'd find suspicious." He frowned slightly, then continued. "No one I hadn't seen before."

"No reports of noise or shadows or anything?"

"No, it was quiet."

"Who walked the north wall last night?"

"Nob, Cully, and me."

"You heard nothing? Saw no one?"

"No one unusual."

"Well, did you see anyone usual?"

He looked uncomfortable. Maybe I was getting somewhere.

"Who was it?" I asked.

"Your Honor, I don't rat on other soldiers."

Ah. A soldier. "George?" No response. "Herman?" Still no response. I didn't want to list every soldier in the Guard. "Sergeant, if you don't tell me, you can explain yourself to the King. And he won't be as understanding as I am."

The soldier's hands clenched, and his eyes turned flint cold. "He can't help himself. Sometimes, he walks the walls like he was still a real guard. Sometimes, he's just sick and heaves his guts up over the walls. But he can't help it. Drink's got a hold on him and won't let go."

"Who?" I asked.

He looked at me, his eyes almost pleading. "Wild Bill."

Wild Bill? "He was on the wall last night?"

The sergeant nodded.

"When?"

"After midnight sometime."

After midnight. The feast was in progress then. Marnie was with Arcus. Herman and George were unconscious. Morganstern Gleb, Emperor Genyoofar, and the King were at the banquet. The banquet where there'd been no poultry, in spite of Genyoofar's known preference for goose. Where the stuffing had been made with apples and no sage and...I reached in my pocket, pulled out the herbs I'd found in the Goose's nest, and sniffed them again. Marjoram—the same aroma as the stuffing, poultry stuffing, poultry stuffing with beef roast. I sank down into my seat, stunned. My voice a whisper, I said, "Thank you, Sergeant, you may go."

"He won't get in trouble, will he, Your Honor?"

"You may go," I repeated.

"Yes, Your Honor."

I left moments after the sergeant did. When I reached kitchen, Bill was dragging the compost barrel outside.

"Bill," I said softly.

"I have to get this outside," he said, his words slurred as much by ale as by effort.

"Bill, I know."

The cook stopped struggling with the barrel and looked straight at me. His dark eyes were watery. "Know?"

"Yes, I know." I held out the herbs. "Poultry stuffing with beef."

He braced his thick arms on the rim, hung his head, and cried. I ordered everyone else from the kitchen, then put my arm around Bill's shoulders. "Why did you kill the Goose?"

"I didn't mean to," he sobbed. "I'd been busy with the banquet, checking sauces, baking pies, stewing fruit, roasting the venison and beef. I'd already made the stuffing then realized I hadn't got a goose. It was too late to get one from town. Market was already closed. Then I remembered the companion goose. Figured I could replace it later.

"I waited 'til no one was watchin', then I went through the garden gate. It was dark, and I didn't see Marnie or anyone else. I crept into the nest. The geese were sleeping. Thought I knew which nest was which 'cause I often brought greens to the geese...but I was drunk. Grabbed a goose and broke its neck quickly; didn't want it to suffer.

"Wasn't 'til I saw the goose in the light coming from the kitchen, I realized what I'd done. Couldn't take the dead Goose into the kitchen—everyone knew what it looked like. Had t' get rid of it, so I stuffed it in a bag and hid it in the garden. Later, I took the bag with me to the walls and dumped it over. Didn't know it'd be found so soon. Didn't mean to kill it, just the companion. I didn't mean it."

No grand conspiracies, no intrigues, just a drunken mistake. I stood there looking at him, not knowing what to do next. I'd proved the peasant boy Thom was innocent, but what about Bill? I could talk to the King, explain the situation. Wild Bill deserved better than disgrace He'd saved the King's life numerous times and had been the hero of the war with the Wildmen.

Maybe I could get Bill a pardon, especially if I explained it was an accident. And if I emphasized the benefits to the economy, such as cutbacks in spending for the army. And now that I thought about it, Squire Plantus' estate would be just the place for a veteran soldier and Royal Cook to retire. I smiled to myself. I don't think Herman would dare complain.

Yes, I'd talk to the King. After all, being the King's half-brother does have its advantages.

A Grain of Truth

I've always loved fairy tales, but sometimes I wondered if the tales were told as they actually happened. (Yes, I know, they're not real.) But I like to make up my own versions.

The winner writes the history—whether it's the truth or not. Heaven knows that Queen Ella wrote her own chronicles, so of course everyone believes her. But I want to set the record straight before I die, even if I'm the only one who reads this account.

My mother was a handsome woman, a devoted wife and mother. Father was a very successful merchant, trading in salt, grain, wine, and fine cloth. My sister Genvieve and I never lacked for food or clothes. We were tutored in Latin and Greek by priests. We learned to play flute and mandolin, and to dance gracefully and to sing. Ours was a happy life. I thought it would always be that way.

When I was eight years old, Father became ill. The physicians bled him, leeched him, mixed herbal potions for him, yet nothing helped. He died three weeks later, leaving Mother grief-stricken but very wealthy. She mourned a full year before she took off her widow's black.

A month later, Baronette Geoffrey de Moreaux first called on Mother. He came to sell the last of his jewels to buy a dress for his daughter. Soon he came to visit, then to woo and court, finally to propose. I didn't like the way he stared at Mother. His face was too much like a fox eying chickens. But his solicitous manner, his gracious speech charmed her. He vowed his love for her and his devotion to Genvieve and me. Mother finally accepted his proposal, and they were married three weeks later.

Moreaux moved us all to his house and introduced his darling daughter Ella. I was stunned to silence with I saw her for the first time. She was twelve and tall for her age. Her hair was the color of golden thread. Her eyes were blue as sapphires. Skin as pale and translucent as skim milk. Lips red as roses. Hands and feet, small and delicate. Her dress was made of pink and white brocade with pearls and lace bordering her neck. She was the most beautiful young woman I'd ever seen, more beautiful than Mother.

"Ella," Moreaux said, "this is your step-mother."

Ella stiffened and glared at Mother.

"And these are your step-sisters Genvieve and Camille."

Ella looked us up and down, then turned to her father. "What ugly toads they are," she said. She stamped her foot and flounced up the stairs.

I was stunned. I knew I wasn't pretty; neither was Genvieve. We looked like Father, dark and plain. But no one had ever called us ugly before. Genvieve started to cry. I put my arm around her and tried to comfort her.

Mother embraced us both. "Why would she say such a thing?" Mother asked Moreaux, appalled.

He shrugged and followed Ella into the house.

Our lives changed drastically. There was no money for lessons or new clothes anymore, not for Genvieve or me. There was always money for what Ella wanted. It wasn't fair.

Mother went to Moreaux and pointed out that it was her money, and that it should be used for her daughters as well.

He laughed. "I'll use the money any way I choose."

"But it's my money!" Mother protested.

"No," he said with a smirk, "it isn't. When you married me, all your wealth and property became mine, to use as I will. *That* is the law."

"But—"

He slapped her so hard, she crashed against a heavy table. "Don't defy me again. Or your daughters will have nothing." He turned and walked from the room.

Ella did what she could to make our lives miserable. She pinched us, kicked us, told us how ugly we were. She delighted in making tears in our clothes, spilling ink in our shoes, taking for her own the few pieces of jewelry we had, making us fetch and carry for her like servants.

Once she told her father that I'd broken his favorite crucifix. I pleaded my innocence. That's when I learned one of the laws of nature and nobility: beauty equals truth equals goodness. Ella was beautiful. I wasn't. So Moreaux believed Ella, and I was punished for doing something I hadn't and for lying about the something I hadn't done. Moreaux beat me with a rod, then locked me in my room for two days without food or water. If he hadn't let Mother see me the third day, I might have died. I'd never hated anyone before, but at ten years old I learned to hate.

I thought things couldn't get worse. I was wrong. My life became an endless series of beatings. Genvieve's, too. One time she broke her arm when Moreaux knocked her down a flight of stairs. I was just happy she was still alive. Moreaux wouldn't spend money on a doctor for her so Mother had to splint the arm herself.

Every day Mother had a new bruise or injury. She changed from a handsome, proud woman to a frightened drudge, afraid to speak, hopeless, but she survived. We all survived—barely.

After five years of hell, we were freed from Moreaux. As he rode home from a neighboring noble's house after an unusually lucky night at cards, he was robbed and beaten to death by highwaymen—at least, that's the official story. Rumors said he was cheating, that the noble sent his own men to get back his money and teach Moreaux a lesson. Moreaux had the grace to die.

Mother was widowed again, widowed and nearly broke. The business Father had built had been leeched of its profits until it was almost bankrupt. Mother still had her tiny dowery, enough to keep us from starving, but not enough to keep servants.

"We'll all have to work and do without if we're to keep a roof over our heads and food on the table," Mother told Ella, Genvieve, and me. "No luxuries, no coaches, no gowns or jewels. We'll have to grow our food, clean our house, take care of each other."

Genvieve and I nodded. We'd been taking care of ourselves since we'd moved into Moreaux's house anyway.

Ella looked horrified. "You want *me* to work?"

"Yes," Mother said. You're the oldest so you can tend the animals during the day and help with the cooking in the evening. Camille, you—"

"Tend the animals!" Ella shrieked. "Do the cooking? I will *not*. I'm not a servant! I won't soil my hands for you! This is *my* house, and you're nothing but common serfs!"

"No," Mother said, "by law this is *my* house now, whether you like it or not." She sighed. "Ella, I know losing your father is hard for you, but we all have to go on. If we want to eat and live in this house, we *all* have to help, even you."

"Never!"

Mother stared at her for a moment, then shrugged. "Those who work, eat. Those who don't, won't. It's your choice."

Ella held out for two days before she started helping with the household.

We didn't have an easy life, but at least it was less painful than when Moreaux was alive. I washed clothes and milked our only cow. Genvieve fed the chickens and swept the floors. Ella grudgingly tended the pigs and sheep, spending as much time away from the house as possible during the day, and she learned to cook soup without burning it. She still called us names and made our lives miserable. o get back at her, we called her Cinder Ella because once when she got a smudge of soot on her face, she fainted from horror.

Mother worked from before sunrise until after sunset, trying to rebuild the merchant house as well as keep what we already had. It took a while, but finally, we didn't have to worry whether we'd go to bed hungry.

Two years after our stepfather's death, Mother received a letter with the royal seal of the king. We were invited to the palace, to a ball given for the crown prince. And the prince was going to choose a bride from the young women attending. Genvieve and I were so excited. We'd never been to a ball; we'd never been asked. Genvieve was still young, only fourteen, but I was sixteen and eager to dance and dance until dawn. Ella seemed almost annoyed.

"Well, it's about time that someone remembered who I am," she said.

"Oh, Mother, can we go?" I asked, almost afraid to hope.

Mother smiled. "I think it's possible."

"But what about clothes?" Genvieve asked. "We don't own anything fine enough for the palace."

"Well," Mother said, "business has been more profitable this year. I think we could afford material for dresses for the three of you."

"But what about you?" I asked.

"I have a dress that will do, one I've saved all these years." Mother patted me on the shoulder. "Now back to your chores. The ball isn't for a week yet."

That week seemed to drag on. Mother secretly bought material and sewed the dresses for us three girls. I begged to see them, but she just laughed and said she wanted to surprise us.

The afternoon of the ball she called us to her room. There on the bed were three satin gowns, the most beautiful gowns I'd ever seen. Genvieve's was violet with silver-edged lace. Mine was scarlet with gold-edged lace. And Ella's was cornflower-blue with white lace threaded with pink satin ribbons.

"Oh, Mother!" I said as I held up my dress. "It's beautiful!'"

Genvieve hugged Mother. "Thank you, thank you!"

Ella just stared at her dress. "You expect me to wear that to the palace? To have the king and the prince see me in that...that ugly rag?"

My sister and I gaped at her.

Mother said nothing for a moment, then, "Ella, your dress is perfectly suitable for a ball. I made it to compliment your eyes and hair, just as I chose flattering colors for your sisters. There's no time to make another dress, nor money. You can wear this or nothing."

Ella crossed her arms and stamped her foot. "I'd rather not go at all!"

Mother sighed and shook her head. "I've done all I can. If you do not like the dress, then stay home, miss the ball. I'm tired of trying to be kind to you."

Ella flounced from the room, slamming the door after her.

Mother rubbed her eyes, then put on a smile for us. "Come, girls, let's fix your hair and get ready for the ball. Who knows? Maybe tonight you'll dance with a prince."

When Mother had finished with us, we looked in the mirror and gasped. We weren't beautiful, but we were striking in our new dresses. And Mother—she was as handsome as when Father was alive. Her auburn hair was highlighted by the dark green dress she wore. I was sure the prince would fall in love with her at first sight.

Mother had hired a carriage from the local inn. When it arrived, she tried one last time to convince Ella to come with us. Ella refused, saying she'd rather die than wear the blue dress. Mother threw up her hands, then hurried us to the carriage. I glanced back at the house as we drove down the drive. Ella was standing by the front door, ripping the dress apart and throwing the pieces on the grass.

When we arrived at the palace, I was astonished. I'd never seen such a building before—pure white stone glowing with torches and lamps everywhere. Gardens of roses scented the air. Music whispered from inside. I just stared for so long, Mother had to shake me from my trance.

I can't recall much of that night, only feelings. My heart pounding, my feet floating above the floor while I danced with several handsome young men— especially Sir Charles de Lenne—joy bubbling inside me. Lights, music, laughter. A voice announcing Crown Prince Malcolm, his dark hair and eyes, his lean handsome face that made me quiver. The gentle rush of swaying skirts as everyone bowed. It was all too wonderful.

Suddenly, silence rolled over the crowd like a wave. I glanced around the hall, trying to see what had happened. That's when I saw her—pale and beautiful as an angel. She wore a dress of purest white that glowed like moonlight. Her golden hair was perfectly curled; her skin, flawless. I'd never seen a woman move as gracefully as she did.

Prince Malcolm was as awestruck as the rest of the crowd. He walked toward her, never looking away from her face, and bowed when he stood before her. She curtseyed to him, then nodded when he asked her to dance.

He didn't look at another woman the rest of the evening. She was the only one he spoke to, danced with, shared a cool drink with. They were alone in the crowded ballroom.

"She's the one," I whispered to Genvieve.

"The one what?"

I chuckled. "The one he'll choose to marry."

Genvieve looked a little disappointed, but another young man asked her to dance and she was soon smiling again.

I was so caught up in the gaiety of the night, I almost missed the excitement. Just as the watchman was announcing the third hour, I noticed the beautiful girl had disappeared. No one actually saw her leave, but she'd vanished like mist in sunlight. Prince Malcolm looked for her frantically. The palace guards didn't see her pass through the gates. There was no sign of her anywhere. The entire court was talking about her as the ball ended in the first light of dawn. The prince was so desperate to find her that he ordered another ball for the next night, hoping she would attend.

I was exhausted by the time we reached home, but I couldn't sleep. I was too excited. "Mother, can we go to the ball tonight? Please!"

She yawned and smiled and nodded her head. "Why not? But we still have work to do before we can enjoy ourselves. Animals to be fed, house to clean." She yawned again. "Well, at least the animals must be fed. Then we can all sleep for the afternoon."

Ella was no where to be seen. I had to feed the sheep, goats, and chickens. We had a light breakfast, then we all went to bed.

That evening, Ella came to the kitchen long enough to tell us she still wouldn't go with us. Mother didn't bother trying to talk her out of staying home. I didn't care. If Ella wanted to sit at home and miss all the dancing, that was her choice. We left as the sun was sinking close to the horizon.

The ballroom was more crowded than the night before. Word of the beautiful girl had spread throughout the kingdom, bringing the curious who had missed the previous ball. The candles had burned down halfway when the beautiful girl appeared at the entrance to the ballroom. I hadn't thought she could've looked more beautiful than the night before. I was wrong. This time she was wearing a golden dress that shone like the sun. Prince Malcolm never left her side.

The ball was grander than the first one. Charles de Lenne and I danced so much, I didn't realize that the night had nearly gone until I heard Prince Malcolm calling for the guards. The girl had slipped away again. No one remembered when she had left.

Genvieve told me that the prince had been talking with the mysterious girl, sipping a cup of white wine and pointing out various members of the court, when she just wasn't beside him anymore. I was beginning to wonder if the girl were bewitched or simply insane. After all, who would leave the prince when he was obviously charmed by her?

We went home at dawn, tired but delighted. Another night to press between the pages of my memory, to be savored in years to come. I knew I'd never be this happy again.

We were all surprised when a messenger arrived with an invitation to a third ball. I thought Genvieve was going to giggle to death at the prospect. I wasn't as excited; two nights of dancing 'til dawn were plenty for me. However, since I probably wouldn't see the inside of the palace for the rest of my life, I decided I might as well enjoy one last dance.

Ella disappeared just before we left. Mother didn't bother to look for her. We'd all despaired of convincing her to come with us. It was her loss.

That night the palace blazed with candles. I danced most of the night with Charles de Lenne. I imagined what it would be like to be his wife but knew my family connections would never allow him to ask me.

Just after the clock struck twelve, the beautiful girl entered the room. This time she wore a silver dress sewn with diamonds that sparkled like stars in the night. The prince stayed by her, took her arm and wouldn't let go. He was in love with her; anyone could see that.

The chimes began to sound three in the morning when the girl started to leave. The prince wouldn't let go of her arm. She struggled, twisted, and finally pulled free of his grasp, then she ran from the ballroom with the frantic prince in pursuit. Guards scrambled to close doors, block stairs, seal gates, but the girl eluded them. This time she left something behind: a glass slipper.

The next part of the official history is mostly true. The prince went from house to house trying the slipper on every young girl in the kingdom. When he came to our house, Ella was with the sheep in the pasture by the woods. Mother sent me to find Ella although we knew she hadn't attended the ball. Mother was always fair.

Just as the prince was leaving, I arrived with a miffed Ella in tow. She demanded to try on the slipper. To our surprise, it fit. Ella was the mysterious girl! The prince was overjoyed. He took her back to the castle, and they were married a week later. Mother genuinely hoped Ella had finally found what she'd always wanted. Genvieve was a bit jealous. I was simply glad for some peace in our house.

Less than a month after that, the king died suddenly. Malcolm was crowned king, and Ella was crowned queen. That's when the lies and rumors began. Mother was accused of hiring men to kill Ella's father. No noble would believe Mother was innocent when the queen swore it was true. Mother was convicted and beheaded.

Genvieve and I were still young enough, we were brought to the castle. Ella made a great show of concern for "her dear sisters". She even discussed the possibility of a marriage between me and Charles de Lenne. He was kind and pleasant, and we became dear friends. I was happier than I'd been since Father died. I'd hoped that being at court my sister and I would be safe. I should've known better.

Late one fall afternoon a servant brought me word that Genvieve had been playing on the battlements and had fallen to her death on the rocky ground below. I knew Ella or one of her lackeys had pushed my little sister; she was afraid of heights. I also knew I was next.

That night, I stole from my room and crept through dark corridors until I reached the lowest outer wall. Mouse-quiet, I climbed down a knotted-sheet rope and ran as fast as I could back to my house. No sooner had I arrived than I heard horses galloping towards me. Ella had discovered I'd escaped.

I fled toward the woods, hoping I could lose them in the quarter-moon dark. Faster and faster I ran along a narrow path. I glanced over my shoulder. Torches flickered between the bare limbs. They were gaining on me. I crashed through briars and branches, scratching my hands and face. I was cold but sweating, breathing ragged mist. They were going to catch me, I knew it.

I almost crashed into a wattle-and-daub hut I hadn't seen in the dark I dove under the animal-hide curtain hanging over the low doorway. Inside a ratty-haired crone shrieked and threw a wooden bowl at me.

"Please, I won't hurt you!" I said as I crouched behind the only chair in the place. "Soldiers—they're coming for me."

She glared at me. "Why?"

Quickly, I told her about Ella, my mother, and Genvieve, and how I was certain I was the next to die.

The crone cackled. "Right you be, right you be. Ella girl wants you dead, dead, dead. Helped her I did and she promised, oh, she promised. A girl child, pretty little thing, for me to raise. Yes, for me. And now I'll catch you for soldiers. Ella girl will be pleased, yes, pleased."

She lunged for me, but I ran from her hut, ran for the woods but got tangled in some briars. I heard the horses pounding closer, closer.

"She be close, she be!" the crone said. "Look for her, she can't be far!"

I heard a hard crack of palm on jaw. "Shut up, witch. My queen sends me to send you to hell."

A scream filled with rage and betrayal pierced the night, clawing at my soul. The soldiers turned their horses and trotted back toward the castle. They weren't after me.

I untangled my cloak from the briars and crept back to the hut. The old woman lay on the ground in front of the doorway, a dark, damp circle spreading across the front of her threadbare shift. Another death by Ella's word.

The crone moved. She wasn't dead! I almost left her, knowing she had tried to betray me into Ella's hands, but I couldn't. I picked up the gaunt body and carried her inside to her heap-of-rags bed. I packed the cleanest rags I could find into the gash in her belly and tried to stop the bleeding.

Claw-like fingers clutched my wrist. The crone opened her dark eyes and stared at me. "Ella girl wants me dead, and dead I'll be, but not so easy she breaks her bargain. Dresses I give her, shoes and carriage, magics to hide who she is, poison no one can tell. And she gives me death." She gasped, shuddered, and clutched my wrist tighter. "Black bottle, tiny, by the crow's claw...take it, pour in wine...make her drink...make her tell truth...make her tell truth...forever..." Her life wheezed out with her last word.

I found the vial and hid it next to my heart. Where was I to go? I had no family, no friends except Charles de Lenne and I didn't want to endanger him. I decided to leave the kingdom and hoped I could survive on my own.

I tried to avoid roads and people, but a border patrol cornered me in a small rift. They dragged me back to the castle where I was tried for Genvieve's murder and treason. Servants and courtiers testified they'd seen me arguing with Genvieve and had threatened her. Only Charles stood beside me throughout the trial, my one true friend, even though I begged him not endanger himself. The way Queen Ella glared at him, I feared he would be the next one to face her wrath.

I wasn't surprised when I was convicted, nor was anyone else except Charles. I laughed when King Malcolm sentenced me to death, but it was bitter laughter.

The night before I was to be executed, Charles was allowed to visit me for the first time since my arrest, a final kindness for the condemned. A good man, a true noble, he wanted to try to rescue me and flee the country. I wished...I wished ...

"No," I said, "you would die along side of me, and I thank you for your bravery. But there is a thing you can do for me." I gave him the vial and told him what to do with it.

He looked wary, and for a moment doubt flickered across his face.

I touched his hand. "It isn't poison, nor is it harmful." I poured a cup of wine, added a bit of the dust from the vial, and drank. "See, it will do her no harm...only...only...make her tell the truth...for the rest of her life."

Charles took the vial and put it inside his shirt, then took my hand. Hope sparkled in his eyes. "My lady, I swear by heaven and on my honor, I will do as you ask."

And for the first and last time, he kissed me.

It is dawn. I hear the soft tread of my confessor accompanied by the heavy boots of the palace guards. I make a good confession and receive absolution, then the guards take me from my cell to the courtyard. I'm not afraid.

Charles is in the crowd, trying to get close enough to touch me. "I've kept my vow, my lady," he calls.

My fingertips brush his. "I love you," I say. I can't stop the words.

"Camille!" He tries to break through the barrier of soldiers, but they are too strong.

I climb the steps and forgive the executioner. Ella is watching from a balcony, celebrating my death as she did Mother's execution—with a cup of wine, wine laced with a grain of the Dust of Truth. And I know that she will not be long in following me to the ax.

The Tell-tale Harp

Fairy tales don't always have fairies in them. But they always have magic. And if they can make one laugh, all the better.

It was the first giant I'd ever seen. He was at least eighty feet tall. His head was higher than the highest turret of the castle. He stood before me—and above me, very far above me—seeking justice. This was definitely the biggest case I'd ever judged as Basilopolis' Minister of Justice.

I'd ordered a dais constructed east of Basilopolis as a makeshift court since the giant—the primary plaintiff—couldn't fit inside the castle. I sat down and faced the accused. The boy couldn't have been more than thirteen years old, thin as a rail and ragged. He looked pitiful in manacles. Not the typical hardened criminal. But the list of his crimes was longer than the boy was tall: three charges of breaking and entering, three charges of burglary, three charges of grand theft, twenty-six charges of destruction of property, one charge of assault with intent to do bodily harm, and one charge of attempted murder. An accomplishment for anyone, much less a boy.

"So, boy," I began when he interrupted me.

"Jack. My name is Jack." His voice was squeaky.

"Jack. Would you explain how one small boy could cause so much trouble?"

His brown eyes glinted, and his jaw jutted out. "I didn't cause any trouble. He did." He pointed a thin finger at the giant, who harrumphed and pulled a white lace handkerchief from the sleeve of his green velvet coat. "He's the one what mashed them houses an' trees an' fields. And he's the real thief."

"How can he be a thief when it was you who stole his property?"

"I jus' took back what was mine. He stole those things from my family long time ago."

I stared at the ragged boy, then at the giant. "Are you saying, Jack, this person stole a hen that lays golden eggs, a large bag of gold, and a golden singing harp from you?"

"Yes!" He stood very straight, chin high. He was either a very good liar or really believed what he said.

"That's absurd," said the giant, his voice a cultured baritone. "That young ruffian broke into my house, stole my property, and when I sought to apprehend him, he tried to murder me!"

"Liar!" Jack shouted.

"I but tell the truth." The giant bowed and swept his green and gold hat across his gold brocade vest. "Reginald Bartholdy, Esquire, at your service, Your Honor."

"He's a lyin' thief and murderer!" Jack said. "He stole our gold an' things and killed my dad 'fore I was even born!"

Reginald rolled his saucer-sized eyes to the sky and dabbed at his nose with his handkerchief. "Utterly absurd."

I gazed from the giant to Jack. "You have proof?"

"My mum'll tell ya." He looked over his shoulder. "Mum, where are ya?"

A pinched-faced woman in a dirt-brown dress wedged her way through the crowd. "I'm here."

"Tell 'em, Mum. Just like ya told me all those years."

"Mistress," I said and nodded to the woman.

"Widow Bonnyclabber, Your Honor." She bowed like a marionette.

"Your son says that he entered Bartholdy's house to retrieve certain items stolen from you. Is that true?"

Widow Bonnyclabber blinked her old honey eyes slowly before she spoke. "Yes, indeed, just like Jackie says. 'Fore his dad an' me was married, my John said he had..." she stopped and scratched her head, as though confused, "all those things, said a giant stole 'em, and swore he'd get 'em back. He left to find the giant 'bout five months 'fore Jackie was born." She wiped her nose on her sleeve. "I never saw John again. But 'bout two months later an old woman brought me a hat an' pipe—John's things—tol' me a dyin' man asked her to bring them to me. Said he tol' her a giant throwed him off a land in the sky and broke his legs and back and he was sorry he couldn't come home." She sniffed and wiped her eyes on her other sleeve.

"So," I said, "do you believe this giant is responsible for your husband's death and the theft of your wealth?"

The widow looked wide-eyed at me and cocked her head. "Well, 'course. How many other giants you know of 'round here?"

None. But then, I hadn't known of any until Reginald had appeared. "I see. Now, tell me what happened."

"Well," Widow Bonnyclabber began, "we was poor. I couldn't keep up the farm by myself. I had t' sell off everything we had 'til a couple of weeks ago all we had left was the house an' one cow an' no food. So I sent Jack to town to sell the cow. That's when the real trouble began." She sighed, glanced at Jack, and sighed again.

"What happened?" I asked.

"He sold the cow—for a handful of beans!"

"But, Mum, they was magic!" Jack said.

I raised an eyebrow. "Magic beans?"

Jack looked at me, his thin brows pulled low over his eyes and his mouth tight. "Well, 'course! How else ya think that beanstalk got so tall?"

"Where did an old man get magic beans like that?" asked Blinn, my young court mage.

"How should I know?" Jack asked fiercely.

I cleared my throat. "Continue."

"See, I was on my way t' sell our cow Daisy when I met this crippled old man on the road an' he offered t' buy Daisy for a handful of beans. Now I ain't dumb enough t' trade a cow for beans an' I said so." Widow Bonnyclabber shook her head at that. "But he said the beans was magic so I gave him Daisy an' took the beans."

"You then went home?"

Jack nodded. "An' Mum was real mad at me. Whapped me up side the head and pitched the beans out the window."

"Wasn't even enough to make soup with," Widow Bonnyclabber muttered.

"Anyway, she whapped me again an' sent me t' bed. Next morning I woke up an' looked out my window, an' there was the biggest beanstalk I ever seen! I mean, it was bigger than a tree and stretched up t' the clouds and beyond."

"Now those beans I could make soup with!" Widow Bonnyclabber said.

"That's when I remembered 'bout the giant and our treasures. I figured I'd go up an' get our things back an' we'd be rich."

"So you climbed up to the giant's land and invaded his home," I said.

"I didn't either," Jack huffed. "His wife let me in."

Reginald's huge mouth fell open. "My wife She allowed you to enter my home?""

"Yeah, she opened the door an' tol' me come have somethin' t' eat. Cooks real good for a giant."

"Yes, but she simply cannot make a decent pasta prima vera," Reginald said, fanning himself with handkerchief.

I looked at Jack. "Can she verify your story?"

"Well, yeah, if she can get down here."

I gazed up at the sky. "Of course, that might be difficult since there is no beanstalk anymore. Blinn?" I looked at the mage sitting beside me.

Blinn scratched his copper hair and scrunched his nose. "I don't know, but I'll look into it."

I turned back to Jack. "So Mistress Bartholdy let you in, gave you something to eat, and..."

"An' tol' me I better go 'fore her husband got home. But all of a sudden, he comes stompin' an' shouting 'Fee, fie, fo, fum, I smell the blood of an Englishman. Be he alive or be he dead, I'll grind his bones to make my bread.' An' so I hid behind a broom real quick 'cause I didn't want him t' grind me up."

Reginald sounded as if he were strangling. "Your Honor, you cannot believe such heinous accusations, can you? I am a vegetarian! I eat no meat, although I do consume eggs and dairy products."

"Oh, yeah?" Jack glared up at the giant. "What about all that shouting?"

Reginald sniffed. "I was not shouting. I was practicing my vocalizations." He cleared his throat, then in a pure—and very loud—baritone, sang, "Feeeee, fiiiie, foooo, fummmm," raised it a note, and sang again. Actually, he had a very good voice. When he finished, he smiled and blushed. "I've never sung in public before. Usually, I sing duets with my harp while she accompanies the two of us."

"That must be..." I rubbed my ringing ears, "unforgettable."

"Truly?" Reginald looked puppy dog pleased. "Perhaps we could sing for you when this unpleasantness is over."

"Um, perhaps." If he could sing a mile from Basilopolis—at least a mile! "Jack, what happened next?"

"Well, he ate his supper, then took a box down from the mantle an' opened it an' out he pulled my dad's bag of gold."

"How do you know it was yours?"

"'Cause it was real little, my size, not giant size, an' the coins were so small, he had t' pick 'em up real careful."

"I'm a numismatist!" Reginald said.

"A what?" I asked.

"A numismatist. I collect foreign coins, so of course, they were small!"

Jack ground his teeth. "Anyway, he was countin' the coins an' sluggin' down mugs of ale—"

"I *never* touch ale," Reginald said, shuddering. "I was sipping fruit punch."

"An' wasn't long 'fore he was snoring loud enough t' shake the walls. I climbed up the table an' grabbed the bag an' ran outta there fast as I could."

Reginald pointed down at Jack. There, Your Honor, he admits he absconded with my collection."

"It's mine!" Jack shouted up.

"Mine!" Reginald shouted down, almost blowing away the dais where I sat.

"Silence!" I shouted. My head was beginning to throb. "Now, Jack, what about the hen?"

"Well, Mum was real excited when I showed her the gold so I figured I'd try t' get back the hen so we'd always have gold. So next day I went back up the beanstalk. His wife let me in again an' then I heard him stompin' an' shoutin'," Jack glanced up at Reginald, "or singin', an' I hid again. After he ate supper, he got the hen, set it right on the table an' said, 'Lay, hen, lay,' an' the hen laid a real golden egg! He drank himself asleep an' I grabbed the hen an' hightailed it home."

Reginald glared down at Jack. "Your Honor, from his own mouth he condemns himself."

"It's my hen!" Jack said, glaring back at Reginald just as fiercely.

"And the harp?" I asked as I held my throbbing head.

"Well," Jack shot an icy glance at Reginald, "Mum was so happy with the hen, I decided t' get the harp, too. Everything happened like 'fore, but this time he didn't drink as much. He pulled out the harp, set it on the table, and said, 'Play, harp, play' an' it set t' playin' a song an' he was singin' with it. Anyway, he finally went t' sleep so I snatched the harp an' started t' run. Then that harp started screamin'."

"Screaming, indeed!" Reginald tapped his foot on the ground, which rippled and shuddered so much, most of the crowd stumbled and plopped down. "She was singing a beautiful aria of utter despair, so piercingly beautiful it woke me from my nap. This knave had her in his foul clutches and was carrying her off. Naturally, I gave chase. I couldn't let him kidnap my dear companion, especially when she was in the middle of her aria.

"I'm not naturally athletic, but I did reach the beanstalk only moments after he did. I was, however, reluctant to descend the vine because..." Reginald blushed and hung his head, "I dread heights, simply dread them. But he had my beauty, my dear harp. What else could I do but cast aside my fear and pursue him down the vine?"

"Admirable," I said.

"Anyway," Jack interrupted sharply, "I shimmied down the beanstalk, ran t' the house, grabbed our ax, an' started choppin' down the beanstalk. I could hear the giant climbin' down so I chopped faster 'til I heard a crack and the whole thing started topplin' over. He hit the ground with a crash that shook houses for miles around."

"And broke my barn!" said one man in the crowd.

"And my orchard!" said another.

"My goats."

"My chickens."

"My wheat."

Reginald pointed at Jack. "He attempted to murder me, calculated and premeditated, and as a result of his actions, significant property was damaged or destroyed. Your Honor, can there be any doubt of his guilt?"

"It's just his word against mine," Jack said.

I sat back and thought for a moment. Jack was right; it was his word against Reginald's. "Are there any other witnesses?"

My harp," Reginald said. "She will testify to the truth of my words. Send for her."

Testimony from a harp? It was unusual, but this entire case had been unusual. "Very well. Bring the harp from the Judgment Chamber."

A sergeant bowed and hurried back to the castle. It was quite a while before he returned, running. "Your Honor, the harp is missing, as are the bag of gold and the hen! They've been stolen!"

Someone had stolen evidence from *my* keeping? "Explain! What happened?"

"We don't know! The guards say they heard and saw nothing. The door was not broken. There are no marks on the floor or latch. But the room was empty when I opened it."

Reginald clapped his handkerchief to his chest. "Do you mean that my property has been stolen *again*?"

"Apparently," I said with a sigh. I turned to my court mage. "Blinn, come with me."

We hurried back to the Judgment Hall. Just as the sergeant had said, the room where I kept evidence was empty. No scratches on the door, no signs of chicken feathers so there hadn't been a struggle. Not even footprints—the castle drudges were very efficient about scrubbing the stone floors until they gleamed. The door guards swore they hadn't heard or seen anything. The boy who fed the golden egg-laying hen claimed it was there when he'd been in the room just after dawn.

"What now, Blinn?" I asked as I gazed at the empty evidence room.

"Well..." Blinn straightened his too-big green robe and scrunched his mouth, "I could check for magic, Your Honor."

"Then do it."

Blinn waved his skinny arm, crossed his green eyes, wrinkled his freckled nose, mumbled something like cronies-candelabra-brandy-eminence, then stared at the door for a long moment. "Aha! There's a faint trace of magic here. Almost too faint. Either it's very old..."

"Which it couldn't be," I interrupted.

"Or it was very weak magic to begin with."

"Can you track it?"

Blinn scanned the room again, then the doorway and the Judgment Hall. He shook his head, sighed, and pulled his robe back up on his narrow shoulders. "Just too faint." He started to go, then added, "Your Honor."

Blinn wasn't much for formalities, but he was the best court mage I'd ever known. "What can you do?" I asked.

"Use my tracker."

I raised an eyebrow. "You have a hound?"

He grinned. "No, a mole."

"A mole?"

"Best trackers for magic. They can smell a trail even twenty years old."

"Then get him—it."

"Her," Blinn said.

"Whatever. We must find the thief quickly."

Blinn ran from the Judgment Hall and returned a few minutes later carrying a tiny grey mole. Around its neck was a thin red ribbon tied in a bow and a delicate silver chain for a leash. Blinn grinned and petted the animal. "Hildie will find our magic thief, won't you, Hildie?"

The mole nuzzled his hand and flailed its feet, as if anxious to start. Blinn put Hildie down near the evidence room and said, "Seek and find."

Hildie scuttled inside the small room as fast as her teeny legs could go. In the corners, under the table, behind the door, she searched everywhere, then scuttled out into the Judgment Hall. I was amazed the little creature could move as fast as it did.

"She's got the scent," Blinn said as he followed her.

I followed Blinn, as did the sergeant and two guards he'd brought with him. The mole padded across the entry hall, out the doors, down the steps, across the courtyard, through the gate, all the way down the main street of town to the field where the court had been set, then scuttled into the crowd.

Blinn shouted, "Please, don't step on her! Don't anyone move! Hildie, Hildie!"

We wove slowly through the audience—it was hard to keep sight of such a tiny animal—until the mole reached the eastern edge of crowd, then headed for the East Road. I called for five more guards to join us, and we all walked down the dry track. The mole kept straight on the road, little nose twitching as her short legs stirred the dust, down a gradually sloping hill, around some flat rocks, beside several fields and into Quindan Woods.

Suddenly, Hildie stopped short. She turned her head left and right several times, took a step forward, sniffed the road again, plodded forward, then side to side.

"What's wrong?" I asked.

"She's lost the scent," Blinn said. "Looks like our thief either dispelled the magic or somehow disguised the trail. The dust looks smooth, as if brushed or swept. Give her a chance; she'll pick it up again. She's as good as any hound on a trail."

The mole inched forward, sniffing from one side of the road to the other, until she paddled forward again.

"She's got it!" Blinn shouted as he followed after her.

The guards and I came after them until Hildie stopped again. She sniffed the edge of the road and walked through a small break in the trees. Her sharp little nails scratched against layers of dry leaves as she led Blinn through brush and briars.

She stopped so abruptly, Blinn almost stumbled over her. I banged into Blinn, the sergeant bumped into me, and the guards followed suit. Hildie scooted out of the way while we struggled to remain standing.

"What's wrong now?" I asked.

Blinn signaled quiet, as if it mattered after the near disaster of moments before. "Watch."

The mole crept forward, making almost no noise. We tiptoed after her until I could see an open space up ahead. She stopped, straightened her tail, lifted one paw, and pointed her nose at the clearing.

The sergeant directed the guards to spread out and surround the clearing. Blinn picked up Hildie, then he and I crept forward.

As we reached the trees at the edge of the clearing, I saw an old man sitting on a long dead log and stuffing a last bit of brown bread in his mouth. He was ragged but clean. White frizzled hair spread from under his floppy hat and mingled with his beard. There was no sign of the stolen items.

Brushing bread crumbs from his mouth and coat, he stood up with the help of a worn walking stick and turned his back to me. That's when I noticed he was hunchbacked. He limped toward the opposite side of the clearing.

I looked at Blinn and cocked my head questioningly. Blinn frowned but nodded. "Be ready," I whispered. He nodded again and fixed his eyes on the stranger, concentrating the way he always did when working on a spell.

I stepped into the clearing and said, "Sir."

The old man started and turned as quickly as his leg let him. His jaw dropped open when he saw me. All the guards stepped from the woods, surrounding the old man. He wheeled to his right but stopped when he saw the guards. Turning his back to me, he halted again at the sight of the guards. He turned a third quarter of a circle, starting to bolt that way, when the guards on that side began advancing toward him. The old man shrieked, reached into a small pouch at his waist, and brought out a closed fist.

"Stop him!" Blinn said, but not in time.

The old man tossed silvery dust into the air over his head and vanished as the particles settled over him. Gone, no shadow, no trace at all.

"He's invisible!" Blinn said.

"Tighten the circle!" I said. "Don't let him escape!"

The guards drew swords and slashed the air at their sides, gradually advancing toward the center.

"Blinn, can you do anything?"

"I'm trying!" The mage put Hildie on the ground, wiggled his fingers, mumbled something like "hats-a-bill-in-context-ray", and clapped his hands. Nothing happened. "Something's blocking my spell!"

A yelp sounded near the eastern edge of the clearing. I'd forgotten about Hildie. She had her teeth sunk into something that tossed her back and forth, right and left, up and down, but she didn't let go, scratching her target with her sharp-nailed claws.

"Guards, grab...whatever the mole's biting!"

The guards piled on the invisible yelper. A strange sight, nine soldiers struggling with thin air and a little grey animal latched onto nothing. At last, the guards had forced their quarry to the grass-and-leaf strewn ground. Clinging dust and leaf fragments partially revealed the culprit.

"Make it let go!" the old man said, kicking at Hildie.

Blinn took the end of the mole's silver chain and gave it a tug. The mole didn't let go. "Hildie, heel!"

She let go, took one last swipe at the old man's leg, then trotted to Blinn's side. The mole sniffed the air and growled low. I didn't know moles *could* growl. She looked very threatening for a mole.

"Tie his hands," I told the sergeant, then turned to the old man. "Where are the things you stole from the castle?"

"I don't know what you're talking about! I stole nothing!"

"Why did you try to escape?"

"Anyone would, if attacked by a group of armed men, even you!"

"Yes, of course," I said sarcastically. "Let's return to the castle. I still have a trial to finish."

Two guards clutched the old man's arms and hurried him along with the rest of us. Because of the old man's limp, it was late afternoon before we reached the outdoor court again. Jack and his mum were still there, as was Reginald the giant. The guards held the old man beside young Jack.

I settled in my chair. "Blinn, can you make him more visible?"

"Well," Blinn scratched his red hair as he sat down beside me, "we could cover him with dust or mud or anything that would stick to him, preferably after drenching him with water. What did you use?" he asked the old man. "Karmallin dust to make you invisible?"

The old man said nothing.

I stared at where the man's face should've been. "Maybe Hildie can convince you to talk."

"All right," the old man muttered. "Yes, karmallin dust."

Blinn leaned toward me. "A little water should rinse it off."

I called for water. Four guards each brought a full bucket and dumped the water over the old man. He sputtered, coughed, sputtered again, and became completely visible.

"Now, where are the items you stole from the castle?" I asked.

He said nothing, just glared at me. That's when I noticed the hump on his back had shifted to the other side—and it was moving!

"Remove his coat," I said.

The sergeant and another guard tugged the coat from the man's shoulders. His hump was a sack!

"Open it."

The sergeant cut the strings holding the sack in place, set the sack on the platform in front of me, and opened it. Out stumbled a chicken, unsteady, head weaving from side to side. It flopped on the wood, gave a scratchy cackle, and keeled over, leaving an ordinary white egg next to it. The sergeant nudged the hen with his boot; the hen didn't move. The sergeant shrugged, picked up the egg, and gave it to me.

Reginald the giant sobbed and dabbed his eyes. "Oh, the poor dear thing, murdered."

The sergeant reached inside the bag and pulled out a smaller bag and a golden harp. The harp had a woman's head and body carved from the frame; the mouth was gagged with a strip of cloth. Rope was wrapped around each string, making it impossible to pluck them. The sergeant removed the gag first, then began unwrapping the rope.

"Thank you, oh, thank you!" the harp's golden voice said. "You don't know how grateful I am to be free from that man's clutches."

"Then he..." I pointed to the old man, "was the one who took you from the castle?"

"Oh, he did indeed kidnap me from that room," the harp said. The emerald eyes turned toward the old man. "You terrible, terrible man! Gagging me, tying my strings. It was dreadful, simply dreadful! I'm certain I'll be out of tune for days!"

"And did that young man in the manacles steal you from Reginald Bartholdy's house?"

The harp looked toward Jack, sniffed delicately, and nodded. "That young knave tore me from my master's care. I don't think I can bear the shock. I am too frightened to sing the horrors I've endured." Her strings trembled a note of fear on the air.

I gazed at Jack, then at the old man, who slouched in front of me. Somehow he looked different, something ...

His beard—it wasn't white any more. More black salted with white. And his hair was crooked. A wig! "Remove that man's hat."

The sergeant removed the hat and a cocked wig of white hair, revealing short hair the color of the beard. So, the man wasn't as old as he pretended.

Widow Bonnyclabber gasped and stepped toward the man. "John?"

He looked frightened. "Marsha?" he squeaked.

"John!" Her voice rose and grew louder as she drew out his name. She clenched her fists and launched toward him.

"Marsha!" He shrank back against the two guards holding him.

"Hold!" I commanded. "Do you know this man?" I asked Widow Bonnyclabber.

"Know him?" she fumed. "I've mourned this rogue for more than fifteen years! This is my husband, John Bonnyclabber!" She aimed a blow at his head. He barely ducked it.

"Your husband?" I repeated, astonished.

"My dad?" Jack said, his eyes wide. "But he's the old man what sold me the beans!"

"Him?" Blinn, Marsha Bonnyclabber, and I all said simultaneously.

Jack nodded vigorously. "Him."

"Good heavens!" Reginald blurted out, nearly deafening all present. "That man invaded my home some fifteen or sixteen years ago. I tossed him over the edge of my cloud."

"John!"

"Dad?"

"Marsha!"

"Thief," Reginald huffed.

"Enough!" I said. "Hear my judgment."

Everyone became silent.

"Reginald, I return your property." I gazed at the dead chicken. "Including the hen and its egg."

The giant gave a sweeping bow. "Thank you, noble judge. You are truly a wise and just man."

"Jack, you will help repair all the damage the fallen beanstalk caused. If I learn that you've failed to perform your duty or run away before the repairs are completed or if you steal anything ever again, you will be outlawed, and when caught, hanged like any criminal." I gave him my most solemn and daunting stare. "Do you understand?"

Jack trembled, his lower lip quivering. He swallowed hard and nodded. I guess he believed me.

I leaned over to Blinn and whispered a question. He scrunched up his mouth for a moment, then grinned and nodded.

"And as for you," I said, staring straight at John Bonnyclabber, "you will help your son repair the damage to the surrounding farms. You will also work for the owner of each farm for one week each year for the next three years. Sergeant, search him for money."

The sergeant found several copper and silver coins.

I gazed at John. "The money is forfeit to your wife, whom I direct to buy several hens and a rooster. You will tend the chickens and live with them in the barn. You will use no more magic nor will you go more than the distance from your farm to this city the rest of your life—which Master Blinn will guarantee with a spell."

I couldn't tell whether John was sputtering from anger or surprise, but I thought his was a just punishment.

"Oh, one more thing." I looked from Reginald to the thick, puffy clouds high above, then back at John. "Do you have any more of those beans?"

The Miller's Daughter

Certain fairy tales puzzled me because the characters would behave in ways that made no sense. For example, after Rumplestiltskin saves the girl from the king's greed by spinning straw into gold, she married the king. I never believed that.

The first time I saw her, she was covered in flour from the top of her golden hair to the tip of her dark leather boots. That's when I fell in love with the miller's daughter.

She skipped along the edge of a stream to a pool and a tiny waterfall that tumbled into it. Stripping it down to her chemise, she waded into the pool and stood under the cascading water. Flour changed into white mud plastered to her. She rubbed her face, scrubbed her hair until the flour was only a spreading circle of white on the pool.

Her hair shimmered like molten gold. Water splashed over her like liquid diamonds. She moved with the grace of a flowing chain of silver. My heart pounded wildly in my chest.

Suddenly, her eyes looked right at me and grew wide. She gasped and smiled. Who are you?" she asked.

"*Just a friend,*" I said.

She sloshed through the water until she reached the end of the pool. "I've never seen anyone like you before," she said as she squeezed water from her hair. She sat down beside me and rung out the skirt of her chemise. "You're no bigger than I am."

My mouth felt dry. I had to swallow and lick my lips before I could speak. "I'm a dwarf, a mountain dwarf."

"A real dwarf?" She clapped her hands and grinned."How wonderful! What are you doing here? Where do you live? Are there any more around here? Would you be my friend? My mother died a long time ago and my father works all day in the mill and I have to help him a lot and I don't have anyone to play with. Please, please, be my friend."

My cheeks flushed with embarrassment. The high pitch of her voice, her small size, the way she spoke and acted–I should have realized before then. The girl was little more than a child, so much younger than I'd first thought. She couldn't be older than twelve summers, probably only ten.

I swallowed hard and smiled back at her. "Yes, I'll be your friend," I said softly. "I'm all alone, too."

She gave me a hug. "My name's Madja. What's yours?"

I started for a moment. "I...can't tell you my name right now. Dwarves only give their names to their dearest and closest friends. And we just met."

She frowned at that. "But someday we'll be dearest and closest friends and then you'll tell me, won't you? When I'm older?"

"How old are you now?"

"I'm ten, almost eleven."

I nodded and smiled. "Yes, someday when you're older, when we're truly friends, I'll tell you my name."

Madja's eyes glittered. "All right. But what can I call you 'til then?"

"Just call me Friend."

She smiled, touched my cheek with her small, soft hand, and said, "All right, Friend."

From that day on we spent part of every day together. She would bring me honey cakes she baked. I told her stories of my people. She sewed me a new jacket and trousers to keep me warm in the winter. I showed her how I could slide into stone and come back out. We played hide-and-seek in the woods. I cherished our time together.

For her thirteenth birthday I wanted to make something special, something I created just for her. I made a silver flower, delicate and shimmering like starlight on water, like moonlight on snow. Even my mother couldn't have made something more beautiful.

When I gave it to Madja, she held it in her hand as if it were a butterfly she was afraid she'd damage. She said nothing at first. Then she looked up at me, her eyes glistening with tears. "Thank you," she said softly. "It's the most beautiful thing I've ever seen."

Then she kissed me for the first time, just on the cheek, gently, tenderly. I suddenly realized that she wasn't a child anymore, although she wasn't fully grown yet. And I loved her, chastely and deeply.

Time passed until she was fifteen summers old. She grew twice as tall as I was. Her hair was like fine gold, waist-long and thick. Her eyes were flawless sapphires. Skin like alabaster and rose quartz. Body as strong and majestic as a mountain yet delicate as a meadow flower. And still she called me Friend even though we were so different.

Her father made her work long hours at the mill, but she still found time to steal away to meet me almost every day. We didn't play many games any more. Mostly, we talked. I told her how I found gold and gems. She showed me how to grow vegetables. I showed her how to make the finest beer. She taught me how to make cheese from my goat's milk.

One day as we sat beside the pool, Madja asked me, "Why are you all alone?"

"I'm not," I said, grinning. "I'm here with you."

She sighed and raised one eyebrow. "You *know* what I mean. You're a mountain dwarf living alone in the woods with no kin, no friends, no people. Why?"

My smile faded. I stared at the water. Words stuck in my throat, choking me. Madja touched my hand. "Does it hurt so much?" she asked.

"Not so much as yesterday," I replied. "But it hurts. It hurts."

"Let me share it with you," she said. "Maybe it will hurt less then."

I hesitated, then nodded. "I lived with my people in the mountains north of here. My father was the best silversmith in a whole tribe. My mother could craft the most intricate items of gold and gems. My sister could spin gold into fine thread and weave the most delicate, shimmering cloth you ever saw. We were happy, so happy, in our halls of stone." I paused, my throat tight.

Madja squeeze my hand gently. "What happened?"

"I was young, almost as young as you were when we first met. Mother sent me down to the deepest caverns to track a new vein of gold. It was the first time she'd given me such an important task. I was so excited and proud. I wanted to do my best, to prove I was worthy of such trust.

"I followed the vein deep into the mountain, moving through the stone slowly, carefully so I didn't lose the vein. When I reached the end, I was so tired, I found the nearest cavern and rested.

"When I woke up, I made a quick sketch of the vein, then headed back home. As I drew near the usually noisy halls of my people, the silence was eerie. I found my family, my friends, my people...all dead, murdered. There were bodies of human soldiers, too. I think they came for our wealth because all the treasures of our halls were gone. And so was everyone I loved."

I squeezed my eyes shut, trying to hold back tears. Even after twenty years the loss was still deep, still raw. I cleared my throat and said, "I buried them all and sealed the gateway to our realm. I wandered for days until I found this place. I built my little cottage, found and tamed my little goat, but still I was alone, so terribly alone." I open my eyes and gazed at her. "Until I met you."

Madja gathered me into her arms and wept with me. "I know what it is to be alone," she murmured. "My mother...she was so kind, so gentle. She loved trees and flowers and animals. Father adored her. Two years before I met you, Mother became ill. Father bought potions, teas, poultices, charms, anything to try to cure her. She grew so thin and week, she couldn't sit up, couldn't get out of bed. She died in my father's arms, little more than skin stretched over bones."

I felt Madja's body shudder with sobs. Finally, she spoke again.

"Father was never the same after that. He did the best he could, but something died in him, too, when Mother died. He worked longer hours at the mill, making it the most prosperous mill in the kingdom. And he started spending the little time he didn't work or sleep at the village tavern, drinking to forget. Soon, the only time I saw him was when he ate the breakfast I cooked or when I had to help him in the mill. I keep house, cook, keep the fire going, try to please him, but he misses Mother so much. He works so hard, so very hard." Madja paused, holding me close. "Sometimes...when he's drunk, he...hits me. He doesn't mean it. He just can't help it."

I wiped away her tears. "Madja, you'll never be alone again. Not ever." I touched her cheek. She turned her face and kissed my palm. "I told you once that dwarves only give their names to their dearest and closest friends. That's true, but there's more to it than that. Anyone who knows a dwarf's true name has power over the dwarf and can make him do whatever he's commanded." I kissed her hand and held it over my heart. "I give you that power over me. My true name is Rumplestiltskin."

Madja's eyes grew wide, and she whispered my name. "I promise, I swear on my life, I'll never tell anyone." She held me tenderly, comforting me while I tried to comfort her. I felt happier and more content than I'd ever been.

One late summer day I waited for the sound of Madja's light step, her voice calling for me, waited until afternoon shadows began to lengthen, 'til the sun touched the horizon and deer came out to graze. Where was she? What had happened? Fear chilled my heart. Was she hurt or ill? I had to know, had to be sure she was all right.

Tree limbs creaked, crickets scritched, and the wind moaned as I crept to the mill. The building was dark, not even fire glow flickering through the windows. I sang Madja's name. She didn't answer. I listened through the stone walls and heard nothing.

Frightened, I slid inside the stone wall as I had slid through the bones of Mother Earth since I was a kidling, drawing strength from the rock. I felt home again, safe and renewed. I was tempted to rest there in the stone, cradled in those cold, comforting arms I'd known so long ago, but I had to find Madja. With the sigh of regret, I slid from the wall and into the room.

I called Madja's name softly, hoping not to disturb her father. Where was she? The hearth was cold; the fire, long dead. She always kept the fire going. I went to her tiny room. The bed was cold and unmade. In the other room her father's bed was empty and unmade as well. The only sound was the scrabbling of mouse feet on the stone floor.

Something was wrong. I knew it. Madja was in danger or was hurt. I could almost feel her pain. I closed my eyes and listened with my heart. There, softer than a whisper, I heard her crying. Not in the mill, no, far away. I followed the sound through the village, up the hill to the town and the king's castle. She was there in that strong fortress of stone, somewhere inside. I kept to the darkest shadows, feeling around the cold stones, listening, listening for her.

Finally, I heard her through the thick wall. I touched it, letting my fingers become part of the stone, and felt despair flowing from her heart as freely as tears from her eyes. Poor, gentle Madja. I had to help her, save her. I slid through the wall as quickly as I could.

The last ray of sunset seeped through the slit of a window and bathed my beloved Madja in its rosy light. She sat on a short stool in front of a spinning wheel, the small kind used for spinning linen. Her hands cradled her face, and she was sobbing, sobbing. Straw in heaps as tall as me lay about the periphery of the room. Dust and chaff mingled with the odor of mold and the chill of winter to come.

"Madja," I whispered.

She sat up suddenly, wiped her tear-streaked face with her sleeve, and looked around the room until she saw me. She dropped to her knees on the stone floor and held out her arms, and I ran to her.

"Oh, Madja, I was so afraid when you didn't come. Why are you here?"

"The king's guards came to the mill," she said, "and dragged me and Father here."

"Why?"

She held me close and kissed my head. "My father," she said, "my father—" She choked up, and hot tears splashed on my hair.

"What has he done?" I asked.

"He'd boasted that...that I could...spin straw into gold!"

"Wodin's blood," I cursed through my teeth. "That fool!"

"The king has ordered that I must spin all the straw into gold by morning or he will kill my father and me."

I gasped. "No! I won't let that happen!"

Madja lifted my chin until I was looking straight into her eyes. "There's nothing you can do, but thank you for coming to comfort me this last night of my life." She smiled sadly and kissed my forehead.

"No!" I pushed her away. "I won't let you die!"

She slumped to the floor and hung her head. "You can't stop it."

"Yes, I can!" I grasped her hands. "I can. I'll spin the straw into gold for you."

She looked at me with astonishment. "Truly?" she whispered. "You can spin straw into gold?"

I nodded. "All that comes from Mother Earth, I can work. Copper, silver, gems and gold–these things I can shape and mold. For you, Madja, for you I will spin this straw into gold."

Her lips trembled. Tears flowed down her cheeks again. "Friend," she said softly, "my dearest friend..." She reached for a leather thong at her throat and pulled a small pouch from beneath her bodice. Opening it, she removed a fine gold chain set with three blood-red garnets. "This was my grandmother's. She wanted me to wear it on my wedding day." She placed the necklace on my palm.

I shook my head and started to give the necklace back, but she folded my fingers over the necklace and said, "I owe you my life and the life of my father. This is so little to thank you with, but it's the greatest treasure I have. Please, take it. Please."

I couldn't refuse. If it were so precious to her, it was more so to me. I placed the necklace inside my shirt, next to my heart. I still felt the warmth of her hand on the gold and wished ...

Dusk filled the room with grey shadows. The king had left no torch, no lamp or candle, so I called glow worms. They came through the slit in the wall, dozens, scores, hundreds of them, crawling across the ceiling, the walls, to light the room to a cool, soft yellow.

I turned to Madja and sat down on the stool. "Rest now while I work. By morning the king will have his gold, and you and your father will be safe."

She took my hand, gave it a gentle squeeze, then kissed it. She pulled her shawl tightly around her shoulders, lay down beside me with her head resting on her arm, and closed her eyes. I listened to her breathing, watched her breast rise and fall. How beautiful she was, like a perfect gem, like hammered gold.

Picking up a piece of straw, I began to sing a song of deep mines, of hidden treasure, of gleam and glitter and shining gold. Pedal pumping, wheel spinning, spindle turning–straw became spool after spool of wire-fine gold. By midnight not a single bit of straw remained.

I sat and watched Madja, trying to understand why I loved this girl, why she touched my stony heart as no woman of my race ever had, ever could. No answer came. I stayed there, watching and wondering, until I heard heavy steps approaching the door. Quickly, I slid back through the wall and outside. Madja was safe. I went home to milk my goat and to rest. Making magic always sapped my strength, but I didn't care. Madja was safe. Madja was safe.

When I woke, it was already late afternoon. I went out and milked my goat, who complained at being neglected. Then I drank a flagon of honey beer and ate some bread and butter. I washed my face, combed my auburn hair and close-trimmed beard, and left for the mill. I couldn't wait for Madja to come to me. I wanted to see her, needed to see her, to reassure myself she was well.

The sun was westering by the time I reached the river. The mill was dark, silent except for the gurgle of water over stones. I sang Madja's name, but she didn't answer. No one was inside.

"Wodin's blood," I cursed. "The king, he still has her."

I raced to the castle through back streets and alleys, hiding from guards and torchlight. Edging around the castle, I brushed my fingers across the stones and listened until I heard Madja weeping. I flowed through the wall and ran to her. "Madja. Madja."

"I was so afraid you wouldn't come," she said as she wrapped her arms around me and help me close. "I didn't know what to do."

"Madja, what happened?"

"The king, the king, he saw the gold," she stammered. "He was pleased, very pleased. And he wanted more." She shuddered, swallowed a sob, and pointed at piles of straw twice as big as before. "He commanded me to spin all this into gold, too, or he will kill my father and me. Can you help me again?"

I smiled. "How could I not? Dry your tears and sleep. I'll wake you when I've finished."

She kissed my forehead. "I..." She sat on the floor and pulled out the small bag she kept around her neck. Opening it, she took out a golden ring, plain and smooth. "This was my mother's ring. It's all I have left of her." She put it in my hand. When I protested, she shook her head. "You have saved my life twice. Take the ring, please."

I finally agreed although I promised to keep it only until she returned home. "Sleep now. I'll wake you when my work is done."

Again, I sang a song of gold and gems, of deep mines and shining caverns. Straw to gold, straw to gold. Bales and heaps of spun gold until dawn's light glowed in the sky. I woke Madja, then flowed through the wall and trudged home, tired but happy.

My goat bleated at me, full of milk and uncomfortable. "There, there, little one," I said soothingly as I milked her. "I'm sorry. I'll have you milked and fed very soon." I sighed and said to myself, "And then I'll sleep."

When I woke, the sun hung just above the treetops, and there was a chill like autumn in the air. Winter was coming, the freezing of streams, icicles on trees, snow weighing down pines. I could smell the north wind inching closer even though summer hadn't given way to fall. I shivered, then milked my goat, ate a bit of bread, and went to find Madja.

I found the mill still dark and empty, and knew Madja was still at the castle. I found her in the room with twice as much straw as the night before.

Madja gazed at me with red-rimmed eyes, yet she tried to smile. "Even you can't spin this much straw into gold," she said quietly.

"I can try," I said. I sat down and immediately started to sing and spin.

"Father took the only other treasure I had," she said. "The silver flower you made for me—he sold it for drink. I have nothing else to give you."

I gazed at her, my throat as tight as my chest. "You've given me something I treasure more than gold."

She put her hand on the spinning wheel to stop it. Cupping my chin in her hands, she kissed me full on the mouth. "When the king frees me," she said, "I'm not going back to the mill with my father. I want to live with you, be with you, be your wife."

I felt dizzy and light-headed, as if I'd been drinking for hours, and my very bones felt hot and liquid like molten rock. Madja, my wife! My heart danced in my chest. Madja, my wife!

I swallowed my joy and took a deep breath. "But first, I must finish this spinning. After that..." I smiled at her and returned her kiss. "After that, I'll wait for you at my house. Sleep now, Madja. Sleep and dream of happiness."

She lay down at my feet, and as I began singing and spinning, she closed her eyes.

All night long I spun heaps, bales, mountains of golden wire from the straw, spun it faster than on the previous night. Even so, I barely finished the last piece of straw when I heard a key slide into the lock and start to turn. Quickly, I melted back into the stone and out the other side. I was exhausted. I'd never used so much magic in so short a time. I stumbled home, milked my goat just enough to relieve her discomfort, then staggered inside my cottage and fell asleep.

The sun was halfway between zenith and horizon when I woke. My goat was bleating piteously. I milked her completely this time, strained the milk, poured it in a milk can, and put it in the spring house. After I washed myself in the pool, I put on my best set of clothes, ones Madja had made for me, and I waited for her. And waited. And waited.

Dusk had melted into night when I finally admitted that she wasn't coming. The chill clutched my heart. The king wasn't going to let her go–ever! Why would he? She could spin straw into gold.

I had to rescue Madja somehow. I ran past the empty mill, the silent village, toward the town and the castle. I prayed that she was all right.

The streets of the town were filled with people singing, dancing, drinking and laughing, celebrating some human holiday. I had to creep through alleys to avoid the crowds. Torches lit all the walls of the castle, making it hard to pick my way unnoticed. Inching along the base of the fortress, I reached the wall where I'd found Madja the nights before.

I listened, hoping I could hear her. I did, but her weeping wasn't coming from the same room. No, she was higher up, at least another floor above me. I clutched at the stones, fingers finding the smallest ledge to grasp, and pulled myself up the sheer wall. Closer, closer to Madja.

I found her in a large room furnished in velvets, brocades, tapestries, and an elaborately carved bed. A man with graying hair lay sprawled across the bed. He reeked of sour wine and heavy perfume. He snored loudly, deep in sleep.

Madja huddled before a blazing fire on the hearth. She wore a satin nightdress embroidered in pure gold thread. Her knees were drawn up to her chest, and she rocked back and forth while she sobbed.

"Madja," I said softly as I ran to her side.

She looked up slowly. For a moment she didn't seem to see me, then her eyes fixed on me. Tears streamed down her face, and she turned away. "Please, go away. I don't want to see you anymore." She rested her forehead on her knees and closed her eyes.

"What's wrong?" I asked, suddenly frightened. "Please let me help. Tell me what's wrong."

She raised her head and stared into the fire. "The king," she said, "the king married me today."

I gasped. "You've married him?"

"No!" she whispered intensely. "He married me! The king marries whom he will. I had no choice, no say! I'm his wife...*his* wife." She covered her face with her hands.

I leaned my cheek against her head and stroked her hair. "We can escape. I can make the stones open for us."

"No," she said. "If I try to leave, the king said he would kill my father. And he would."

"What has your father ever done to deserve your loyalty? He beat you, worked you hard while he drank."

"But he's my father. He raised me after Mother died. He did the best he could." She started weeping again.

"Shhh," I said, "don't cry. It'll be all right."

Madja shook her head. "No, it won't. The king's cruel, greedy, and always drunk. And he wants a son within a year." She shuddered. "The servants told me that most of the time...he can't...he can't..." She glanced up at me, her cheeks flushed. "He's had four other wives. None of them had children. All the wives died suddenly. And I'll be next. I'll be next."

I felt helpless, as helpless as the day I found all my people massacred. There *had* to be something I can do. "I'll help you, somehow," I murmured.

"Can you make him able to give me a child?"

I sighed and shook my head. "That's not the magic of my people. I find things underground, work magic of earth and stone, gems and gold. Growing things, living things, these are the realm of elves, and I don't know where to look for the elves. But I'll search for them if you ask me. I'll go to the four winds if you ask it."

Madja wrapped her arms around me and help me close. "No, I couldn't bear for you to be gone for so long."

"Anything I can do, anything in my power, I'll do for you."

She became still, frozen. Her breathing was shallow and quick. "Give me a child."

"I told you, I don't know the magic."

She caressed my cheek. "No, not magic. Give me your child."

I stared at her. "But I'm a dwarf. I don't know if I *could* give you a child."

She kissed me. "Try," she whispered against my lips.

I did.

Every night I came to be with her. Sometimes, the king was passed out in the bed. Sometimes, he wasn't even there. We'd sit by the fire, quietly talking about our hopes. She'd fall asleep holding me. Just before dawn I'd slip from her embrace and leave.

The moon had waxed and waned and waxed half full when she told me she was carrying our child. I was so surprised, I couldn't say anything for a few moments. Truly, I hadn't thought it possible. Now, I believed *anything* was possible.

I smiled. I grinned. I laughed so loud, Madja had to caution me to quiet.

"Now you will be safe," I said.

"For a while. Until the child is born." Madja paused. "I pray it's a son."

I didn't care whether it was a boy or girl, but a boy with insure Madja safety. "I pray for a son, too."

The whole country rejoiced at the announcement of a royal heir. Madja was cared for, watched over so closely, I seldom found her alone. When she was, it wasn't for long. At least, the king didn't hurt her. However, Madja told me that he beat the servants more often.

All through the winter snow and ice, we waited. The spring rains came, and we waited. Spring had almost given way to summer when Madja's pains came on her early one morning. By midafternoon the midwife announced that the queen had given birth to a healthy son; the kingdom had a prince and heir.

That night I crept to Madja's room. She looked thin, pale. Her forehead felt feverish, but her hands were cold.

"Madja." I breathed on her hands and rubbed them warm. "Madja, my love."

Her eyes flickered open. She smiled weakly. "You're here." She closed her eyes again, resting a moment, then said, "Look at our son."

The lace-draped crèche was almost too tall for me to look into. I pushed a footstool over to the side and climbed up.

I've seen many things that brought joy to my heart: gems that glitter like rainbows, jewelry fit for royalty, arches carved from polished granite, statues of purest marble. None of those things made my heart swell so much in my chest, made my blood pound with pride and love as did that baby lying in the crèche. His hair was as golden as his mother's, but his pug nose was like mine. He was the size of a human baby and was as handsome a little boy as I've ever seen.

I touched his hand, so soft and tiny. His fingers curled around my finger. His eyes opened, dark as smoky topaz, and he gazed at me. My son. My son. A pain so sweet rose in my chest, it brought tears to my eyes.

"He's beautiful," I said softly.

Madja gave me a warm languid smile. "Yes."

I stayed the whole night with her, just happy to be near her and our son. Nurses came when the child cried. I faded into the stone until they left again, but I watched over the two people I loved more than gold and jewels and life itself.

For the next month it was harder to find time along with Madja. Servants came and went at all hours, tending the baby until Madja could. Her son was prince and heir. He had all the attention a prince could have.

Madja's father didn't come to see the baby until he was several weeks old. Dressed in wine-stained velvet and stumbling drunk, her father arrived late one evening. I barely had time to fade into the wall and watch them. The miller stared down at the baby, then grinned at Madja.

"Made our fortune, girl," he said, his tongue thick and slow. "A boy on the first try. The king made me a duke. After all, can't have a plain miller for the king's father-in-law." He laughed so hard, he woke the baby. The newly made duke put a finger to his lips and said, "Shhh, Prince Johann. Grandpa is gonna go drink a toast to you."

He staggered from the room, banging the door shut.

Madja picked up the crying baby and sat on the edge of the bed. She rocked and crooned to our son until he went to sleep again, then she put him back in the crèche. I stayed with Madja until dawn warned me it was time to go.

Three full moons after that, I came to Madja and found her lying on the floor and crying. Her dress was ripped. Her lip was bleeding. Bruises blotched her face and shoulders.

"Who hurt you?" I asked, anger burning like a forge in my heart.

"The king," she said as she wiped the blood from her mouth. "He wanted me. He was drunk." She wrapped her arms around me. "I tried to get away from him, but he caught me and he hit me and hit me and..." She buried her face against my neck, trying to stifle her cries.

"Oh, Madja, you can't stay here anymore," I said. "I can take you and the baby somewhere safe, somewhere away from here."

"Where? How?" she asked hopelessly. "I can't pass through walls the way you do. And I can't just walk out the castle gate."

"No, but I can command the stones to open a doorway for you. We can climb down a rope and flee this place."

She was silent for a moment, then she said, "Yes, my love. Anywhere we can be together."

"Never!" a voice shouted.

I jumped up and saw Madja's father standing with his back against the open chamber door.

"So you're the one," he said through gritted teeth. "I knew something was strange." He glared at Madja. "It's *his* get, not the king's. Isn't it? *Isn't it?*"

"Father, don't, please," Madja said on her knees. "If the king ever thought the child wasn't his—"

"He'd kill you, the child, and me, too," her father said. "But he's not going to find out, not from me. I like living here and being a duke. Nothing's going to take that from me. Nothing. Especially not some gutter dwarf named Rumplestiltskin."

I froze. My throat tightened.

Madja gasped. "How...where did you hear that name?"

Her father smiled, just a hint of his yellowed teeth showing. "From you, daughter dear."

"I never!" she said, shaking her head vigorously. "I never told anyone!"

"Ah, but my dear, you talk in your sleep. I heard you mention that strange word. I finally realized it was a name, a special name, for someone very special to you. And here he is." Her father swept his hand toward me. "I suppose he's the one who turned the straw into gold. I might just make him do that for me from time to time."

I lunged at him, but Madja held me back. I asked her why. She shook her head and said, "Wait."

"Listen, dwarf," her father said. "I hold your life in my hand. I really don't want you dead. You *are* valuable. But I can't let you take Madja and her son out of the castle. They are my guarantee of a good life. So I think I'll forbid you to come here anymore."

"No!" Madja cried. "Father, don't!"

"Shut up, girl."

"No!"

"Shut up, girl, or I'll beat you worse than the king did!"

Slowly, Madja stood up straight, a cold, hard glint in her eyes. "I accepted everything because I couldn't let you die. You're my father, I loved you, but you weren't worthy of my sacrifices."

"Sacrifices," he said with a careless laugh. "You went from miller's daughter to queen to mother of the crown prince. Didn't sacrifice much. And look what we gained."

"What you gained," she shot back.

He shrugged. "What I gained. And I won't lose it. Ever." He turned to me. "Rumplestiltskin, by your name I command that from this day on you are forbidden to come inside the castle, not through the walls, not through the floors, nor through the gates. Be gone!"

Forces, stronger than iron, stronger than the bones of Mother Earth, dragged me toward the castle wall. I fought, but I knew I couldn't win. He'd invoked my true name. I was his slave. I flattened against the stone, struggling not to slide into it.

"Take us with you!" Madja cried. "Don't leave us!"

It was hard to concentrate, but I sang to the stone and opened a doorway through the wall beside me. "A rope!" I gasped as I fought to keep the door open. "A rope."

"Oh, no, dwarf," her father said. "She stays here."

That's when Madja hit him with the footstool. He sagged to the floor, blood streaming from his head.

"Hurry," I groaned. "I can't hold the door open much longer."

Madja grabbed the satin ropes from the bed curtains and tied them together. I hoped they were long enough to reach the ground.

"Tie one end to the bedpost," I said weakly. "Now bind the child to you, then climb down the wall."

Madja bound our son to her chest as securely as she could. She crept through the doorway, wrapped the rope around her hand, and let herself over the edge. When I was certain she was down the rope far enough, I stopped singing, and the opening started to close. I began to sink into the rock.

Suddenly, I heard a shriek. Madja father pushed to his feet and lunged at the rope. He cursed Madja and tried to pull her up. He was halfway through the opening when the stone closed around him. For a few moments he screamed, then was silent.

I reach the outside and skidded down the wall, touching the ground just after Madja did. We ran from the castle, ran through the town, down the road to her village. We circumvented the houses and reached the mill. Madja stuffed a few of her belongings in a bag, then we fled to my cottage.

I tied a rope about my goat's neck, packed my tools and utensils and treasures, including Madja necklace and ring, and we left. We hurried through the woods to the river. I sang stepping stones from the river bed, held them while we crossed the river, then sent them to rest beneath the water. I hoped that not even the best tracking dogs could pick up our scent.

Three days later we reached the ancient hall of my people. I broke the seal I'd placed there when I'd left so many years before. Dust and silence greeted us, but Madja smiled at me.

"Dust I can take care of," she said as she shook out a ragged sheet from a long-unused bed. And soon these halls will echo with children's laughter."

"Children?"

She winked at me. "After all, Johann needs brothers and sisters." She sat on the edge of the bed and began to nurse our son.

I glanced around the deserted halls, then gazed at my wife and son; what I'd lost and what I'd found. My heart filled with joy and love. I wasn't alone anymore.

The Djinn Bottle

This is the first story I sold. Marion Zimmer Bradley was kind enough to buy it for her magazine, and she encouraged me to continue writing, as she did so many other writers. I am so grateful for her advice and kindness.

Adossa sat on a wooden stool, kneading a lump of clay in the cool of morning, when she noticed five strangers riding along the river bank toward her thatched hut. With her forearm she smoothed a few grey strands back to a topknot and shaded her cave-black eyes from the river's glare. Few people from the city ventured this far upstream, especially in the summer heat, unless they were seeking her. She wiped her hands on her roughly woven dress. Thinking of enough gold to buy wheat for winter, she watched the riders approach.

One of the strangers wore a scarlet coat over a white robe, a shining scimitar thrust beneath the red-gold sash. A ruby brooch fixed a feather to the scarlet turban. His skin was like fired clay; he held his black beard high. He was lean and well-disciplined, and his ebony eyes darted everywhere.

Handsome, Adossa thought as her eyes followed the lines of his face and body. *Handsome but dangerous.*

Reining his black stallion, he looked down at her. "I am Elrahad, Tarkhan of Beshtakeen."

"My lord." Adossa bowed just enough to be respectful, watching him as one watches a dangerous animal. "And why does the Tarkhan of Beshtakeen seek out this humble potter?"

He smiled with a cordiality that Adossa knew was feigned. "I have heard that no other potter in the land is your equal."

"You honor me, O Tarkhan." She glanced at the other four riders in white and gold uniforms, then at Elrahad with apprehension.

"A few of my guards," he said in a nonchalant tone, dismissing their presence. "I want you to make a bottle."

"A bottle?"

"Yes. Make it exactly as I wish and I will give you one hundred gold pieces."

A gleam in her eyes, Adossa smiled and bowed. "What kind of bottle do you wish?"

"A bottle to hold a djinn."

He answered in such a matter-of-fact tone that Adossa repeated the words to herself to be certain she'd heard correctly. "My lord, you ask the impossible. No earthly container can hold a spirit."

"Yours can." Elrahad sounded certain. "Otherwise, I would not have come."

Adossa straightened and shook her head. "My lord, you have been misled. I am but a potter, and though I know the secrets of clay, I have no skills in magical arts. No human can trap a djinn."

The Tarkhan leaned forward and smiled slyly. "The Emir of Abustan showed me the magic bottle you made for him. Make one for me."

Adossa started. "The Emir...showed you his bottle?"

Elrahad's smile broadened

Feeling cornered, she studied him slowly with narrowed eyes. "So...you wish to trap a djinn. What color and for what purpose?"

Elrahad sat erect and stared down at her. "The purpose and color are not important."

"But they are. Each color of djinn has unique powers and protections. I must use the right clay and glazes for each. If you try to capture a blue djinn in a bottle made for a red djinn, he will merely laugh at you and crush you beneath his feet. So," she stared back at him with audacity, "if I am to make the correct type of bottle, tell me what I ask. Why do you wish to trap a djinn?"

Elrahad remained silent.

"I must know in order to speak the proper spell," Adossa said with restraint, "or the djinn will not be able to use his powers from within the bottle."

"To become Sultan of all Talukistan." He spoke as if to justify his motives. "The old Sultan is weak; his son is a half-wit. The Sultan's grand Vizier is as old and muddled as the Sultan himself. When he dies, the realm will be thrown into chaos. War, hunger, death–Talukistan will suffer unless a strong leader takes control. *I* want to be that leader, and I need the djinn to help me."

Adossa's voice had a hint of sarcasm. "A noble cause, but it could be the end of you."

"Not if your spell is correct."

Knowing she couldn't dissuade him, she sighed. "And what color?"

The man scowled at her then answered slowly. "A red djinn."

Adossa's eye widened. "The *marid*, elemental spirit of fire! All the *marid* are deceitful and dangerous!"

Elrahad nodded. "Dangerous but powerful."

Glancing at the guards again, the woman stepped back nervously. "My lord, I cannot do as you ask! *Marid* are too powerful!"

"*Two* hundred gold pieces. Enough to buy some goats, wheat and oil for several years, bolts of fine cloth, and even a few precious oranges."

Adossa swallowed hard. As much as she wanted the money, she shook her head. "I dare not! Not even for two hundred gold!"

The Tarkhan's jaw tensed and his eyes burned. "Do you wish your son to live?"

She gasped. "Shamal? You have my son?"

"Yes, and his wife and children." He paused while the potter considered his words. "Make the bottle, and I'll return your family *and* give you the gold."

Adossa's rage blazed like her kiln, but her voice remained quiet. "You will have your bottle, Tarkhan."

"How soon?" Elrahad toyed with the hilt of his scimitar. "The Sultan might die any day."

Adossa pounded the clay on her board. "One week."

"In one week I will return." Turning his mount, Elrahad spoke softly to his guards, then spurred his horse to a canter.

Adossa watched as three Tarkhan guard disappeared downstream. The fourth guard dismounted and remained, his onyx eyes on her.

For a week Adossa worked hard, shaping the clay, letting it dry, and worrying about her son. She ground the colored rocks, mixed the glazes, and thought about her daughter-in-law. She fed the fire in her kiln until the stones glowed like sunset and she prayed for her grandchildren. On the seventh day she brushed away the cold ashes and stones and took out her creation.

Elrahad arrived the next day with the three guards. He looked down at her with amused confidence, then dismounted. "Where is the bottle?"

"Here!" The potter handed him a cloth-wrapped bundle.

Elrahad removed the covering, then gasped.

The bottle was a foot tall with curving handles on either side and a tight fitting stopper. The glaze sparkled with the fiery depth of a ruby. On one side of the bottle was a five-pointed star inscribed in a golden circle.

"Beautiful," Elrahad whispered as his fingers caressed the bottle.

"Yes, it is," the potter said with quiet pride.

"Now, how do I trap the *marid*?"

"Take this honeycomb," Adossa said and handed him a covered crock. "Press out the honey. Melt the wax. Dip the stopper in the wax and say these exact words:

"*Come, O Marid, spirit of flame! By the power of fire, I summon thee! By the power of earth, I hold thee! By the power of wind, I bind thee! By the power of water, I command thee!*

"The djinn will be enslaved to you by the spell. Now, O mighty Tarkhan, where are my son and his family?"

"They will remain my guests, until I have my djinn." He tossed her a large pouch. "Here is your payment. You are truly a great potter."

Adossa glared at him but said nothing.

After rewrapping it, Elrahad placed the bottle and the covered crock in a sack which he tied behind his saddle. He mounted his stallion and gazed down at Adossa with satisfaction. Turning, he rode south to his palace, the four guards following him.

Feeling the weight of gold in her hands, Adossa watched them, anger in her eyes but a hint of a smile on her lips.

Adossa was digging clay just after sunrise the next day when a hot wind roared up the river valley from the south. She cowered face down in the mud, shielding her head with her arms.

A booming voice shook the ground and shattered trees. "Hail, Adossa!"

Peeking over her sleeve, Adossa spotted a figure *ten* times as tall as her hut. His skin was red; his eyes were like black opals. Sharp teeth gleamed like daggers of pearl. In his right hand he held a human-sized figure trapped in a golden cage.

Sitting up, Adossa smiled and bowed respectfully. "Hail, O mighty Zah-Rin!"

"It is good to see you again, mistress of clay," the *marid* said. His voice stirred great waves in the river, and shook Adossa's hut. "I thank you for the Tarkhan. Surprised he was that I did not climb into the bottle. He became quite furious and demanded I make him Sultan. Nearly to tears I laughed myself at the way he chanted the spell!

"Safe is your family; tomorrow they will be home." Zah-Rin poked the cage and grinned. "My new pet will amuse me for many years. For this, Adossa, one wish I grant you."

The potter smiled. "I have all I need, and now..." She glanced with satisfaction at the miserable figure in the cage. "I have the only thing I could want."

The djinn guffawed, flattening Adossa's house and every tree for a two-mile radius. "I like you, potter!" He grinned wickedly and slapped his thigh. With a wave of his hand, he restored the hut and raised new trees along the river bank.

Elrahad cried, "But the Emir of Abustan!" His knuckles whitened as they clutched the golden bars. "I saw the bottle! I *saw* the djinn!"

"Of course, you fool," Adossa said without pity. "He was bound by his own kind. Zah-Rin asked me to make that bottle so the Emir could control the djinn during his imprisonment. I *told* you, no human can trap a djinn."

Carefully, Zah-Rin placed the crimson bottle beside her. "May you live a long and happy life, mistress of clay!" The *marid* then disappeared, his laughter mixing with Elrahad's wail.

Standing, Adossa picked up the djinn bottle and walked to her hut. She set the bottle on a shelf–beside four similar ones she'd been compelled to make over the years.

Djinnxed

The Tales of the Arabian Nights were also a favorite of mine growing up. Genies, flying carpets, great voyages–these still live in my mind.

For the 10 millionth time, Zhumaii paced his window is present, counted the cracks in the walls, sang every something new, and cursed his fate. "That mortal wizard commanded me to abduct the Sultan's favorite concubine! I had no choice! And for this the Sultan imprisoned me! If I am ever released, I shall slay the first mortal I see. Then I shall find the Sultan and the wizard and slave, as well!"

Suddenly, the cells started shaking, causing July to the bare floor. He heard a loud pop rush of wind. Sunlight poured in from above. Surprised, he stared at the warm, yellow light, then he yelled with joy and slew upwards toward the opening. He stretched to his full height and looked eagerly about for whoever had freed him.

Standing on a white sandy beach was a tiny man, strange close to being wet. He held a dark bottle in one hand, its stopper in the other. The man's mouth dropped open as he stared up in Zhumaii.

"Bow, O mortal!" Zhumaii said. "Pray to your gods, for I am Zhumaii the blue djinn, and I am going to kill you!"

For a moment the man didn't move. Then he ran toward Zhumaii, hugged the djinn's gigantic pale blue ankle, and said, "Oh, thank you! Thank yu ever so much!"

Zhumaii blinked his emerald eyes, uncertain he'd heard the man correctly. "Mortal, I mean to kill you!"

"Yes, I know!" The man said with a lopsided grin. "I'm so grateful! Could you do it right now?"

Is he mad, the djinn wondered cautiously, *or just a fool? Killing a madman brings ill luck.* "You wish me to kill you?"

"Oh, yes, if you would." The man nodded vigorously, swayed, then rested his head against the djinn ankle before he looked up again, grinning. "You are a genie, are you? I never thought I'd be so lucky!"

Irritated, Zhumaii asked, "Why, mortal, should I give you what you desire? Why do you wish to die?"

The man plopped down on the sand, grabbed a pale green bottle marked "Brandy," took a gulp and coughed. "You don't want to hear my story."

Zhumaii stared at him, then threw up his hands. "I have not heard a new tale since Kasim the Blind told me about the merchant and the twin dancing girls with their enormous..." He paused, delight shivering through him.

"You must've been in there a long time," the man said.

Zhumaii rubbed his chin. "I do not know."

The man shrugged. "Doesn't really matter. Sit down, and I'll tell you my troubles."

Confused, Zhumaii lowered himself to the warm sand side the man.

"Oh, my name is Franklin. Franklin Virgil Gates, III," the man said and stuck out a hand to the djinn.

Ignoring the hand, Zhumaii said, "and I, Franklin Franklin Virgil Gates, III, am Zhumaii Ali ben Yusef, fourth tarkon of the blue djinn, captain of the Great Djinn's legions, Lord of the summer winds."

"You certainly are blue," said the man, brown eyes wide as he scanned Zhumaii from head to toe. "And call me Frank."

"As you wish," the djinn said, "and you may call me Zhumaii."

"Do you mind if I ask you a question?"

"Ask what you will, Frank," Zhumaii said.

"You're a djinn, not a genie? What's the difference?"

Zhumaii's lips curled, revealing sharp teeth. "Genie is a mortal word which angers us. Often, the utterer's tongue is ripped out."

Frank patted his soggy chest. "I'd never offend a person with a racial slur! I'll never use that word again." Abruptly, he laughed. "Of course, since I'll be dead soon, I won't have a chance to."

Zhumaii grinned wider. "That is good."

"Anyway, where was I?" Frank frowned and scratched his stubbly cheek. "Oh. I was trying to drown myself when I found your bottle and opened it."

"Why were you trying to drown yourself?"

Frank's shoulders slumped, and he shook his head. "You wouldn't believe. Nothing in my life has gone right. Do you know what it's like to be smarter than all the other kids in town?" He glanced up at Zhumaii. "No, I guess not. Anyway, I swore I'd leave when I grew up, and I did. Got a scholarship to UCLA to study computers—"

Zhumaii cocked his head. "UCLA? Computers?"

Frank raised a bushy brow. "University of California as Los Angeles. And a computer, well, it's like a..." he scrunched his mouth, tapped his chin, then brightened, "like an abacus, a counting machine. Sorta."

"Ah," Zhumaii said.

"I graduated in only two years and started Lasertronics to build computers. I had a rich wife, a son, a huge estate, a yacht, summer home, cars, horses, stocks, everything a man could want."

Zhumaii didn't understand all of that, but he said, "Then you are wealthy and much favored by the gods."

Frank snorted, "I wish! My vice president in charge of accounting embezzled sixty percent of the profits last year, claimed a loss on taxes, and left a set of books implicating me!" He barely caught himself before he toppled to the side. "Sure, I've skimmed a little, cheated on taxes, used every loophole I could, but nothing like he did. Now the IRS is confiscating everything not in trust for my kid. And I'm looking at years in prison for tax evasion!"

Vice president? Embezzled? IRS? What did these words mean? "I have heard it said that man's wealth is in his family. Is not your family well?"

Frank groaned. "My wife just filed for divorce. She wants to marry her fitness instructor! She says I only wanted her money. Sure I did, but I didn't need it after my company became successful."

He sniffled and hugged his bottle. "My son's in Tibet, getting in touch with his inner self, turning his back on the world. Of course, he used my money to get to Tibet and keeps drawing from my account." He took another drink. He looked so dejected, Zhumaii almost felt sorry for him.

"But what of your trade?" Zhumaii asked. "Do you not find satisfaction in your work, building these computers?"

Frank cringed. "Foreign companies make chips cheaper than I can buy here, and have clones out as soon as mine hit stores. They underbid me on big contracts, lure my best engineers away, and even tried a takeover. I only managed to keep the company by getting a loan—just before the bank went belly-up. Now the new owners want to foreclose." He drained the bottle, brandy trickling from the corner of his mouth. "I'm ruined! Nothing left! That's why I want you to kill me, see?"

Zhumaii stood up and scowled at Frank. "Yes. I see that you are indeed a miserable mortal. To kill you would be merciful." He raised his foot to crush Frank, then halted. Zhumaii's eyes widened, then he smiled and set his foot down beside Frank. "But I am not merciful. I swore that I would slay the first mortal I saw when I was free, in revenge against the mortal wizard who caused my imprisonment. But allowing you to live would be the greatest curse I could give you. May you only die of old age and never prosper."

"I...I won't die?" Frank staggered to his feet. "No—wait! You said you would!"

Zhumaii laughed. "Farewell, O most miserable of men, and may you live many years." He launched into the midday sky, while Frank's shouts of "You can't do this to me!" faded behind him.

Zhumaii was free at last. It was good to breathe fresh air, feel the warm sun on his back, and hear the whisper of wind, the song of sea birds, the crash of waves. Soon he would reach the lands of silks and spices, camels and caravans.

"Now may the descendants if the Sultan and of the wizard yet live." He grinned, anticipation as sweet as honeycomb in his mouth. "But not for long."

A Woman of Vision

This was one of the first stories I ever wrote. When I went to a writers workshop, I discovered one of the attendees was part of a through the mail workshop and had read this story. She and I still part of a writers group that has been together for nearly thirty years. This is still one of my favorites.

"Filea! Come back here!" Exasperation made my voice harsh as I picked up her discarded bundle of belongings from the grassy roadside. Brushing the dust from my off-white blouse, leather jerkin, and dark brown trousers, I gripped the hilt of my broad sword and yelled, "This road's not safe, and we have to reach Zylona before the gates close for the night!"

Filea laughed at my frustration as she ran farther away.

"I'm not sleeping outdoors when I can have a warm bed and a stomach filled with hot food. Fi!"

Her blond hair falling to her waist, Filea ran gracefully through the thick grass. She picked red clover to make a garland for her head and nibbled yellow-flowered sour grass. Lifting her pale, oval face toward the late afternoon sky, she smiled and began to turn in circles. He blue frock hugged her breasts and hip, a delicious temptation to any man. Her face glowed with the blush of youth, her body blooming into womanhood, but her deep blue eyes revealed a mind that would always be a child's. I was her protector, her keeper, her sister, her twin.

Filea and I were identical twins, except I was more muscular and looked older. Worry and fear had added lines and creases to my face and a cynical glint to my eyes. Though I'd been born with healing powers called ramoojin, now I had only the limited telepathy of my people. However, I had a quick eye and quicker hands and feet. I needed them to keep us alive in the hostile lands we traveled.

The two of us had wandered many lands in the eight years since we'd fled our home in Amajin: the mountain peaks of Rothen where the natives live on yak milk and where tons of snow could crush a person at a whisper; the rock-strewn desert of Kolkoth where nomadic tribes drove their goats from oasis to scrub grass meadows and where sand snakes waited for unwary travelers; Stryend-By-The-Sea where date palms grew and bitter-skinned oranges were held more precious than gold; and Far Samdi of gilded temples and vibrant silks, of thieves and harlots and death in dark alleys. We'd survived all these. Filea had grown more beautiful and graceful while I'd grown stronger and more agile.

We were on our way to Zylona, walled capital of Hamadeen. Now that the Kallisi hordes had been driven out, the land was safe to visit. I'd hoped to earn some money at the Midsummer Festival, the celebration of the first harvest. My sword and Fi's dancing had always provided for us, but more than once he'd had to flee when her visions had fired Villagers' suspicion and anger. I knew that somehow I had to prevent Filea exhausting herself while dancing at the festival. We needed the money, but I felt uncertain about going to Zylona.

I stood beside the dusty road and watched Filea dancing. She was completely unaware of danger that might be lurking nearby. Anger and resentment rose in me. Sometimes I almost hated her. No...no, I didn't hate her. I just wanted to be able to think about my own needs for once: a home, children, a man who loved me–things other women enjoyed. Instead, I had to think of Fi's welfare. She was free of responsibility. I was the one who always worried, who lay awake wondering where our next meal would come from, how long I could protect Fi. I sighed, knowing I couldn't forget my responsibility, and knowing, too, that I wouldn't turn away from it even if I had the opportunity. I loved my sister. I was just tired and edgy.

Shifting my backpack, my shoulders aching from the pull of the straps, I ran after Filea. "Enough!" I said, irritated. "You can dance in the city. We'll find a warm place to sleep and some food. Now, let's go!"

Dragging her back to the road and handing her bundle toi her, I hurried her toward Zylona, shining white amid the grassy plain. Horsemen, wearing the king's red and gold livery with their scimitars flashing at their sides, and gaily colored wagons passed us. We trudge on, foot-sore and tired. Our empty stomachs growled. Filea grew cranky and pouted because we'd walked half the night and all day without more than a few minutes rest. Finally, she plopped down on the grassy shoulder and refused to take another step.

Just then, another wagon lumbered beside us and stopped. The driver was an old woman, as homely and portly as Filea was beautiful and slim. The woman's skin was like blotchy leather. Her mouth was a nearly toothless gash across her pig-like face. She had hands so broad and thick that I was amazed she could bend them enough to grip the reins. Grey-black hair was slicked back into a knot and held in place with two ceramic rods. Her dress was a mosaic of fabrics. But the one thing that attracted my attention was her one good eye, her other one hidden by a patch. Golden and feline, her eye gleamed with cunning.

She surveyed us thoroughly, scratched her bristly chins, and pursed her lips before speaking in a raspy but kindly voice. "You two young girls look worn out, you being just babes compared to me, me being older than the sea, and it's a hot day, the sun beating down so hard, though not so bad as last year, and I thought, me seeing you sitting beside the road all worn out, that you might like a ride to Zylona, the road being unsafe for such pretty children as you and the city being a mile yet and the gates closing at sunset, and would you accept a ride in my wagon?"

I gaped at the old woman, astonished she'd said the entire speech in one breath.

"Yes!" Filea jumped to her feet and started to scramble up on the seat.

"Fi!" I shouted, tugging at my sister's arm. Caution had become automatic with me. I didn't know anything about the old woman, not even her name.

The driver scowled at me, chubby fists on sprawling hip. "Fie on you, too, you ungrateful snip, and may you have blisters as big as hen's eggs on your feet at day's end!"

While I was distracted by the driver's outburst, Fi wriggled from my grasp, darted around the front of the wagon, and climbed up on the seat beside the woman.

"No, I mean Fi is her name!" I said, frustrated by Fi's behavior but anxious not to offend the old woman. "Filea. And I'm Elan."

"Oh, I see." The old woman grinned at me as Filea removed her thin boots to rub her feet. Stretching her massive arm out to help me up to the wagon seat, the driver continued, "Filea and Elan, two fine young girls come, I think, to see the wonders of the Midsummer Festival that's like nothing else you'll ever see, no matter where you may journey from Zylona, and my name is Old Matty, though I had another name once, but I don't remember what it was because everyone's called me Old Matty for so long, but it doesn't bother me at all, and I imagine that you've never been to the festival or Zylona so I'll take you babes under my care, so to speak, and show you the cheapest places to room, the friendliest taverns, and the best spots to set up your business, and if I may ask, what are you selling, seeing that you have no wares to hawk, and where do two such lovely children come from, if I may ask?"

Open-mouthed, I stared at Old Matty a long time before I could answer, trying not to trip over my words. "Filea's a dancer, and I'm a fighter, a sword for hire, but usually I guard Fi."

Old Matty chuckled and slapped her thick thigh. "Aye, indeed, and such a pretty thing needs guarding along this road, what with bandits watching for merchants and others going to the festival, and don't I know it well, being I was attacked on my way to Zylona last year, not that I had anything worth stealing, just pottery I make to sell at the festival, but those robbers didn't know that so they stopped me and searched my wagon, naturally finding nothing they wanted, and you certainly are lucky I came by when I did and..." Old Matty rattled on as she confidently guided her team along the road to the city.

Zylona's walls were constructed of white stone, whether limestone or marble I couldn't tell, and topped with merlons like the teeth of some giant beast. Four white minarets stood above the walls. And in the center of the city, rising high above the fortifications, was the onion-shaped dome of the king's palace, gilded and gleaming in the sunlight.

From Old Matty's chatter I learned that, although she'd been born in Zylona, she lived near a village about three miles east and north. Her husband had died twenty years ago, leaving her with four sons and two daughters to support by selling the pottery she made. She journeyed to Zylona for three days each month except at midsummer when she stayed for the entire festival week. She never mentioned what had happened to her eye. I didn't ask about it, out of consideration for her–and because I had an uneasy feeling that I'd be expected to answer questions about myself, questions I didn't dare answer.

Fi and I were the last members of a tribe of Jin. For millennia out people had wandered all the lands from the northern mountains to the southern sea, from the eastern deserts to the vast western plains. Jin had warred against no one, killed only for food, and lived in harmony with the land and with each other.

Then from across the sea had come the humans, the *kreeyagen*, which in our language meant "the ones who kill when not hungry." Our people couldn't understand the newcomers. Jin had tried to live in peace, offering gifts and friendship and sharing the land. But the humans would not share. We had power which were no more magical to us than breathing or laughing, but the humans had viewed our abilities with awe, envy, and suspicion. They struck out at us from fear.

Hunted by the *kreeyagen*, the Jin had scattered into small tribes, driven into hiding. Over the years the tribes lost contact with each other. Whether the other tribes had died out, were massacred, or were too remotely hidden, we didn't know. For over two thousand years my tribe had lived in Amajin, a heavily wooded hilly region north of the kingdom of Zraylin. We'd feared we were the only Jin surviving.

All Jin had the power to reach each other's minds in times of fear or worry, but some had special gifts. Aurojin were males who could see ores and gemstones through solid rock so miners could dig more directly for what they sought. The kirojin were young boys who understood the speech of animals and even walked safely into dens of lions. Some women, called felojin, could weave a charm for luck or love into a kerchief or scarf while other, called ramoojin, could heal minor wounds immediately or speed the healing of more serious injuries. I had been ramoojin, though I'd lost that power. But the rarest and most prized were the khoroojin, the young girls who danced like butterflies, like gazelles, until exhausted. Visions of the future would come to the dancer then, warnings of danger or promises of prosperity. Filea was khoroojin.

The khoroojin's power vanished at age sixteen, being linked in some unknown way to the time,m of choosing mates, but Filea was born with a mind that never grew older than a child of eight summers. Her ability had remained with her although she was now twenty-five. She was a wonder, a unique treasure unlike any in the history of the Jin.

We arrived at Zylona's iron gates as the sun touched the western mountains. Lines of people waited while the city guards questioned every visitor. Some were mounted, some on foot, some led pack animals, and some carried packs on their own back. All were trying to gain admittance before sunset shut them outside the protection of the high stone walls.

Old Matty patted my hand with her paw. "Now, don't you worry about getting inside, little Elan, because Old Matty's well-known to the guards, and even the sun will hold a while until I'm well inside, and then I'll conduct you to an inn I know, the innkeeper being an old friend of mine, and you can stay the night there if you like, and Lyedy, that being the innkeeper's name, you see, Lyedy will treat you fairly, you being a friend of Old Matty."

For some reason, I trusted her. She was so huge that she dwarfed everyone else and made me feel secure.

Finally, the wagon stopped before the gate while two guards approached us.

"Well, look who's come to grace our festival again this year." One of the guards greeted the old woman with a wink. "Old Matty, a queen among women! And it looks like she's brought a couple of princesses with her." He stared at me with contempt. "At least one princess...and a solvadish."

I didn't understand the word, but the meaning was unmistakable. I'd found the same attitude in most places I'd been. Often, a female mercenary was considered just below a prostitute, an affront to the natural order of male supremacy. Some societies had even worse words for me.

The other guard grinned at Filea. "Just what we need to complete our celebration. I'll see to it personally that you'll enjoy yourself, if you understand me."

"Will you?" Fi clapped her hands with innocent excitement.

"Forget it, Fi!" I said through clenched teeth, my hand gripping my sword hilt as my temper flared.

"But, El, I want to!"

The first guard jabbed his comrade in the side, pointed to me, and said, "All she needs is a man to teach her what a woman is good for, and I'm just the man to do it."

As the guards leered openly at Filea and me, Matty took out her whip, shook it, and scolded them. "You ill-begotten sons of camels, you watch your tongues or I'll teach you some manners, you being disrespectful to two ladies such as these, them coming to the festival for the first time, and maybe the last, what with gutter-spawned rogues like you speaking so rudely to them, so you apologize, and maybe I won't lay this whip across your ugly faces."

"Matty, you wound me!" the first guard replied. "I merely offered to show these two lovely ladies the wonders of our city."

Matty snorted, still brandishing her whip. "I know exactly what you were offering, and don't think you can fool me with your innocent looks because I know what kind of *wonders* you meant, but these two are under my protection and if any harm comes to them, I'll peel the skin from your backs with this whip, if you understand me!"

The guard laughed. "Indeed, we do! We have no intention of angering you, Matty. The whole city would riot if you ordered it."

"And don't you forget it, you disgusting excuse for a man, and your mother should be ashamed of you!" Matty slapped the reins to start her team through the gates.

"I don't have a mother," the guard said, laughing heartily, "or a father either."

Matty held her chins high. "That doesn't surprise me even a little, you dirt-eating worm-riddled bastard!"

"We love you, too!"

"Some guards they are," Matty grumbled as she glared at them, although I knew she wasn't serious, "a disgrace to the garrison, but don't you let them bother you because Old Matty'll watch out for you and I've lots of friends here so don't you worry because you're safe with me."

We drove through a short, dark tunnel and emerged in a broad street clogged with animals, wagons, and jostling people, all pressing toward the bazaar to find the best spot to sell their wares. Mud-plastered houses, two-stories high and jammed wall to wall, lined the street. Cloth awnings shaded the recessed doorways. The air was thick with dust and the sweaty odor of animals and humans crowded into a small space at the end of a hot, sticky day. Voices haggled over merchandise in the shops or railed at the slow pace of those ahead of them. Donkeys and camels brayed impatiently, longing for a cool stall and food. At every intersection of street and alley, the blind, lame, or disfigured begged for alms. Children, well-trained in the thieving arts, wove through the mass of visitors. Old Matty discouraged the rascals with a scowl and a wave of her whip.

Matty turned left out of the press of people and headed south on a street little wider than the wagon. Passing shops and houses identical to each other, Matty turned right on a broad street, shadowed and quiet. Near the end, where I could see the palace dome thrust above a courtyard wall, Matty halted before a wooden door. A black kettle was painted on a red sign which heralded the building as an inn.

Leaping from the wagon seat with unbelievable grace and agility, Matty stood with fists on her hips and bellowed, "Where's the thieving owner of this dung heap of an inn?"

It was the shortest sentence I'd heard her say since we'd met.

The door banged open, and out stalked a man as huge as Matty but not as ugly. Thick, grey hair was cropped short as was his beard. Green eyes glittered in a pock-marked face. The rolled-sleeve shirt he wore could have fit the horses. His stained apron could have served as a sail. His legs and arms were twice as thick as those of a blacksmith, and the tread of his feet shook the ground. "And just what brainless gutter-rat is stupid enough to call my inn a dung heap?" he shouted.

Matty glared at him. "I'm the one that called this decayed wreck a dung heap, and that's kind compared to what I should have said, but since there are children present, I curbed my tongue rather than describe this establishment with the accuracy it deserves!"

The innkeeper's face broke into a grin, and he slapped his thigh. "Matty! I'm glad to see you! I'd begun to wonder if you'd make the festival this year!"

"And why shouldn't I?" Matty said with a grin as she sauntered toward him. "The year I miss the Midsummer Festival, Lyedy, will be the year I'm lying in my grave, and that won't be for many years because someone has to keep rascals like you honest, and it might as well be me!"

Lyedy hugged the old woman, then turned to Filea and me.

"Friends of mine," Matty said, her face crinkling with a smile, "this being Filea, and this being her sister Elan, and this..." she pointed at the innkeeper, "is Lyedy Solls, innkeeper, and you better treat them fairly or I'll spread a tale that you use rats in your stew and keep bugs in you bedding, and you know that everyone in the city will believe Old Matty."

"For you, Matty, I'll serve them like queens." Lyedy bowed respectfully to us. "Come, young friends of Old Matty, the best rooms in my inn are yours for the duration of the festival, and food, wholesome and hearty, cooked by my wife."

I hesitated, remembering the five copper regals in my pouch that were our only wealthy, and wondered how much the best rooms and meals cost. Filea eagerly jumped from the seat, but I hung back. I guess my uncertainty showed in my face, because Lyedy said,

"During festival week, most guests pay at the end of their stay, when they've sold their wares."

"Thank you," I said relieved.

Lyedy studied us. "What do you bring to Zylona?"

"Filea's a dancer," Matty answered before I could, "and Elan's a mercenary looking for work, and if you know anyone who needs an extra guard during the festival, what with thieves trying to steal everything possible, then you tell him about Elan, as fine a fighter as I've seen in all my years."

I was startled by Matty's praise and disconcerted by her gaze. She'd never seen me fight, but if I could find work on her recommendation, I'd do my best to be worthy of her faith.

Lyedy scratched his jowls ang gave me a look somewhere between skepticism and distaste. "I know of several who might be interested in an extra sword, but not many will hire a woman. I'll send my boy Yamal to ask within the hour, but don't expect too much. Silas and Rogon will stable your team, Matty. Now, come inside. Rest and eat while I prepare your rooms."

Matty and Lyedy entered the inn single file, barely squeezing through the doorway. Filea skipped behind them. I followed more slowly, wondering if we would earn enough to pay for the rooms and keep food in our bellies for a while.

As I entered the common room of the inn, I noticed it was crowded with people. All of them were gaping at Filea. Most people I'd seen in Zylona had dark skin and black hair, which made Filea even more exotic to the inn's guests.

Three young men dressed in fine clothing stopped drinking their wine as they stared at my sister. Rising unsteadily, they swaggered toward Fi. One man blocked her path, his wolfish grin revealing yellow teeth. "Come, join us at our table, my pretty one."

I stepped in front of Fi. "No."

He ignored me and spoke to her. "We can share a cup of wine."

"She doesn't want to sit with you," I said firmly, my eyes narrowing.

"And are you her keeper?" one of them asked.

"I'm her sister," I said. I moved my hand toward my dagger, prepared to fight.

The drunken man licked his thick lips and moved closer. "I see. You can join us, too."

As he eyed me, I shuddered. Anger, hot and deadly, flared in my heart. In a quiet voice that betrayed my rage, I said, "Get out of our way."

I suppose he didn't think I was serious. Men often underestimated me, believing I was just a woman and no match for them. Some had died from that belief. Whatever his reason, he grabbed my arm and tried to pull me to him.

Drawing my dagger too quickly for him to react, I whipped the blade's point to his throat and pressed just enough to hurt but not enough to cause serious bleeding. "I said no!"

Cursing, his two companions started for me. Lyedy stepped behind them, grabbed their cloaks, and jerked the men off the floor. Calmly, but leaving no doubt that he was serious, Lyedy said, "Leave now or I'll break you into pieces and feed you to my hounds."

With a last glance at Filea and me, the man I had at knife point stepped back, grumbling, and signaled for his companions to follow him. Furious but resigned, the two men nodded, and Lyedy released them. They exited the door without looking back.

Watching with relief, I trembled. I would have killed them if they had pressed me. Deep inside, the voices of my ancestors cried out against the rage I felt.

Lyedy turned to face me. "My apologies, Elan. They won't be allowed through my door again."

Matty, Filea, and I followed Lyedy to a square table near the counter which separated the common room from the kitchen. Lyedy served us thick stew, crusty bread, and a dry red wine, all of which I downed with ravenous concentration. I didn't worry too much about young men swarming after Filea. I'd always discouraged them with a few words of warning backed up with my sword. There was greater danger than a few easily rebuffed advances: the discovery of our heritage.

"Tag, tell us the story about the Jin," came a voice from directly behind me.

A deep, rich voice gave a vibrant laugh and said, "Oh, I've told it so many times, you could tell it yourself."

"Ah, but none of us has your talent. Please?"

Tag laughed again. "All right. Hear now the tale of the prince and the evil Jin."

I nearly choked. Even in Zylona, Fi and I weren't safe. My face felt cold, and I shivered. Memories, as sweet as the first sip of wine and as bitter as the last, blurred my vision.

Fi and I had been orphaned eight years before. While gathering wild berries, we'd received terrified images from our parents. We'd raced through the hills and arrived in time to witness another attack of Zraylin against our people. I'd dragged Fi behind boulders on the hill above our home and watched in horror as Zraylin soldiers slaughtered every Jin in the village, including our parents and two younger brothers and an older sister. Weeping silently with my hand clapped over Filea's mouth, I'd held her until the murderers had left.

I think I buried my heart that night as I'd buried my family and friends, but somehow I'd found strength within me, a strength like steel: cold, hard, razor sharp and unyielding, the strength to survive. I'd taken up an abandoned Zraylin sword to fight, to kill if necessary, in spite of millennia of non-violence. My rammojin powers had vanished, perhaps destroyed by hatred. I was Jin, but like my sister, I was flawed.

As I stared into the wine, someone touched my shoulder, and I jumped, startled. Looking up, I saw Matty staring at me with her golden eye. For some reason, I thought she sensed the bitter anger that burned like acid in my heart, but she didn't mention it.

"The festival begins at dawn, Elan, and we all need rest so we're up before the sun and set up our booths, so off you go to bed, and may the gods send you peaceful sleep." She gave Fi and me a hug and a pat on the cheek.

Lyedy's wife, Lori, guided us to our rooms on the second floor. She was a full-figured woman in a blue dress with white apron, grey-black hair wound into crown. I liked the warm smile she gave us, but when she indicated that Fi was to have a separate room, I refused.

"My sister always sleeps in my room," I said softly. "She's afraid if she's alone."

"I understand," Lori said, nodding, her eyes glancing at Fi. "I'll see that another bed is brought into your room. Is there anything else I can bring you?"

"Some hot water for a bath." I longed to wash the dust from my skin and soak my sore feet.

"You'll have it in a few minutes." Lori gave me a motherly smile before she left, closing the door behind her.

"El, why didn't you want me to sit with those men?" Fi asked me, her tone curious rather than indignant.

I hesitated, not knowing how to explain. "They weren't kind men."

"But they seemed so nice."

"Well, they weren't!" My tone was sharper than I'd intended. "They wanted to hurt you, and I wouldn't let them. Don't worry, Fi. I won't let anyone hurt you, ever."

My sister looked puzzled. She never seemed to realize why other people would harm her.

Lori soon appeared with two buckets of hot water to mix with cold water from the pitcher beside the basin. Two young men, very attractive and obviously Lyedy's sons by their looks, carried a bed frame into the room. A girl of perhaps fourteen years, a younger version of Lori, dragged in a mattress. While the men went to fetch tubs, Lori and the girl spread and tucked a sheet over the mattress, then a sheet and light coverlet over all. Lori and the girl left but came back with two more buckets of hot water. The sons returned with two tubs, towels, and soap. Lori filled both tubs with water, then she and her children left.

I told Fi to strip off her clothes and wash. I dropped my clothes in a heap and stepped cautiously into the steaming water, letting my feet adjust to the heat. I lowered myself into the tub and relaxed. My eyes closed as the warmth soothed my tired body. The water felt so good, I nearly fell asleep. Shaking my head, I lathered with the soap, then rinsed.

"Did you notice the men who brought in the bed and tubs?" Fi asked as she made a soap bubble.

"Why?" I said, wondering if I should be concerned for her.

Fi grinned impishly. "One of them was watching you."

"Oh?" I was surprised to be noticed by a man and more surprised that Fi had noticed. "Which one?"

"The one with the green eyes. He likes you."

Embarrassed, I blushed, my heart beating quickly. "Don't be foolish, Fi. Just wash up."

Fi had dried off and was pulling a gown over her head by the time I stood up and stepped out of the tub. She jumped into bed and pulled the sheet over her. Shivering, I dried quickly and donned my gown. I slipped under the cool sheet and lay my sword beside me from habit. Forgetting my doubts and fears, I snuggled deep in the soft bed.

A knock brought me to my feet, sword in hand, my senses alert, my muscles coiled to fight.

Matty opened the door, a wide smile on her face until she saw my drawn sword. "You're safe here, little Elan," she said as I sheathed my weapon and returned to bed. "No one will hurt you as long as Matty and Lyedy are watching over you, so sleep peacefully, child, and tomorrow you can start work for Scrivvins the jeweler, his shop being right across from my stall, and there'll be room for little Fi to dance beside my wagon so you can keep an eye on her while you work."

Matty lumbered over to Fi and kissed her forehead. Fi looked up at the mountain of a woman and smiled, a light in Fi's eyes as if she remembered something. Then she lay down and curled up like a cat. Matty covered her, stroking Fi's hair until she slept.

"Such a pretty child she is," Matty said softly, sadness in her golden eye as she shook her head, "and a child she'll be all her life, and such a burden that is for you, Elan, so hard to bear, yet you bear it well and with love, to your credit, for you have strength, such strength that comes only from suffering, and you've suffered, as your eyes tell me."

I said nothing, astonished she could see so clearly. Like a knife her gaze cut through me, laying open my heart, revealing all my doubt, anger, and terror.

Since the chair beside my bed wasn't large enough or sturdy enough to support her, Matty sat on the floor. "Fear only breeds fear, Elan, and trust breeds trust, and you'll find that I'm as trustworthy as I am ugly." She held up her hand to stop my protest. "I know what I look like to those who see me, but I know what most don't, you see, because I know what's in here." She thumped her massive bosom. "And if I'm satisfied with myself, then I'm happy, so remember, Elan, be happy with yourself, and others will see you, not as you appear, but as you are."

"Thank you, Matty." My throat was tight. Tears I refused to shed seemed to drain to my heart, splashing down like spring rain on frozen ground, thawing, warming, bringing life again.

Matty smiled. Perhaps because of the soft moonlight, she didn't seem as ugly as when I'd first seen her.

Long before dawn I woke up, refreshed and ready to begin work. Even Fi was excited, barely able to sit still during breakfast. Lyedy's sons Silas and Rogon had already hitched up Matty's team by the time we'd finished eating. With Filea and Rogon beside Matty, Silas and me on the drop gate, we headed for the bazaar, the young men accompanying us to lead the horses back to the stable.

The bazaar was directly east of the gate of the palace's outer courtyard. When we arrived, other merchants and craftsmen, who had parked their wagons and carts wherever available the night before, were already setting up tables and spreading out their wares.

Before leaving with Rogon and Matty's team, Silas introduced me to my employer. "Master, this is Elan. Lady, this is Scrivvins the jeweler."

The thin, balding man stared at me with skeptical eyes. "Usually, I don't hire women. However, Lyedy gave you a recommendation so I decided to take a chance on you."

"I thank you, sir," I said. "I'll serve you faithfully."

Grunting, he turned back to setting out his stock.

"Don't mind him," Silas whispered as he leaned close to me. "He's always like that. I know you'll do fine. I'll see you when the market closes." He smiled warmly, then left.

My heart fluttered a little. If I weren't always so wary, if I could forget my responsibilities and just be an ordinary woman for just a while…I glanced at Filea standing beside Matty's wagon. Resentment crept into my heart. No, I'd never be just an ordinary woman. I was responsible for Fi and would be for the rest of my life

As Matty opened the sides of her wagon and propped the hinged walls with sturdy poles, I inspected her wares with surprise. She said she made pottery, but calling her work mere pottery was like calling a flawless diamond a common rock. Her vases and jars were graceful and smooth; the glazes, rich, with a depth like looking into a clear stream. Plates and bowls, pots and cups, all were functional yet with an elegance that would brighten any home.

The first customers were other merchants, weighing with keen eyes the value of their competitors' goods. I wandered through the aisles with Fi in tow, feeling the fluid silks and thick furs with envy. Fi sniffed the aroma of fruit pastries while I examined finely crafted daggers and swords. Nearby, a rotund man in green silk pants, red silk shirt, and yellow silk vest proclaimed that Izolda the Great would reveal the future for two copper regals. Not wanting to take a chance that Izolda had the gift of farsight, I hurried on to the animal pens, dragging a protesting Fi with me.

The sun had risen well above the eastern wall when buyers and lookers came from their inns and homes. Everyone wanted to touch and smell, to test and examine carefully, to haggle and argue until both buyer and seller were satisfied with the exchange of money and goods.

I stationed myself beside Matty's wagon across from Scrivvins' table and took out my mother's silver flute to play as Fi began her dance. Scrivvins had agreed to allow me an portion of every hour to accompany her.

Filea wore a diaphanous dress of royal blue, revealing enough to tempt the most saintly yet still retaining a quality of innocence. The color enhanced Fi's fair skin and golden hair. A gossamer veil matching her dress covered her face below her eyes, which I'd carefully outlined with kohl to draw the onlookers' attention. She was beauty such as young men worship and old men dream of.

I played a lively tune as she began her dance, her finger cymbals tinkling in time with the music. Her hips swayed as she circled the area. Fi whirled, her skirt nearly standing straight out. Hands over her head, backs together, she made a half turn left then right alternately, moving past the growing crowd of spectators who stood in silent awe of her liquid grace. She removed her veil and swung it behind her then before her, teasing the crowd with glimpses of her face. Then she flung the veil away, and Old Matty picked it up.

I slowed the tempo as Fi began her hand dance, moving her hands and arms enticingly like serpents. Bending backward impossibly far, Fi seemed to weave a spell with her fingers, the ching of her cymbals drawing the watchers into the enchantment.

Finally, I changed to a quick, exciting rhythm. Fi leaped like a gazelle and landed spinning. She shimmied back and forth, side to side. Her body seemed to ripple like a field of wheat moved by the wind. She whirled, her gleaming hair flung out, then collapsed to one knee like a broken flower. Her hair cascaded over her face. She crossed her hands in front of her. With one last ching of her cymbals, she ended her dance.

As always, Fi's performance was a success. Copper regals and a few silver ones showered the ground at Fi's feet as people shouted their approval. If every crowd were as enthusiastic, we'd have enough money to feed us for several weeks.

Fi stayed beside Matty while I worked for the jeweler. During the day, I foiled two pickpockets from preying on Scrivvins' customers, spotted a team of three women who tried to palm several gems, and apprehended an audacious thief who grabbed a gold chain and fled. When I tried to stop him, the thief sneered at me, drew a sword and dagger, and attacked. I disarmed him with little difficulty while the jeweler shouted for the city guard. Before I left for the day, Scrivvins gave me one silver regal, a generous sum, and asked me to return the next day. His bony face smiled with satisfaction. The bazaar closed at sunset to make room for the dancing to celebrate Midsummer's Eve. Fi was already on the wagon seat with Rogan and Matty so I climbed on back with Silas. We said nothing kin the way to the inn. My thoughts were occupied by the wonderful sights of the bazaar. The weight of coins in my pouch reassured me that Fi and I would have money to live on for a while.

When we stopped before Lyedy's door, Silas scrambled out then offered to help me down. I laughed, jumped to the cobblestones, and followed Matty and Fi through the door.

That evening Matty, Fi, and I joined Lyedy's family in their private quarters for supper. Afterwards, we sat around the table while Lyedy told us about the war against the Kallasi and how Hamadeen had triumphed.

"It's a good thing it's all over," Lori said, her arms crossed as she glared at her husband. "Lyedy was talking about joining the fight himself."

Matty laughed. "The Kallasi wouldn't have had a chance."

Everyone laughed at that, even me. It had been a long time since I'd felt the warmth of gathered family and friends. When everyone retired for the night, I lay in my bed, hugging that warmth to my heart as I fell asleep.

The next day went much as the first, except I saw the three young men I'd met at Lyedy's the day we arrived. The one who'd felt my dagger at his throat glared at me, called me "Solvadish," and spit on my boots. His friends grabbed his arms and dragged him away, cursing me as they disappeared into the crowd. Scrivvins gave me a look that said he wondered if he'd made a mistake hiring me.

Nothing unusual happened until the third day of the festival. The sun was halfway between zenith and horizon, and Fi had just finished dancing more gracefully than ever. The audience tossed copper and silver coins which I knelt to gather.

It was then I noticed a man among the crowd who didn't throw a coin, a man who drew my attention in spite of myself. Taller than the other spectators, he had cropped hair and beard, both blacker than raven feathers. His dark, lean face was more handsome than any other I'd ever seen. His red and gold silk coat and the gold jewelry he was so freely spoke of his wealth. He had the body and manner of a disciplined warrior, and he seemed confident of himself and of his right to deference from others. With deliberate steps, he approached Fi as she picked up the coins on the ground.

"You dance like a goddess," he said with awe, offering her a gold regal.

My mouth dropped open. A gold regal would feed the two of us for several months. He handed the coin to her as if it were insignificant. Distrusting him, I moved closer to Fi.

She blushed, and her eyes shone with pleasure. "Thank you, sir."

"I am Prince Kaleed." His stance showed he expected to be known.

I stepped beside Fi and helped her stand. "I'm Elan, and this is my sister Filea. We are honored by your praise."

"Sisters." Turning dark, seductive eyes toward me, he studied me thoroughly. "Yes—yes, I see it."

"Twins." Held by his mesmerizing stare, my voice faltered. I felt as if my secrets were exposed and my soul was open to him. I was terrified by him—yet excited, too.

He gazed at me for a long moment then gave me a smile that was disarmingly friendly. "Your sister dances very well. Would she be willing to dance for the king? I could arrange it easily. Her beauty and grace should be seen in palaces where she would be appreciated. She would be well paid for her performance."

"Oh, El, to dance for the king!" Fi said as though she'd been given a new toy.

"How much?" I asked with direct practicality.

"Would ten gold regals be sufficient?"

I nearly choked. He'd offered more than a year's wages for one dance. "When would you want her to perform?"

"This evening, one hour after sunset. The king is giving a feast for a visiting prince. Your sister's dancing would be the perfect entertainment. And you..." he paused as he stepped closer to me and added firmly, "you, of course, will play for her."

My voice quavered as I tried to avoid his eyes. "She goes nowhere without me."

"Where may I send a palanquin for you?"

I hesitated. His forceful gaze made me uneasy yet at the same time intrigued and tempted me. Still, I felt reluctant to reveal where we stayed. "We will present ourselves at the palace gates at the appropriate time."

"As you wish." He bowed but never took his eyes from my face. He turned to go, then faced me again. He leaned so close, I felt his warm breath and smelled his musky perfume as he whispered, "The hours will seem long until tonight." Four of the king's guards appeared to escort him as Kaleed turned to leave.

My hands shook as I counted Fi's earnings.

Matty appeared bedside me and said softly, "You have caught the eye of a powerful man, Elan."

I glanced at the lines of bowing people which marked the prince's procession and felt as if I teetered on the edge of a chasm. "Who...who is he?" I asked with a trembling voice.

"He is the son of the king's beloved sister, who died, and after the king's infant son, Kaleed is next in line for the throne, and he's captain of the armies of Hamadeen and the honored hero of the wars with the Kallasi hordes and is much beloved by the people of Zylona for his generosity to the poor, but beware, little El, for I see darkness in his face and danger in your future."

Her words heightened my constant fear of discovery, and I turned sharply towards the old woman with dread. "Are you gifted with farsight?"

She smiled and patted my cheek. "No, Elan, but I often see more with one eye than most do with two, so remember my warning," she said, glancing around to see if anyone could overhear us, "and know that you can depend on me to help you."

Grateful for her concern, I grasped her forearm and gave it a firm but gentle squeeze before I returned to work.

In all the years Filea and I had wandered, we'd never made a true friend. Fi hadn't seemed to mind, being happy wherever she was, but I'd felt the loneliness of our lives. Always fearing discovery, fearing to open myself to the hurt that comes with caring, I was touched by Matty's concern.

Silas and Rogan arrived in time to help close up Matty's wagon. I sat in back with Silas. My stomach churned, and my fingers drummed against the wooden floor as we rode to the inn.

"Did you have an interesting day," Silas said, startling me.

"Yes," I said, avoiding his eyes, "a most interesting day."

"Elan..." He cleared his throat, seeming anxious and a little shy. "I wondered, I mean, I thought perhaps, this is, if you'd like, we could, uh, join the dancing in the bazaar tonight—if you're not too tired."

I was so seldom the object of anyone's attention, especially when in Fi's presence, I was caught off guard by his suggestion and turned to study him.

His green eyes were wide with hope. Honesty and respect shone in his lean face. There was no secret self he kept hidden from others. He was just as he appeared: warm, open, compassionate.

"I'm sorry, but Filea and I are to appear at the palace tonight."

"The palace!" He gaped with astonishment, then gave me a disappointed smile. "Maybe another night during the festival?"

"Perhaps," I said, trying not to encourage him.

As soon as we reached the inn, we jumped down to the street and left the men to stable the team and wagon.

Fi and I ate little supper. She couldn't dance her best on a full stomach. I was too anxious. We went to our room to wash and dress in our best, since we were to be in the presence of royalty.

I sighed as I brushed Fi's hair. "I wish I could have bought you a new dress to wear tonight." I braided the sides and fixed them at the back of her head with a leather thong. "You should look radiant for the king. Imagine the money you'll receive tonight! Probably enough to keep us in food for months!"

Filea giggled. "Or silks."

Someone knocked on the door.

"Come in," I said.

Matty and Lori entered, carrying two dresses of finest silk: one, bright pink and the other, blue as the summer sky. The midriffs were sheer; the hems, embroidered with golden thread. A matching veil and satin slippers accompanied

the dome's center by an iron chain, the golden sun reflecting light for the entire room.

Perhaps fifty guests, attired in silks, sat on satin cushions at low tables in a semicircle before a marble dais. A group of musicians sat on the right side of the room. And on the dais, amid purple cushions, sat three imposing men in scarlet robes. Prince Kaleed was on the left. The man on the right was obviously the visiting prince that Kaleed had mentioned. But there could be no doubt that the man in the center was King Alifa'ar. The king had the same lean face as his nephew but lined with age. Alifa'ar's face showed compassion and gentle wisdom that Kaleed's lacked.

The slave led us to the dais, knelt, and touched his forehead to the floor. "O great King Alifa'ar, ruler of Hamadeen, descendant of gods, master of winds, may you live forever, I present Filea the dancer and her sister Elan the musician, to entertain you and your guests."

I genuflected, tugging at Fi's elbow so she'd follow my example.

The corners of the king's eyes crinkled with humor. "Prince Kaleed speaks favorably of your dancing."

"May we be worthy of his praise," I said humbly. I'd learned humility was essential in life when in the presence of powerful people who could have me killed.

Taking out my flute, I sat down on a cushion beside the musicians who waited for me to set the tempo and begin the tune. Fi walked to the center of the hall and spread her veil over her shoulders. Standing tall, her arms stretched over her head, backs of her hands touching, she waited for the music to start.

I played two lines of music solo. The musicians joined in after that. Fi stood motionless except for her hands, the ching of her cymbals matching the lively tempo. Slowly, she began to pivot on her right foot, swinging her left hip out with each tiny step, changing to her left foot when she'd completed a circle. Stretching her arms straight out to her sides, she swayed her hips right, left, right-left-right and repeating, shimmying her shoulders, fluttering her abdomen.

She removed the pins the held her veil and began the veil dance. Holding the veil straight out, she swung it left, right, back again, then circled her body with the filmy fabric. The spectators' eyes followed her every move. With arms raised she dashed around the hall, the veil flowing behind her, then she flung it away. She ran to the center of the room and struck a pose that signaled the hand dance.

The music became much slower, quieter, with a mysterious almost mystical tone, flutes and drums dominating the sound with two long beats, then three quick ones. Fi moved like the undulations of a snake following the swaying of a flute. Gradually, she descended to the mosaic floor and with sinuous elegance, slithered toward the dais.

I noticed that the musicians seemed to be prolonging the dance. I also noted that Prince Kaleed glanced occasionally at the band, nodding slightly. The head musician nodded back. Kaleed turned toward Fi, watching, watching. He was plotting something, but I didn't know what precisely.

At last, the band moved into the third phase, a frenetically energetic segment that led to the climax of the dance. I could see that Fi was exerting herself more than she had all day. I cringed and stopped playing. I stood, clutching my flute helplessly.

No, Fi! I thought frantically to her mind. *Not here! Not before the king! The kreeyagan will know! Don't do this!*

I can't stop, El! Fi's thoughts cried back. *Help me!*

The music continued, more insistent, as though it controlled Fi. She danced with every bit of strength she had left, spinning, spinning like a dervish, her body flushed and glistening. Finally, the music ended.

Panting for breath, her hair damp and clinging to her arms, Fi sank to the floor and lay prostrate at the foot of the king's dais. She lifted her face slowly and propped herself up. For a long moment Fi stared at the king, then she screamed. And in that moment, I saw what she saw, felt what she felt. I shared her vision.

I saw the king sitting on his throne. A cloaked and hooded shadow, dark as midnight, crept up behind him. A silver dagger with jeweled hilt and curved blade flashed from the shadow's robe and slashed across the king's throat. Air gurgled from the gaping wound while blood spurted and stained the king's gold robe. Clutching at his throat as his life seeped through his fingers, the king fell from his throne. The shadow walked toward the body. Convinced that life had fled, the shadow threw back its hood and revealed a face. Then I screamed.

The room filled with puzzled demands from the guests. The king commanded quiet, ordered the musicians to play again, and called for more wine. From somewhere I heard a chilling word whispered: Jin. Glancing at Kaleed, I saw him smile slowly. He knew our secret!

I didn't wait for our payment. Jamming my flute under my arm strap, I raced to Fi's side. I jerked her to her feet and dragged her from the hall, past guests and guards. As we reached the doors, the guards blocked our way. I looked back at the king and saw him nod to the guards, who stepped aside and let us pass.

We hurried through the hallway, retrieving my sword on the way. We reached the porch on the courtyard before Fi collapsed. I knelt, flung her over my shoulder, and stood with some difficulty. I ran as fast as I could across the moonlit courtyard toward the gates opened to the bazaar.

As I approached the gate, I slowed my pace and smiled at the guards, hoping to cover my edginess. "Drunk already! Can't have her sprawled unconscious in the king's presence."

One of the guards gave me a lecherous grin and elbowed his comrade in the side. "You could leave her with us for the night."

"It would serve her right," I said in the same spirit, "but you might get caught, and I wouldn't want two attractive men like you to be flogged. Suppose we meet tomorrow when you're if duty and she's awake. I'm certain we'd all enjoy ourselves more than tonight. Just name the place and time."

"Noon tomorrow at the Dancing Wench?" the guard said.

"Noon tomorrow at the Dancing Wench." I had no idea where the place was nor any intention of being there. "Until then."

His eyes already burned with expectant pleasure.

I hurried through streets still clogged with dancers until finally I reached Lyedy's inn. Matty was in the common room, sipping wine and spinning a tale for the innkeeper and his wife who had chosen not to join in the celebration. I slumped against the doorway to catch my breath.

Matty jumped to her feet and rushed to take Fi into her arms. "Child, what happened?" Matty said as Lyedy and Lori joined her. Lori took Fi from Matty.

"Matty, Fi and I must leave Zylona immediately! Lori, will you help me gather our belongings? Matty, can you sneak us out of the city in your wagon? Lyedy, what do I owe for our stay here?"

"Wait!" Matty said, grabbed one of my arms, and forced me down to a bench beside Lori. "Now you just sit down there and tell me why you have to leave right now."

"Our lives depend on it!" I started to stand, but Matty pushed me back down to the bench.

"What do you mean, your lives depend on it? If anyone's threatened you, I'll see he's brought before the king to answer for it!"

"You don't understand! It's the king's men that will come for us, or rather Prince Kaleed's men!"

Lyedy whistled his surprise while Lori clapped a hand over her mouth.

Matty studied me closely. "What have you done?"

If my only concern had been myself, I'd have lied and tried to sneak out of the city, fighting if necessary. But Fi wasn't able to fight or even move. I had to keep her safe, whatever the cost to me. Clearing my throat, I said, "Matty, it's not what we've done. It's what we are."

I told them everything, including the strange vision that somehow I'd shared with Fi–something that had never happened before–and about the face of the shadowed assassin: Prince Kaleed.

Lyedy gasped.

Lori's dark eyes were wide with wonder. "I'd always thought Jin were a legend passed down in stories told to children!"

I shook my head. "Kaleed knew what we were when he invited us to the palace. I don't know how, but he did. He prolonged the dance deliberately in order to provoke a vision, but why? What did he hope to learn? Or did he want to confirm his suspicions?

"If we stay here, Kaleed will find us and force one of us, robably Filea, to reveal her vision, and that will be our death. If we try to flee, we'll be caught. I'm certain he's alerted the city guards to watch for us by now. If we warn the king, he may keep us prisoners if only to have Fi's talent available in the future. If we don't warn him, we'll be just as guilty of his murder as Kaleed. So, what should I do?" I stood and paced the floor, considering my options but knowing they were limited by Fi's condition.

Matty stroked her chins. "The city gates are locked, and you couldn't escape that way even with my help, and Kaleed knows you're staying here, so we must move you to safer place, and I know several places in this city where the guards will never find you, places you can hide until Fi's well enough to travel, and as for the vision, I think you should warn the king tonight."

"But how?" I said pointedly. "I can't risk going back to the palace. Kaleed would certainly catch me."

A slow grin spread across Matty's face. "If you went in the front gate, but there are more ways into the palace than that route so just you trust Old Matty." Turning to Lyedy, she continued. "My friend, I think the cellar is the place for these two."

"The guards will search there, too!"

The other three exchanged amused glances before Lyedy explained. "There's a hidden trap door in the cellar that leads to a maze of caves and passages beneath the city. I've heard it said that some use the tunnels for smuggling goods or people in or out of Zylona, though, of course, I wouldn't know of such unlawful activities." He grinned. "You and Fi can hide in one of the small chambers while we arrange for your safe passage."

"But what about—" I began when Matty interrupted me.

"No time for that now, El, because the guards will come any minute, and you must be hidden, and I must be back here chatting calmly, even appearing a little drunk, when they arrive to search, and no," she said as I started upstairs to collect our belongings, "leave your things just as they are so the guards will believe that you haven't come back here, but don't you worry for I'll get them to you as soon as possible or at least before you leave."

Lori handed Fi to Matty, Lyedy led us to the trap door in the kitchen. Lyedy climbed down the ladder first with a lantern in his hand. He set the lantern down on the dirt floor, then held out his huge arms to take Fi as Matty lowered her down carefully. Matty descended the ladder. I followed. Lori came down a few moments later with blankets, a water skin, and a basket of food.

Matty took Fi from Lyedy again, then he moved a stack of flour sacks in a few minutes, revealing another trap door. Opened, it revealed a ladder descending into darkness. Lyedy took a lantern and climbed down, barely squeezing through the opening. Matty lowered Fi, who was still unconscious, through the hole to Lyedy's waiting arms.

Matty turned to me. "Don't you worry, El, because you've three friends here, meaning Lyedy, Lori, and me, who know more about Zylona than all the king's guards put together, and things will work out fine, so just trust Old Matty."

I did, more than I'd trusted anyone or anything for years except myself.

Lori handed me the blankets, food, and water. "Matty and I are going back upstairs to the common room. The guards could arrive any second, and we want to be there to delay them as long as possible. Good luck, Elan. May the gods keep you safe." She called down to Lyedy, "Bring up one of the small kegs of wine when you come upstairs. That will be the excuse for not being with Matty and me."

I climbed down the ladder, picked up a lantern, and followed Lyedy as he led me through dank passages hardly wider than he was. Soon, I lost all sense of direction in the twisting, looping tunnels. At least the guards couldn't find us down here. They'd be lost within the first few intersections.

Finally, Lyedy turned left into a small chamber, cold and damp, stacked with goods that were probably illegal. "Spread out a blanket on the two crates for Fi and light that lantern on the crate over there. You might as well sleep, too. You'll be safe here. After the guards have left, Matty will come here, and you two can plan your visit to the palace."

Lyedy brushed my cheek as my father had done in days lost forever. "Don't worry, Elan. Matty's watching over you, and the gods watch over Matty."

Taking one of the lanterns, he left us, the glow of light on the tunnel walls fading as he went. I wrapped in a blanket, lay down beside Fi, and tried to keep her warm. I wondered how soon she would awaken, how Kaleed had recognized us as Jin, and if there really were gods who watched over Matty.

I slept for maybe an hour when someone shook me. Startled yet not wanting to frighten Fi, I swallowed a curse and blinked my eyes clear.

Matty bent over me, a hand to her mouth to signal silence. She beckoned me away from my unconscious sister and walked to the tunnel where we could talk.

"What's happening above," I said eagerly.

"The king's men came looking for you just as you said they would," Matty said, her eye blazing with anger, "and they searched the entire inn, dumping out trunks and chests, and taking all your belonging, I'm sad to say, and looking through every room in the inn, even the cellar, though they didn't find the trap door, thank the gods, and then they searched the stable, including my wagon, breaking my wares, as if I could afford to live on nothing for the next month, and I called down every curse my dead husband ever taught me, and finally they left, and they weren't too happy to be angering Old Matty!"

"They probably won't come back right away," I said, tapping my lower lip, "but they'll return if they can't find us anywhere else. So, how do I reach the palace and warn the king?"

Matty's eye glittered like a flickering fire. "It's not as hard as you may think and not as easy as you might hope, but don't worry, little El, because Old Matty will show you the way she use to sneak inside the palace, me being much younger and thinner in those days, and though I can't fit through the passages now, the years weighing heavily on me as you can see, I'll tell you just how to find the king's rooms so you can warn him in time, hopefully without being discovered by the prince, and here are some of Silas' clothes, since a dress isn't practical for the places you'll be going tonight, and your daggers, which I hid before the soldiers came."

I stifled a smile, still amazed that Matty could say somuch in one breath. I glanced at my sister. "What about her? Will she be safe alone?"

"I'm certain she'll be all right, seeing I'll only go with you part of the way and then come back to guard her myself so just trust Old Matty."

I removed my leather arm bands and set them and my flute next to Fi. Wiggling out of the dress I'd worn to the palace, I kicked the garment into a heap along with the slippers and veil. The black trousers fit well. The shirt was a bit too baggy, but I cinched it up as I buckled my sword around my waist. I rebound the leather straps around my arms and slid the daggers beneath the bands. A hooded cloak and soft leather boots completed my outfit. I picked up my lantern and turned to Matty. "All right, let's go," I said.

"You follow close to me," Matty said, "because others use these tunnels, not this particular one, but a few of the passages we'll cross are used by those whose names would bring a chill to the most hardened soldier in the ranks, if you understand me, but you're safe with Old Matty, at least as far as I go with you, though you won't have too much trouble after that because most of the scoundrels don't venture near the palace tunnels anymore, so let's go because the sooner we go, the sooner I'll be back to guard Fi."

We each took a lantern. I worried about leaving Fi in the dark, but since she showed no sign of waking, I covered her with my blanket, then left the room.

How Matty led me through the twisting passages without a map or some sign scribed on the rough-hewn walls, I couldn't tell. I was lost in the maze after three turns. Passages crossed and branched, slanted down or climbed up. Some were wet, water trickling down the stone walls. Some were dry and dusty, thick with webs. Some showed footprints of recent visitors. Matty navigated the tunnels with certainty, as a seasoned mariner navigates the sea.

It seemed we'd walked miles of passages when Matty halted and pointed to a very narrow opening. "This is where I leave you," she said, "and you must go on alone, and don't you worry, you'll reach the palace just fine, if you remember my instructions, and just to make certain, I want you to repeat what I told you."

I sighed. All along the way Matty had drilled me in the exact route to the palace until I'd said it four times perfectly. "Narrow passage to a three branch. Right tunnel. Pass two left openings, one right, one left, three right. Take the next right, then next left. Straight to a wall. Press the stone three hands from the floor on the left. Opens to the lowest cellar of the palace. Climb up to the next cellar and go beneath the steps. Push on the center stone to reveal a secret door. Follow the passage to the stairs. Climb three flights of steps. Turn left. Go thirty-three paces exactly. Push on the right wall, and I'll be in the king's chambers."

"Perfect, and now you go quietly, especially when you get near the cellar because someone may be in there bringing up more wine, with all the celebrating, so be careful, and may the gods watch over you."

I turned to go but stopped and looked at her with inquisitive eyes. "Matty, how do you know this secret way to the king's chambers? I mean, how did you ever find it?"

Matty winked at me, her eye glowing with a sweet memory or long-forgotten dream. "I wasn't always a potter, you know, nor was I always married nor as full-figured as I am now, being a little too broad to fit through certain tunnels ahead, and I wasn't uncomely either, having soft skin and shining hair like ebony and delicate face and graceful form, and that's how I managed to catch the king's eye one day in the market square, and on occasion I'd visit him by way of the secret passage I've revealed to you, though that was many years ago and we were little more than children, but they were sweet days, sweet memories I treasure in my heart."

Nothing could have surprised me more than more than Matty's confession. Looking at her now, I could hardly imagine she could have attracted a king.

Matty patted my cheek. "By using the secret passage, Ali will know you come from me and believe you, so off you go, little El, and good luck and..." she paused, then added, "and tell Ali that–that I remember."

She turned and lumbered back down the passage we had come, leaving me alone.

I followed Matty's instructions, amazed that she had ever been slim enough to move through the narrow tunnels. Once I had to turn sideways and wiggle through a part where the tunnel had caved in and partially blocked the path. Dust and cobwebs covered my cloak and set me to coughing.

Finally, I reached the wall to the cellar. Pressing my ear to the wall, I listened for voices or the sound of feet. It was fortunate I did because I heard two voices bellowing at each other, although I couldn't quite understand what they were yelling. I waited until I heard nothing, then carefully measured three hands from the floor on the left and pressed the stone. A low narrow door swung slowly into the tunnel, revealing a large cellar. Kegs were stacked two high and two deep, except in front of the secret door. Two kegs had been removed from that spot just before I'd entered the cellar, so I had no trouble climbing in.

I crept to the ladder and climbed up to the closed trap door. I listened to assure myself that no one was above before I pushed the door open enough to slip through to the upper cellar. Shelves lined all the walls except directly behind the wide steps that led to the palace kitchen. Quietly tiptoeing to the empty wall, I pressed the center stone.

A dark corridor, hardly wider than my shoulders, opened before me. It smelled of ashes and dust and air which hadn't been circulated in half a century. I wondered if I could breathe it and survive long enough to reach the king.

No time to worry about that, I thought to myself as I heard voices above coming closer.

I pushed the door closed and shut myself in the stone corridor. I crept as silently as possible, knowing any noise I made might be heard and reveal my presence. The walls were smooth and dry but as cold as a cave which had never seen a ray of sunlight. Silas' clothes were heavy, but a chill ran through me like cold hands brushing my neck. Every step stirred up dust which threatened to gag me. I held part of the cloak over my nose and mouth just to be able to breathe.

I reached the stairs and began to climb, an eerie echo accompanying each step I took. By the time I reached the top, I was lightheaded from exertion in the bad air. Turning left, I had to concentrate to count thirty-three paces. As I counted the last step, I rested against the wall, breathless and dizzy. I knew I had to find the secret panel or I'd die where I was, lost and forgotten, leaving Fi at the mercy of Kaleed's schemes.

I leaned against the right wall and pushed with desperate strength against the stones. At last, the wall opened a little, as though something were blocking it. My left foot against the left wall, I pressed my shoulder against the door and pushed until it moved. I stumbled through the opening, past an ebony table which stood askew from the wall. Panting and pale, I dropped to my knees.

When I looked up, King Alifa'ar stood before me in a night robe, a scimitar in his hand. The expression on his face was hard to read. He seemed wary, surprised, and amused all at once. "And who are you that stumbles into my chamber by a secret path?" he said, his tone more curious than frightened.

I threw back my hood and answered, though still short of breath. "I'm...Elan...the musician."

"Ah, yes." He nodded, recognizing me. "Your sister is quite enchanting, but she has a most unsettling ending to her performance. How did you find your way here? No one knows that secret passage but me."

"One other knows, Your Majesty, one you knew in the days of your youth, one who loved you and still holds you in her heart with much affection and respect, one who sent me with an urgent message for you."

The king stared at me for a moment, then closed the secret door and replaced the table. He hung the scimitar above the table and offered his hand to help me up. "I think I'll hear your message."

Leading me to a lounge with a bolster pillow, he poured me a goblet of strong wine and sat down beside me. The wine was sweet and burned my throat, warming me quickly.

"Now, what is this message you have brought me?" he said, a fire kindling in his dark eyes.

"Truthfully, I have two messages. The first is this: Tell Ali that I remember."

His face softened as if his youth had been restored to him for a moment. His eyes glittered. His larynx bobbed as he swallowed. I could tell that he remembered also.

Clearing his throat, he said, "And the other message?"

"The other message is from me–actually from my sister and me. Your life is in danger, Your Majesty. Prince Kaleed means to kill you."

"And how do you know this?"

"Because I saw it! Fi saw it! That's why we screamed after the dance!"

"Saw what? How?"

I took a deep breath. I was afraid to reveal my heritage, yet I knew I had no choice. "Your Majesty, my sister and I are Jin."

"Jin?" the king said, surprise in his voice. "Prince Kaleed was discussing the existence of such a people several years ago with an ambassador from Zraylin. Are you saying you are truly a Jin?"

"Yes. Fi was born with a special gift. She has visions of the future, not all the time, just after she's danced until exhausted, like tonight. She saw a vision, and somehow I shared that vision with her. We saw Prince Kaleed kill you. You must stop him."

"Really?" said the object of our discussion.

Although a little wobbly, I leaped to my feet and drew my sword, ready to defend the king.

Prince Kaleed stood in the doorway of the king's chamber, fingering the hilt of his scimitar. He gazed at us with eyes narrowed to serpentine slits.

"Guards!" the king shouted.

"Don't bother," Kaleed said coldly. "I sent them away while I spoke to my uncle in private."

"How dare you!"

The prince slid his eyes toward me. "I didn't expect to find you in His Majesty's bedroom. I'm certain I could accommodate you much more satisfactorily than an old man. But I'm sure you're not here merely for a night of pleasure, although I'm confident you'd provide that. No, I imagine you've told the king of the vision your sister had tonight. She's khoroojin, isn't she?"

I held my tongue, though mentally I hurled at him every curse I'd ever heard in all my wanderings.

The prince began walking toward us. "What did she see? Where is she? My guards have searched everywhere in Zylona for you two."

"She's safe from you!"

"Is she?" he said. "No matter. You are here."

"That won't help you!"

"Stop this!" Alifa'ar said. "Kaleed, explain yourself."

"Why should I?" Kaleed said bitterly.

"Because I'm the king."

"Not for long. I will be king when the sun rises this day. You will be dead." He gazed at me. "I'll find Filea, even if I must raze Zylona to its foundations. Your sister's power will be of great use to me as ruler of Hamadeen."

"Even if I were to die tonight," Alifa'ar said, "you wouldn't be more than a regent for my son."

"I think your son will become deathly ill tonight, and your consort will kill herself in despair. That will leave me as the only male heir to ascend the throne. It should be mine, was mine until your son was born."

"The palace guard will thwart your plans."

Even as the king spoke, I felt him press something against the back of my arm: a dagger. *At least he'd not totally defenseless,* I thought.

"The palace guard is mine, and the army as well." Kaleed's eyes blazed, yet I detected a hint of pain behind the anger. "I've served Hamadeen all my life. My body bears the scars of my battles to defend this land. I would have died to protect Hamadeen and its people. I've earned the right to rule."

"Not while I live, nephew."

"No," the prince said softly, regret in his face, "not while you live." His hand strayed to his weapon.

I placed myself between the two and faced Kaleem. "Thencome, prince, try to take his life, but you must face me first."

"This is not between you and me, Elan," Kaleem said.

"It is now." I drew my sword and poised to fight.

Kaleed sighed and drew his scimitar. "If it must be, then so be it."

I tore off my cloak and flung it at him, hoping to startle and distract him. He simply batted it aside.

At that moment, Alifa'ar hurled his dagger at Kaleed, but the prince was too quick. The dagger sailed past him as he dodged to one side. With venomous fire in his eyes, Kaleed charged us. In one continuous motion, he blocked my sword and punched me in the abdomen so hard I doubled over and gagged. Kaleed kicked the king in the groin, then smashed a solid blow to his uncle's jaw, slamming the king against the wall. Blood smeared the stones behind Alifa'ar's head as he slid to the floor, crumpled and deathly pale. His chest was still. Kaleed nudged the king's body, then wheeled toward me.

I was skilled in swordsmanship myself, but I realized from the way Kaleed moved, he surpassed all I'd learned. Kaleed was a deadly opponent, feline, agile, a master swordsman. Our swords clashed, metal ringing with a hand-jarring clang. I knew from the first strokes, I was unprepared to face a scimitar. Kaleed moved differently than I did, handled the scimitar unlike my broad sword. He used a sweeping diagonal attack while I used a more straight cut and thrust. Fortunately, his weapon was more unwieldy than mine. I was quicker, but he was stronger than I.

Kaleed drove me back step by step until the lounge was directly behind me. He delivered a blow so hard, my arm felt half numb. I lost my balance and fell to the lounge. Quickly, I rolled to the floor on the other side and barely avoided his next strike. Taking advantage of his momentary surprise, I leaped up and swung my blade toward his neck. Kaleed was too fast. He twisted to his right and suffered only a slight scratch along the right side of his chest.

He swung at me and raked down the length of my left arm. I thrust my sword at his chest. He parried. He retaliated. I blocked. His blows wore me down, pushed me back until I was against the king's bed.

I missed a parry. Kaleed slashed a deep gash on my sword arm near the shoulder. I dropped my weapon, lost my balance, and toppled to the bed with Kaleed on top of me. He grabbed my wrists and stretched my arms out on the bed.

"Now you are like any other woman," he said, hunger in his eyes, his body tense against mine. "Like any other woman." He paused and studied my face. His grasp relaxed, and his eyes lost the hard-edged desire that had shone in them. His voice became soft, almost gentle.

"No. No, you are not like other women, Elan. I knew that when I saw you at the bazaar. You intrigued me as no other woman ever has. You are strong and quick and intelligent, my equal in all things. And you are beautiful. I need such a woman as my consort." Slowly, deliberately, he bent to kiss me.

He's called me beautiful, his equal, and had asked me to be his queen! No man had offered me so much. For a moment, I almost responded to his kiss, but only for a moment. I jerked back and spit in his face. "I won't be the consort of a murderer!"

Humiliation filled Kaleed's face as he tightened his grip on my wrists. "So be it," he said "I would have made you queen of Hamadeen. My beloved queen! I would have given you everything I have, everything I am." He halted, his forehead lined with anger, and perhaps, hurt. Then his eyes grew hard and cold. "But I will know the pleasure of you before I kill you. I'll find your sister. She will be my special concubine, warming my bed by night and dancing for visions by day. Now where is she?"

I glared at him. "I'll die rather than tell you!"

He leaned close to my face and whispered, "But you will tell me, Elan, and then you will die."

He kissed me hard, bruising my mouth. I struggled against him until I had enough leverage to knee him in the groin. He screamed like a wounded animal mad with pain. He grasped my throat and choked me. I clawed at his hands, but to no avail. They were like a vise tightening around my throat.

I realized I was going to die, and I was frightened, not for myself, but for Fi. Who would take care of her? Who would protect her from people like Kaleed? Those thoughts troubled me as a dark veil seemed to cloud my sight. I fumbled for a dagger in my armband, my ears ringing and my chest feeling like it would explode. Finally, I levered the weapon out and grasped the hilt. With all the strength I had left, I drove the blade into the side of his neck.

His eyes registered astonishment, anger, pain, and fear in succession. Blood and spittle bubbled from the corners of his mouth. His hands relaxed around my neck, and he slumped against me.

I lay still a few minutes, gasping for air, then heaved Kaleed's bloody corpse off me and struggled to my feet. As I stared down at the dead prince, a lump formed in my throat. *Fi's safe,* I thought, *and the king–the king!*

I hurried to where Alifa'ar lay crumpled and knelt beside him. I placed one hand on his neck and the other on his chest. I felt a pulse, faint and weak, but I knew he was dying. "If only I were still ramoojin!" I said, bitter and angry at my helplessness.

As if in answer to my cry, I felt heat flowing down my arms. A blue flame seemed to surround the king and me, not burning us but warming, soothing, healing. Within seconds, I felt his heart beat stronger, and his breathing was easier. Even my wounds were partially healed. I shook my head in amazement. My power had returned!

The king moaned.

"Your Majesty..."

He opened his eyes. "Kaleed?"

"He's dead," I said.

Alifa'ar closed his eyes, grief shaking his body. "He was like my own son."

Dizzy and unsteady, I slumped to the floor with exhaustion.

Suddenly, the king's eyes grew wide. "My wife and my son! Kaleed said they would die tonight!"

Forcing myself to stand, I grabbed my sword. "Where are they?"

"Down the corridor to the right and across the hall."

I raced as quickly as I could and arrived in time to back stab a guard who was struggling with the young queen. Her son lay crying in his cradle, unharmed. Escorting the queen, who carried her child to the king's chambers, I found the king talking to a bearded soldier.

I knelt before the lounge where the king was sitting. "Your Majesty, the queen and prince are safe."

Alifa'ar embraced his young wife and son, comforting her and caressing his son's cheek.

"By your leave, I'll return to my sister." I stood, swaying unsteadily, and turned to go.

"Wait," the king said. "Stay with us here at the palace. You'll be safe, and I'll provide you with anything you desire."

I shook my head. "I thank you, but we can't remain in Zylona. Fi's talent is too tempting to ambitious men. You may protect her for a time, but one day you will die. Who would keep her safe then? I'm her only kin. I'll protect her as I always have."

Alifa'ar took my hand. "I am indebted to you. How may I reward you?"

"Kaleed promised Fi ten gold regals for dancing."

"You shall have twice that," the king said. He nodded to the other man who left. "I owe you not only my life but the lives of those I love. Is there nothing else you desire?"

"Forget us," I said. "Forget who and what we are. That's all I ask."

"If that is your wish." The king motioned to the soldier who had returned. "This is Tomar, my oldest, most trusted friend and new captain of my army. He's begun arresting those guards loyal to my dead nephew. Tomar will escort you so that you may be certain no one will harm you."

"It isn't necessary."

As I turned to leave, the king touched my arm. "I promise that your secret will go with me to the grave. Please, let me have the assurance that you are safe."

Too weary to argue, I nodded my acceptance.

"If some day your path leads you back to Zylona, you will be welcomed in my palace as an honored guest."

"I'll remember." I doubted I'd ever come to Zylona again.

He looked deep into my eyes, and leaning close, in a voice so low that only I could hear, he said, "And tell the one who sent you to me that I remember also."

I nodded and left with Captain Tomar.

Stars were still twinkling in the early morning sky when we emerged from the palace. A palanquin waited at the courtyard porch, and Tomar held the curtain for me to enter. I climbed inside, collapsed on a satin pillow, and slept until Tomar shook me gently.

The palanquin had stopped outside the inn. Tomar helped me exit then escorted me to the door. As I started to enter, the captain asked me to wait then took a pouch from his belt.

"His Majesty asked me to give you these," he said. Opening the leather bag, he withdrew two silver chains with silver medallions and handed them to me. Each was inscribed with an eagle, the symbol of Hamadeen, and three words in some language I didn't recognize. "These are for your sister and you. They signify that you are under the protection of the king of Hamadeen."

"Please, give my thanks to His Majesty."

"Also in the pouch are twenty gold regals." Taking out another pouch, he handed it to me. "This is to be given to one you know. You are to tell that one that the king is grateful for sending you to save his life."

"I will." Impulsively, I clasped his forearm.

He turned and marched beside the palanquin, disappearing into the grey night before dawn lit the sky.

I walked into the inn. Lyedy and Lori were bustling about the inn, preparing for breakfast. When they noticed me, I was assailed with questions from both sides.

"Please wait." I clapped my hands over my ears to shut out the chaos. When they had calmed down, I dropped my hands and said, "I'll tell you what happened. Just let me sit down."

They did. Lori brought me some wine and joined her husband at the table.

I told them everything, ending with the silver medallions. Well, no, I didn't tell them how I'd healed the king and my wounds. I didn't know how to tell them about that. I didn't understand it myself. How had I regained ramoojin power? How had I shared Fi's vision? Maybe I'd had the powers all along. Maybe they were innate to all Jin. I just didn't know.

"Where's Fi?" I said anxiously.

"She's still safe in the chamber below," Lyedy said. "Matty's with her. Now we know you're safe, I'll bring them both upstairs."

A few minutes later, he emerged from the cellar with Fi, who was still sleeping. Matty trailed behind him. While Lyedy carried Fi up to her bed, with Lori following, Matty rushed forward and hugged me, worry in her eye. "Are you all right, child, and did you warn the king, and is he alive, and what happened to Prince Kaleed?"

I was exhausted, but I repeated my tale for her while she nodded, wide-eyed.

"And didn't I tell you everything would be all right if you could just talk to the king, him being a truly good king, and it happened just like I said it would, so see, you just trust Old Matty."

I smiled and tried to imagine what she'd looked like so many years ago when she'd loved a king and he'd loved her. Leaning close to her, I pressed the pouch in her hand and said, "This is for the one who sent me to save the king's life. He is grateful. And," I dropped my voice to a whisper, "he told me to say that he remembers, also."

Matty held the pouch as it were the most beautiful, most delicate flower she'd ever seen. A tear collected at the corner of her eye and trickled down her cheek. I saw love shining in her face, a quiet, deep love that had lasted through years of separation. I wondered if I would ever find love like that.

I tried to stand, but my legs buckled. Matty leaped up to catch me. With her arm around my waist, she helped me upstairs to my bed before I lost consciousness.

When I woke, it was late morning.

"It's about time you woke up!" Fi sat beside my bed and fidgeted crossly with her hair. "I thought you were going to sleep all day again!"

"No, but I wish I could." I groaned, rolled over, and buried my face in my pillow. "How long have I slept?"

"Two days!"

"Two days!" I said as I jerked my face toward her.

"Yes!" Fi flounced across the floor. "Matty's waiting downstairs for us. We're leaving as soon as you get out of bed."

"What do you mean?" I bolted upright, but she was already out the door. I crawled out of bed and found a tub of water sitting on the floor along with soap and a towel. A kettle of water steamed on a hook in the fireplace. Over a chair beside the hearth hung a new set of clothes complete with new boots. I stripped off Silas's clothes, which I'd slept in for two days, then dumped the kettle of hot water into the tub, stepped in, and eased into the warm water. Though my wounded arms were still stiff and sore, I washed and scrubbed off the dust and cobwebs which still clung to my hair. Drying by the fire and donning my new clothes, I went downstairs.

Matty was pacifying an impatient Fi in the common room when I joined them.

"Fi, what makes you think we're leaving?" I asked.

Matty answered for her. "Well, little El, you've had an exciting time at the Midsummer Festival, but I've been thinking you might have had enough excitement for a while, and seeing that all my wares are broken and I've nothing left to sell, although the king sent me a generous compensation for my goods and a commission for numerous items beside, there's no reason for me to stay in Zylona, and I thought you might like to ride with me, being that's how you came here, so what do you think about leaving right now?"

Stunned by Matty's speech, I thought about her offer. It was too dangerous for us to stay in Zylona. Someone else might try to use Fi's talents. We had enough money to last us for a long time so nothing held us here. I gave Matty a grateful smile. "I'd like that very much."

Fi cheered with glee.

"And I was thinking," Matty continued, "since you two don't have a home of your own, maybe you might stay with me, not that it would be permanent, mind you, but just for a while until you decide where you're going next, and you can relax without worrying, and you'd be safe with my family, and you could take peaceful walks in my woods, and maybe I could teach you a potter's trade."

"I'll think about it, Matty." It would be wonderful to stay with her, at least for a while. I was so tired of traveling, of worrying, of guarding every word. I wanted to lay down my sword for a while and just enjoy life again. I would be good not to be afraid, to be free of responsibility, if only for a few days. And Fi would be safe with Matty.

We gathered our belongings, which had been returned by Captain Tomar along with new clothes for both of us, and loaded them into Matty's wagon. Silas hitched the team.

"We never had our dance," he said, disappointment in his face.

"I know."

"Won't you stay for the rest of the festival?"

"I can't."

"Perhaps you'll come back next year?"

The hope I read in his face made it nearly impossible for me to refuse. "Perhaps. I'd like to dance with you."

And as I said it, I knew it was the truth. If he were Jin, I'd have been tempted to stay with him.

I climbed up beside Matty and Fi, and we drove away, waving to Lyedy, Lori, and Silas. We took back streets to avoid the bazaar, still at the height of the festival, and arrived at the city gate at midday.

After we drove through the tunnel and beyond the gates, I looked back at Zylona. Hanging from the walls were twenty bodies, one of which was Kaleed. I shuddered and turned away. I could have been hanging there in his place. Yet something in me mourned his death. He might have been a good king, and I...I could have been...no. I could never have been his queen. I shrugged off the thought.

I think Matty could read minds. Certainly, she seemed to know something was bothering me and gave my hand a comforting squeeze. As the sun neared the horizon, she turned to me, and trying to distract me, said, "Would you like to see something beautiful?"

"If you want to show it to me," I said, wanting anything to dispel the image of Kaleed's dead body from my mind.

She reached between her ample breasts, took out a delicately painted box, and handed it to me. Carefully, I opened the lid.

Nestled in white fur was a topaz carved like a rose. It sparkled in the waning sunlight, glittering like Matty's golden eye. The king had remembered her eyes, her flashing, piercing eyes. I wondered what had come between the two young lovers, why they'd never married.

"Sometimes love isn't enough, El," Matty said softly. "Sometimes other things are more important than the feelings of two individuals."

I understood. He was a king; she, a commoner. Kaleed had been *kreeyagen*. I was Jin. Some chasms were too wide to bridge.

The sun sank in the west. Twilight cast its eerie shadow on the land. When stars began twinkling overhead and a full moon rose above the surrounding thicket of trees, a golden-red glow of firelight appeared ahead of us. Matty reined the horses before the closed door of a wooden house.

"Where are we, Matty?" Fi said curiously.

The door opened. Light and laughter and delicious aromas tumbled out, warming my heart.

Matty put her huge arm around Fi and gave her a gentle hug. "We're home, child."

"Home?" Fi's eyes brightened. "El? Are we home?"

Matty gazed at me and smiled.

"Yes, Fi," I said quietly, "We're home–for a while."

Touched by the Gods

Sword & Sorceress is a wonderful anthology series begun by Marion Zimmer Bradley and continues still today. I was lucky enough to sell this story to Sword & Sorceress XXI. If you love sword and sorcery, you should definitely read this series.

I woke suddenly, aching as if I'd been trampled by cattle. My throat was dry as Zindol's Desert, but my hair and skin were damp. I didn't recognize the room I was in. The closed shutters lit in little light, and the hearth fire had burned down to a dull red glow. Finally, my eyes adjusted enough to see a middle-aged woman sprawled like a plump rag doll in a chair beside my bed. Her clothes were a brightly colored patchwork.

Of course, I thought, my mind starting to work. That's the fashion in Thallingar. I sat up, groaning, muscles punishing me for moving.

My companion yawned. "Are you awake, Elan?"

I groaned again, pulled a wool blanket over my breasts, and shivered. Who was she? She seemed familiar. Yes, Althea, the innkeeper's wife. I was in the Full Barrel Inn.

Althea touched my forehead. "Fever's gone. Tomorrow or the day after, you can get up."

I started to ask what she was talking about when I remembered. My twin sister Filea and I had come to Thallingar a few days before the autumn Full Moon Fest to look for work, Fi as a dancer, me as a sword-for-hire. Instead, I'd caught a fever. It must have hit me quickly, too quickly for me to use my healing power, and that made me uneasy. Usually, I felt an illness in time to heal myself. Not this time. I didn't know how many days I'd been in bed, but I stank of sweat.

"How long have I been sick?" I asked, smoothing my hair behind my ears.

Althea beat my pillow into a soft mound, then eased me back to it. "Ten days. Didn't think you'd survive. Many don't live past the third day. You've a strong spirit."

I shivered again, but this time from fear. Ten days? Where was Filea? Who'd taken care of her while was sick? What frightened me was that someone might discover Fi's ability to see visions while dancing, might learn we weren't human. I could take care of myself in the world. But Fi, she was so vulnerable, trusting. I was always afraid for her.

We were identical twins with sun-gold hair and eyes like summer skies. I'd been born first, normal. Fi was born breach after a long and difficult labor. Her body grew to womanhood. Her mind didn't. Sometimes, I wondered if the gods had given her the gift of dance in recompense, as if they ever felt pity or remorse.

"Where's Fi?" I asked in a raspy voice.

Althea paused half a moment, less perhaps. Only a fighter like me would've noticed. She smiled and tucked the blanket under the feather mattress. "She's being well cared for. Save your strength. Don't worry."

Something was wrong. I read it in Althea's grey eyes, in the slight tremor of her mouth. "I want to see her," I said, trying not to betray her anxiety.

She didn't look directly at me. "Not safe for a visit yet. Wouldn't want her to catch Quick Fever, would you?"

At least, Fi wasn't ill. Somehow, I knew Althea wasn't lying about that. She tensed. Her fingers curled into her palm. She was hiding something. A warning screamed in my head, but I was still too weak to do anything about it, at least with Althea present. I decided I wouldn't push her. Better to be cooperative. "No, I don't want her to get sick. Just let me see her when it's safe."

Althea relaxed and managed a genuine smile. "Of course. Rest now. I'll bring food later."

"What time is it?" I asked in a tired voice.

"Early evening." She added wood to the hearth and stirred the coals to life.

I yawned and let my eyelids droop. "I think I need rest more than food."

Althea studied me. "Then sleep. I'll bring food in the morning. Water's in the pitcher."

She poured me water, which I drank slowly. When I handed her the cup back, she said, "Call if you need anything. I'll hear. My room's next door."

Good to know, I thought as she left.

Pretending sleep, I listened. Floor boards creaked in the hall. Hinges squeaked as someone opened my door but didn't enter. A moment later the door shut, the lock clicked, and footsteps faded away. Someone wanted me to stay here, but why? And who? Outside were answers, and I meant to find them.

I lay very still and summoned the quiet fire hidden in my Jin soul. Warm healing blue flames flowed through me, around me, chasing pain and renewing strength. As my body healed, my mind cleared. I remembered things I should've noticed befire, that should've alerted me: the intense look in Dask's eyes as he spoke; the sudden interest Royan, chief priest of the Temple of Geddering the Merciless, took in Filea; the wide-eyed citizens watching my sister dance, whirling like a blue and gold butterfly.

Fi was in trouble, I knew it. I felt no cry mind-to-mind in the Jin way, but I sensed danger. I'd tear down every building in Thallinger to find her.

Moving with the silent stealth I'd learned from wild animals I'd played with as a child, I got out of bed and pulled on blouse, pants, boots, and cloak, all the color of forest shadows, just right for being unseen at night. My clothes felt strangely loose; the fever had made my normally slender body even thinner. Streaking my hands and face with charred wood to hide my lightly tanned skin, I strapped my sword to my back beneath my cloak, slipped daggers into wrist and belt sheaths, then crept to the window and lifted the latch. I was lucky. The shutter hinges were leather and didn't squeak when I pulled one side open a crack.

I was on the second floor, looking out on Merchant Street which ran from the North Gate to Temple Square. Twilight was fading into a clear autumn night on the Plain of Anrathoth. A crescent moon hung like a silver of orange peel above the Yorbid Mountains on the western horizon. A few people hurried past, eyes watching everywhere. Though Thallingar was known for swift, merciless justice, thieves and murderers still lurked there. Only the foolish or desperate traveled at night. I wasn't foolish.

At last, no feet echoed on stones. No eyes or steel gleamed. I pulled my hood low over my face, eased the shutters open, and climbed out the window. Clutching the sill, I relaxed my legs to absorb the shock, then let go. I landed in a crouch with no more noise than a leaf, dagger in hand in case I was wrong about the street being deserted. I wasn't. I melted into the alley behind the inn and headed for Choley's Tavern and the one person I hoped could tell me what I needed to know–Dask.

Every city had a section where life was miserable and death was easy to find. Thallingar's was called Darkway, and Choley's Tavern sat in the center of it. There was little color in Darkway, even in daylight: light gray and dark gray, black and brown. Smells were much more varied, from mildly offensive to stomach-turning putrid. Darkway's denizens never noticed.

Actually, Darkway wasn't too dangerous during daylight if you carried weapons openly and walked down the center of the streets. At night, ten armed mercenaries might not be enough to keep you alive. Only Darkway's inhabitants and priests were relatively safe after sunset–the former because they knew every escape route; the later because no one dared anger the gods.

I crept from shadow to shadow through filth-covered alleys, past limp bodies I didn't bother checking for life. At last, I reached the street beside Choley's. Rough voices and heavy footsteps made me flatten against the stone wall. Two men, swaggering drunkenly, argued as they passed down the street before Choley's. Shortly after, I heard the soft thunk of steel entering flesh. One or both wouldn't see sunrise.

I slunk around the corner and into a recess below a wooden sign, a frothy mug painted on it. I listened to sounds seeping through the wooden door, laughter, pounding on wooden tables. Someone was singing a bawdy tune. I rubbed off enough of the char-black to look dirty but not disguised. Pulling my hood lower over my face, I pushed open the door and went in.

A few eyes turned in my direction, then dismissed me. Minding one's own business was normal at Choley's. The owner stood behind the bar, drawing mugs of beer and singing along with his customers. His voice was as rich and vibrant as the giant Bell of Seaside. Dask had told me Choley was an ex-mercenary. He was built like a blacksmith and needed no bashers to handle unruly drunks. His leathery face was square, marred by many lines. At least two weren't natural.

The tavern was dark, smoky, and smelled of sweat, filth, and spilled drink. I scanned the crowd 'til I located Dask, Second Priest of the Temple of Gedderin. He'd been one of the first people to greet Fi and me when we'd arrived in Thallingar. His grass green eyes had made me nervous, but in a pleasant way. I'd played my silver flute; Fi had danced. Dask had followed every ching of her finger cymbals, every flutter of her veil. I'd worried about his interest, but after the dance, he'd turned to me.

"Are you and your sister staying in Thallingar?" he'd asked and leaned close to me.

I'd pulled back a bit. "At least until the fest is over, unless I've found work by then."

"What kind of work?"

"Mercenary."

He'd raised a sandy eyebrow. "Perhaps," he'd paused and given me half a smile, "I could help. I know the captain of the guard and most merchants. I'll inquire about work."

I'd thought he'd been concerned about us as part of his professional duties, but if he could help, I wasn't too proud to accept. Dask had been charming and amiable. We'd sent our time in his company, except when Fi'd danced and I'd played. He'd introduced us to his fellow priests, including chief priest Royan. I'd had the feeling Dask was flaunting us, but he'd treated us both with the greatest respect.

The last evening of the fest Fi'd wanted to go to bed early. Dask had escorted us to the inn, said good night to Fi, and asked me to join him for supper. I'd smiled and agreed.

Dask had hesitated a moment, then said, "Would you accept this?" He'd pulled out a black and red scarf and held it out to me. The followers of Gedderin wore such scarfs during the festival. I'd looked at it, touched it, then shook my head. "No, I'm not a believer."

Dask had frowned, then gave me a weak smile. "Then keep it as a remembrance of me."

I sighed and smiled back. "All right."

We'd shared a good meal at a tavern near Temple Square. Dask told me tales of Thallingar while I'd eaten. I'd felt edgy, a vague sense he wanted something from me.

As we'd left the tavern, I'd shivered though the night had been warm. Before we were halfway to the Full Barrel Inn, I was shaking, dizzy, and barely able to stand. The last things I remembered before I'd passed out were Dask's arms around me and his quiet voice chuckling.

I wove my way through the tables to the unoccupied end of the bar and waited until Choley wandered my way. Plunking two copper coins on the wooden counter, I said softly, "A mug of ale for me and one for you, if you'll let me buy it."

A crow-feather eyebrow raised slightly as he stared hard at me. He picked up one copper with surprising agility, considering how huge his fingers were, then slid the other coin back to me. "I don't drink while I'm working, stranger, but thanks for the offer. Maybe later when Ramy takes over."

My hand froze above the coin. How did he know I was a stranger? Of course. My accent betrayed me. I clutched his wrist and said in a hushed voice, "I need some information."

His dark eyes narrowed, pulling at a scar on his left cheek. "Information's expensive." He held up his other hand as I stuck my free hand in my pouch. "Sometimes information costs more than coins."

I released him, my hand trembling from the strength I felt in him. "I'll pay the price, but I need answers."

"Answers can kill."

"No, just unanswered questions."

He scrunched his thick lips. "When Ramy comes on duty, we can take a room upstairs." He grinned as I jerked back. "Just business, nothing more."

"All right," I said slowly. "How long?"

"About half an hour. Go up now if you want."

Should I watch Dask or stay out of his sight? "I'll wait."

"Suit yourself." Choley grinned as he went to wait on someone at the other end of the bar.

Dask seemed unaware I was watching him. I'd learned that the best way not to be noticed was to act as if you belonged, make no effort to hide. I didn't want anyone wondering about me.

Sooner than I'd hoped, crippled old Ramy limped in. Sidling between tables, he went to the bar where Choley handed him a rag and told him to make correct change. From Choley's tone, I figured Ramy couldn't count higher than the fingers on one hand.

Choley motioned for me to follow him. I didn't want to let Dask out of my sight, but I went. The stairs creaked as I climbed after Choley. I glanced at the crowd. No one paid any attention. My imagination was making me skittish.

Choley led me down a dim corridor barely wide enough for him, pushed open a door, and waited for me to enter. I glanced in and was surprised to see only a large table and six chairs. Choley grinned at me, obviously pleased with himself. I slipped past him and sat down, my back to solid stone. He closed the door with deliberate delight, sauntered to the table, and sat down facing me.

"Now, to business," he said. "Price will depend on what information you want."

I hesitated. How much could I really trust him? I leaned close enough so he could hear me and whispered, "I want to know where Dask has my sister."

A lecherous smile pulled at his lips. "I don't keep track of his women."

Barely controlling my anger, I tossed back my hood. "She's not one of his women! She's a dancer, my sister. You may have seen her at the Full Moon Fest. She looks exactly like me."

Choley grinned again. "Cleaner, I hope."

I gritted my teeth and continued. "She's very..." I searched for the right word, "child-like."

His eyes flew open wide. He sucked air through a space between yellowed teeth and stood up. "Can't help you."

I grabbed his arm. You know where she is, don't you? Tell me, please!"

"Beyond help. Leave here if you want to live."

"I won't leave without her! Where is she?"

There was pity in his eyes as he shook his head. Where you can't reach her. Where no one can."

"She's not dead. I'd know if she were."

Shoulders sagging, Choley looked down at me. "Not yet," he said softly. "Why'd you bring her here? Didn't you know what they do to people like your sister?"

I shook my head, ice spiders in my stomach.

He sat back down, ran his hand through a tangle of blue-black hair, and gazed straight at me. "There's a sect of Gedderin, not officially sanctioned, called the Innocents." He frowned and spat on the floor. "They believe the childminded are touched by the gods, given visions too beautiful or too terrible for their minds to bear. They're given back to the gods on the moonless night after the autumn full moon. Of course, the Temple priesthood won't admit the sect exists, even though some of them are part of the Innocents–like Dask. I didn't think they'd find a victim this year because tomorrow night's the ritual. They probably thought your sister was sent by their god just in time."

"They'd have to kill me before I'd let them hurt Fi."

"Very likely," said Choley. "I'm surprised you're still alive. I'd have killed you first."

I jumped, startled, clutching the table until my knuckles turned purple-white. "I think they tried." I told him about my sudden illness.

His jaw tightened, and his eyes became slits of ebony. "Sounds like that scarf Dask gave you was infected with Quick Fever. Over half those who catch it, die. You must be stronger than you look." He shook his head. "The innkeeper and his wife, never suspected they were Innocents."

"Where would they be keeping her?"

"In the Temple. You'd have to fight the whole priesthood to get her back."

"If I have to, I will." I stood up and turned to go.

I'd almost reached the door when Choley called, "Wait."

I looked over my shoulder at him and saw him digging his chipped nails into the table.

"I..." He paused, brows pulled together. "I've made a good life here and want to stay, but if you need another sword, mine's still sharp."

I gasped. "If you're found helping me, you'll be a fugitive–or worse."

His face crinkled even more. "Oh, well, never did like the Innocents. Beside, Darkway's getting dull."

I stared at him incredulously. Darkway was probably more exciting, in a deadly sort of way, than any other place I'd ever been. I walked back to the table. "My name is Elan. I can't offer you much, but what I have is yours." I held out a leather bag containing all the money I had.

He took the bag, weighed it in his broad hand, and tucked it inside his shirt.

I assumed he accepted. "It has to be tonight, but first, I have to talk with Dask. Do you have a place we wouldn't be overheard?"

Choley's face looked like crinkled parchment as he smiled. "A room below my living quarters behind the bar. I use it for...private...business."

"All right, I'll grab Dask after he leaves here. Just be at your back door when I knock."

"Might make it easier for you." Choley reached deep in his pocket, pulled out a small hinged box, and opened it.

My mouth fell open. Silver-gray dust half filled the container. Dream Dust. Possession was death in Thallingar. One pinch relaxed a person, gave him exquisite pleasure; two made him unconscious, brain damaged; three killed him. Choley had enough to keep half the population of Thallingar happy for a year or dead in one night.

He closed the box and slipped it into a pocket. "I'll put some in his drink. You'll have no trouble with him."

I swallowed hard. "Let's hope he hasn't left yet."

Dask was sitting at his table, drinking with three companions, as we descended the stairs. I watched Choley amble through the crowd, greeting those who were leaving and welcoming new arrivals. He spoke to the table directly behind the priest, turned, and stumbled against Dask's back.

"You shhpilled my drink, Choley!" Dask sputtered while his companions leaped out of the path of flowing mead.

Choley looked apologetic. "Sorry, priest. I'll get you another. No charge."

Dask glowered as Choley called old Ramy to sop up the mess. Choley took the mug, refilled it, and returned it to the red-haired priest. As Dask drank, a contented smile bowed his wide mouth. Green eyes clouded. Freckled skin flushed. His head wobbled from side to side like a huge, burnt orange flower on a spindly stem.

Dask's friends wandered away since he ignored them. After a while, he looked around the vacated table and lurched to his feet. Walking as if the floor constantly shifted, he reached the door and sagged against the wall. His hand inched toward the latch, grasped it, and raised the bar. He staggered outside into Darkway. Choley looked at me, barely nodded, and vanished through the curtain behind the bar. I waited a few moments, then walked to the door and left.

My eyes took half a second to adjust to the darkness, but my ears picked up the unsteady shuffled of feet on cobblestones. I peeked around the corner and saw Dask zigzagging down the street, holding his head stead with one hand, smothering laughter with the other. I checked the shadows for lurkers but saw no one. Like a night hawk, I glided silently toward my prey until I was an arm's length behind him.

Suddenly, Dask looked back over his shoulder. His face turned so pale, it looked like a full moon in Darkway's streets. He tried to step away from me, tangled his feet in his robe, and fell hard on his hip.

I dropped to a crouch. That much noise would attract people I'd rather not meet. I tied his hands and feet, stuffed cloth in his mouth, and heaved him over my shoulder. I nearly gagged. He smelled as bad as the rest of Darkway. It wasn't easy to stand up. Dask was heavier than he looked. On the third try I made it, but my back ached from the strain.

I heard soft leather against stone, the barest rustle of cloth. Darkway's inhabitants were coming to investigate. I headed for Choley's back door.

I tapped against the wood. The door made no sound as it opened from dark alley to darker room. I hurried inside. Moments after the latch clicked into place, yellow sparks glittered like star showers from a flint-struck steel. A candle sputtered to life and gave the room a translucent golden glow.

"Follow me," Choley said. Candle in hand, he led me through heavy curtains to another room.

Embers in a fireplace cast a crimson light. Choley set the candle on a table, threw back a frayed rug, and opened a hidden trapdoor. Retrieving the candle, he climbed down a wooden ladder, set the candle in a lantern, and came back to the ladder. "I'll take him," he said.

Dask squirmed as I transferred him to Choley's broad shoulder. The wooden rungs creaked from the added weight but held. I grabbed the trapdoor, flipped the edge of the rug over it, and pulled rug and door together over the opening as I descended to the hidden cellar.

Choley tied Dask to a chair, made a slip knot in a rope, and looped it around Dask's neck. I stood before him until his eyes fixed on me with clear recognition.

"You thought I'd die, didn't you?" I asked, my voice soft as snowflakes.

Dask struggled against the ropes until Choley tightened the noose. "Still," Choley whispered in Dask's ear. "Stay very still."

I moved a chair in front of Dask and sat down. "I'm going to take the gag from your mouth. Tell me what I want to know, and I may let you live." I removed the cloth. I should've guessed Dask would scream.

Choley jerked the rope so tight, Dask turned nearly as red as his hair. Bending close, Choley said, "No one can hear you, so speak quick and soft."

Our prisoner panted as the rope loosened around his throat. I could read my death in his eyes.

"Where's my sister?"

He didn't answer, just glared hatred at me.

Choley pulled the rope just enough to worry Dask. "Where is she, priest?"

"In...in the temple," he growled.

I took out my dagger and ran the flat side of the blade along his cheek. "Where?"

His eyes opened so wide, they looked like they might fall out of their sockets. "At the top of the central tower. Six Innocents guard her. If you try to save her, she'll be killed. You're helpless to stop it." His smile cut deeper than his words.

"If she dies, you will, too."

He laughed. "If I die, you won't leave alive either."

"Don't!" Choley grabbed my arm.

Blood leaked down Dask's face from a shallow cut, a cut I hadn't realized I'd made. I dropped the knife and fled to a dark corner. My heart thumped hard against my ribs. I wanted to kill Dask, to see his blood soak into the ground, and those thoughts made me sick. The world had taught me to fight, to kill to survive, but my ancestry taught peace. Sometimes, I thought the conflict would shatter my mind like crystal handled too roughly.

A firm hand on my arm made me jump. Choley stood beside me, creases in his forehead. I swallowed hard and blew out the air that fear had trapped in my lungs.

"Sorry," he said, on brow raised. "Didn't mean to startle you. What's troubling you?"

Only a handful of people knew Fi and I weren't human. Could I trust Choley that much yet? If I hoped to save Fi, I had to. "Watch and listen," I said, then strode to the chair before Dask.

Facing him, I reached toward his red-stained cheek. He flinched, fear in his eyes. With a corner of my cloak, I dabbed the blood away from the wound. I touched his face, then reached inside myself. Faint blue flames flowed from my hand and licked at the cut until it healed without a scar.

"H—how'd you do that?" Choley stammered as he clutched the ladder.

I looked straight at him, knowing I was putting my life and Fi's in his hands. "I'm Jin. So is Fi."

His face scrunched in a puzzled frown. "But Jin are just stories, tales for children."

"No, we're real. So are our powers. I'm a healer. Fi sees visions while dancing. My people had many gifts."

"Had?" He paused as if he were repeating my words to himself. "Where are your people? Why are you here?"

"Dead." I told him of my people, massacred by humans who'd feared our gifts. I still heard my mother's screams, saw my dear friend Jenise run through, felt my little brother die–always with me, even after eight years, as fresh and raw as the day it happened. I shuddered, drove the painful memories back to the dark cell in my heart, where I kept them locked away. I looked at Choley and waited for him to speak. He didn't, but Dask did.

"It's true your sister has visions?" His eyes took on the gleam of religious fervor. "Then she's truly sent to us. She'll be an excellent sacrifice, the perfect expression of our devotion to Gedderin. The believers would die rather than let her escape."

I'd always been afraid of Dask's type of fanaticism. I sent a pleading look to Choley.

He looked from me to Dask. "He's right."

"What?" I sputtered. "How can you say that!"

"Even if you rescue her from the temple, the Innocents won't give her up. They'll trail us 'til they recover Fi. Unless we offer them something they want," he smiled as he stared at Dask, "like their priest."

"A trade? Fi for him? Would they really do it?"

"Never!" Dask spat. "When they know your sister has visions, they won't exchange her, even for me!"

Choley strode to him and bent down until they were face to face. "The Innocents don't know she has visions. Only the three of us do. I won't tell them. Elan certainly won't." Choley's eyes took on a gleam that made me as jittery as it did Dask. "And *you're* not going to tell them anything."

Dask's eyes widened. He started to speak several times, his mouth opening and closing like a beached fish, but no sound came.

"All right," I said, breaking the icy tension. "I'll rescue Fi tonight, then we can leave the city."

"No," Choley said.

"No?" I gaped at him. "We can't stay here after I've invaded the temple!"

"Oh, we'll leave," Choley replied, then poked my chest, "but you're *not* going to rescue Fi."

Anger made my voice like cold steel. "Yes, I will."

Choley shook his head. "I won't let you."

"Why?"

"Because it's suicide."

Disgusted, I turned away, but he grabbed my arm and jerked me back to face him. "Look, Dask has already told you there's no way you can reach Fi without alerting her guards. She'd be dead in seconds–and so would you. Let's go for a straight exchange. Best chance with least risk."

I started to argue, but he was right. Slowly, I nodded. "How will be get a message to the Innocents?"

Choley rubbed his square jaw. "One of the Alley Cats."

"Alley Cats?" Had he trained cats as messengers?

"Darkway's orphans. They call themselves the Alley Cats. Quiet, fast, deadly, know every back alley, rooftop, and unlocked door and window in the city. We give them a message for the innkeep, since he's an Innocent."

I nodded. "Good. Set the exchange point outside the city, somewhere we'll have the high ground and a quick escape route. Make it at least an hour's ride west of the city and late in the day. That way the sun will be in their eyes, and they'll have to make the trade fast and hurry back before the city gates close for the night. Only problem we have is getting out of the city ourselves."

Choley gave me an appreciative smile. "No problem. We'll just take one of the carts I use for my, uh, other business and drive out at first light. I'll handle the rest since I know the city better than you do."

Suddenly, I felt very tired. I'd healed twice without resting. Can I sleep here for a few hours? I need a little rest, and I can't go back to the inn."

Choley nodded toward the ceiling. Sleep in my bed."

I gasped, embarrassed.

He held his hands up to stop my reply. "Don't hear words not spoken. I said 'you,' not 'we.' I won't be sleeping tonight, too many things to do."

I gagged Dask again, then followed Choley up the ladder. His room was separated by a dark velvet curtain from the room with the trapdoor. Lighting another candle with the first, he turned to go, but I stepped in front of him.

"Want me to stay?" He grinned at me and winked.

"No, Choley, I want to thank you. You're giving up a profitable business to help me."

"Who says I'm giving up anything? Figured I'd have to leave someday if my smuggling was discovered, so I made plans long ago, just in case. Money, escape routes, new city, everything waiting until needed." He grinned again. "Guess now's as good a time as any to move on."

"But–but you don't have to help. Why?"

The grin crumbled to a somber stare, and a quiet sigh escaped his thick chest. I've guarded caravans through deserts so hot my sweat sizzled as it fell to the sand. I've climbed through mountains so cold I thought I'd lose fingers and toes. I've fought wars for causes I didn't believe in, just for money. Nothing I've done ever made a difference in the world, made it better. Now I have a chance to save one life." He stood tall, almost regal as he gazed at me.

"And..." he paused, eyes narrowed, "I watched my brother and his wife and their two children die of Quick Fever, life sucked out of them like a weasel sucks eggs. In a week's time I lost all the family I had." He eyes glinted with the anger his voice revealed. "And Dask deliberately exposed you to Quick Fever, to make certain you died! That's why I'm helping you!"

He disappeared behind the curtain. Moments later I heard the side door open and latch again.

A warmth swirled in my chest. The good in humans always surprised me. A person here or there still gave me hope that humans would someday value compassion as much as the Jin had.

I stripped off my boots and cloak, unbuckled my sword, then lay down on the wide, firm bed. Staring at the candle-wraiths playing on the ceiling, I wondered if our plan would work, if I'd ever see Fi again.

A quiet baritone voice cut through my dreams. "Elan, we have to go."

I opened my eyes to see Choley standing in the doorway, curtain draped against his arm. "Time already?"

"Yes. What we have to do requires dark." He let the curtain drop between us. I dressed and hurried to the main room.

Choley was opening the trapdoor as I arrived. "I've got the wagon and three extra horses tied up outside. We'll put Dask in a barrel and sneak him out of Thallingar with the rest of the supplies I've packed."

I handed him a lit candle as he started down the ladder. "What about the message?"

"Won't be delivered 'til a couple of hours before sunset. The Innocents won't have enough time for a sneak attack." He gave me a wink. "Don't worry. Nothing can go wrong." As he reached the bottom, I heard him mumble, "I hope."

When I joined him in the secret room, he was pouring a cup of wine. "Take off his gag," Choley said.

Dask was bleary-eyes but still angry. As soon as I removed the cloth, he cursed me with plague after plague.

Choley held the cup in front of Dask's face. "Thirsty?"

Dask turned his curses on the tavern keep, but Choley just smiled and tossed back a few of his own. "Look, priest, you can drink this wine and fall asleep, or I can pound you unconscious. That'll take longer and feel lots worse–for you, that is. I'd enjoy it. So what'll it be?"

Dask snickered. I guess he didn't think Choley would really hit him. Dask was wrong. His jaw sounded like pottery breaking as Choley's hand smashed against it. Green eyes rolled back into a head that wobbled like a poppy with a broken stem. I thought Dask would've been out for hours from a blow like that. Instead, his eyes focused on Choley, glittering emerald bright.

"Thirsty now?" Choley asked.

Dask opened his mouth and swallowed as Choley held the cup.

"Good." Choley turned to me. "When he's out, we'll leave."

Dask became slack-jawed and dull-eyed in moments and was soon limp as a rag doll. His breathing slowed, and his lids closed, but he smiled in his sleep.

Choley hefted Dask over his shoulders and climbed the ladder. I followed, shut the trapdoor, and went to the side entrance. I snuffed the candle and cracked the door enough to check the alley, hidden in gray light before dawn. No movement, no sound, no gleam of eye or steel. I opened the door. Choley carried Dask to the wagon parked beside the door, shoved him into a barrel, and secured the lid. We piled bundles around it, then climbed onto the driver's bench.

Dawn blushed the sky as we reached the western gate. A caravan waited for the first shaft of sunlight announcing a new day and the opening of the gates. I was edgy as we passed the sentries, but they didn't stop us. We followed the caravan, just another wagon on the western trade route.

We reached the mouth of the western pass through the Yorbid Mountains–the site chosen for the trade–in two hours. Choley showed me his secret path into the mountains. We took Dask's barrel off the wagon and hid it in a crevice, then Choley drove farther up the path. I stayed behind to watch Dask and set traps to block pursuit. Beyond that, all I could do was wait and hope.

The westering sun was hot on my back when Choley took Dask from the barrel. He was as unwieldy as wet clay and about as cooperative. It took both Choley and me to lever him out.

When Dask was sitting on reddish sand at the mountains' base, I noticed something was wrong with him. He looked like a sack of grain, even acted like one, not moving from the position in which he'd been placed. I thought he might still be asleep and shook him. There was no reaction. He was a shapeless heap, moving only when moved. I grabbed his chin and forced his eyes to meet mine.

That's when I saw it–that subtle lack of awareness I was so familiar with. I'd seen it in my sister's eyes. I felt sick and wanted to scream at Choley. He'd put Dream Dust in the wine, too much, causing brain damage. I could do nothing for Dask. My healing power had its limits.

"Why?" I cried as I turned to Choley. "You didn't have to destroy his mind! I just wanted my sister back alive!"

Choley glared at me. "You really think the Innocents would give up Fi for him without good reason? They're sacrificing someone tonight. It has to be one of the childminded. Better him than her."

I started to argue, but he cut me off.

"Suppose we traded him for her, and he'd told them about Fi's visions. You think they'd let any of us live? Now, at least, we'll all survive, and he'll see his god face-to-face. I'd say he'd getting what he deserves."

My vision rippled like heat waves above desert sands. My soul cried, but I knew he was right.

Dust clouds from the east distracted me. The Innocents had come to make the trade, about ten riders. Hopefully, one of them was Fi. I took my dagger from its sheath, knelt beside Dask, and held the blade to his throat.

Choley took his bow from his shoulder, nocked an arrow, and aimed it at the lead rider. "Stop there," Choley called when they were fifty feet away. "Where's the woman?"

The lead rider signaled. A man rode forward, leading a horse. Fi's wrists were tied to the pommel. She looked pale but unharmed. I had to grit my teeth to keep from crying out.

The leader shrugged back his hood. It was the chief priest Royan. *He* was the leader of the Innocents. "We've honored our part," he growled, "but we require proof of the truth of your claim before the exchange."

I looked askance at Choley. What did Royan mean?

Choley didn't relax his aim even a fraction. "Examine him. He has visions and is touched by the gods."

Cautiously, Royan dismounted and walked toward me and Dask. I watched the chief priest like a desert viper. Royan stooped before us, gave me a cold and deadly glare, then searched Dask's face.

Dask startled both of us by speaking, his voice high-pitched and awed. "Blue flame. Blue flame touched me. Touched the hurt and made it go away."

I trembled and nearly dropped my dagger. Even now, Dask remembered my healing power. His words meant our deaths.

To my surprise, Royan's eyes grew wide. He sucked air through his beard-hidden mouth. "He is indeed touched by the gods! We have our sacrifice!"

I almost gave a prayer of gratitude to the Jin gods, except I didn't believe in them anymore.

Quickly, the Innocents cut Fi's ropes, and two men built like stone towers set Dask in her place. Royan stared at me. His voice was ants crawling on my skin. "We'll remember you."

He wheeled his horse and galloped toward Thallinger, followed by the others.

Fi ran to my open arms, and I hugged her so hard she whimpered. "Fi, are you all right? Did they hurt you?"

"Time for that later." Choley's eyes flitted across the landscape. "I don't want to stay here, just in case."

We mounted our horses and followed the secret path, now half-shadowed. As we rode, I thought about Dask and felt an ache in my chest, a hollow feeling like despair. Dask had tried to kill me and Fi for his god's sake. Choley had ruined Dask's mind from a sense of poetic justice. Royan hadn't cared who suffered as long as he had his proper sacrifice. I'd just wanted to save my sister's life.

I'd been among humans for years. I'd served them, fought them, killed them, but I'd never understand them.

Hidden Scars

Elan the Jin is one of my favorite characters. I have more stories about her and her sister Filea in my head. Someday I hope to write a book about them.

The anguished scream was like a blow to my head as I sat in the common room of Crossings Inn. Jumping to my feet, sword in hand, I scanned the perimeter of the room through narrowed, blue eyes. Silence, as if the world held its breath, replaced the singing that had warmed the customers' hearts as much as the ale had warmed their blood. Everyone, even the mercenaries I commanded as guard master of Choley's caravan, gaped at me as if I were a madwoman.

A hand clutched my right wrist. I hadn't seen Shad move, but my second-in-command pulled me around to face him, eye to eye. White streaks in his dark chin-length hair made him seem older and hardier than his thirty years. His grey-brown clothing gave him the look of his namesake–Shadow Weaver, or in the Heddokhan tongue, Skadus Wefen, god of dark magic and night secrets.

"Elan," Shad said, his voice as soft as moonlight and as cold as a stream in winter, "stop."

"Didn't you hear that scream?" I whispered intensely.

"What scream?"

"Are you deaf? I heard a man scream."

Pulling me closer, he stared at me with wide, chestnut eyes framed by a lean, leathery face. "I heard nothing."

"But—"I stopped, another scream echoing in my mind. I cradled my temple in one hand until the pain stopped, then smoothed a strand of golden hair back to my long braid. Sucking in a quick breath, I shivered with excitement as I realized what was happening. I'd heard a Mind Cry, the limited telepathy of my people. Somewhere nearby was a man of my own race, a Jin!

Pictures cut like jagged lightning through my head. Swords flashing silver-red as they pierced bodies. My sister sobbing against my shoulder while we hid from the invaders. My mother's dead eyes staring at the sky. Blood seeping from Father's chest. Blood everywhere. Brothers, neighbors, friends, dead all dead.

My heart pounded blood through my body. For so long I'd believed my sister Filea and I were the only Jin to survive the murderous jealousy and suspicion of humans. Suddenly, I'd discovered another Jin lived. I knew he wasn't from my tribe. I'd buried them myself after soldiers from Zrailin had massacred my family and all the villagers of Amajin.

Somehow, I had to find this kinsman and quickly. The Mind Cry was only used when in danger or pain. I clenched my sword tighter and swore softly in frustration. Until I heard the Mind Cry again, I couldn't follow it.

"Elan," Shad hissed as I came back to the present, "sit down, now, quietly."

For half a heartbeat I was irritated with him for giving me orders, but I knew he was right. Shad seldom spoke to anyone unless he thought it was necessary or imperative. In the two years we'd worked the caravan together, I'd come to rely on his judgment, yet I resented his interference now. I rubbed my aching wrist, which Shad finally released. Still trembling, I sheathed my sword, sat down at the table, and stared at my empty mug.

"Innkeep," Shad called as he sat down beside me, "the master needs her cup refilled."

"Hah!" the horse-faced man behind the wooden counter replied. "Seems she's had too much already!"

That broke the uncomfortable quiet. Everyone laughed and resumed talking. The innkeeper sauntered to the table, took my mug, filled it with sweet mead from a keg behind the bar, and brought the mug back. My hands didn't shake tool much as I sipped the pale gold liquid. I ignored the jibes directed at me until one villager, whose face was like a knobby apple, grinned at me drunkenly and asked,

"Hey, Swordwife, how about having a different weapon in your bed tonight?"

I stiffened, though I knew he was joking. Swordwife was one of the kinder terms I'd been called. Some countries used much worse for female mercenaries. Giving him an exaggerated scanning, I answered sarcastically. "That could be dangerous, but since you're unarmed, I'd be safe enough."

That brought a chorus of guffaws from the crowd. Even the target of my slight laughed.

"I see your tongue's as sharp as your sword," he said, then called for a toast to me.

A few toasts later, a pair of men two tables away stretched knotted arms and pushed back their bench. "Much as we hate to leave good company," said the pug-nosed man, "we have to get back home." He took a small pouch from between his leather jerkin and his dingy gray shirt. Extracting a blood-red crystal the size of a pea, he held it to catch the firelight, then tossed the gem to the innkeep. "Another round for everyone, Cort."

The innkeep's eyes bulged frog-like. "Milo, where did you find this?"

A smug grin crossed Milo's face. "Now I'd be a fool to say, wouldn't I?"

"Isn't stolen, is it?"

Milo laughed. "Of course not. We're not thieves."

His companion gave the innkeeper a lop-sided grin and said, "We got a slave that can smell gold and gems."

I nearly choked. A man who sniffs or perhaps sees ores and precious gems through rock or earth–he had to be an aurojin and the kinsman I was seeking. My knuckles turned purple-white from gripping my mug so tightly. I leaned forward, pretending to stare at the mead, and listened closely to the conversation.

For half an instant Milo paled, then he grinned and winked at the innkeep. "Sure, Lannie. And last week you swore you saw a pack of flying dogs. Then there was the time he said the trees had eyes and talked to him."

Everyone laughed at that.

Milo locked his arm around his companion's neck and patted him on the cheek. "Come on, Lannie. You're drunk. Time to go home."

"But Milo!" Lannie squealed. He struggled uselessly, his dirt-brown hair falling in his eyes, but he wasn't a match for his stronger and taller partner.

Milo kept a firm grip on Lannie's neck. "Is our wagon ready?"

"All loaded," the innkeep said.

"The wine, too? Lannie's partial to wine, you know." He winked at his companion, then looked back at the innkeep, who nodded and grinned. "Then I'll see you in a few weeks." Milo half dragged Lannie out the back door.

Turning back to his counter, the innkeep smiled and muttered to himself, "A slave that smells gold. What a tale."

I tried not to stand too quickly after they left. "We leave at sunrise tomorrow, men. I'm going to take a walk to clear my head, then I'll check on the horses. When I come back, I don't want to see one of you still here."

Some of the men grumbled as I strode toward the front entrance, but I knew they'd finish their drinks and head for bed. We'd been on the road for twenty days from dawn to twilight, and the men looked worn out. None of them would bother to see if I came back.

Closing the door behind me, I pulled my hood low over my face and clutched my cloak close against the crisp night air. I kept to the shadows cast by the waning autumn moon as I sneaked around the building. At the back corner I saw the two miners hitching a team of stocky horses to a small cart in the middle of the innyard.

"That was stupid," Milo growled. "You want the whole world to know about him?"

Lannie cringed and seemed to shrink. "No, I...I didn't mean it."

"You never mean it!"

Lannie jerked as if he'd been struck.

Milo looked at him, anger softening to exasperation on his moonlit face. "Oh, never mind. Get the gate for me." Milo climbed onto the driver's bench.

Hurrying to the innyard gate, Lannie pushed it open. Milo flicked the reins to start the team. The cart inched through. After Lannie closed and latched the gate, he climbed up beside Milo, and they turned north out of town.

I took one step toward the stables when a rough hand clapped over my mouth. A powerful arm wrapped around my waist, pinning my hands to my side. Fear froze me for an instant. Being held helpless was the one thing I couldn't cope with. Shaking my head furiously from side to side, I worked my mouth free. I bit my attacker's hand so hard, I tasted blood. When he cursed through gritted teeth and loosened his grip, I rammed an elbow in his gut, threw my head back against his chin, and stomped on his foot. He stumbled and let go of me. Whirling, I clasped my hands together and smashed them against his jaw so hard, his head snapped back. He staggered into the moonlight, and I gasped.

Shad wiped dark streaks from his mouth with the back of his hand. "What in the seven hells are you doing?" he said angrily.

"Why in the seven hells did you sneak up and grab me like that?" I shot back.

He gagged and spit on the ground. "I didn't want you running off by yourself."

"That's not your concern."

"Yes, it is. If you disappear, the caravan suffers, and we all lose money."

My face felt hot in the cool wind. "You'll get your promised share! Now go back inside and go to bed."

"No.

I clenched my fists. "No one challenges my authority on this caravan."

"I do," he said. "This time you're wrong."

I stared at him incredulously. He'd never defied me before. It took several moments and a tight swallow before I could speak. "After we reach Far Samdi, your contract is ended."

He straightened and gazed at me, eyes glittering like dark gems in the moonlight. "So be it." He spit on the ground again. "But until then, you go nowhere without me. Now tell me what you're doing?"

I glanced at the inn gate, knowing Milo's cart was well down the road. "Shad, I don't have time!"

"Then tell me on the way."

"You can't go with me."

"You can't stop me."

I chewed my lip thoughtfully. Why did he have to interfere at that moment? Glancing at the inn gate again, I decided I couldn't waste more time arguing. "All right. But we have to go now or we'll lose them."

"Who?"

"Milo and Lannie."

We sprinted to the stables, saddled our horses, and led them from the yard. Once outside the gate, we mounted and took the same road Milo's cart had.

The moon peeked through leafless branches arching overhead. They clashed in the chill night wind like skeletal hands clapping. Even though the road had a thick layer of soft dust, the horses' steps seemed to echo too loudly.

"Now, why are you following Milo?" Shad asked, sounding almost playful, as we rode side by side. "Hope to steal some gems for yourself?"

"No," I said softly.

"Then why?"

"I want the slave."

Shad chuckled. "So you *do* plan to steal something."

"Not quite. I plan to free him."

Reining his horse, Shad shifted in his saddle to look straight at me. "Why?"

"He's one of my kin."

He rested his arm on his thigh and leaned toward me slightly. "And how do you know that?"

"Because he sees gems through rocks."

Shad shook his head and flung his hands up. "And I suppose you can, too."

"No, all I can do is this."

I leaned toward him and touched his split lip. Blue flames flowed with healing warmth from my hand to his injury. When I took my hand away, he touched his lip as his mouth sagged open.

"Skaduswif," he whispered, drawing back from me.

Shadow wife. Sorceress. Witch. I shouldn't have been surprised by his reaction. Humans had always reacted with fear of Jin and the inborn powers we had. Peaceful, never warring or hating, Jin had been unprepared to defend themselves against the blind fear that drove humans to destroy what they couldn't understand.

My shoulders slumped, and I whispered, "No, Shad, I'm no sorceress. I am ramoojin, a healer."

"And...and the slave?" he stammered.

"Aurojin, one who sees ores and crystals in the earth."

"You're really a...a Jin?"

"Yes."

Cold sweat beaded my face. I swallowed hard and waited, afraid he's shrink from me with horror as other humans had. My sister and I had been alone for so long, apart from those around us. For Jin, who were joined to each other by bonds of loving acceptance, the loneliness was almost unbearable.

Shad said nothing, just stared at me, until I couldn't endure it anymore. Tears blurred my vision and felt like icicles on my face. Shad's silence was worse than the contempt and suspicion I'd received from others.

At last, he spoke. "I'll help."

"Why?" I asked.

"Because...because I understand, more than you think I do." He did something I'd never seen him do. He unlaced his leather wrist bands and removed them.

Even in the moonlight I could see the scars, scars of manacles, of infected sores, of slavery. A sob rose in my throat as I caressed the white marks on his dark skin.

"No one should be a slave," he whispered.

"Freed?"

"Escaped. And fugitive. I killed my master."

"Why?"

Avoiding my eyes, he started lacing the wrist bands back in place. "He sold my wife, Verinya. She was a slave, too. Sold her to a whoremaster. After I'd escaped, I tracked them for weeks. The night I caught up with the caravan, I confronted the whoremaster, demanding he let Verinya go. He cursed and told me she was dead. A waste of money, he called her." Shad choked, unable to speak for a moment. Slowly, he raised his dark eyes Tears, like liquid pearls, trickled down his cheeks. "She carried our child. When her new master found out, he'd beat her, hoping she'd miscarry. She did...but she bled to death."

I wanted to put my arms around him, comfort his as I'd comforted Filea when our parents were murdered, but I didn't. Instead, I touched his arm, and Shad stiffened. I felt his fears, shared his memories. I saw a family torn apart because his father had offended a powerful man. Years of shame while chained in the brothels of Stryend-by-the-Sea. And the loss of his wife and child. Shad's pain seeped into my soul, pain like a fist striking my chest, almost more than I could bear.

Grasping his arm, I gave back healing, blue fire flowing from my hand, healing the scars on his body, but also healing the scars on his heart, scars no one had ever seen. His eyes widened. His lips parted and sucked in a short breath. Hand covering mine, he gazed at me silently. Relief–that's what I read in his face, felt in his heart. Relief and gratitude. Several times he started to speak, then shook his head.

"We'd better catch up to Milo," I said, slumping in the saddle. Healing drained my strength as much as physical work, and I'd used it twice in one night without sleeping.

Shad simply nodded.

We rode for perhaps half an hour more when I felt the Mind Cry again. The sound cut my soul like a dagger, pulled me like an unseen rope toward the woods on the right.

"There's a worn track here," Shad said, pointing in the direction I was drawn. "I think the wheel marks are fresh."

I nodded, gave him the mercenary's hand signal meaning "Proceed quietly," and led the way along the path.

The moon was almost overhead when I spotted a yellow glow throw the tangled woods. I signaled Shad to dismount and silently slid off my horse. After we'd tied the reins securely to a tree, Shad and I crept forward until we lay on a leaf-covered bank just beyond the light.

Four men sat before a blazing fire, drinking and laughing. I recognized Milo and Lannie. The other two were huge. One was red-haired. The other looked like a brown bear.

"Good ale!" said the red-haired man. "Wonder if our little gold sniffer would like some."

"Ah, leave him alone, Del," Milo said slowly, as if he were unsure he'd used the correct words.

Del laughed and elbowed the bearish man. "Leave him alone, he says."

Bear grinned at Milo, showing more gum than teeth. "Why, we're just trying to be friendly with him."

Milo sloshed his drink on his legs, stood up cursing, and spilled the rest. "Tarbin's third eye!" he shouted as he tried to wipe the ale from his pants. He glared at the bearish man. "Hollis, I told you to leave Keddith alone! I won't tell you again! He's mine, and he's going to make us all rich, so you better not hurt him!"

Hollis looked as innocent as a fox caught with a chicken in its mouth. "Me? I would hurt a fly."

"No, you wouldn't. Flies annoy people. Look, I know you too well. If I find any more marks on him, I'll throw you out of this deal."

Hollis instantly sobered and stood up. "Not if you're dead."

Milo's hand strayed to his belt knife.

Lannie and Del quickly stepped between the other two.

"Stop it!" Lannie said as he pushed Milo back. "We're partners! If we start fighting each other, we all lose."

At the same time Hollis strained against Del's grip.

"Stop now," Del said, his eyes gleaming like polished mahogany, "or I'll break your arms. No fighting, understand?"

Grumbling, Hollis stopped struggling, jerked away from Del, and stomped toward his bedroll. Lannie released Milo, who muttered something then left the fireside. Del looked at Lannie and shrugged. Both men sat down and finished their ale.

My eyes followed Milo as he walked about half a dozen feet from the fire, crossing directly in front of my hiding place. Another man was huddled against a stake there, the manacles on his wrists attached by chains to a ring about six feet off the ground. His threadbare clothes were as dirty as his skin and hair. His face was hidden thin arms propped on knees pulled tight against his chest.

Milo knelt beside the man, and in a concerned voice, said, "Are you hurt?"

He lifted Keddith's chin until the firelight glowed showing seeping red welts on his face. Milo touched the slave's back gently, looked at the blood smearing his hand, and cursed softly.

Now I knew why I'd felt the Mind Cry.

"I'm sorry," Milo said. "I won't leave you alone with Hollis again."

Slowly, Keddith looked up at his master. In the wavering light I could see his eyes, the sky blue of my kin, but with a dull hopelessness that made my own eyes burn. Something dark and seething pulsed in me, wanting to give Hollis the pain he'd given. Yet even as that desire clouded my thoughts, shame wrong a sob from my Jin soul. I clawed the cold dirt I lay on, eyes closed.

Shad's hand on my shoulder startled me so I crunched dry leaves as I jerked away. Instantly, I flattened, face down, as did Shad, hoping no one would investigate. After eon-length moments, I heard Milo say,

"I think that pack of wild dogs is nosing around again."

Del laughed. "No, that was no more than a rabbit."

"Rabbit or not, better put plenty of wood on the fire."

Shad and I lay still, listening to the clunk of wood and the crackle of flames. My chest hurt, and I realized I was holding my breath. Slowly, I exhaled then took a few short gulps of air. We waited, the cold soaking through our cloaks until we had to grit our teeth to keep them from chattering.

After what seemed like hours, I heard the miners snoring. I rose from the cold ground where I lay watching. Keddith was shivering as he slept, his limbs pulled up tightly against his chest. Signalling Shad to guard my back, I crept from the edge of the woods to Keddith's side. I bent close, my lips brushing his ear, and whispered, "Kinsman, I'll free you."

Keddith's eyes shot open. He stared at me as if I were a demon. "All my kin are dead," he said.

I shook my head and touched his cheek. Healing flowed from my hand, blue flames soothing his wounds until not even scars were left. I sat back on my heels, my shoulders sagging, and took a deep breath. Healing drained my strength as much as physical work, and I'd healed twice in one night without sleeping.

Keddith sat up and touched his cheek. His eyes seemed suddenly alive, like spring flowers which had only slept beneath winter snows. "Ramoojin, who are you?"

Motioning for quiet, I glanced around the camp. The miners still slept. Shad had positioned himself between me and the glowing embers of the fire. I looked at Keddith and whispered, "Elan."

I took his wrist and examined the manacles. Choley, the owner of the caravan and my friend, had taught me a little about locks, but I knew I couldn't open these without the key. I waved Shad over. "Can you undo these?" I asked.

Shad looked them over, then shook his head. "Not if you want me to do it quietly.

Keddith glanced suspiciously at Shad, then said to me, "He is not Jin. Why do you travel with *kreeyagen*?"

"Later," I said. "Shad, check the ring. See if you can pry it open."

A soft chuckle made me jump. Sword in hand, I stood beside Shad, who was also in fighting stance.

"Don't bother," Hollis said with a hungry glint in his hazel eyes. He held a sword in one hand and a club-like branch in the other. "He's not going anywhere...and neither are you two."

Behind me, I heard Keddith inhale sharply.

"Elan, why are you using a weapon?"

I looked over my right shoulder and saw the horror I'd heard in Keddith's voice reflected in his face. He stared at me incredulously, as if I'd gone mad. Jin didn't use weapons, didn't kill, but I did. I'd had to learn to kill just to survive in the human world. I was still tormented by the deaths I'd caused, the lives I'd taken. Keddith couldn't understand that, not yet, maybe never.

I couldn't have turned my gaze toward Keddith for more than a few moments, but they were enough for Hollis to attack. He roared like an animal and charged at Shad. From the corner of my eye, I saw the branch swinging toward my left side. I tried to spring away but knew I couldn't avoid the blow. Relaxing my body to absorb the shock, I rolled as the branch connected. I hit the ground hard but was only bruised.

As Hollis hammered at Shad, I saw the other men waking,

Seven Hells of Ky-Ros, I thought. *Four against two. We've got to kill Hollis quickly to have any chance.*

Pushing myself upright, I swung at Hollis, grazing his side. He spun toward me, his face twisted with hate, and tried to smash my skull. Shad's blade plunged through Hollis' back just above the leather belt around his thick waist. I struck Hollis' arm, slicing down to bone. Bright crimson blood spurted from the gash, splattering my leather jerkin. He shrieked and dropped the branch. His movements were slower, as if he fought in a mud pit. Seeing Lannie approaching and Milo and Del grabbing their swords, I left Hollis to Shad.

Lannie's eyes registered surprised recognition. "Why?" he stammered and hesitated.

I didn't answer. My sword raked a deep furrow across his chest from shoulder to hip. He fought back but he wasn't sword trained. Soon he lay on the ground, bloody breath bubbling from his slashed throat.

Del attacked, and as our swords connected, a numbing shock ran up my arm. I had to use both hands to hold the hilt. Del was just as strong as Hollis but had the calm concentration a good swordsman needed, making him more dangerous than Hollis. Despite Del's size, he was quick. His every move seemed planned; every blow, well timed. He toyed with me, as a cat plays with a mouse, not yet ready to kill. Soon I had shallow but painful cuts on my face, arms, and thighs. One gash on my left arm was bleeding worse than the others. I was already fatigued from fighting Hollis and using my ramoojin power, and I missed a parry. Del's blade swept toward my throat. Just when I thought I'd sucked in my last breath, Shad's sword blocked Del's with a teeth-rattling clang.

I stumbled away and came face to face with Milo. He also recognized me, and his pause gave me the advantage. Batting his sword away from me, I kicked his knee with all my remaining strength. He toppled like a cut tree and clutched his leg, cursing. I really didn't want to kill him. Even though he was a slave master, he'd been kind to Keddith.

"Give me the key," I said, sword point pressed to his chest, "and I'll let you live."

Milo's eyes bulging, he fumbled inside his leather vest until he withdrew a black key on a thong. I took it and sighed with relief. Palming the key securely, I pounded my fist against his jaw. His eyes rolled back. His mouth hung open. He wasn't unconscious, but he was in no condition to fight.

Dropping the key inside my blouse, I turned to help Shad. Del had etched my companion's body with a network of fine cuts, none of the critical but all in areas of acute sensitivity. Shad was weakening, recovering more slowly, retaliating less often and less effectively.

I launched a kick at the back of Del's knee. The blow didn't hurt him. It merely threw him off balance a bit, but his next stroke missed. Shad dodged left and drove his sword into Del's side. Howling and with a jaw-cracking punch, Del sent Shad sprawling on the hard ground. I plunged my sword into Del's back. A scream of despair burst from his mouth as he crumpled to his knees. My sword pulled free. His life pumped scarlet from his chest. Turning his head, he looked up and me, blood trickling from his mouth, disbelief in his wide brown eyes. He crashed to the ground like some ancient pillar which had lost its support, and his dead eyes stared accusingly at me.

As Shad got to his feet, I noticed Hollis' body, his head separate from the rest. The surrounding dirt had turned into rust-brown mud. My stomach heaved, but

I clamped my teeth tight against the twisting inside. A little faint, I staggered to Keddith and pulled out the key.

He gaped at the blood on my hands and clothes, and he recoiled from me. "You killed! You used a weapon to kill! You are not Jin! You are *kreeyagan*, a killer without need!"

Anger tightened my jaw and narrowed my eyes. Grabbing the front of his ragged shirt, I said, "There was need, kinsman. I saved your life."

"I would rather be dead than see one of my people become like the *kreeyagen!*"

I jerked him toward me until we were only a breath apart. "Would you? Would you truly? I've seen death, more than you ever will. I saw my parents, my brothers, a sister, my friends and neighbors murdered by *kreeyagen*. Only my sister Filea and I survived. I buried my entire tribe, and I swore I'd never let anyone take my life without a fight. I want to live, and if I have to kill to live, I will. You're free now. You can go where you will, do what you want, but you'll find that in the human world, you won't survive without killing." I released his shirt and stabbed the manacle lock with the key.

He didn't resist as I removed the shackles. I couldn't meet his eyes because some of what he'd said was true. In some ways I had become like the humans. A Jin would give his life to protect others, but he wouldn't take a life to do so. My heritage always clashed with reality. I'd had to find a way to live with my choices.

Shad's voice cut through my thoughts. "Where's your treasure?"

Looking toward the reddish embers, I saw Shad standing over Milo, sword poised against the miner's throat.

Larynx bobbing as he swallowed, Milo tried to shrink away from the metal point. "Inside the mine, in a wooden chest."

Feeling tired and dizzy, I stood slowly and shuffled toward them. "Shad, it's his wealth. We don't need it."

"Neither will he."

Before I could stop him, Shad drove his blade into Milo's throat. For a second the miner's eyes grew round. He tried to scream, but his breath escaped through the gaping hole in his neck.

I screamed at Shad. "Why? You didn't have to kill him!"

Blood streaking Shad's face and clothes, he looked at me with cold, pitiless eyes. "He was a slave master. He deserved death."

Tears rippled my vision. The ground seemed to rise slowly toward me until two strong arms circled my waist and supported me.

"Ramoojin," Keddith whispered in my ear, "heal yourself."

Shivering, I leaned back against him. "No, Shad needs healing."

"But he just killed Milo!"

I hesitated, then said softly, "Jin, would you have me withhold healing from the injured?"

For a long moment, he didn't answer. When he did, his voice shook. "No, that isn't the way of our people."

Letting Keddith brace me up, I reached toward Shad.

He grabbed my wrist and stared at me, his eyes like cave shadows, his dark brows drawn together. "Heal yourself."

"I'll heal both of us."

"I'll heal eventually. Why use your power on me?"

A final tear trickled down my face. I gave him half a smile. "Because I'm Jin."

Blue flames flowed down my arm to Shad's hand and to all his wounds. Minor cuts disappeared. The more serious ones clotted and closed. Even my own wounds began healing.

Shad inspected himself, a sigh of awe escaping his lips. Gazing at me, he said, "Thank you."

His voice sounded like echoes in a well. My vision darkened, my bones turned to jelly, and sparks seemed to explode in my head as I collapsed.

I woke in a bed, Shad sitting by my side. His eyes were red, and his face looked grey. I started to sit up, but he gently pressed me back down.

"Don't move," he said.

I rubbed my eyes and yawned. "Is it morning?"

"Yes, two days later."

"Two days!" I sat straight up, pulling the coverlet against my bare chest. "We have to make up the lost time! Where's Keddith? Have the drivers harness the horses. We'll leave in the hour."

"Quiet!"

I flopped back against my pillow, astonished. "What?"

"Everything is ready. We're just waiting for you to get dressed."

"And Keddith?"

"He's going with us. Seems he wants to meet your sister, wants to know if she's as...unusual as you are."

"Oh." I thought about Filea and Keddith, and I wondered what that meeting would be like. "All right. I'll be ready in a few moments." I scanned him carefully. "You look like crow bait."

"Better to look like than be."

We both smiled, then he left. Shivering in the cool room, I dressed quickly. I wondered who'd undressed me, but I thought I knew. Hurrying down the stairs, I was greeted by Cort the innkeeper.

"I see you are well, guard master," he said with a wide grin. "I fear my mead is too potent for you."

Ah, he thought I'd just drunk too much. I smiled back sheepishly. "I'll have to stick with ale from now on."

He laughed and gave me the tally of our expenses. I paid him for an extra day. He thanked me for my generosity.

Sunlight stabbed my eyes like pins as I stepped into the innyard. All the wagons were ready to leave. Keddith, his pale skin and golden hair no clean, sat beside the driver of the first wagon and smiled at me. Shad held the bridles of both our horses. Taking my reins, I swung up into my saddle.

"My contract?" Shad said as he settled on his own horse.

"At least until we reach Far Samdi," I said as I wove the reins between my fingers. Turning toward him, I saw his lips drawn tight and a dark brow raised.

"And then?"

I couldn't help but smile at him. "Well...who else would I find to sit by my bed while I sleep off too much mead?"

A Prayer for the Dead

I remember seeing on TV the devastation of hurricanes, fires, earthquakes. People had lost everything. And I saw news crew interviewing others around the country sympathizing with the victims. One person who was interviewed said, "It's terrible, but what can I do?" I wanted to tell that person, "Do whatever you can to help. Give money, send food or clothing, help rebuild. Just help."

The dead stayed dead. That was a fact of life. They were buried with solemn rituals and rivers of tears. Friends and neighbors sympathized with the bereaved family, bringing food and drink and comfort. But nothing changed the fact that the dead stayed dead.

"Except in Aldagar," Livvona sighed as she answered the knock at her door. Perhaps because the land had a history of wizard wars or because the lines of magical forces met there—whatever the reason, the dead often left their intended final rest and roamed the desolate hills and scrub grass plains, seeking... what?

It was Livvona's vocation to discover what the dead were seeking, then lay them to rest—permanently. At least, that was how people viewed her work, like the four men standing before her, all from the village of Eldon Green.

Livvona sighed again, glancing at the half-finished cloth on her loom. She'd started weaving four months ago, just after High Summer's Day. Every time she'd added a few inches, another group of petitioners had appeared at her door. This time she'd been home for a full day before the men of Eldon Green had knocked at her door.

"You've got to rid us of a Cold One," insisted Taygus, the leader, a nut-brown man who stank of smoke and iron. "He's killing our children!"

"Killing children!" she said, astonished.

Taygus nodded.

"Just children?" Livvona asked, puzzled.

Taygus nodded again. "Cold Fever's already taken three."

"Oh, he's not killing them himself."

"Same as if he did! You've got to stop him!"

Livvona finger-combed a strand of graying hair from her face. Being a priestess of Sorwe the Gentle, she was compelled to help anyone who asked. "I'll come."

"If we leave now, we can reach our village by noon tomorrow," Taygus said. A double arch of black brows frowned together above his sharp nose.

Sighing, Livvona shuffled to the shelves lining one end of her hut. Wooden boxes and ceramic bottles and crocks sat in neat rows, color bands indicating what each contained. Potions for milk fever. Potions to keep locusts from crops. Potions for luck.

She put several containers carefully in her bag, along with food and a reed pipe.

"We've no time for music," Taygus growled.

"Then I pity you," she said as she slid the strap over her shoulder.

King's Road, running north toward Aldagar's capital, was deserted except for a man leaning heavily on a staff. The ragged sling on his left arm almost his the mercenary's tattoo on his hand. Livvona stopped to check his injury, but Taygus tried to drag her away.

"Forget him! We found you before he did!"

Jerking from his grip with a strength that left Taygus looking shocked, Livvona glared at him. "Everyone who needs my help gets it. He's hurt. I have to help."

"But the Cold One! Our children are dying!"

"The time I give this man won't make any difference," she said quietly, but her tone was hard as stone.

Taygus started to say something but closed his mouth in a tight frown.

She cleansed and rebandaged the soldier's wound, and gave him the blessing of Sorwe. He gave her thanks and a copper coin in return, then trudged southward.

Her companions said little the rest of the way, except Morthat, the youngest of them. He walked with a loose, easy gait. His eyes were like clouds heavy with life-giving rain.

"Tell me about the Cold One," Livvona asked.

"He came—"

Taygus interrupted Morthat. "I'll tell her what she needs to know."

Morthat lowered his gaze instantly and moved out of Taygus's way.

Taygus looked down at her with eyes of iron. "I'll answer your questions."

Giving him a smile meant to put him at ease, she said, "Then tell me about the Cold One."

Taygus kept his expression blank, staring straight up the road as they walked. "What d'you want to know?"

"When did the Cold One appear?"

Taygus blew out a slow breath. "Ten days ago. A boy named Micah came running from the goat pasture and said a man had crept up from behind and hit him. All the men grabbed their weapons and went after the man." Taygus shivered, although the air was warm. "We found him–it–a Cold One. Skin blotched red from Blood Plague, eyes like the fires of Kedder's hell. We threatened it, but we knew we couldn't harm it. It said it'd kill all our children."

Morthat broke in then. "Our healer died several weeks ago. We heard about your power over Cold Ones. That's why we came to you."

For a moment, Taygus looked as if he might strike Morthat. Slowly, anger drained from Taygus's leathery face to be replaced by pain. "Yes, that's why we came to you. You have to send the Cold One to Kedder's endless fires–before it kills anyone else!"

Livvona shuddered. Taygus's anguish was like a blast of winter.

"Why does he only touch your children?" she asked.

"How should I know?" Taygus snapped at her. "It's a Cold One! Who knows why it does what it does? That kind hats life, all life!" His voice softened, and a tear wavered at the corner of his eye. "Any life." He stared at the road a few moments, then looked up at her sharply. "What difference does it make, anyway? It's a Cold One. You're a priestess. You're supposed to banish it."

"Yes," Livvona said softly as she stared at him, "but I have to know why he's plaguing you before I can put his soul to rest."

Taygus mumbled something she couldn't make out, then picked up his pace. Even Morthat had difficulty keeping up with him. Livvona was grateful when Morthat offered to carry her sack and gave her his walking stick to lean on. By the time they made camp, she was exhausted.

No one talked much that evening, except when Livvona prayed over the meal. The men chorused the proper response, but without sincerity. She watched them, withdrawn, their eyes avoiding hers. They hid behind invisible walls of fear and distrust...or was it something else? She didn't know. What she did know was that pain was Taygus's shield, a pain so sharp it had carved deep wounds in his soul. What could hurt a man like him down to the core of his being?

Livvona fell asleep, watching Taygus and wondering.

Taygus had been right. After turning off King's Road and walking for several hours, they arrived midday at Eldon Green–a dozen stone huts clustered between meadow and woods. All the inhabitants poured from behind locked doors to greet the men.

Livvona could almost taste fear in the air. Hands clutched children close. Eyes, red from lack of sleep, glanced everywhere. But hope flickered in faces as the villages at Livvona.

"Taygus!" a woman's voice cried. From one of the buildings ran a middle-aged woman, her ash-grey eyes wild, her chestnut hair loose and tangled. She plowed through the crowd and tumbled into Taygus's arms, sobbing.

"Ada! Ada, what's wrong?"

"She's dead! Raelyn's dead!"

Anguish filled Taygus's dark eyes and cut deep lines in his forehead. "Raelyn?" he whispered. "Goddess, no. Not her, too." He buried his face against Ada's thick hair and wept. "What about the boys?"

"Alive, barely," she said.

Livvona touched Ada's shoulder. "Show me where they are. I can still save them...I hope."

Wiping tears on her grey sleeve, Ada ran to her house, a neat stone building with a forge to the left. Inside, near a blazing hearth, were four cots. A blanket covered a tiny form on one. In the other cots were three young boys, pale as moonlight.

Livvona touched the smallest boy's cheek. Sweaty but cold as frost. Breathing so shallow, she could barely detect it. Body rigid and deathly pale. Just as she feared. Cold Fever in its last stage. Even with the potions she'd brought, she couldn't be certain the children would live.

"Get tubs, troughs, anything large enough to hold the children. You have to bathe them in hot water, as hot as they can stand, to stop the Cold. I'll make a potion that will help. Force them to drink it. It should keep them alive until I can banish the Cold One."

Ten other children were also ill, she was told, but none was seriously as Ada's children. Taygus refused to leave Raelyn's body. He sat in a chair beside the hearth and rocked her, singing a lullaby. He stared at the fire, withdrawn, not answering when Ada pleaded with him to help with his sons.

"Raelyn was our only daughter," Ada said as she sank to a stool beside Livvona, who stirred a kettle of potion for the children. "Taygus adored her." Looking toward her husband, she blinked back tears. "One day, some of the children slipped away to play at the edge of the woods. We should've watched them closer. That's when the Cold One found them. Imsen and another boy died right after

Micah. That's when Taygus went to find you. Too late...too late for Raelyn." She hid her face in her hands and cried.

Livvona felt cold and sick, remembering how forceful Taygus had been when she'd stopped to help the mercenary. Had that delay caused Raelyn's death? No, surely not. It had taken only a little while to clean and dress the wound. It couldn't have made the difference. Still, doubt bothered her conscience.

When the potion was finished, she sent for the women whose children were ill, giving a cupful for each child. "This should be enough for now. I must talk to the rest of the villagers before I meet the Cold One, but first I need some sleep."

"Please, stay at my house," Morthat said. Livvona hadn't noticed him hovering at the doorway. When she hesitated, he continued, "I live alone, so you'll be undisturbed."

She smiled. "I'll check the other children, then come."

Morthat smiled back, smoothed back his golden-brown hair, then left.

Livvona checked all the children, making certain the potion was being used properly, and gave them Sorwe's blessing. As she trudged to Morthat's house, she leaned heavily on the walking stick he had lent her. She felt old suddenly, tired, and she wondered if she were strong enough to deal with the Cold One. Too late to send for another priestess. She had to face him now, whether she was ready or not.

Morthat had moved his bed before the hearth and provided a thick fur to spread over the blankets. "I'll guard the door while you sleep."

She smiled at him. "Thank you. Wake me well before sunset."

He nodded and left.

Huddling under the covers, Livvona breathed the slow, calming prayers she'd learned so many years ago, then fell asleep.

She moaned as Morthat woke her, not wanting to leave the warmth of the bed. "So soon?" she whispered.

"Yes. The men are outside, as you asked."

Joints creaked as she pushed back the blankets and sat up. This would be the last time she gave a Cold One peace. Somehow, she knew it. She tugged her sack over her shoulder, the weight like lead. "May I use your walking stick a while longer?"

"Of course," he said, offering his arm for support.

She smiled, shook her head, and preceded him from the house.

All the men were there, all but Taygus. Livvona heard his voice singing softly to his dead child. She would have to heal him later.

"Stay inside tonight, all of you," Livvona said. "Bar doors and windows, and don't step outside until dawn." She started to leave.

"I'll come with you," Morthat said.

She didn't stop or even look back at him. "No. I need to be alone and undistracted tonight. Sorwe will protect me. Stay inside."

There was a momentary silence, then hurried footsteps and closing doors.

Walking west across the wide meadow, Livvona looked for a place for the confrontation. The setting sun dyed everything blood red and rust orange as it crept toward the mountains. At last, she chose a slight rise with a clear view on all sides. Shadows spread across the meadow as she searched for a flower, finding a tiny but fragrant butterdrop. From her sack she removed a square of fabric and spread it on the ground. Sorwe's symbol, an outstretched hand, glittered golden on the silver cloth. She placed the flower and a small dish of honeycomb on it, then sat crosslegged on the ground, shivering as the chill air seeped through her clothes and into her joints. Taking the reed pipe from her sack, she prayed a protective circle around her as she watched the final sliver of sun sink behind the mountains.

The moon rose milk-white and full over the trees. Livvona began to play her pipe softly, a tune filled with summer skies and bubbling streams, warm days and pleasant nights, woman's love and child's laughter. The music glided on the night wind, growing stronger as she played.

Suddenly, she felt a draught of cold that even Kedder's fires couldn't warm. A graveyard stench made her stomach lurch. he Cold One was near. Her hands shook, but she kept playing.

Soon, a shadowy form covered with rotting clothes stood before her. Even in the moonlight she could see dark stains on his skin, signs of Blood Plague that had killed him, but lesions of decay marked him as well. He stared at her, eyes glowing like a forge, burning with hate.

"Who ar-re you?" he asked, his voice like dry leaves.

"Livvona, priestess of Sorwe the Gentle, healer, peace giver." She held the pipe between her palms and bowed. "And who were you?"

"Wer-re?" His laugh was cold as ice, sharp as steel. "No one."

"But you had a name."

"Yes-s," he said slowly. "Sethim. My name was-s Sethim."

She bowed again. "One who was Sethim, I offer you gifts. Breathe the scent of the flower, and remember the perfume of spring meadows. Taste the sweetness of honey, and remember the satisfaction of good food and mead. Hear the music of my pipe, and remember the songs of birds and the laughter of children. All these are the joys of life."

He looked down at the butterdrop, then knelt and touched it. A tear oozed from his eyes and fell on the flower, coating it with frost. Jerking his hand away and standing quickly, he glared at her.

"The joys-s of life have no m-meaning to m-me," he said. "Only sor-r-row and r-reveng-ge."

"Revenge? You seek revenge against children?"

"No!" The force of his voice was a gale against her shields. "Not against-st children! Against-st their parents-s!"

"Why? What did they do to you?"

"They know." The hellish light in his eyes burned brighter. "They know well. J-justice for their crim-me!"

One seeking vengeance—a true revenant, she thought shivering. The power of his hate, his rage, pounded against her circle of protection. This was going to be harder than she'd imagined. Revenants didn't reveal their purposes readily, and they weren't banished to the grave by prayers alone.

She pushed against his hate, gently, without threat, then spoke again. "But you're killing children! Four are already dead, and more will die."

He squeezed his eyes shut and turned his face from her. A sob heaved his hollow chest. "No...I...No."

As his hate wavered, Livvona pressed him. "Today a little girl died, one who'd never harmed you. She died slowly, painfully, Cold Fever stealing the warmth of her life away. You killed her! Why?" She thought she'd touched his compassion, stirred his pity. His reaction wasn't what she'd expected.

"They killed m-my daughter-r!" he shouted at her. "Death-th for death-th!"

The fury of his hatred slammed her back against the cold ground. Gasping for breath, she rolled slowly to her side, pushed up on her elbow, and met his gaze. "The villagers...murdered...your daughter?"

"Yes-s!"

"How?" she whispered. "Tell me the truth, Sethim, and by Sorwe I swear justice will be given to them."

Sethim hesitated, anger and pain flitting across his ulcered face.

"Did the villagers of Eldon Green murder your daughter?"

"Yes-s! No. But they killed her-r!" His shoulders sagged, and he closed his eyes. "We fled our-r village in the west because of the Blood Plague, but I didn't know we alr-ready had the sickness. I was trying to reach the Temple of Sorwe when I found the village. Chellaine was-s unconscious-s by then. I shouted for a healer. They told me to go away. I begged, I pleaded for help, but they threw stones at us-s and drove us-s into the woods." He sank to the ground as if weak. "Chellaine died a short time later. I dug her grave with my fingers-s and buried her. Not long after that, I died, too."

Livvona's thin brows pulled together as she closed her eyes in shock. Only one other village in Aldagar had ever acted as Eldon Green had. A barren desert covered the remains of the cursed place. "Sorwe forgive them."

"No!" Sethim pounded his rotting fist against the ground. "They deserve no forgiveness-s-s! When they came for me, I swore they'd pay for Chellaine's death-th, that none of their children would live!"

Horror clutched her heart and forced tears from her eyes. Her stomach felt as if she'd eaten a half-cooked lump of dough, and her throat was a raw and burning as if she'd vomited. Why did children often pay for their parents' sins? And what sin was worse than lack of compassion?

She swallowed hard before she spoke again. "You know what it is to watch your child die, helpless to stop it. You know how she suffered. Do you want other children to suffer as she did? To feel the burning fever, the freezing chills? To be too weak to breathe, too tired to live?" She summoned the images of the sick children of Eldon Green, showing him their pain, forcing him to feel their suffering, hear their sobs, see life drained from them by Cold Fever. Her voice became soft, gentle, as a mother whispering to her child. "Will stealing their lives give life to Chellaine?"

"No," he said, leaf-tangled hair falling over his face as he hung his head. "But what justice is-s there for her death-th?"

Livvona considered his question. What would be justice for the villagers' actions? "I don't know. But I will. By Sorwe I swear I will. Tomorrow, come to edge of the village at sunset. Justice will be done."

He looked at her, eyes narrowed, brow creased with doubt. At last, he spoke. "I'll wait one more day."

She nodded. "That's all I ask."

He turned and started toward the woods, but over his shoulder he said, "One day only. And I swear that if your judgment isn't true justice, you'll be the first-st to join me in Kedder's hell."

Sethim merged into the night shadows, taking his killing cold with him. The fiery gleam from his eyes remained with Livvona for hours.

The last stars were fading when Morthat met her halfway to the village.

"I couldn't stay in the village while you were out here alone. I watched from here, to make sure you weren't hurt. Are you all right?" he asked. "Let me help you."

Even though she was drained and barely able to stand, Livvona pulled back from his offered hand, leaning heavily on the walking stick to keep from shaking. "No."

"Is he...gone? Forever?"

"No." Her voice was sharper than she'd intended. "Why didn't you tell me the truth?"

He flinched, then stared at his feet, his shoulders drooping. When he met her gaze finally, his face was pale, his cheeks sunken. "I wanted to. Sorwe knows, I tried, but Taygus said you wouldn't help if you knew. I...I couldn't let the children die."

Putting an arm around her waist for support, Morthat told her the truth while the two of them walked. The village healer had just died when Sethim had stumbled into Eldon Green, marks of Blood Plague covering his body. "There was nothing we could do to cure him or his little girl. I wanted to give him food and water, but Taygus said no, and the others agreed with him." He hung his head. "I should've anyway."

Livvona gave his arm a light squeeze. She understood the villager's fear. Blood Plague spread quickly and was always fatal unless treated by a healer. But to do nothing, to drive the sick away with stones ...

When she and Morthat arrived at Eldon Green, they were surrounded by the villagers.

"Is he gone?"

"Are we safe?"

"Will the children live?"

Livvona stared at each of them, her mouth tight, her eyes narrowed. Not one could meet her gaze for long.

"Sorwe forgive you all," she said, her voice soft but piercing. "I know."

The villagers shrank from her, shame coloring pale cheeks.

"But they had the plague..."

"We had no healer..."

"We would've died..."

"There was nothing we could do..."

She raised the walking stick with hands, then pounded it against the ground like a forester splitting logs. "You could've built a shelter of sticks and hides outside the village! You could've given them food and water and firewood, and sent for a healer! You could've cared! See what your fear and lack of compassion has cost you!"

Heads turned away. Hands muffled sobs. Eyes fixed on grass, sky, woods, anywhere but on her.

Morthat bowed his head, lines cutting across his high forehead. "Priestess, I knew it was wrong, but I didn't stop them. I did nothing. What punishment do I deserve? What will give the Cold One–and us–peace?"

Livvona shook her head. "I don't know. I must pray and ask Sorwe's guidance. The Cold One will come at sunset. Then, I will give you my judgement."

The strength her anger had given her disappeared. She walked toward Morthat's house, stumbled, and felt his arms catch her.

"Please. Let me help you," he said.

Too tired to argue or answer, Livvona leaned on him. He guided her to his house, helped her into bed, and built a new fire on the hearth.

Shivering beneath the blankets, she prayed. *Lady Sorwe, goddess of healing, show me what is justice for Sethim and Eldon Green.*

She waited for an answer to come, as it always had before. This time there was silence within. All she heard was Morthat adding wood to the fire, and the echo of her words: "Let me help." The words became visible, letters written in light and blood that changed into hands reaching out. Livvona smiled as she drifted to sleep. She had her answer.

Morthat stood beside Livvona as the sunset turned the world to flame. Behind her, the villagers shuffled uncomfortably. She shielded her eyes against the red glow, watching, searching.

Out of the sunlight came a shadow, a darkness without warmth of life. Preceded by a blast of soul-chilling cold, Sethim approached, his eyes glowing brighter than the sun. "It is-s time, priestess of Sorwe. Show me justice."

She nodded slightly and turned to the villagers. "He asked for your help; you refused him. He asked for shelter; you drove him away. He asked for pity; you showed him fear. You caused the death of this man and his child. You murdered them as surely as if you had driven swords through them. Their blood has stained your fields and pastures, and Sorwe's face is turned from you."

Terror paled faces as villagers gasped and sobbed. Her curse meant no blessing at birth, no prayer at death, and no healer between.

Shaken, dark eyes haunted, Morthat sank to one knee and reached out to her. "Priestess, please, show mercy!"

"Mercy!" Sethim said, eyes like bonfires. "What mercy did you show Chellaine or m-me?"

"Peace!" Livvona said, glaring at Sethim. "Death for death. That's what you said. They caused two deaths, you and Chellaine. Count the deaths here, Sethim. You've caused four deaths, taken four innocent lives. You'll have to answer to Sorwe for them!"

Livvona looked back at Morthat. "Mercy? Can you give life to the dead?"

"I would if I could," he said. "I'd trade my life for theirs, if it were possible." His eyes widened. "Is it?"

She shook her head. "Only the goddess can give life. But you can give what she demands as payment."

"Anything."

"She asks your life."

Morthat's thin brows arched and met above his sloping nose. "But you said...but they can't...I don't understand."

"'Let me help you.' Twice you've said that to me. That is what you must do, what all of you must do." She swept her hand toward the villagers. "Offer your help to everyone who needs it. Eldon Green will be a haven for the sick, the homeless, the hopeless. No one will be turned away, ever. Life for death."

The villagers glanced at each other, then nodded at Morthat.

"Thank you," he said, a smile almost bowing his lips.

Turning to Sethim, Livvona said, "Life for death. Is this justice?"

He was silent for a moment, then he said, "Justice...and mercy."

"Then be at peace, Sethim. Rest in the gentle arms of Sorwe."

The fire in his eyes mellowed to the soft glow of dying embers. "Peace be yours, priestess-s-s. May we meet again beyond this world." He bowed, turned, and walked with stiff, halting steps toward the woods.

Livvona started to follow, but Morthat stopped her.

"How can we care for the sick? We have no healer."

The corners of her mouth twitched as she held back a smile. "You do now."

She hobbled after Sethim, reciting prayers for the living and prayers for the dead.

Swordfish and Saucery

I like resourceful characters, and I love to create magic spells from simple things. And I especially love a little twist at the end.

The door of the Swordfish Inn banged open, startling Ilsimar as she scrubbed the bar for the expected noon crowd.

"Dent my door, will you?" she called, throwing down her cloth and smoothing back a strand of rust-colored hair from her eyes. "As if I have money to replace doors constantly."

She stopped as the silhouetted figure stumbled inside. It was Jace the miller, her erstwhile suitor from the town of Crossings. Thick chest heaving, he tried to speak, but no sound came.

"What in the name of Sorwe is the matter with you?" she asked as he sank into a chair.

Face flushed, he gulped for air. "Tarvin's crossed the border!"

Ilsimar laughed. "Again?" King Tarvin of Lassa was notorious for failed attempts to enlarge his tiny realm.

Jace pounded his calloused fist against the table. "No! You don't understand! This time he's brought a couple of sorcerers with him!" He paused, sucking in a breath. "They stripped Crossings of everything valuable, and the people are being sent to the slave markets of Nisra! I barely escaped to warn you! They're coming here next, and they won't stop until they've conquered all of Aldegar!"

Surprised and suddenly afraid, Ilsimar said nothing but fetched a large mug of mead for Jace. He guzzled the pale red-gold liquid and wiped his mouth with the back of his hand.

"When did they attack?" she asked.

"Yesterday morning. I rode all night."

She chewed her lower lip. Yesterday. Tarvin might reach Rosedale tomorrow, depending on how many men he had and how fast they could travel through Farrup Woods. She called the two boys who worked for her. "Ben, find Master Cal and tell him to come immediately, then go to the chapel and ask Healer Vivianne to join us. Tullee, take care of Jace's horse. Quickly now!"

The boys dashed out the door like hounds on a rabbit trail, past a pair of curious girls and into the early summer morning. Ilsimar refilled Jace's mug and took a cup of wine herself. *Lady Sorwe, what can we do?* she wondered as she downed the wine.

Cal the blacksmith arrived moments later. "What's so important, Ilsie?" he asked with a wide grin as he strode to the table.

"Tarvin's at Crossings."

He grinned. "Made it that far before his men decided to go home? Must be a record."

"This is serious, Cal! The villagers are being sent to Nisra!"

"Slaves?" Cal's dark eyes bulged, and his jaw dropped. "Tarvin's taken slaves?"

Ilsimar nodded.

The blacksmith shook his head. "We've got trouble."

"Trouble? What trouble?" Healer Vivianne stood in the doorway, leaning on her staff. Her plated hair glowed sunlight yellow, but her eyes were storm-cloud gray. She joined them at the table.

Ilsimar turned to Jace. "Tell us exactly what you saw–everything. Any detail might make the difference."

Jace squeezed his eyes shut for a moment, forehead drawn in tight lines. "I was on my way back from delivering flour, and everything was fine, peaceful. Then I saw them–hundreds of men and horses landing on the river bank from rafts. I *know* they hadn't been there a moment before. They mounted on shore and attacked."

Cal looked incredulous. "How in the name of Sorwe did that bunch of farmer-turned-soldiers take out the border garrison?"

"They didn't. The sorcerers hit the barracks with something–fire, lightning, I'm not sure. The building just exploded and killed most of the guards. I saw a few soldiers on horseback riding east, but they were the only ones to escape. Then the Lassans attacked Crossings. The villagers were no match for the soldiers." Jace paused for a gulp of mead before he continued. "I crept through Old Barney's vineyard and climbed on the inn roof to see what was happening. Everyone was rounded up and held in market square, except the innkeeper and his family. Tarvin and the two sorcerers made Old Barney put them up in the inn. I waited 'til dark, then crept away and came straight here."

"The sorcerers," Ilsimar interrupted, "what did they wear?"

"Purple and silver robes."

"Great," she muttered. "Masters. We *are* in trouble."

Cal raised a soot-colored brow. "You know magic, don't you? You went to Volyn's school."

"But I didn't reach master rank. I'm no match for them."

Jace grabbed her arm. "But you have to do something! Tarvin'll be here tomorrow, maybe sooner!"

Ilsimar scrunched her lips and stared at the table. "We can't run fast enough to avoid Tarvin. Not enough wagons and horses. We can't fight, not against trained soldiers. Vivianne, are there any Cold Ones running around you haven't sent back to the grave? If you could turn them toward Crossings, they could cause some havoc and delay Tarvin a while."

The healer shook her head. "Sorry. I banished the last undead three weeks ago. Of course, it's always possible for new ones to pop up at any time."

"We can hope. Anything to scare off Tarvin."

Cal rubbed his chin, smearing it with more charcoal dust. "Why won't they go home this time? Lassans don't like to be away from their fields for long. That's why Tarvin's always failed before."

"Must be the sorcerers."

"All we gotta do is wait 'til the Lassans have had enough and decide to go back home. If only we could make them homesick."

Ilsimar's head snapped up. "What?"

Cal cocked his head and looked puzzled. "I said, I wish we could make 'em homesick. You know, make 'em want to go home. Why?"

She drummed her fingers on the table. "I...I'm not sure, but...great Sorwe...if it could work."

"You know how to stop Tarvin?"

She drummed faster, then stopped. "Maybe. I can't promise. If the sorcerers are masters, they might detect what I'd be doing. But then, they might not."

Cal threw up his arms and said through gritted teeth, "What are you talking about?"

Ilsimar stared absently at the table. "Something simple. Tarvin's sorcerers might not expect that." She stood and arched her back slowly to stretch her tight muscles. "And now, we have to make plans."

"So," Vivianne said, "what do we do?"

Ilsimar winked at Jace, then smiled. "We make a feast for Tarvin."

It was just after midday when the first of Ilsimar's alarm spells, set about a mile from Rosedale, was tripped. Ilsimar watched the clouds of dust betraying Tarvin's approach, when she felt the second alarm spell, she signaled the musicians. Flutes and pipes, lutes and drums, mandolins, rattles, and tambourines, all played a lively tune. Young women with flowers in their hair and bells on their ankles danced in the road while girls scattered petals in the dust. Boys waved pennants; men, their hats. And everyone cheered as Tarvin, flanked by two middle-aged men in purple and silver, halted before Cal, Vivianne, and Ilsimar.

Cal bowed with a grace that surprised Ilsimar. "Welcome, Tarvin, King of Lassa, mighty warrior, great conqueror. How blessed is Rosedale that you favor us with your presence. We beg you to enter our village and accept our hospitality."

Tarvin frowned, pulling more lines in his round cheeks, then raised a sandy eyebrow. He turned to the snow-blond sorcerer on his left and mumbled something. The sorcerer looked straight at Ilsimar, the whispered back to Tarvin.

"I accept your offer," Tarvin said as he sat up as straight as his thick belly allowed. He turned his gaze to Ilsimar. "And who are you, sorceress?"

Ilsimar curtsied slowly, blushing as intensely as she could. "You honor me, Your Majesty. I am Ilsimar, but I am no sorceress. I studied at Volyn, but I never mastered more than the easy magics—practical spells to chase rats and ants from my kitchen, preserve food and improve its flavor, wards against thieves—"

"Sound alarms against invaders," broke in the blond sorcerer.

Ilsimar blushed again. "Yes, O Master..."

"Galt," he said. "And this is Keld."

"Master Galt. Master Keld." She bowed to each. "Alarms are one of the highest magics I can do. I was never strong enough to learn the great spells. But some people say I'm a sorceress in the kitchen. I learned the use of culinary herbs quite well." She smiled at him. "Please, Your Majesty, masters, I ask you to honor my inn by staying in my best rooms and allowing me the privilege of serving you."

Tarvin glanced from Galt to Keld. The both smiled a sly half-smirk and nodded to the king. Tarvin gazed down at her for a moment, his eyes glittering like emeralds, then said, "I accept your offer, yes, most definitely. And I look forward to being served by you."

Ilsimar had an uncomfortable feeling he implied more than he said, but she forced a smile. "If you and your companions will follow me..."

Turning to a lean man in a studded black leather vest, Tarvin said, "Captain, set up camp around the village. Confiscate all weapons."

"We've gathered all our weapons in a pile at the edge of the village," Ilsimar said quickly, "to save you time and trouble. And we have food and drink in the square for all your men–and dancing."

"Later, yes, perhaps later," Tarvin said, waving his hand to dismiss her.

With Cal and Vivianne beside her, Ilsimar led the way back to town, the musicians still playing, women dancing, girls scattering petals before Tarvin. Garlands of flowers hung from poles and draped windows. The aroma of whole pigs, roasting slowly over pits of glowing coals, filled the air.

Ilsimar stopped at the inn door, opened it, and bowed. "Enter and be welcomed, King Tarvin."

He stared at the sign over the door for a moment before he dismounted. "A swordfish. Most unusual, most unusual."

"My father was a fisherman, and he was especially fond of swordfish." Ilsimar told Ben and Tullee to tend the horses, then she escorted the king, the sorcerers, and ten guards toward their rooms. "Would you like to bathe, Your Majesty? The road is dusty and hot."

"Yes, I would."

"And you, also, masters?" she asked.

Galt and Keld nodded.

Hot water will be brought in a moment. After you have refreshed yourselves, please come to the common room. There will be feasting, music, dancing, and other entertainments. I hope you will be pleased."

Tarvin smiled, and his eyes were cold and hard. "We shall see, yes, we shall see."

She bowed and hurried to the kitchen to inspect the meal.

The common room had been cleared of all but three tables, two placed perpendicular to the other. The center table was covered with an embroidered linen cloth and set with pewter plates and mugs. Finger bowls, with rose petals floating on the water, sat beside linen towels just as Ilsimar had seen at a banquet once. A platter of sharp cheese was flanked by bowls of summer fruits and early vegetables. Chairs had replaced the usual benches. Things looked as elaborate as she could make them in the short time she'd had. "Now, if everything else is ready..."

"Ready?"

Ilsimar started as Galt spoke behind her, almost in her ear. She caught herself before she called out a plague of lice on him, and she smiled as she faced him. "Y-yes, Master Galt. The meal...if the meal is ready, I'm ready to serve you, King Tarvin, and Master Keld."

He returned a disarming smile, but his aqua eyes showed no hint of friendliness. "His Majesty and Keld will be down shortly. But I'd like some wine right now."

"Of course, master." She went to the bar, took out a bottle of spring wine, and filled a mug.

"Join me," Galt said as he took the wine.

"If you wish." Ilsimar took another mug and filled it from the same bottle. She raised it and said, "Sorwe's blessing."

Galt copied her action but hesitated until she took a sip, then he tasted it, too. "Quite good," he said, "and not the least poisoned."

Ilsimar looked shocked. "Master Galt, why would I try to poison you?"

He just smiled back at her. "Cherry wine, isn't it? But I taste something unusual."

"Jasmine flowers and almonds. It's a specialty of Rosedale."

Galt raised his mug to her, then finished the wine. Tarvin, Keld, and his guards joined them moments later. Ilsimar showed them to the table, then called Tullee.

"Fetch Healer Vivianne."

The boy scurried out the door.

"Do you expect someone to be ill?" Galt asked, his eyes narrowed.

Ilsimar laughed. "No, of course not. Vivianne is very skilled at the lute. I thought His Majesty might enjoy some music while he ate."

"Yes," Tarvin said, "yes, I would."

"Wine, Your Majesty?" Ilsimar filled his mug from the open bottle. "Master Galt has already sampled it for your protection." She flashed a sweet smile at Galt.

Tarvin sipped the wine, then took a long drink. "Ah-h-h, I haven't tasted spring wine like that in ages."

"I'm honored you enjoy it." Ilsimar bowed, hurried to the kitchen, and came back with two more bottles of the wine. One of the girls she'd hired to help serve followed with a plate of bread rounds. Two other girls brought more bowls of fruit and vegetables to the side tables. After serving the king, Ilsimar poured wine, and the girls served bread to the others.

Vivianne arrived with her lute, and so did two young men who could juggle and do tumbling. Cal came soon after, carrying a yoke to entertain with feats of strength. Ben and Tullee carried the roast pig from the outside pit to the spit in the common room, where several chickens, a leg of lamb, and a quail already dripped basting fat on the embers. Ilsimar put a final glaze of honey on the quail before she slid it onto a plate and presented it to Tarvin. A spicy, sweet chutney and a rhubarb relish were served with the meats. Fruit and vegetables were replenished; mugs were kept full of wine. Vivianne played; jugglers juggled; and Cal lifted four men, holding onto ropes at the ends of the yoke, off the floor. The guards cheered, and Tarvin clapped. Even Galt smiled his pleasure.

After filling the mugs again and serving honey-glazed shortbread for dessert, Ilsimar stood before Tarvin and curtsied. "And now, Your Majesty, I ask permission to entertain you with my simple skills."

Guards sprang from chairs and drew swords. Galt and Keld mumbled spells of warding against harm.

Tarvin glared at her and said in a quiet, threatening tone, "Beware, little sorceress. I am well protected, very well protected. You shall die if you try to harm me."

Frightened by Tarvin's cold gaze as much as by the glint of cold steel, Ilsimar sank to one knee and stared at the floor. "Your Majesty, I swear by Sorwe, I wish you no harm. Even if I did, I know that with a wave of the hand, Master Galt or Master Keld could shatter any spell I'd weave." She raised her gaze slowly until she looked straight at Tarvin. "I only wish to entertain you."

Half a smile twitched the corner of Tarvin's mouth. "Then do so–carefully."

With a glance and a nod to Vivianne, who began playing a Lassan ballad, Ilsimar stood and made a graceful curtsey. "Your Majesty, masters, soldiers of Lassa, I am no sorceress, but I have learned little magics: how to season a special sauce, how to make venison as tender as lamb, how to grow the sweetest fruit and to keep wine from turning sour." She waved her hands. "And...how to call fireflies in the daytime. Come, little night lamps."

Through windows and door came tiny blinking lights, zipping around the room until they formed a circle of glittering light over Ilsimar's head. She put her thumb and forefinger together like a ring. The fireflies flew through it, but when they came out the other side, they formed a solid circlet of gold. Ilsimar tossed the circlet in the air and whispered a spell. The gold became fireflies again.

"Marvelous!" Tarvin said, clapping his thick, stubby hands. Keld smiled. Galt looked surprised.

"Master Keld," Ilsimar said, "choose a fruit from the bowl in front of you." Keld selected a peach. "Master Galt, split the peach and give me the seed."

Galt cut the fruit, separated the halves, then stared up wide-eyed at Ilsimar before he handed her a seed, small as an apple seed but silvery. She took a clay pot, already filled with dirt, and planted the seed. "Life, little seed."

A tiny silvery tendril pushed through the soil, growing thick, until it nearly burst the pot. Delicate silver flowers blossomed in moments, the fell petal by silver petal to the floor. Leaves like polished silver sprouted and grew, almost hiding silver apples the size of a robin's egg. Ilsimar picked one and offered it to Tarvin. His eyes widened as he reached for it, but he hesitated.

"It isn't poisoned, Your Majesty," she said. "Let Master Galt or Keld examin it. But I promise you, you've never tasted anything as sweet, as delicious as this. I'll even taste it first." She took a small bite, then held the apple out to Tarvin.

Keld held his hand near the apple, muttered something, and nodded to the king. "It is safe, Your Majesty."

Tarvin nibbled the apple, the popped it in his mouth. "Excellent, truly excellent!" he said, still chewing the fruit. "I must have that tree!"

"It is yours, Your Majesty." Ilsimar smiled shyly, curtsied, and offered apples to the sorcerers.

Galt examined his fruit carefully. "This isn't one of the little magics. I know masters who couldn't do this."

Ilsimar's blush wasn't feigned. To have Galt's approval was gratifying.

She bowed again. "And now, I call colors. Red from the strawberry." She pointed at the bowl of fruit. A ball of red light sprang from it and hovered above her. "Orange from carrot. Yellow from squash. Green from mint jelly. Blue from blueberries. Indigo from cloth. Purple from plum." She held her hands above her head, palms toward Tarvin, and slowly drew them apart. The globes of light stretched into bands that arced from wall to wall. "A rainbow without rain."

A grin crinkling his jowls, Tarvin banged his mug on the table. "Magnificent! You must come to my court and entertain me always!"

"I'm honored, Your Majesty." Ilsimar glanced at Vivianne, who began a Lassan love song. "I have one more gift for each of you. Your Majesty, what is your favorite flower?"

Tarvin cocked his head, then said, "The Cammis rose."

Touching the rainbow's red band, Ilsimar whispered a spell. Red mist swirled in her hand and formed a rose, crimson with a white heart, fragrant and in the height of its beauty. She presented it to Tarvin. He inhaled its scent and sighed, a tear wavering at the corners of his eyes.

"Beautiful," he murmured, "simply beautiful."

"Master Keld?" Ilsimar asked.

Keld looked thoughtful a moment. "A butterdrop. Near my home there are meadows filled with that wild flower."

Ilsimar touched the yellow light, which filled her hand and shrank to a tiny golden flower. She handed it to Keld.

"It reminds me of home," he said softly. "I haven't been there in many years...many years."

Galt started and rested his chin in the crook of his hand while he stared at Ilsimar.

"And you, Master Galt?" she asked.

He didn't answer for such a long time, Ilsimar thought he hadn't heard her. "Master?"

Galt looked straight at her, and a slow smile bowed his mouth. "A shadow lily."

Ilsimar shivered but reached up to the very edge of the purple light. A mist so dark it was almost black churned in her hand, coalescing to a lily, soft as velvet, dark as midnight. Shadow lilies grew in the darkest part of dense forests and were used in conjuration of ill and distillation of poison. "Beware, master," she whispered as she place the flower in Galt's hands.

His eyes glittered as he leaned close to her. "As always...sorceress."

Ilsimar stepped back, worried. Did he know what she had planned? No, surely. No one could, no one but the Sorcerer Lords. Galt wasn't one of them.

She touched the blue light. Bluebells, the most common flower of Lassa, appeared in her hand. She gave them to the captain and the guards.

"And your favorite flower?" Galt asked her.

Ilsimar jumped, startled by his question, but caught herself before she cried out. "Uh, the trumpet flower."

Out of the air he plucked a trumpet flower, orange as carrots and as large as his lily. "For you, Ilsimar."

His voice was a caress; his touch, an invitation. Blood flowed hot through her; heart pounded against her ribs. She shook off the effect, gulping for air.

Swallowing to relax her thoat, Ilsimar began to chant softly:

"Jasmine-almond-cherry wine,
Honey sweet, refreshing mint,
Silver apple–magic fruit,
Homeland flower, lively lute,
Though you wander, though you roam,
All these things will draw you home."

"No-o-o!" Galt's eyes widened with panic; his jaw dropped. "No! Stop! I can't..." He struggled to his feet and reached for her. "You..." he gasped, "you did this. I should've known...I should've known." He dropped back to his chair and closed his eyes. The same contented smile that appeared on all the other guests at the feast tugged at Galt's mouth.

Ilsimar's chest hurt. She let out a breath trapped inside. Her knees buckled, and she collapsed on the wooden floor. She felt chilled, in spite of her heart pounding and worn out. Too much magic at one time, and especially the last spell. Cal and Jace grabbed her arms and lifted her to her feet.

"What did you do to them?" Jace asked as she sank into the chair Vivianne had vacated.

"Home Wish," Ilsimar whispered, leaning back against the cool stone wall.

"What?" Jace and Cal asked together.

"Home Wish. The spell I created for my Master Test. It could create the desire to go home or remain home. The lords of the Sorcerer Council didn't think it was good enough to grant me master rank. Foolish, simple magic, they called it." Ilsimar gave them a weak smile.

Cal looked worried. "Will it last?"

Ilsimar nodded. "Galt and Keld might find a way to break it in time, but the others won't. When they wake, Tarvin will take his army back to Lassa and stay home from now on."

Cal whistled a sigh. "Not bad for simple magic. I didn't know you were that powerful."

Vivianne prayed away Ilsimar's fatigue. "Will you go back to Volyn to try for master rank again?"

Smiling, Ilsimar shook her head. "I don't want to leave my inn or Rosedale." Her smile broadened. "You see, I drank the wine and ate the honey. I tasted the mint and the silver apple, and I took the trumpet flower. When I cast the Home Wish, I cast it on myself, too."

Hope

Every day, the news shows the tragedy of war and how it affects generation after generation. How can we end war? Is there any hope for peace? I have to believe there is.

Everything in the healer's sanctum was in order. Boxes and bottles of medicines lined narrow shelves on one wall. Healing herbs hung from rafters. A gold embroidered white cloth draped the altar to Sorwe the Gentle. Everything was as it should be. Except the healer was gone. And so were the village children.

Kneeling, Garilynn quickly breathed the Swordmate's prayer to Sorwe, then she stood and turned towards the villagers who crowded at the open doorway. "How long have your children been gone?"

"We don't know," said Karrick, the stick-thin leader of Village-On-War-Road. "Sometime night before last. Damned Paramites!"

Garilynn blinked and frowned. "Paramis is responsible for this?"

"Who else?" Karrick said and spit on the ground.

Garilynn sighed. The countries of Paramis and Aldegar had been at war so long, no one living remembered a time the two kingdoms hadn't been fighting. And this small border village had seen more than its share of fighting.

"Please!" said a red-eyed young woman who elbowed her way to the front of the crowd. "I want my baby, my Torry! Bring him back to me! Please, please, bring him back!" She buried her face in a blond man's shoulder and sobbed.

"I will," Garilynn said as she touched the woman's arm. Turning to Karrick, she said, "Tell me everything–what you heard, what you saw, anything that might help me find the children. And I need something to drink."

"Come." Karrick motioned her to follow him.

Sweat, engendered by the noon sun, trickled down Garilynn's lean face and dampened her short, black hair as she stepped outside. Even this far north the summers were sticky and hot. Her leather armor chaffed as she and the villagers crossed the wide dirt road to the largest stone building in the village–The Last Hope Inn.

Karrick opened the solid wooden door. "Enter and welcome, Swordmate," he said.

"Sorwe's blessings on you and yours." Garilynn ducked her head and went in.

The inn was dark and cool, a welcome relief from the hot sun. Baking bread and simmering stew scented the long, narrow room. Garilynn's stomach grumbled. It had been hours since her pre-dawn breakfast.

"Food and fresh water for the Swordmate," Karrick called to the kitchen. He led Garilynn toward a long table near the cold hearth.

As soon as Karrick and the other villagers joined her, Garilynn said, "Tell me."

Karrick mopped his high, freckled forehead with a corner of his not-so-clean apron. "Yesterday morning I woke up and found our little girl wasn't in her bed. Sometimes in the morning she crawls out and goes to the kitchen for something to eat so that's where we looked first, but she wasn't there. We looked all over. That's when we heard shouting outside. We ran out and found others looking for their kidlings."

"My daughter and two sons," one man said.

"My sons," said another.

"My little girl."

"My boys."

"My grandson."

"All the kidlings," Karrick said. "All gone. We searched the woods, the plains, the fields all the way to the border, even searching last night with torches, but we found nothing. Not one clue to where they were. Damn the Paramites! Cowards! Making war on babes!"

Garilynn frowned in thought. "Why would Paramis take your children?"

"Because Paramites are evil!" Karrick said, pounding his fist on the table. "They're animals. They've killed us for generations."

"But why take children and leave you alive? Children are tno threat to them."

"Not now, but someday," Karrick said. "If they kill the next generation, then they've won."

"Then why didn't they kill everyone?" Garilynn said. "That would have ended the hostility now and forever. And how did such a large force evade the border guard, steal the children, and make it back to Paramis without anyone hearing or seeing anything? And what happened to your healer?"

"I don't know!" Karrick said. "I don't know! That's why we need your help. You've got to get our kidlings back. We'll fight, too. Most of us have served in the king's ranks. We've got to hurry and get there before...before..." He choked back a sob.

A stout woman with greying hair set a mug of water, a wooden bowl of stew, and half a loaf of bread in front of Garilynn. The woman's eyes were bloodshot, and her cheeks were red and raw from crying. She glanced at Karrick, the clasped her apron to her mouth and ran back to the kitchen.

"Your wife?" Garilynn asked.

He nodded.

"Sorwe comfort and keep her," she said softly. She raised her palms up, whispered a thanking to Sorwe, and took a long gulp of well water so cold, her teeth tingled. Wiping her mouth with the back of her hand, Garilynn turned to Karrick. "Where do the tracks lead?" she said, then dipped a chunk of bread in the stew.

"No tracks."

Garilynn blinked at him. "No tracks?"

Karrick shook his head.

"But there must have been some signs."

"No footprints leading from the houses, from the village, none. Almost like someone swept the streets clean."

Garilynn frowned. There had to be signs. People didn't just fly away. Or did they? Magic? Could a mage have stolen the children? Garilynn swallowed two bites of stew and gulped more water. "Show me where your child slept."

Karrick stood and led her to a bedroom behind the kitchen. "There." He pointed to a smaller room beyond.

She stood in the doorway, closed her eyes, and prayed to see. She knelt, touched the threshold, but felt no magic. Not on the floor, the windowsill, the bed clothes, the small embroidered pillow. But wait, something tingled her fingers as she touched the pillow. A scent of rosemary, chamomile, roses, peppermint, and something vaguely familiar filled the air, wholesome, soothing, peaceful. There was magic *in* the pillow. "Where did she get this?" ` `

"Our healer, Maywen, gave it to her to ease the nightmares she'd been having since..." He squeezed his eyes tightly.

"Since what?"

"Since her brother was killed by Paramites." He slumped against the door frame, and his voice cracked. "Kint was searching for a lost calf. Five damned Paramites beat him with clubs and rocks until..."

"How do you know they were Paramites?"

"I saw them!" he said through gritted teeth. "I was searching for the calf, too. I came out of the woods above the plain and saw them beating him. I shouted at them and ran to help him. The Paramites ran back across the border. I carried him back to the healer, but she couldn't do anything. It was too late."

Karrick blinked his eyes, swallowed hard, and looked away. His hands curled into fists. His narrow shoulders heaved up and down. After a few moments, he gazed back at Garilynn and continued.

"Our little girl saw Kint's body and started screaming. Justie didn't eat or sleep for three nights. So Maywen gave the dream pillow to ease her dreams. It seemed to work. Justie hadn't had nightmares for two nights. I thought everything was going to be all right. I mean, yesterday I woke up feeling better and more hopeful than I'd felt since Kint died. Then I found Justie missing." A tear leaked down his cheek. "Please, Swordmate, my wife can't bear to lose another child. I can't. Find Justie. Bring her home to us. Find whoever took her and let them feel Sorwe's judgment."

Garilynn grasped his arm firmly but gently. "By Sorwe I swear, I'll find her, her and all the children."

His eyes widened, and tension eased from his jaw. "Thank you," he whispered. "May I keep the dream pillow?"

Karrick nodded. She stuffed the pillow in her backpack, then the two of them went back to the table. Garilynn grabbed a chunk of bread and looked longingly at the stew. Sighing, she went out into the thick summer air.

Garilynn scanned the dusty road through the center of the village for any sign. There were only boot prints and shoe prints, none of the child-size. She even checked the edges of the road, but they looked as smooth as if they'd been swept clean. She stared at the dust. It looked *exactly* as if it had been swept smooth. Someone had tried to hide a trail.

With Karrick beside her, she searched house for signs: footprints, broken windows, torn clothing or bed linens. Nothing seemed out of place: no signs of struggle, no hint of how the children were spirited away. But on each bed was a dream pillow.

"Were all the children having nightmares?" she said as she glanced about the final house.

Karrick shrugged. "I don't know. Many were. Especially after my son died. Maywen gave all of us pillows so the kidlings wouldn't be afraid."

Garilynn took the dream pillow from her pack, held it to her nose, and breathed in the scents. Soothing, restful, peaceful, so peaceful. She breathed deeply and held her breath. Warmth crept through her, relaxing her. She was so tired. She needed sleep, needed to close her eyes. After so many nights on the hard ground, she could finally rest in a soft bed. Sleep crept into her eyes, loosened her muscles, eased her mind. Yes, she would sleep without worries, without fear.

"Swordmate!"

Garilynn snapped open her eyes as Karrick shook her. "What happened?" she said.

"You fell asleep! You were standing there with the pillow, and you fell asleep!"

Garilynn dropped the pillow instantly and rubbed her eyes. "I must be more tired than I thought."

Lines gathered across Karrick's forehead, and he raised one eyebrow. "You should rest more, Swordmate."

"All right." She lay down on the bed and closed her eyes.

"Swordmate! What is wrong with you?"

Garilynn sat up and blinked. Why had she suddenly tried to nap? Simply because Karrick had said she needed rest? She stared at the dream pillow and realized with the strange scent was: Joy-on-the-Mountain. The spell herb made one relaxed and compliant. Healers didn't often use it, usually only when a patient resisted treatment. She finger-combed her hair from her forehead. "Let me be for a time. I must pray for guidance. Sorwe will show me where your children are."

Karrick started to speak, then nodded. The two of them left the house, and he went back to the inn.

Garilynn felt the villagers watching her as she strode to the healer's cottage. Fear flowed from them like water from a spring. She felt relieved when the cottage door closed out their grief.

Taking her sword from its sheath and kneeling before the cloth-draped altar, she held her sword on her palms and raised it shoulder high. "Lady Sorwe, hear my prayer. Merciful Sorwe, you who see and know all that is, show me the way to the children. Guide me to what is lost, and let me deal justice and mercy to whomever has committed this dead. Gentle goddess, tell me what I must do."

She placed her sword before the altar and bowed her forehead to the floor. When she sat up, the golden hands on the altar cloth glowed as if the sun had come from the heavens and rested in the palms. The light was so intense, it hurt her eyes. Brighter and brighter until the light was unbearable. Garilynn huddled on the floor, her arms crossed over her head and her eyes squeezed shut.

With her eyes closed, she saw tiny feet walking a path were plants, grass, and trees parted, the flowed back over the tracks. She saw the Sword, great constellation of the northern sky. And she saw cupped hands stained with blood and washed with tears.

Slowly, she opened her eyes and gazed at the golden hands. The light had dimmed until it was the mellow glow of embers, then it was just golden thread on a white cloth. She raised her hands and her face to the ceiling. "Thank you, Lady Sorwe." She picked up her sword, sheathed it, and left the cottage.

The villagers milled around the doorway, their eyes filled with hope.

"Can you find them?" Karrick said.

"I know where to look," she said.

"Then let's go." He tugged off his apron.

"No."

"No?" His eyes widened; his hands clenched. "It's my daughter out there. I'm going whether you agree or not."

"And me," said a man.

"And me," said two more.

A chorus of voices followed, all insisting they go.'

"No!" she said. "I must go alone. If you all go, you will alert the one who took your children and we may never find them." She held up her hands at the villagers' angry cries. "I am the right hand of Sorwe. She will guide me where I must go. Have faith in her love for you and your children. And trust that I will bring them home to you."

Many grumbled. Karrick glared at her a while but finally nodded. "Sorwe guide you, Swordmate."

She nodded, then turned toward the border. She'd almost reached the edge of the village when she heard running footsteps behind her. She turned and saw Karrick's wife carrying a waterskin and a small shoulder pack.

"Water and trail food," the woman said.

Garilynn slid the straps over her head and across her chest. "Thank you," she said. "I'll find her for you."

Tears trickled down the woman's face. She wheeled and ran back toward the inn.

Dust covered Garilynn's boots and left grit in her mouth as she walked down the hill toward the border. When she reached the flat plain, she turned north toward the deep forest. She knelt and searched the ground, lifting the grass and wild flowers until she finally found one small footprint. Picking her way carefully, she found another footprint, another, and another, always pointing north until she reached the edge of the forest.

She gazed west, toward the border. The sun was almost halfway between zenith and horizon. Would she be able to find the children before dark? She hoped so. The forest after sunset would be as black as a cave.

Sunlight glinted on metal moving across the plain. Garilyn shaded her eyes to see what caused the glint. A mounted soldier with a metal helm galloped up the road toward the village.

"Hail, guardsman," she called.

The soldier reined his horse, stared at her for a moment, then said, "Hail, Swordmate. I've news for the village and for you. Paramites from Warren-On-The-Hill attacked the border guard!"

"From the village across the valley?"

The soldier nodded.

"Merciful Sorwe! Have they crossed the border?"

"No, but they will soon. They went back to their village to gather more fighters."

"Gather more fighters? The border guard defeated them?"

"No, they weren't fighters. They were just villagers armed with whatever they could find, but we routed them. They swore they were going back for reinforcements, soldiers this time."

"But why did they attack?"

The soldier threw up a hand and looked disgusted. "They claimed we'd stolen their children. As if we'd want them."

"Wait," she said slowly. "*Their* chldren are missing?"

"That's what they said. Since night before last."

"The children from Village-On-War-Road are missing, too."

The soldier's eyes widened. "Now the Paramites are gathering an army. Could be here by tomorrow morning, afternoon at the latest. I've got to warn the village and bring as many reinforcements as possible. And we can certainly use your sword."

"I can't join you," she said. "Sorwe has set me to find the children. I *must* follow Her will. When I find them, I'll join you at the border. Warn the village. Tell them about the Paramite children. And tell Karrick I will keep my vow. Sorwe's blessing on you."

"And on you." He clapped his legs against the horse's sides and galloped on.

Cold crept up Garilynn's back. The Paramites' children were missing, too. That could lead to only one thing: war. Not just a skirmish but an all out war. *If* she didn't find all the children in time. Less than a day.

"Sorwe, guide me straight and true." She stepped into the forest.

The light dimmed to a cool grey-green. The air was close, stifling, overwhelming with the scent of damp earth and decades of spicy dry leaves. Garilynn searched for a path, brushing away leaves with a short dead branch she'd picked up. A footprint here, there, farther on, to the left, down a small hill, along a creek.

Finally, she spotted grass that had been trampled in a circle. A small strip of linen cloth lay under a small stone. Footprints led into the circle from the southwest and out of the circle from the north, no attempt to hide the path.

The light turned to grey then darker grey until Garilynn could barely see where she was going. Keeping close to the creek, she walked until she could barely distinguish trees from the night. She stopped, took out her flint and precious band of steel. She gathered what sticks and dry leaves she could see nearby and struck the steel with flint until sparks caught the tinder. Smoke twisted from the pile, then a tiny flame nibbled at the fuel. Soon she had to add larger twigs to satisfy the fire's appetite.

"No time to sleep," she decided. "I need light."

She found a branch for a torch, bound dry grass and twigs to one end with a strip of cloth, then held it in the small fire until the grass blazed and the twigs caught. She splashed water on the burning pile of twigs until no smoke rose from it, then walked on.

The torch burned down, and she fired another one. Night air made her skin damp and cool. Her eyes ached, and she kept going, following the crushed leaves and broken branches. She couldn't stop. No time to sleep.

Late in the night, maybe even on toward morning, she saw a twinkle of yellow light ahead. Her torch was down to a stump of embers. She held it down low to keep from being seen. Creeping silently between trees, past briars, she slid the torch into the creek and approached the flickering light.

A wide glen opened before her, a large bonfire in the center. Circling the fire were at least two score sleeping children, dark-haired children from the village and tow-headed Paramite children. They were covered with blankets and had a ring of pale blue flowers around their heads. Joy-on-the-Mountain again.

A woman rose on the other side of the fire. Greying brown hair flowed over her brown robe. A dagger in her hand glinted in the firelight. Go away!" she said, her voice sibilant.

"I am the right hand of Sorwe. She knows what you have done. You used the dream pillows to soothe the children's fears and make them compliant enough to follow you. You used the blessing of Sorwe's healing sleep to keep the parents from frim waking while you stole their children. You have broken your vows to harm none, and Sorwe weeps for you. She sent me to bring these children back to their parents and to bring you to the judgement of Sorwe."

"You can't have them!"

"Don't you understand? They *have* to go home! Even now forces are gathering on both sides of the border. People will die. Their parents will die."

"Good! Let them all die! Then the fighting will stop, and the children will grow up safely! They won't hate each other because they live on different sides of a valley. No more children will die because of their parents' hate." The woman glared at her.

Garilynn stepped closer to the fire. "Maywen," she said in a gentle voice. "Maywen, I know you love the children." She edged around the fire. "I know you loved Kint."

"I brought him into this world," the healer said, her eyes shimmering with tears. "I was the first one to hold him.His eyes saw me before they saw his mother. I salved his hurts, taught him prayers, watched him grow until he was almost a man. And they killed him! Their hate killed him! No more! I won't lose another child to their hate!"

Garilynn edged closer. "Maywen, I know you're grieving for Kint. So are his parents. And now you've taken their only remaining child. Think of the grief you've caused them."

"No! I've grieved for all the children!"

"So do I. And so does Sorwe."

"Then why doesn't She stop the killing? Why didn't she save Kint?"

"I don't know." Garilynn moved within a few feet of Maywen. "But you have to take the children back to their parents."

"No. I'll raise these children together. They won't know they are enemies. And finally, when all the soldiers, all the parents, all the hatreds are gone, then I'll take the children back to the plain and we'll build a new village without hatred and anger and killing. And the children will be happy and safe. And their children. And their children. And their children. I'll save them all."

Maywen lunged at her, slashing with the dagger. Garilynn ducked and rolled to her left, then crouched and knocked the healer off her feet with a leg sweep. Maywen fell on her back hard, knocking the breath out of her. Garilynn straddled the healer and grabbed her wrists. The healer struggled wildly and slashed a long shallow cut down Garilynn's right arm. Blood soaked the torn edges of her sleeve.

"Maywen!" Garilynn forced the healer's wrists to the ground. "Look at me! Look at my arm. You've drawn blood. You want to kill me, don't you?"

"Yes! No! I...I have to save the children! Protect them!"

"Violence only breeds more violence. Isn't that what you want to stop? The endless circle of violence that kills all the one you've loved?"

The healer stopped struggling and stared at Garilynn.

"You can't do this. You've stolen this children from people who love them, from people they love. How long can you keep them here? How will they feel when they can't find their parents, their families?"

"But they're happy! All the children play together and like each other. They don't hate each other, and they won't ever if they stay with me."

"You have no right to do this, even if for the love of the children."

"But I can't watch one more of them die in my arms like Kint. I can't bear it."

"Then help me stop the war. Help me take them back home. You've shown them that there's no reason they should be enemies. Trust in Sorwe to keep their friendship for each other."

Maywen lay very still, then glanced around at the sleeping kidlings. "How can I be sure? How can I be sure?"

"You are a healer, a priestess of Sorwe. Ask her." Cautiously, Garilynn released the healer, stood up, and backed away.

Maywen sat up and rubbed her wrists. Slowly, she stood, brushed dirt from her robe, and smoothed her hair. She gazed at the sleeping children, then raised her hands to the sky, closed her eyes, and murmured a prayer. After a few moments, her hands fell to her sides, and tears streamed down her face. "You're right, Swordmate. Their parents' blood will be on my hands if they die in battle. I tried to stop the killing, but my way is the wrong way. Merciful Sorwe forgive me." She sank to her knees and wept.

Garilynn hurried to her and shook her shoulder. "There's no time to cry. We have to take the children back before the battle begins."

The healer looked up at Garilynn. Yes. We must go back before more blood is spilled."

Maywen stood and began breaking the ring of flowers on the children's heads.

Garilynn helped, shaking the children awake. "Wrap in your blankets," she said. "We have a long way to go tonight."

The children stretched and blinked their eyes.

"Where's Papa?" a little girl said.

"Where am I?" an older boy asked.

Garilynn smiled and stroked the girl's hair. "It's all right. We're going to find your papa. Is that all right?"

The children looked at each other and nodded.

When they were ready, Garilynn made torches for the healer and herself. Maywen led the way; Garilynn followed the last child. The children didn't grumble in spite of stumbling over rocks and tripping over twigs, and they moved quickly.

But is it quickly enough? Garilynn thought, worried. She prayed they'd reach the border in time.

The night changed from violet to indigo to grey-blue. Dawn wasn't far away. Garilynn's heart pounded. *Will we make it? Can we stop the war?*

Light brightened to grey, the grey-green. Dawn had come and gone. Droplets of sunlight splashed on the highest branches of the trees and drizzled down to the forest floor. Far ahead yellow peaked through the tree trunks. They'd almost reached the road.

Midmorning sunlight momentarily blinded them as they emerged from the forest, but Garilynn could still hear well enough. Scores of booted feet pounded the dry road to her left from the village, and just as many running feet approached from her right, from the Paramis side of the border. The war hadn't started, but soon would.

Black spots floated before her eyes, then cleared. Maywen, the children, and Garilynn were at the edge of the plain and between two companies of soldiers. "Follow me!" she said, motioning to the healer.

She ran straight across the plain to the road and stopped in the middle, facing Paramis. "Stand behind me, between them."

Maywen stood at her back facing Aldegar. The children huddled close on either side. Shouts rang out from both sides as the soldiers called for the children to get out of the way.

"No!" Garilynn shouted and held up her hands. "We will not move! There will be no fighting today! See, I have found your children! They are well and well-fed. No harm has come to them. They have been cared for with love and kept from harm. There is no reason to fight."

"They stole our children!" said a Paramis soldier, pointing at the Aldegarans.

"They stole ours!" an Aldegar villager said.

"No, they didn't!" Garilynn said above the din. "Only one person is responsible for this, and that person will face the judgment of Sorwe. I am a Swordmate, the right hand of Sorwe. You of Aldegar know what I am. And even you of Paramis know that Swordmates speak only truth."

The soldiers on both sides quieted, though many grumbled.

"We demand justice," said a Paramite officer.

"No, you want revenge," Garilynn said. "I will deal fair and true justice to the one who did this."

"But they're out enemies!" said Karrick, who had pushed to the front of the Aldegar ranks. "They're Paramites! They all deserve to die!"

"You want to kill Paramites?" she asked. "Then here." She picked up a little Paramite boy who was perhaps four years old and handed him to Karrick. "You want to kill Paramites so much, then kill him."

Karrick looked stunned. The Paramites cried out and raised their weapons.

"Hold!" Garilynn raised her hands and glared at the Paramites. "You want justice. Justice you'll have." She turned to Karrick. "Go ahead. Kill the Paramite. He's the enemy, isn't he? A death for a death?"

The little boy snuggled his head against Karrick's shoulder and closed his eyes. Karrick stared at him, then the man's eyes softened. He stroked the boy's fine blond hair and rested his cheek against the boy's head. "No, I can't."

"But he's a Paramite."

"*He* didn't kill my son. He's an innocent."

Garilynn touched his arm. "Yes, he is. They all are."

Karrick gazed at all the children and nodded.

"Papa," said a soft voice.

"Justie?" Karrick searched through the faces until he fixed on a little girl. "Justie!" He knelt to catch his daughter with his free arm. He kissed her, hugged her close, and cried into her hair.

The Paramite officer walked up to Karrick and held out his arms. "My son," he said.

Karrick looked at the boy and nodded. Before the Paramite took the boy, Justie wrapped her arms around the boy's neck and gave him a kiss on his cheek. "You play with me tomorrow, okay?"

The boy gave her a sleepy smile and said, "Okay."

Karrick and the officer stared at each other.

"There will be no fighting today," Garilynn said.

"No fighting today," Karrick said.

The Paramite nodded, took his son, and turned back toward his home. The children ran to the waiting arms of their fathers, who swept them up, hugged them, and turned back toward their homes and families.

Garilynn and Maywen watched as the soldiers walked away. "How did you summon the Paramite children?" Garilynn asked.

"I disguised myself as a peddler and went to Warren-on-the-Hill. I sold dream pillows to as many parents as possible, then waited 'til nightfall and whispered to the children to follow me."

"You must face the judgment of Sorwe now," Garilynn said.

"Yes, I know."

"You know what you did was wrong, don't you? Even if you did it out of love, it was still wrong."

"Was it?" Maywen said softly. "Look." She nodded toward Village-On-War-Road.

Garilynn looked at the Aldegar villagers. All the children were waving over their fathers' shoulders.

"Now look there." Maywen pointed toward Paramis.

The Paramite children were smiling and waving back.

Soul Healer's Song

I met Jo Clayton at a convention in St. Louis, and I liked her immediately. We went to a panel on non-traditional vampires and vampires in other cultures. We were both fascinated by the mythology of the Chinese vampire, and we agreed we'd both write a story about one. This is for you, Jo.

Xiu Mei found the farmer sprawled in the road, his body torn to pieces. His face was as pale as cotton cloth and barely recognizable. Only last week she had bought wheat from him, a robust man in the strength of his life. Now he was like hunks of meat on a butcher's table.

She knelt beside the body, held her hands palms out, and began the soul song of eternal peace. A breath of air brushed her palms, and she gathered it in her hands. Shaping the air into a sphere of calm and comfort and promised rest, she spread her hands to enlarge the sphere until it covered the body completely. "May your body be safe from evil, and may your higher soul and lower soul both find peace in the next world," she sang.

What had killed him? Bears? Wild dogs? What could rip a man apart like that?

Her dark eyes widened as she stared at the body in the dusty road. No blood pooled in the dirt or oozed from the body. No blood. No blood at all.

She gasped, stumbled back from the body, and dropped her healer's bag of herbs. "Chiang-shih!" she whispered. "Vampire!" And she knew evil had come to her village.

Grabbing up her blue cloth bag, she ran down the dirt road to her village at the foot of the steep hill. She passed children laughing in the warmth of an early autumn morning, women haggling with merchants at the market, the village elder's great house and walled garden. Finally, she reached her own one-room stone cottage.

"Grandfather!" She flung open the door and ran to the bed in the corner. "Grandfather, please! You must help me!"

Grandfather wheezed and opened his red-rimmed eyes. "Little Plum, what is wrong? Did the birthing not go well?"

"Yes, a fine, strong boy." She started and glanced at the ceiling. "I mean it was only a girl, sickly and deformed. She probably won't live out the day." She shuddered, hoping she hadn't drawn the jealous attention of the gods to the child. "But Grandfather, on the way home..." Xiu Mei gulped a breath and brushed a strand of sweat-damped black hair from her mouth. "A farmer–the one we buy grain from–I found him dead in the road!"

Grandfather sighed. "Death comes to us all. It is part of life. Soon it will come for me." He coughed and closed his eyes.

No, Grandfather, please!"

"Yes, even to me. Do not worry, Little Plum. I have lived many years and have many sons and grandsons–and one very wise granddaughter. All have brought honor to our family."

"But you do not understand!"

"Have you told the man's family? The burial must be as soon as possible to satisfy his souls."

"Please, listen!" She shook him, then realized what she had done and quickly released him. Kneeling beside the bed, she bowed to him. "Forgive me, Grandfather, but you must listen to me! The dead man–he was torn apart! But there was no blood! No blood at all!"

The old man's eyes opened wide with surprise and fear. "Are you certain?" he whispered.

She swallowed hard and nodded.

"Chiang-shih," he hissed.

Xiu Mei held his thin, trembling hand. The skin was dry as paper and too cold. How many times had she held that hand when she was little? It had always been so strong and reassuring. How could it feel so feeble? "Grandfather, you were physician to the old mandarin. You know the secrets of keeping well and healing the sick and much more. All these things you have taught me to help the living. But do you know how to defeat the undead?"

Grandfather tried to sit up, but a hacking cough shook his whole body. He sank back against his pillow and gasped for breath.

Xiu Mei reached for a cup of water on the small table beside the bed. She spooned in powdered onion from her bag, and honey and mashed apple from a bowl. Softly, she began a song of soul healing over the cup, weaving harmony of body and spirit to strengthen Grandfather's soul and make the medicine more potent. The cup began to glow and warmed in her hands. The liquid began to steam. Peace and comfort surrounded them like a blazing fire on a cold day.

Levering Grandfather up until he was almost sitting, she held the cup to his mouth. "Drink slowly, Grandfather," she said. "It is hot."

Grandfather took a sip, another sip, coughed, took another sip and another, had a coughing spasm, then took several more sips. Finally, he began to breathe easier, slower, and he relaxed against her arm. "Little Plum," he said, "there is a way...to fight the chiang-shih...but I do not have the strength. *You*–you must fight the chiang-shih."

Xiu Mei nearly dropped the cup. "Grandfather! I-I cannot fight the chiang-shih! I am no warrior!"

"Strength of arm will not defeat the vampire. Strength of heart and spirit can. Your heart is good, and your spirit is strong. You have the gift of healing souls as well as bodies. It is the rarest of magics I know, and you are the most gifted soul healer I have ever seen. But you must also have the courage to face the vampire. You must...you must." Grandfather slumped against the pillow as Xiu Mei slid her arm out from behind his back. "Now call the elder and the chief citizens. There is much we must do and much I must teach you before the sun reaches its rest."

Xiu Mei huddled by the shuttered window facing the center of the village. Fear slithered across her shoulders and down her back. Her left arm clutched a drum to her side. Her right hand ached from gripping the striking stick so tightly. She thought of every soul healing song she knew: one for a broken heart, one for the loss of a loved one, one for encouragement, one for forgiveness, one for driving out evil humors in a wound, one for binding a wound, songs for little sorrows, songs for great sorrows, and so many other songs. But none of them eased her own souls.

Like everyone else in the village, she had sprinkled iron filings across her threshold and on every windowsill so the chiang-shih could not enter. "Iron burns the chiang-shih as fire burns us," Grandfather had said. She had placed garlic cloves in the four corners of the room and rubbed garlic on Grandfather and herself. "The odor of garlic is repugnant to chiang-shih." Now all she could do was wait and pray.

The full moon was high and blue-white like fresh milk when she heard a knock at the door. Startled, she fell backward and almost dropped the drum. She did drop the striking stick. Grandfather stirred but did not waken.

There was quiet for a few moments, then a voice outside said softly, "Xiu Mei? Xiu Mei, are you awake? It's Cheung."

"Cheung?" Xiu Mei's heart quivered with joy and surprise. "It has been so long since you left."

"Yes, too long. I have missed you so much."

She opened the door just a little and glanced around the darkened streets. "Cheung." She gazed at him, moonlight on his strong chin, his dark eyes, and high forehead. He was just as handsome as the day their marriage contract had been arranged. Even though his name meant "good luck", she thought she was the fortunate one to be betrothed to so handsome and kind a man. She blushed and hoped he could not tell it in the darkness. "I missed you, too."

"I feared I might never see you again. The last caravan I took through the northern districts was attacked, and I was injured. But as soon as I was well, I came back to you. I wanted to look on your face before I returned to my father's house. Please, my wife-to-be, may I come in?"

"It is not seemly that you should come to my house so late, nor is it safe. Chiang-shih walk the night."

"Chiang-shih!" he whispered. He shuddered and shrank closer to the door. "And my father's house is at the far edge of the village. Please, let me stay with you until sunrise. Then it will be safe to walk the streets. Please, Xiu Mei."

She gazed at the young man as she had so many times before. Glancing up and down the darkened streets, she nodded. "Quietly. Grandfather is sleeping." She opened the door wide and stepped back.

Cheung stepped toward her, then howled like a wounded dog. Rage burned in his eyes. Hate twisted his mouth. "What have you done?" he screamed.

She looked down at the threshold. Moonlight glittered on the line of iron filings, and just barely touching the line was his footprint in the dust. Tears filled her eyes, and her heart went cold. No, oh no, not Cheung, not him!

"The drum!" Grandfather called. "Remember: chiang-shih cannot bear loud noises! Strike the drum!"

She struck the drum with her hand as hard as she could. Cheung clapped his hands over his ears. Other drums joined Xiu Mei's. Cheung roared and ran from the village. The drums went on for a few moments longer, then one by one they stilled.

Xiu Mei closed the door, dropped the drum, slid to the floor, and wept into her hands. "Grandfather, it was Cheung!"

"I know, Little Plum. I saw."

"Why him?" she cried. "Why did it have to be him?"

"I don't know." Grandfather sighed. "Usually when one dies, both his souls ascend to the next realm. But sometimes, when one dies with great rage in his heart or dies violently or is killed by one of the undead spirits—as Cheung must have been—the lower soul, the soul of earthly hungers and desires, refuses to ascend, refuses to accept that he is dead. Then he becomes the chiang-shih, trying to satisfy his hunger by draining life from others." He gazed at Xiu Mei. "I am so sorry, Little Plum."

"What am I to do?"

"You are a soul healer. You must heal his lower soul and give him peace."

The first rays of sunrise seeped through the door as Xiu Mei checked her bag of herbs and supplies. "Garlic for protection. Drum and iron filings for defense. Red peas to bind. Embers for fire. Water and food and blanket for strength. Have I forgotten anything?"

"No, you know everything I can teach you about chiang-shih. All else you need, you have inside you," Grandfather said. "Courage is your armor, and compassion is your weapon. Listen to your heart and follow its wisdom."

"I will, Grandfather." She bowed respectfully, slipped the healer's bag over her shoulder, and turned to go.

"And come back with tomorrow's sun, Little Plum."

"I will, Grandfather," she said. *I hope.*

She followed Cheung's tracks from her threshold north along the dusty road through the village. The footprints led up into the hills past the spot she had found the farmer the day before. Sometimes, she lost the tracks in the scrubby grass, but she searched until she found the trail again. Over hills, through woods and a narrow dale, beside a small brook, until about midday she spotted a cave tucked between two pillars of stone. The tracks led to the entrance.

His resting place," she murmured.

Quickly, she set down her bag and began the preparations just as Grandfather had told her. "Red peas set in a half circle stretching from side to side at the entrance to his resting place will bind him in this place. He cannot cross a boundary of red peas. Gather wood for a small fire to keep you warm at night. Measure your height against a tree, then find a stick that is an arm's length longer. Make a circle that wide and ring it with garlic and iron filings. And rub garlic on yourself. Step inside the circle with the drum and your belongings, and never leave the circle—not for any reason—until after sunrise. Your life depends on it.

Speak to him of beauty and goodness that his lower soul will remember the man he was, but do not listen to his words for he will deceive you and lure you to your doom if he can. Heal him, Little Plum. Sing his souls to rest."

Preparations completed, she stepped into the circle. She had had so little sleep the past two nights, what with the birthing and waiting for the chiang-shih, she was exhausted. She rolled her blanket up into a pillow and lay down to rest until sunset.

She woke just as the sun was sinking behind the hills. "It is almost time," she whispered. She poured the embers from the clay jar and added twigs to coax a flame into life. Kneeling, she prayed.

As she stood, she looked at the cave entrance and gasped. The circle of red peas was gone! An ant struggled to carry off the last one. Cheung was free to leave the cave and kill again!

She grabbed her bag and rummaged through it for the box of red peas. The sun was nearly gone! If she hurried, maybe she could make another barrier.

Emptying the red peas into her hand, she started to step beyond the circle when Cheung lunged straight at her from the cave. She staggered back inside the circle, barely missed the fire, and fell against the drum, which rolled out of the circle beyond her reach. The peas flew from her hand and scattered in the dust. Rolling into a crouch, she stared at Cheung.

He paced before her, unable to cross the garlic and iron circle. "Have you come as a bride for our wedding night?" he asked with a smile.

Xiu Mei tried to blink back her tears, but they rolled down her smooth cheeks. "I cannot be your bride, Cheung. There will be no wedding night for us. There will be no children to continue your family name, no grandchildren to warm our last years. There can be nothing for us now. Only this one night of sorrow and healing."

"Come to me, and you will never know sorrow again," Cheung said. He sat down in front of her. "Xiu Mei," he said with the gentle tone she knew so well, "you know me better than anyone else. Do you believe I would hurt you? We grew up together. We played pebble games and raced snails and chased butterflies. I knew even as a child that you were the one I wanted to marry." He paused and gazed at her shyly. "Do yu remember what I gave you before I left with the caravan?"

Xiu Mei nodded, tears drying on her face. She tried to speak, but her throat was too tight and dry. A sip of water from her waterskin helped.

"Yes," she whispered, "I remember." She reached inside her jacket for a small cloth bag, opened it, and pulled out a dried flower, still blue and delicately scented. "True love, Grandfather calls it. I have kept it next to my heart."

"Xiu Mei, my beautiful plum, my true love, come to me. Come to me. Come to me." His words were like silk against her skin, soothing, inviting, comforting. He held his arms out to her, and she wanted to run to him, wanted to feel his arms around her, rest her head against his chest, and listen to his heart beat.

"You are my good luck, Cheung," she said. She stood and slowly took a step toward him. *His heart beat*, she thought.

"Come to me, Xiu Mei. I have waited for you all my life."

"And I have waited for you." She gazed into his dark eyes and took another step. *His heart beat.*

"We will be together forever," he said softly, his voice like flower petals.

"Forever," she whispered and took another step. *His heart beat.* Another step. *His heart...doesn't beat!* She looked down and saw that her foot had almost crossed the circle. Stumbling back, she shook her head and rubbed her eyes. She felt off balance, as if the sky were the earth and east were west.

Cheung was on his feet, holding out his arms to her.

"Xiu Mei..."

"No," she said, her heart aching. "No, we can never be together, for you are dead and I still live. But I must give you peace and send you to the next realm."

Anger filled his eyes like dark fire. "Never! If you will not come to me, then I will hunt other prey and drink their blood. Stay here in your sanctuary while I feast elsewhere." He turned from her and stepped away.

"No! I cannot let you leave!" She started, then sang his name.

Cheung halted, as if his feet were mired in mud. She sang his name again. He turned to face her slowly, as if he strained against chains that held him.

Singing! Singing would hold him until the sun rose! And when the warm rays of the sun bathed his body in light, his lower soul would see and know that he was truly dead, and he would be free! But could she sing all night? She had to! For his sake.

She sat on the ground and sang his name again, over and over. Soon he was sitting before her again, struggling to move but unable. She sang to him every lullaby she knew, every playtime rhyme she had ever sung, every ballad and folksong she had ever heard. She watched the full moon rise in the sky and wished it would fall quickly to its rest. And still she sang.

Cheung pounded the ground, dug his fingers into the dirt, but he couldn't leave. The music held him stronger than chains of iron.

Xiu Mei's throat grew hoarse. Her lips were dry. But she dared not stop singing. She held her fingers under the mouth of the waterskin, let a few drops of water fall on them, then moistened her lips. Her head ached. Sleep pulled at her eyes. Still she sang to him of the beauty of a newborn child's face, the joy of a gentle breeze, the sound of nightbirds singing, the feel of walking on soft earth, and the fragrance of wild flowers.

The moon was nearly gone and dawn edged the clouds magenta when her voice cracked. Cheung struggled to his feet, triumph in his eyes. She tried to sing again but only a hoarse caw came out.

Cheung laughed. "Your voice is gone. You cannot hold me with your songs any longer. I will find a resting place before the sun comes, and I will come for you another night. You have failed, Xiu Mei." He turned toward the cave.

Tears streamed down from her burning eyes. What could she do? She needed strength and rest, but there was no time.

Strength and rest - like a woman in childbirth needed! How many times had she sung the soul song of strength and rest as she birthed a baby? She calmed her mind, centered her thoughts, and began the song.

Her voice was only whisper at first, but it was enough to halt Cheung. Warmth began in her chest, spread throughout her body. Her voice grew stronger, more sure and steady; her body, refreshed. She marveled at the vigor coursing through her. She had always sung the soul song for another, never for herself. Now she felt born anew.

Cheung wheeled back toward her. "No," he whispered as he stood with his hands clenched. "Let me go, please, Xiu Mei. Let me go. Don't let me die."

"I cannot let you die, Cheung, for you are already dead although you deny it," she sang. "See now the sun, how its light shines on you and reveals the truth."

Sunlight crept over the hillside, flowing over them like liquid gold.

"No!" he wailed. "No! Xiu Mei, please!" His body was bathed in sunlight, warm and golden. He reached out to her, anguish on his face. "Xiu Mei," he whispered.

For a moment, he gazed at her, his eyes clear, then he smiled gently. "I am free, Xiu Mei, free, thanks to you. Farewell, my true love. I will wait for you in the next realm." Slowly, he fell to the earth like an autumn leaf and lay still in a pool of sunlight.

Xiu Mei stepped from the circle and knelt beside him, her tears falling on his body. She sang the soul song of eternal peace, just as she had for the farmer, then she touched Cheung's face for the first and last time.

"Farewell, my husband who never was," she whispered as she rose to find wood for a funeral pyre.

The Boy Who Cried Dragon

This is my version of "Scared Straight", fantasy style.

The doorknob turned easily. Jimmy couldn't believe his luck. Only the fifth house he'd tried in the neighborhood. No car in the garage. Excitement pulsed through him, just like before. He had broken into three other places in the past month. Not to steal; he didn't need to steal, not with ready access to Mom and Dad's credit cards. No, he did it the first time to prove to his friends he could, to prove he was invincible. Now he didn't want to stop. He needed the thrill of that brush with danger.

There was a small pet flap at the bottom of the door. Jimmy frowned a moment. If it was for a cat, there was no problem; the cat would be out at night. If it was for a dog, though, he didn't want to tangle with the animal, no matter how small it was. Jimmy pushed the back door open just a bit, shined his flashlight through the crack, and peeked in. Just to the right of the door was a litter box. Definitely a cat. Jimmy relaxed and slipped his short, thin body inside.

It was quiet, no sound but the squeak of his Airwalks on the vinyl floor. A dim yellow light glowed above the wooden kitchen table. The room was neat, no dishes in the sink. A bowl of cat food sat on the floor and a bag of Meow Mix on the counter. The white double-door fridge was filled with an assortment of food and drink; leftovers here, a few fruits and vegetables there, mostly meat in the freezer. He helped himself to a canned cola, smiled as he popped the tab, and walked down the short hallway, past the stairs on the left.

The lights popped on when he entered the living room. Throat dry, skin cold, he jumped back, spilling soda on his black hooded jacket. Immediately, the lights went out. He edged back into the room, and the lights came on again. "Must be some new gadget," he mumbled as his heart slowed to near normal.

Little hearts, diamonds, spades, and clubs were woven into the thick, closed curtains and upholstery. The carpet was bottom-of-a-well black. Torch-shaped lights hung on either side of a black and white marble fireplace. A large TV sat in one corner, but there was no VCR, no stereo system, not even a Walkman lying around. Not that he really wanted a Walkman; he had three at home. He just wanted something to prove to the guys he'd been here.

The other side of the room opened to a library, heavy wooden shelves filled with old books. The desk was cluttered with papers, pens, and a collection of pewter and plaster figures—dragons, unicorns, fairies, and some creatures Jimmy had never seen before. The place smelled of old age and old leather. He shrugged and headed back to the hall for the stairs.

The dark wood banister was smooth and warm and spoke of years of polishing with lemon-scented wax. It reminded him of Grandma. Her place always smelled like that. The same black carpet as in the living room flowed up the stairs. The stairs creaked as he climbed.

Jimmy reached the top and looked down a hallway that ended in a closed door. Four other doors, all shut, led off the hall.

He opened the first door on the left. Lights snapped on automatically, just as in the living room, and revealed a rose-pink bathroom, spotless and clean, with a bare medicine cabinet, neatly folded towels, and barely used soap. Across the hall from the bathroom, a narrow door opened to a linen closet filled with new towels and sheets. The next door led to a bedroom with rows of tiny bottles on a shelf, nothing worth stealing. Opposite was an empty room without even dust on the wood floor. The air was stale and had a faint tinge of something. Smoke, spice, maybe perfume—Jimmy couldn't quite put his finger on exactly what, but the scent seemed out of place in there.

The last door, the one at the end of the hall, revealed a pale green room with a dark wooden four-poster bed, a chest of drawers, a dresser, and an oval gilt-framed mirror. A foot-long wooden box shaped like a treasure chest sat on the dresser.

Jimmy smiled as he hurried over to the box. It was held shut by a tiny gold padlock. Jimmy pulled on the lock, but it stayed in place. "Heck with it," he muttered, set down his soda, took, out his pocket knife, and tried to pry off the tiny lock. He twisted, turned, pounded; finally, the lock cracked, broke, and fell off with a sound as loud as thunder.

Jimmy jumped, the crouched with his knife poised to defend himself. His eyes darted around the room, but nothing else happened. He blew out his breath, turned back to the chest, pushed up the lid, and gasped.

Inside were silver and gold rings, bracelets, necklaces, and chains, all glittering with jewels and gems. He ran his fingers through the jewelry. Was it all real? He stared for a moment, then stuffed it all into the pockets of his jacket and went back to the hall.

He had started downstairs with his prize when he heard a sound: low, barely audible, like the whoosh of a revolving door. For a split second he feared the owner had come home. He listened for a moment, but heard nothing except a throbbing in his ears and realized he was holding his breath.

Cold sweat trickled down his forehead. His stomach twitched nervously. Bracing one hand on the wall, the other on the banister, Jimmy tiptoed down the stairs. The living room was dark, no sounds or shadows. *I'm outta here,* he thought, and sprinted for the dimly lit kitchen.

A low growl startled Jimmy. He flattened himself against the refrigerator doors and zigzagged the flashlight around the kitchen, his eyes frantically searching the shadows. He saw no one, no movement. He started inching toward the back door. The growl grew louder, closer. Jimmy grabbed a long-handled skillet from a pot rack on the wall and held it like a baseball bat.

"I'm not afraid of you," Jimmy said, although his hands shook as much as his voice.

Eyes blinked in the dark near the floor, yellow eyes with each pupil shaped like a magnifying lens viewed sideways. Jimmy turned the flashlight on the eyes. There by the door stood a house cat, black and gold, sleek and shiny.

A cat. Jimmy laughed at himself. Scared by a cat. If the guys ever found out...

He started to walk toward the back door again, but kept the skillet ready in case the cat tried to claw him.

"What are you doing in my house?" a bass voice boomed.

Jimmy wheeled around, looking for the speaker. No one was there.

"I said, what are you doing in my house?"

Jimmy's hand tightened on the skillet. "Where are you?"

"Here, thief."

"Where?" Jimmy cried.

The cat took a step forward and smiled.

Smiled? Jimmy shook his head. *No way,"* he thought. *You're losing it, Jimmy.*

He swung the skillet at the cat, which nimbly sidestepped the blow. Jimmy grabbed the doorknob. He turned it, yanked as hard as he could, kicked it, pounded and yelled at it. The door didn't budge.

Jimmy turned and ran for the living room, but the cat blocked his way. It was bigger now, the size of a half-grown collie, and its fur was slicked down against its body. Jimmy swung the skillet at it again. The cat batted it out of Jimmy's grasp with talons that left deep furrows in the metal.

Jimmy gasped. The cat's feet were no longer soft, padded paws. On each foot, three scaly toes stretched forward and one back. Golden-edged scales crept up the legs, covered the tail, armored the growing back, sides, and belly. The long neck had two parallel lines of horny ridges from the top of a wide head to the tip of the serpentine tail. And the head–a huge scaly triangle of smoking nostrils and dagger-like teeth.

Jimmy stared, mouth desert-dry and hanging open. The creature was gigantic, way too big to fit inside the kitchen, much less the house. That's when he noticed that the painted walls were shimmering, sliding away to walls of dark stone, rough and uncut, like the walls of a cave. The ceiling was as high as that of a cathedral, with a hole at the top where moonlight dripped through. A cold breeze brushed his face. The taste of ashes filled his mouth.

"Now, thief," the bass voice echoed through the cavern, "return my treasure."

Jimmy gazed up at a black-and-gold dragon, bigger than a Learjet. Smoke twirled lazily from two broad nostrils, and a black forked tongue flicked out at Jimmy. No, it wasn't a dragon, it couldn't be! Dragons were fairy tales! "The soda— there must've been something in the soda," Jimmy muttered.

"I did not mind that you took a soda," the dragon said, "which was not tampered with, by the way. I *was* annoyed that you came to my house uninvited, especially when I was not here to greet you. But when you broke into my chest, that angered me. Return my treasure, boy, or I will eat you." The dragon grinned miles of teeth. "I may eat you anyway."

"You're not real!" Jimmy said. "This place isn't real!"

The dragon crept closer. "Of course, it is real. Where else would a dragon live but in a cave?"

"But I was in a house." Jimmy backed up a couple of steps. "I *know* I was!"

The dragon snickered, strands of smoke rising from its nose and intertwining. "Yes, it looked very real, did it not? The human wizard I keep to mind the house for me does an excellent job."

"But you're not real!"

The dragon smiled a very unpleasant smile. "Most people think that. I try to keep it that way." The smile faded. "Now, boy, give me back my treasure."

Jimmy couldn't believe this was happening to him. "You can't be real, you can't be real!" he cried. He spun around and dove into a tunnel directly behind him. His flashlight barely illuminated the slick rock floor just in front of his feet. The jewelry in his jacket flopped hard against his thigh as he ran. The narrow passage bent left, dipped down, then back up, bent left again, then turned sharply left opening into a large cavern.

Jimmy screeched to a halt. There was the dragon again, right in front of him. Cold sweat trickled down Jimmy's neck, and he retreated until he felt rough stone pressing against his back.

"You did not think that you would get away from me, did you, boy?" the dragon purred.

Jimmy looked side to side, then sprinted for another opening just a few feet to his right. The dragon laughed. Jimmy ran and ran, stumbled, and ran some more, past glowing green moss, over slime slick rock. Something metal clinked on the rock floor. A ring or bracelet fallen from his pocket? Jimmy didn't stop to find out. He just kept running.

The path rose gradually, then leveled off. Suddenly, Jimmy slipped on the slimy rocks and tumbled down a steep incline, through a doorway to a large cavern—the same cavern he'd fled.

The dragon was waiting for him, eyes narrowed. A single flap of its wings slammed Jimmy to the floor. "There is no escape, boy. Now, give me my treasure!"

Jimmy rose slowly. He put his shaking hands into his pockets, pulled out the jewelry, and tossed all of it as close to the dragon as he could throw. "There! Okay? So let me outta here. Please?"

The treasure glittered as the dragon gathered it in one claw, sniffed it, breathed in deep, then carefully placed it on top of a huge heap of other gold and gems. The dragon turned back to Jimmy and stretched its giant head down until their faces were only inches apart. Jimmy's eyes watered and burned from the dragon's breath.

"For the rest of your life," the dragon rumbled in his face, "I will haunt your days. I will stalk your dreams. I will be in every shadow. My eyes will see you in the darkest night. If you ever break into another house, I will know it and I will come for you. Do you understand?"

Eyes popping, Jimmy gulped, shivered down to his toes, and nodded.

"And now, boy,"—the dragon gave him a toothy grin—"I am hungry...and you smell like dinner."

A shriek bubbled out of Jimmy's mouth. He wheeled and ran to another tunnel, higher and wider than the others, slick with moss and water. The passage twisted right, left, and right again. He tripped and fell down a sharp slide, scratching his face. The flashlight slipped from his hands, rolled away, and blinked out. He was alone in the dark–alone, winded, and terrified.

"Do you enjoy excitement, danger?" came the dragon's voice close, too close, behind him. "Is this dangerous enough for you, boy? s this enough excitement?"

Fear surged through Jimmy like fire, spurring his legs into motion. He jumped to his feet and head away from the dragon. The path rose steeply; he slipped halfway up and scraped his hands raw. He ran as fast as he could in the dark, left hand touching the wall of the tunnel, right hand weaving in front of him. Running, running, stumbling over fallen stones and stepping in sudden pools. His clothes were torn, muddy, and soaked with icy water. His chest hurt as he sucked in air, and his muscles cramped from the damp cold.

The roar of the dragon drove Jimmy faster, faster, on and up until he saw a pinpoint of light ahead. He ran until he thought his muscles would tear apart, lungs burst, his heart explode. But he didn't stop, not with the light so close ahead and the dragon so close behind.

He scrambled up a scree-covered slope. Rocks slid from under his feet, pebbles shifted, pitched him to his knees, sliced into his palms. *Move, keep going, stay ahead of the dragon.* The smell of smoke was so thick, Jimmy thought he'd choke to death. *One more step, just one more step.* There! Just in front of him! The light, the light! He'd made it! The light–the red and white flashing lights.

Hands grabbed Jimmy and forced him face-down on the ground. "Don't let him get me!" he wheezed into the damp grass. "Keep him away!"

"Spread 'em," said a gruff voice. "Hands on your head."

Another pair of hands ran down his sides, down the inseams and the outside of his legs, in his jacket pockets. "Nothing."

"You live here?" the gruff policeman asked.

Jimmy tried to answer, but he was still out of breath and exhausted. It hurt just to suck in air.

Just then a car drove up, and a white-haired man in a business suit stepped out. "What's happening?" he asked as he hurried across the lawn. "This is my house." He pulled out his wallet and showed his driver's license to the officers.

"Break-in, suspected burglary," the gruff cop said. "A neighbor reported strange sounds and lights going on and off in your house. We caught this punk running out the front door."

"You'd think a neighborhood like this would be safe from thugs." The old man shook his head and glared at Jimmy. "No place is safe anymore."

"Cuff him," said the gruff policeman. "You have the right to remain silent. Anything you say..."

The other cop pulled Jimmy's wrists together behind his back and slipped the hard plastic loops around them. Both cops pulled Jimmy to his feet.

At that moment, a black-and-gold cat jumped from the shadows and clawed Jimmy's leg. Jimmy howled. The cat leaped away and sprang into the old man's arms.

"There now, Dragon," the old man cooed as he stroked the cat's fur, "did that bad little burglar scare you?"

"Dragon?" Jimmy cried. "Its name is Dragon?"

"Yes," the old man said sharply.

"But...it *is* a dragon."

The gruff policeman leaned in close to Jimmy's face. "Are you giving up the right to remain silent?"

"No!" Jimmy said, and nodded toward the cat. "But it changed into a dragon! I saw it! It chased me all through the house, and the house turned into caves and tunnels, it kept chasing and chasing, and it was going to eat me! Don't let it get me, please! It's not a cat! It's a real freaking dragon!"

"Great," muttered the other cop, "another insanity plea."

"But it *is* a dragon! I'm not crazy! I'm not!"

"Come on," said the gruff cop. The two officers pulled Jimmy to the squad car, bent his head down, eased him in, and closed the door behind him. The cops got in the front seat, the gruff one driving, the other reporting in on the radio.

Jimmy stared out the window at the old man and his cat. Yellow eyes blinked at Jimmy. A wisp of smoke curled from the cat's nose, and a black forked tongue flicked out. The old man held out his hand and took a lit pipe from thin air. He puffed it once. Then old man and cat both smiled smugly at Jimmy.

"Look!" Jimmy screamed. "See? I told you! It's a dragon! A dragon!"

The gruff cop chuckled as he drove away. "Tell it to the judge, kid."

Jimmy huddled in the backseat, miserable, scared, and hopeless. Fat chance a judge would believe him. No one would, not his mom and dad, not his friends, no one. Why did he have to pick that house? He'd never do it again, never, never, never.

Suddenly, Jimmy heard a voice inside his head, the bass voice of the dragon. "Remember me, boy, and remember what I told you." There was a pause, a sound of smacking lips and of glittering jewels being sifted and falling, then, "I know your smell. And I never forget a smell."

The Reluctant Vampire

Marion Zimmer Bradley said she wanted an entire issue of her magazine devoted to short-shorts: stories 1000 word or less. It's difficult to construct an entire story in those few words. This was my story that she bought.

Sharon woke with the worst headache she'd ever had, worse than her monthly migraines, even though it wasn't quite that time yet. This one was different. Her mouth was dry. There was a grapefruit-sized knot in her stomach. Her golden eyes pulsed in rhythm with her throbbing head. Hunger clawed her stomach like a wild animal.

Sitting up slowly, she realized she was still wearing her party dress. "What in the world did Trevairin put in my tomato juice?" she groaned. "Probably slipped in vodka–and after I told him I can't drink alcohol. I'm going to kill him."

When she stood, her legs felt like rubber bands. Cradling her head, she shuffled to the kitchen, opened the fridge, and took out a bottle of orange juice. The gurgling of liquid splashing into the glass echoed like Niagara Falls in her head. She popped two aspirins in her mouth, took a drink, then gagged. It tasted like mustard and cayenne pepper mixed with powdered charcoal. She ran for the toilet but didn't quite make it. When she'd cleaned up the mess, she trudge back to the kitchen and heated water for tea.

Pulling up a corner of the window shade, she saw crimson clouds in the September sky. A glance at the clock told her it was 7:33 P.M., just past sunset. "Oh, no! Mr. Jamison'll fire me for sure. No excuses."

The fragrance of the almond-mint tea soothed her anger slightly, as she inhaled the steam. Her breath swirled tiny tornados above the cup until the tea was drinking temperature. But when she tried to swallow, her throat tightened. She choked and tea splattered the table and her dress. She slowly wiped her mouth and watering eyes.

"Trevairin Drogolo's going to wish he was dead!"

She stripped off her dress, went to the bathroom, and turned on the shower. The hot water felt good; she hadn't realized she was so cold. By the time she stepped out, she felt more alive and much less irritated. Blow-drying her short, ebony hair took a few minutes, but she couldn't wipe the mirror clear enough to use her curling iron. She threw up her hands and sighed. *Well, I'm not going over there to impress him, just to remove his head from his shoulders.*

The air outside her apartment was crisp and autumn-spicy. She knew the full moon was hiding behind the trees and buildings, just waiting for the perfect moment to rain silver light on the city.

Trevairin's place was in an upper middle-class neighborhood, usually fifteen minutes away by interstate. Sharon made the trip in ten. Screeching her car to a halt before the large glass and brick house, she jumped out, slammed her door, and strode to the front porch, where she leaned on the doorbell.

The heavy oak door creaked open. Suddenly looming before her were the dark eyes and swarthy figure of Trevairin, dressed in black Levi's and shirt. He didn't look at all surprised to see her.

"Come in, Sharon. There are some people I would like you to meet." Leaving the door open, he turned around and sauntered down the hallway.

Sharon stood motionless, the words she'd practiced all the way over gone from her thoughts. Without protest, she followed him into his den. Four men and three women lounged in casual, dark-colored clothes. When she hesitated in the doorway, they all smiled at her.

Taking her hand, Trevairin led her to the room's center.

"Tonight we add another member to our family. Sharon, we welcome you." His lips brushed her hand.

She shivered from his touch. Suddenly, she regained hold of why she had come. "Look, Trev," she said, jerking her hand away and poking his chest, "spiking my drink wasn't funny or nice. I told you alcohol makes me sicker than a dog. And because of you, I've probably lost my job. I don't suppose it matters to you, but I have to work for a living, unlike you rich people."

A slow, toothy smile lit Trevairin's face. "My dear Sharon, you do not have to work if you do not wish to. You are welcome to stay with us now."

Sharon glared at him. "That's the last thing I'd do!"

One of the women–who seemed vaguely familiar–moved toward her. "Sharon, you belong here. You're one of us. We all have the same blood."

Sharon gaped at her. "Excuse me? Are you claiming to be my long lost relative or something?"

"No," the woman said, a feral look in her grey eyes, "newly found relatives. Trevairin did put vodka–and blood–in your drink last night. You've shared blood with us, and now we're blood kin."

Sharon shook her still pounding head. "This is getting too weird. Good-bye, Trev, and thanks for nothing."

She turned to leave, but Trevairin clutched her arm and spun her to face him. His narrowed eyes gleamed intensely.

"Sharon, you are my bride. At the party, I made you like myself–a child of the night."

With more force than she'd intended, she slugged him in the stomach. He doubled over, and she backed away.

"I'm not married to anyone," she began, icy calm. "If you cooked up a wedding last night, I can have it annulled 'cause I wasn't sober. As for being a vampire..." She flicked her long, sharp nails, and ran her tongue over her emerging canine teeth. She smiled as she read terror in their eyes. "Werewolves can't become vampires."

Teddy Bear, Teddy Bear

The song in this story is an old time jump rope rhyme I learned in elementary school, but the song always made me sad.

Teddy moaned in his sleep again. Without thinking, Mark Emery reached for his son's hand but froze, a sob of dying in his throat. Touching Teddy would only hurt the boy.

Early morning summer the sunshine glared through the hospital window. Mark rested his stubbly chin on the cold steel bed rail. His throat was dust-dry, his eyes watered, and his head ached from lack of sleep.

He plowed a hand through short, oil-damp hair just behind his ear. Fingertips brushed the brain jack in his skull—just like the one in Teddy's skull. Teddy had pleaded for months to have a brain jack before Mark had given in. He'd even written the virtual program *Star Quest* for his son's tenth birthday. Teddy loved to challenge Mark to a game and had finally won. Never again. Never again.

The private room was mist green, a color meant to soothe, but it brought him no comfort. There was almost as much computer equipment in the room, monitoring Teddy, as in Mark's office at home. Mark stared at I. V.'s, oxygen tubes, red LED readouts of vitals, the eerie green line indicating heart rate, the wildly spiking line that registered pain. So much pain, and there was nothing Mark could do to stop it.

Teddy's dark-circled eyes were closed in drugged sleep. God. What happened to the freckled-faced boy who'd been so excited about their trip to the mountains? Gone, like the healthy glow of his skin and the sparkle of his smile.

Three days ago, all the nerve cells in the ten-year-old's body had been blitzkrieged by a rare virus, causing continual pain. One in a million chance, the doctors said, even the specialists who were called in. No effective antibiotic, and with nanotechnology still only bio-medical researchers' hope, the only treatment was dulling morphine until ...

Mark clenched his teeth and covered his eyes, but tears leaked between his fingers anyway. His throat was so tight, it hurt to breathe. Why did his only child have to suffer like this? Why Teddy?

For a moment, a memory flashed across Mark's mind: his wife Loraine, dark brown hair falling limp around her face as she lay in a hospital bed, life snatched from her by a burst blood vessel in her brain. Had it been only four years ago? Teddy looked so much like her–especially now, lying there so pale...so pale. Dammit! It wasn't right that he was hurting so much!

Teddy whimpered, the sound bringing more tears to Mark's tired, aching eyes. He couldn't even hold his son, like when Teddy was younger and had nightmares. No way to comfort him.

If only Loraine were here now. She used to hold Teddy on her lap, sitting on the edge of his bed, and rock him back and forth, whispering against his fine brown hair. "Hush, Teddy bear, Mama's here. Don't cry."

Teddy bear. Loraine had always called him that. She'd sung him a special song, one passed down for generations. Mark could still hear her soft, alto voice.

Teddy bear, teddy bear, turn around.

Teddy bear, teddy bear, touch the ground.

Teddy bear, teddy bear, tie your shoe.

Teddy bear, teddy bear, that will do.

Helpless anger built inside Mark. He wanted to throw furniture across the room, hit someone, something, until his hands hurt more than his heart. But that wouldn't help Teddy. Nothing could do that.

Dr. Harrison came in, shirt as wrinkled as his face. "Mark," he said, frowning, "you've been here all night again, haven't you?"

Hands still clenching the bed rail, Mark turned away and shrugged.

"You've got to get some rest. Go home."

"Why?" Mark muttered.

"Because you look like hell. I bet you haven't had a shower or changed clothes since Teddy was admitted."

Mark scanned the doctor's lean face. "You don't look too good yourself."

Harrison rubbed the peppered stubble on his chin. "I've been here since early yesterday. Cardiac patient. After rounds, I'm going home. You should, too."

"I can't!" Mark said. "If he wakes up, I want to be here. I *have* to be here." He swallowed hard. "Doc, can't you do something for him? Anything, please! He's hurting so much."

"Don't you think I'd do something if I could?" Harrison's voice was raw and strained. "If only there were some way...some way." Shoulders drooping, he hung his head.

"He didn't even have our trip to the mountains. He said he wanted to stand on top and touch the sky. And now..." Mark gazed at the thin little face etched with pain, "he'll never do it."

Harrison sighed long and slow. "Only in his dreams."

Mark nodded mechanically, then halted. Dreams? In his dreams? Excitedly, Mark clutched Harrison's wrist. "Doc, how much longer?"

"A couple of days before the pain becomes so bad, drugs won't do any good. Maybe another day or two after that, not more than three."

Two days. Oh, God...could he make a dream in two days? Would it work? Maybe, just maybe! Hope thumping in his chest, Mark jumped to his feet. "Doc, I'll be back!" He ran towards the open door.

"Get some rest," Harrison called after him.

"No way," Mark said to himself.

Late afternoon sunlight gilded the walls in Mark's office. Typing the last of the virtual reality program, he saved it, then looked up at Jason Gills, his sometimes assistant and longtime friend. "Done," Mark said as he leaned back in his chair and rubbed his eyes. "Now we need to test it."

Jason shook his head. "No way. You need some sleep first."

"There's no time!"

"Make time." Jason's brown eyes glinted beneath a fine veil of golden hair that fell across his forehead. "You've been going ninety miles an hour since yesterday morning. No sleep, nothing to eat except half a sandwich. You want to be able to run this for Teddy, don't you?"

Mark glared at him. "Why the hell do you think I've been working on it instead of being at the hospital?"

"Well, you won't have the strength for it if you don't rest a while."

Mark turned back to his terminal. "I don't have time for this."

"The hell you don't!"

Mark spun around, aghast. Never in the sixteen years they'd known each other had Jason ever cursed. Astounded, Mark sputtered, stammered, tried to think of something to say. Jason didn't give him a chance.

"If you love that boy of yours as much as you say you do, you'll get a few hours sleep before we run the program for him. Otherwise, you can do it without me."

"But I can't do it without you! You know that!"

"Yes. I do." Jason firmly planted his fists on his hips. "So, old buddy, you sleep until seven, I wake you, and we both haul all this stuff to the hospital. Right?"

Mark started to protest, but Jason said, "Right," with a do-it-my-way-or-else tone.

Too groggy to argue any more, Mark let his shoulders sag and closed his burning eyes. "What the hell. Let me call Dr. Harrison first, then I'll sleep."

"Good. I'll pull the covers down on your bed right now." Jason patted Mark's shoulder, then gave it a firm but gentle squeeze. "I know," he said softly. He wheeled and hurried from the room.

What would he do without Jason, Mark wondered as tears gathered at the corners of his eyes and his throat tightened again. Jason was a true friend, who'd kept him working, kept him busy after Loraine's death. And now with Teddy, Jason was still looking out for Mark. Not many people had friends who cared enough to tell the harsh truth. Mark knew he was one of the lucky few.

He reached for the phone, dialed Dr. Harrison's number almost before he realized it. When the receptionist answered, he said, "This is Mark Emery. I want to speak to the doctor."

There was a momentary silence, then she said, "Dr. Harrison is at the hospital right now. If—"

"Teddy?" Mark broke in.

"No. You can call and have him paged."

"Thanks." Mark hung up and dialed, hung up at the busy signal, dialed again, then waited at it rang. The receptionist transferred his call to the third floor—surgical.

After being on hold for a maddeningly long time, Mark heard Dr. Harrison's voice. "Hello?"

"Doc, Mark Emery. I want you to get permission for me to bring some equipment up to Teddy's room. I don't care what you have to promise, I want clearance to bring my stuff up tonight, about eight."

"Mark...what kind of equipment?"

"Computer equipment."

"Why?"

"For Teddy, like a last wish."

Silence.

"Doc?" Worry twisted in Mark's stomach, corded chest muscles. "Please!"

Harrison cleared his throat. "All right. I'll find a way for you to bring it in."

Mark's eyes blurred until he wiped his sleeve against them. "Thanks," he whispered. "See you then." He hung up the phone and stared at it for a while before he stumbled toward his bedroom and toppled across the turned-down covers, already asleep.

Mark and Jason outside Teddy's room, Dr. Harrison looked grim. "Teddy's worse."

Mark felt as if the floor had suddenly fallen out from under his feet. "How bad?"

"Even morphine isn't helping. His breathing and heartbeat are erratic. I may have to put him on life support at any moment. I'm not certain I can let you do...whatever you're planning on doing."

Mark grabbed Harrison's arm. "Doc, I have to do this. If..." His voice caught in his throat. An ache crept from the center of his forehead down to the center of his chest. "No. Since he's going to die, I have to do this."

Harrison frowned, shrugged, and stepped aside.

Mark and Jason set up the computer between Teddy's bed and the empty one near the window, the bed Mark would take.

Harrison stood just watching, sometimes frowning, sometimes looking puzzled. "What will this do?"

Plugging the brain link cables into the multi-jack com port, Mark stretched one cable to his son's bed. He smoothed the boy's dark brown hair from the brain jack on the left side of his head. Mark steadied the opposite side of Teddy's head while sliding the cable link in place, cringing when his son sobbed. "It'll give Teddy the one thing he wanted before he...before he..." Mark couldn't go on.

"You don't really know if it'll work, do you?"

"It should."

"But you don't know what it might do." Harrison grabbed Mark's wrist. "To him or to you."

Mark didn't answer.

Suddenly, the vitals monitor began beeping rapidly.

"What's wrong?" Mark cried.

Harrison checked the wildly bouncing green line. "Heart!" He grabbed a vial and a small syringe, filled it full, expelled the bubbles, then injected the liquid into the IV.

"Oh, God, not now!" Mark pleaded. "Not yet!"

The monitor kept its furious staccato for stomach-twisting moments, then slower, slower, until Harrison blew out a cheek-puffing sigh and wiped his forehead. "He's stable. For now, at least."

"For now," Mark whispered, running fingers through his hair.

"Your turn," Jason said, pointing to the empty bed.

"No!" Harrison said. "What if you'd already been hooked up to him? You might have gone into cardiac arrest yourself! Or you might be in a coma, too! What if he *dies* while you're linked? You could die with him! I won't let you do this!"

"I have to!" Mark shouted. "For Teddy! One last chance to be with my son! Please, Doc, let me be with him for as long as I can! Please!"

Harrison hesitated, a frown in his eyes.

"Please," Mark said.

With a sigh, Harrison nodded. "But only if I hook up monitors to you. And at the first hint of problems, it stops. Agreed?"

"Agreed," Mark said. He slipped his shoes off, climbed onto the stiff-sheeted bed, lay back, and pushed his hair away from his brain jack. Jason slid the link cable in, the click echoing in Mark's teeth. It always did that.

Harrison called for a second cardio-pulmonary monitor and EEG unit. As soon as they arrived, the doctor attached the leads to Mark's chest, wrists, and head, the switched the machines on. "Remember, first sign of trouble..."

"Ready?" Jason asked.

"Ready." Mark gazed over at his son, then at Harrison. "Teddy?"

Harrison checked the vitals again, then sighed and nodded.

Jason sat down before the terminal, put his fingers on the keys, then hesitated. Looking at Mark, he said softly, "Enjoy the vacation."

Mark tried to smile but couldn't. He turned his head 'til he was staring at the ceiling. Closing his eyes, he listened to the tap-tap-tap of fingers on keys, the quiet whirl of the cooling fan inside the computer, the low rumbles and high beeps as the program began running.

Mark's face felt springtime warm, a yellow glow seeping through his closed eyelids. He took a deep, slow breath, then shivered as cold spread through his chest. Blinking to adjust to bright light, he sat up and looked around. Pine-covered mountains inscribed the wide grassy meadow where he sat. The June sun had only been up a couple of hours, but it was already chasing the night chill away.

Teddy lay close by, still, his chest barely moving. He was wearing a quilted red and blue jacket and knitted red hat, just like Mark was wearing.

"It worked." Mark smiled to himself. He crawled to Teddy's side. "Teddy, wake up. We're here. Colorado. Just like you wanted."

Teddy winced, stiffened, then his eyes fluttered open. "Dad?"

Mark nodded, his smile widening.

Teddy glanced around, his eyes growing rounder each moment. Sitting up in short jerks, he braced himself on the thick grass and turned his head from one side to the other. "Oh, Dad," he whispered. "Oh, Dad! We made it! We're here, we're here!" He scrambled to his feet, stretched out his arms, and shouted. "I made it! I'm here!" A joyful chorus of echoes shouted back at him.

Mark started to hug him, but stopped suddenly. "Teddy, how do you feel? Is the pain still there?"

A puzzled look crossed Teddy's face. "I...don't think so. I don't hurt at all." Color drained from his face. "Dad, am I still in the hospital, sick?"

"Yes."

"It wasn't just a bad dream." Teddy stared at the ground for a while, then gazed up at Mark. Tiny lines pulled at the corners of his mouth, gathered between his thin, straight brows. "Is this one of your computer games like we used to play?"

"No, not quite." Mark's voice shook almost as much as his hand did as he smoothed his son's hair from his eyes. "It's something special I made just for you– a vacation trip, just the two of us, like we planned. Everything we wanted to do, talked about, we can do now."

Teddy cocked his head and chewed his lower lip. "Everything?"

Mark knelt on one knee. "Everything."

"But is it...real?"

"As real as if we'd flown to Denver and driven into the mountains ourselves."

Teddy flung his arms around his dad's neck, and Mark hugged him back, cautiously at first, then he locked his arms around Teddy, pressing him to his chest. *He's so big*, Mark thought as tears rippled his vision, *and so small*.

"Dad?"

Mark pulled back and forced a smile. "What?"

"How long have we got?"

"I don't know."

A cloud blocked the sun for a moment, chilling the air, shadowing Teddy's face. Blown by a brisk wind, the cloud passed quickly, and sunlight brightened the meadow. Teddy's smile was brighter, but tinged with sadness.

"Then let's go, Dad. I want to touch the sky."

Mark nodded and held out his hand. Teddy put his small, lean hand in his dad's and curled thin fingers around it, and they started walking toward the mountains.

The meadow wasn't very wide, but it took quite a while to cross it. Mainly because Teddy stopped every few feet to point at something new.

"Look, Dad!" Ground squirrels playing tag with a red fox among the burrows.

"Wouldn't Mom like these?" Tiny yellow, blue, and white flowers scattered among the grass and mossy rocks.

"Oh, look!" Far down the meadow a few magnificent elk, their antlers like small trees.

"Up there! Up there!" A shaggy mountain goat, perched on a shelf of rock.

Granite pebble. Small, icy stream. Metallic flash of rainbow trout. A fat yellow marmot, mountain cousin of the groundhog. White, straight trunks of aspen trees topped with a cone of green spade-like leaves. And the scent of pine and earth and rain. Teddy ran here, darted there, joy and the crisp air coloring his cheeks red.

The meadow merged into the mountain side, a gradual slope to the right, a sheer rise on the left. Aspens stopped at the edge of the meadow. Towering telephone pole pines covered the mountain side to the tree line, except for a swath far to the right. That part of the slope was blackened and nearly bare. No, pine seedling has pushed above the charred ruins. Teddy found a dozen or more. "It'll grow back in no time," he said.

Mark smiled. "No time at all."

They climbed at an angle, away from the burned area. Pine needles and branches crackled under foot and made the going slippery. Several times Teddy slipped, and Mark caught him.

"Dad." Exasperation in his voice, Teddy wrinkled his nose and plopped his fists on his hips. "I'm all right. Really. I'm not going to break anything, you know."

"I know, but..." Mark spread his hands, scrunched up his shoulders, and gave a sheepish grin. "I just do it without thinking. Sorry."

"Well...well, okay." Teddy glanced up the mountain, then grinned. "Race you to the top."

"All right–hey, wait!"

Teddy was already charging up the slope, yards ahead. Mark leaped after him, scrambling over mossy stones and decaying pieces of trunks. He caught up with his son just above the tree line. Stubby grass covered the thin soil. Grass gave way to moss and lichens. They disappeared under a veil of snow.

"We're...almost...there," Teddy said, his words a white mist.

Mark just nodded. Even though he knew this was just a computer program, virtual reality, he felt tired; his feet, leaden. Just a bit farther, just a little more.

They reached the top as the sun hung low in the west.

"Dad," Teddy gasped, "we did it! We climbed the mountain! Look down there! The whole world! Hills and clouds and rivers and cities and oceans–all down there, and we're up here. Here at the top of the world. We did it. We did it." His voice faded 'til it was a whisper.

"Yes." Mark put his arm around Teddy's shoulders. "We did."

Teddy looked up at the blue sky, smudged nose now as red as his cheeks. His arm pressed close to his side, he bent his elbow and began to reach up, up, until his hand stretched high above his head, fingers grasping at the air.

A wisp of opaque white brushed his fingertips, and he jerked his hand back. "Oh-h-h!" He looked up at the sky, then grabbed Mark's arm. "Oh, Dad! Did I touch a cloud?"

Nodding slowly, Mark said, "You touched the sky, Teddy bear. You touched the sky."

Teddy's eyes shown brighter than sun on snow. "I touched the sky." He reached up again, fingers fluttering in the light breeze. "I touched the sky."

He dropped his arm to his side; his shoulders sagged. "Dad, I'm tired. I think I'd like to rest now. Could I just sit here for a while?"

"Sure," Mark said, his voice raspy from more than the cold mountain air. "We can stop the program now, if you want."

"No! No, I just want to sit here and look at the sky for a while."

Mark sat down on a flat slab of rock. "Sit on my lap. It's been a while since you've done that."

Teddy gave him a "I'm-too-big-for-that" look, but sat on his dad's lap anyway. Leaning back against Mark's shoulder, Teddy stared at the sky, a doleful smile on his chapped face. His eyelids drooped; he snapped them open. They drooped again. This time he didn't open them all the way. After struggling for a while, he closed them at last and snuggled against Mark's chest.

"I touched the sky," he murmured.

Arms wrapped around his son, Mark rocked him gently, humming the Teddy bear song, virtual tears freezing ice trails on his face.

Teddy bear, teddy bear, stamp your feet.
Teddy bear, teddy bear, clap the beat.
Teddy bear, teddy bear, reach up high.
Teddy bear, teddy bear, touch the sky.

A teeth-tingling click woke Mark. When he opened his eyes, Jason was standing beside him, the link cable coiled in his hand. All the room lights were on; curtains, closed tight.

Mark tried to speak, but his throat was tight, dry. Finally, he croaked out, "Teddy–how is he?"

Jason said nothing, just turned away.

Pushing up on his elbow, Mark gazed over at the other bed. Teddy lay there, a relaxed smile on his face. The cable link had been removed. Dr. Harrison stood beside the bed, dark circles under his eyes, wrinkles deeper than Mark remembered. Harrison reached for Teddy's vitals monitor, silent now, and pushed a white button. The green heartbeat line, the red LED pulse and respiration readouts all went black.

Mark rolled out of his bed, pulled off all the leads attached to him, and stumbled toward his son, legs unsteady and quivering. Teddy's hand still felt warm, alive, but the tick of Harrison's eyes and the trembling at the corners of his mouth told Mark it wasn't so. Sliding his arms under Teddy, Mark clutched him so tight, his own ribs ached. Or maybe not his ribs; maybe his heart. This time, real tears streaked his face.

"At least, he had his last wish," Harrison said softly. "And he wasn't in pain, was he?"

"No." Mark wiped his eyes on his sleeve. "He said he didn't feel any pain."

"That's what the readout said. Pain stopped as soon as the program began. Could you do that for other people?"

Mark was too exhausted and too hurt to think about it. "I don't know. Maybe."

"If you could, you'd end a lot of suffering. Just think about people crippled by arthritis, paraplegics and quadraplegics, people who've been injured or burned, children like Teddy. You could take away their pain and give them freedom they wouldn't have otherwise. You could grant wishes for the hopeless and dying. You could do for other children what you did for Teddy."

"I don't know!" Mark cried. "Later. Just not now, please!"

"All right," Harrison said gently and held up his hands. "We'll talk later." He turned to go, but stopped, reached across the bed, and touched Mark's shoulder. "I'm sorry."

Mark nodded, no words left. Harrison wheeled and strode from the room.

"I'm so sorry, Mark," Jason said as he packed away the cable links. "But Doc's right. Do for others what you did for Teddy. He'd want you to, you know that."

Mark looked down at his son. Yes, Teddy would want him to do it–take away some of the suffering in the world. Why not? "I'll do it for you, Teddy bear."

Jason halted, multi-jack unit in his hand. "That's it!"

"That's what?" Mark asked, puzzled.

"The Teddy Bear Project. That's what we'll call our new corporation."

The Teddy Bear Project. There couldn't be a better name. "All right," Mark whispered. "In his name."

Jason nodded, then pushed the computer equipment towards the door. "Uh, I'll just take this back to the office, then come back for you. Okay?"

"Okay."

Jason pushed the rolling cart to the hall and shut the door behind him.

It was quiet in the room. Mark smoothed Teddy's hair from his face. "I'm here, Teddy bear. Dad's here."

He picked up his son and rocked him, singing softly.

> Teddy bear, teddy bear, climb the stairs.
> Teddy bear, teddy bear, say your prayers.
> Teddy bear, teddy bear, turn out the light.
> Teddy bear, teddy bear, say good night.

Banana Oil

This was my first attempt at a short-short for MZB's Fantasy Magazine. I'm almost embarrassed to admit that this is partially based on an actual incident.

Cherry Boite had just arrived at Hanson's Lake when she heard the laughter, not nice laughter at that. She climbed off her bike, chained it to the bike rack, and ran toward the shore, her shoulder bag slapping her hip in time with her flopping sandals. She stopped beside some cottonwood trees at the edge of the beach.

Marcie Collins and Yvonne Lasalle, the two most conceited girls in eighth grade, were tossing a bent straw hat back and forth with a couple of boys, and laughing out loud. In the center of the group, trying to catch the hat, was Cherry's best friend Sue Parrish." Sue said as she lunged at Marcie.

"Like where did you get that ugly thing?" Marcie asked, holding the hat high out of Sue's reach. "Your dad bring that home from his garbage truck? Your mom steal it from one of the houses she cleans?" Marcie tossed the hat to one of the boys.

Sue ran toward the boy, who threw the hat to Yvonne. "Give it back" Sue yelled. Her face was so red, her freckles almost didn't show up.

Yvonne smiled as sweet as a rattlesnake. "You want it, garbage girl?" She waited until Sue had almost reached her, then Yvonne tossed the hat into the lake. "It's all yours."

Sue stared at the hat. Tears filled her eyes, and her bottom lip quivered.

"Well, go get it," Yvonne said.

Sue just hung her head.

"Hey, guys, why don't we, like, help her get her hat?"

"Sure thing," one sun-blond boy said.

The guys grabbed Sue's arms; Marcie and Yvonne each grabbed a leg.

"No!" Sue hollered and kicked, but it didn't do her any good. The four carried her to the lake and threw her in.

Sue splashed and sputtered and finally stood up in chest-deep water. Her soggy straw hat floated by. She grabbed it and held it up to let the water drain off. Even from where Cherry stood, she could see the hat was ruined. Sue slogged to the shore, ran across the hot sand to her beach towel, shoved all her stuff in a canvas bag, then ran for her bike. Her eyes were red, and Cherry could see tears running down her face.

Cherry started after her but knew Sue didn't want company right then. Furious and thinking of all the things she wanted to say to Marcie and Yvonne and the boys, Cherry thought of something her mother always said. "Don't get mad at stupid people. They aren't worth your time." Mama said lots of things like that. Things like: Drink lots of water, it's good for you. You don't have to use magic to get things done. Don't get mad at stupid people.

No, I won't get mad, Cherry thought, clenching her fists. *I won't get mad. I'll get even.*

She looked toward the beach. The boys had gone on down the lake shore. She'd take care of them later, maybe send poison ivy to curl around their bare legs. However, Marcie and Yvonne were still on the beach.

Marcie sat down and dumped the contents of her green and white canvas purse on her Aztec-print beach towel. "Great! I left my suntan oil at home!"

Yvonne collapsed on the towel beside her. "Oh, no! What are we going to do? This is, like, a major tragedy!"

Cherry watched from the cool shade of the cottonwood. Most people didn't look as upset when told a dear relative had died as those two girls did over suntan oil. Of course, Yvonne and Marcie probably didn't care about relatives much. They were Barbie dolls.

"You could use something else," Cherry called, putting on her calmest, friendliest face.

Yvonne and Marcie gave her a "how-dare-you-speak-to-us" glare and continued to sulk. They treated everyone with equal contempt. Cherry decided to try again. "There are things you could substitute for suntan oil."

"Really, tree freak?" Marcie asked sarcastically.

Yvonne cocked her head toward Cherry and smiled unpleasantly. "And what would 'nature girl' suggest?"

Tree freak. Nature girl. Yvonne and Marcie didn't know just how applicable those terms were. Plants talked to Cherry. She leaned against the rough bark and felt the tree sway, felt it growing, felt its life.

Yvonne and Marcie couldn't understand that. They'd thought it was amusing to fill Cherry's lunch tray with leaves and berries, and they'd been the instigators of the "poison-ivy-in-the-gym-clothe" incident.

Clearing her throat, Cherry forced a smile. "Do you have baby oil with you?"

Marcie sniffed disdainfully. "If we had some, we wouldn't need the suntan oil"

"What about hand lotion?"

"No."

"Any margarine in your picnic basket?"

Marcie shook her head.

Suddenly, an idea began to form in Cherry's head. "What about fruit?"

"Fruit?" Marcie looked at her, then at Yvonne, then they both stared at Cherry.

"Fruit," she repeated. "You know, oranges, lemons, something like that."

The girls looked puzzled.

"Why?" Yvonne asked.

"Some fruits have lots of oil in them," Cherry said. "Surely, you know that, don't you?"

They didn't reply, just looked at her skeptically.

"So do you have any fruit?"

Doubt narrowed their eyes, but they both nodded.

Yvonne opened the plastic cooler beside her towel and extracted a large bunch of yellow bananas. "Will these do?"

"Well..." Cherry played with a wisp of dark auburn hair that had escaped her French braid. "It'd be better if they were brown-speckled, but they'll work." She walked slowly toward them, sand sneaking inside her sandals. She knelt beside Marcie's towel. "First, eat the banana."

The girls glanced at each other, shrugged, and started to peel the fruit. It seemed half an hour before they'd finished nibbling.

"Okay," Cherry said. "Now take the peel and rub it all over your skin."

Marcie put the inside of the peel against her skin.

"No!" Cherry shook her head. "The outside, that's where the oil is."

They rubbed the banana peels all over. Marcie did Yvonne's back; Yvonne did Marcie's.

Cherry surveyed the girls carefully. "You're all set. The banana oil will do just as well as suntan oil. Just lay out and soak up the sun."

They didn't bother to say thanks. Walking back to the shade, she leaned back against the rough bark of the cottonwood. The trunk pulsed with life, breathing, reaching toward the sun. A cool breeze rustled the leaves, and white puffs of cottonwood fibers floated through the air like summer snow.

"Cherry Ann Boite, you should not have done that."

Cherry jumped to her feet as Mama's whispery voice came from behind her. Turning quickly, she watched as her mother materialized from the tree trunk. She wore a gossamer dress with a wreath of oak leaves on her head.

"Mama!" Cherry gasped and scanned the area anxiously. "Someone could've seen you!"

Her mother frowned at her, face like polished oak, eyes glinting angrily. "I'm a dryad, young lady, and I've had a lot more practice moving in and out of trees than you have." She planted her hands on her waist. "And that's not the point. You shouldn't have done that to those girls."

"But, Mama, they were so mean to Sue, to everyone! They deserved it!"

"Maybe, but that's still no excuse for your actions. You are grounded. I want you to go home immediately and go straight to your room. When you father hears about this..." Mama shook her head and pursed her lips.

Cherry nodded slowly. "I'm sorry. I know I shouldn't do things like this." She hung her head a moment, then looked back at her mother. "But you know, you were right about something."

Mama looked puzzled. "About what?"

Cherry looked at the two girls stretched out on their towels, their backs slowly turning lobster red, and she tried really hard not to grin. "You don't have to use magic to get things done."

Trick or Treat

My writing group sometimes would have everyone take a phrase or sentence and all of us write a story about it. This first sentence was our starting point. It's amazing how different writers can start with the same beginning and create completely different plots.

The first one came at three a.m.

Ellen heard quiet scratching at her front door, like a tiny dog trying to get in. Only thing was, Ellen didn't have a dog. Or a cat. Or family. Or anything to comfort her or brighten the silent house.

She'd fallen asleep on her pink-and-blue striped couch. No reason to go to bed. Tim wasn't there anymore. He hadn't been able to look at her, to stand the empty house, to bear the guilt that had driven him to alcohol and away from her.

A large bowl still filled with Halloween candy sat on the coffee table between her and the TV. No costumed children had come to her house that night. The cute little princesses and black-dressed witches, the cowboys and hobos, the Gypsies and Power Rangers, vampires and ghouls had all passed by without stopping.

Some old black-and-white Cary Grant movie played on the TV, although the sound was so low, she could barely hear the dialogue. Arsenic and Old Lace—that's what it was. She recognized Raymond Massey as the homicidal brother Jonathan.

The scratching again. Ellen sat up and shuffled to the door. She looked out the peep hole but saw nothing. "Must be the wind."

She started to turn away when she heard tiny nails scratching on the heavy wooden door. She undid the chain and turned the knob for the dead bolt when she heard a small, breathy voice.

"Trick or treat."

Ellen cracked the door open and looked out. Dried leaves swirled in the frosty breeze. Sycamore branches clattered against the roof. And there on her porch, silhouetted in the stark yellow street light, was a child, a little girl in a white satin and lace dress, a lace and tulle veil on her head like a bride or like she was dressed for her first communion. Just like—oh, no, please—just like little Jenny had been buried in.

Sounds—screeching brakes, screaming metal against metal and shrieks of pain—streaked through Ellen's head from the grave of her memory. "No," she whispered, clutching at her temples and squeezing her eyes shut. "Go away. Go away!"

Images bled from unhealed wounds—Tim's face streaked with blood, his eyes so filled with pain as he knelt beside their daughter, the paramedic covering Jenny's face with a sheet and shaking his head.

"Trick or treat," the girl said again.

Ellen opened her eyes and stared at the girl. "What--" Ellen's voice cracked. She swallowed and tried again. "What are you doing out at this time of night?"

"Halloweening."

"Sweetheart, that was over at nine. You shouldn't be out here by yourself. Where are your parents?"

"Gone. They left me all alone."

"Dear God," Ellen whispered. She opened the door wider. "What's your name, sweetheart?"

"Amy."

"You come on in here, Amy. I'll help you find your parents."

The little girl hesitated. "Mommy told me not to go in strangers' houses."

"Your mommy was right, but it's awfully cold out there. You must be freezing. You should've worn your coat. You could come in and warm up while I try to get help."

"I'm not cold," Amy said. She held out a tattered bag. "Trick or treat."

"But..." Ellen sighed, then smiled. "All right." She fetched the bowl from the coffee table and stuffed a handful of candy into Amy's bag. "There now. Come on in, and I'll try to find your parents." She set the bowl on a small half-moon table by the coat rack, but when she looked back at the front door, the little girl was gone.

"Amy!" Ellen rushed out on the porch and scanned the front yard frantically. "Sweetheart? Come back! You shouldn't be out here alone! Amy!"

The only reply was the whisper of leaves swirling on the sidewalk.

Ellen ran down the side to the back yard, calling Amy's name, around the other side and back to the front porch. "Amy! Come back!" She looked down the street, across and up the other direction. No sign of the girl. "Amy, please answer me! Let me help you!"

Only the wind—the cold, cold wind—answered. For a moment Ellen considered going to the neighbors for help but changed her mind. She was still a stranger there even after six months. She ran inside and straight back to the kitchen. She grabbed the portable phone from its cradle, hit the speed dial button for the police, and waited while the rings turned into recorded message. Suddenly, she heard scratching at her door again. She slammed the phone into the cradle and raced down the hall.

"Amy, why'd you run away?" She flung open the door, but Amy wasn't there.

Two little boys, dressed up as dirty ragamuffins, stood on the creaky porch, and each held out a grubby paper sack. One was half a head taller than the other. Both had purplish-black bruises around their eyes and splotched on their faces and hands. They even smelled as if they'd rolled in garbage. "Trick or treat," they both said.

"Oh, boys, have you seen a little girl in a bride costume?" Ellen stammered as she dropped candy in their sacks. "And what are you doing out at this time of night? It's way past your bedtime. You shouldn't be here."

"It's the only time we could come," the taller boy said. His voice was raspy and lisping.

"You should be home in bed. Come inside and I'll call your parents." Ellen took the shorter boy's hand. It felt cold, like holding a chunk of ice instead of flesh. A stench of rotting meat crept through the air. "What the..." Ellen gasped and jerked her hand back.

The two boys backed away, but behind them Ellen saw two more children trudging up the sidewalk. And across the street a group of five. And from the neighbor's yard three more. Children, children coming from everywhere.

"Trick or treat," they said. "Trick or treat, trick or treat."

"Oh, dear God, no," Ellen whispered, shaking, her eyes wide but threatening to tear up, as she backed away from the door.

Children shuffled across her lawn, dozens and dozens of children. Some so small they were barely able to walk, some just hitting their growing streak into adolescence, most just at the school age Jenny had been. Children, children everywhere, too many children.

Closer and closer they came, shuffling across the cold hard lawn. Children whose faces were ulcered and oozing, whose clothes were rotting and stained with yellow clay, who stank of worms and formaldehyde and death. Dead children, coming closer, coming to her, coming for her.

Ellen screamed and slammed the door, bolting it against them.

They kept coming, up the stairs, onto her porch, scratching at the door, scrabbling at the windows, pounding on the siding. "Trick or treat," the dead children murmured. "Trick or treat. Trick or treat!"

Ellen put her palms over her ears and pressed hard, trying to keep the voices out. "Go away!" she said.

"But we came for you," the children said. "We came for you."

"No! Go away!" Ellen ran to the kitchen, grabbed the phone, and dialed 911. There was silence on the line, no ring, no dial tone. The phone was dead, dead, just like the children. She clutched the phone, glanced frantically around, and shouted, "Go away! Leave me alone!"

The back door creaked, and the knob turned slowly. Ellen lunged for the chain and deadbolt, but the door opened before she could reach them. There stood little Amy, looking deathly pale in her bride's costume.

"Go away!" Ellen begged.

"We can't," Amy said softly.

Ellen dropped the phone and flattened against the wall. "Leave me alone! Leave me alone!"

"We can't." Amy walked toward her. Other children followed, dripping leaves and dirt and ichor across the white vinyl floor. "We can't," Amy repeated, shaking her head slowly.

"Please, please." Ellen edged back toward the living room, her back pressed against the dark wine wallpaper. "Please, go away. Go away." Fear rose like cold fire in her throat and fell like hot rain from her eyes. She tripped on the hall throw rug but didn't fall. "Go away!"

She darted for the front door, unbolted it and flung it open to flee, but her way was blocked by more children, all pressing to squeeze through the door. She shrank back as the children crept closer until she stood in the doorway of the living room.

"Please," she cried, arms clapped around her chest, shivering, "please, please, leave me alone!"

Amy stepped closer. "But you *are* alone. You are all alone."

"Go away, please, please."

Amy reached out to touch Ellen, but Ellen shrank back. Amy sighed. "Your loneliness called to us. You wanted children to come to you tonight, to stop at your house for candy, to make you feel you are still needed, didn't you? Didn't you?"

"Yes," Ellen whispered. "I wished...I wished they'd come to me."

"That's why we came to you. We heard your wish, felt your loneliness, and we came."

Ellen flinched and hugged herself for warmth. "Why? Why me?"

Amy looked up at her with dark, gleaming eyes. "Because..." She smiled, a sad tiny smile. "Because we know what being alone is. Because we need you as much as you need us. We need you. We're so lost and lonely. Please, let us stay."

Ellen's knees buckled, and she collapsed to the floor. Tears streamed down her face. She held her arms out to Amy, and the little dead girl rushed into Ellen's arms.

The other children surrounded Ellen. "Mommy," they said, "we won't leave you. We'll be here every night. We'll always love you." They hugged her, stroked her hair, touched her with their cold, cold hands.

Ellen hugged them back, her heart filled with joy. She had a house full of children who loved her, needed her, who would never go away. At last, she wasn't alone any more.

Proverbs

A friend of mine once told me, "You look like a sweet little grandma, but you have a dark side to you." This story comes from that dark side.

"A place for everything, and everything in its place," Grandma used to say. Even maggots. What would happen to the world if there were no maggots to take care of all the dead things? Decay is part of life, and maggots are efficient waste handlers. The government should pay farmers to raise maggots to break down the mounds of garbage choking this country.

Grandma knew lots of proverbs, and I learned them all in the years she raised me. "Cleanliness is next to godliness," and Grandma tried to make me as godly as possible. She used the same brush on me she used to scrub the hardwood floors in her house. I almost hated the bathtub by the time I was old enough to wash myself. Grandma was never satisfied unless my skin was red and raw, and smell like Castille soap.

I never could keep my room clean enough for her, no matter how hard I tried to please her. She always found a piece of lint or cobweb hiding in the back corner of my closet or my few blouses and skirts weren't hanging straight enough, or the quilt wasn't smooth on the bed. That's when she practiced another of her proverbs: "Spare the rod, spoil the child." She wasn't about to let me spoil so she beat me nearly every day.

I thought Grandma was like all parents, that she treated me the way mothers and fathers treated their children. However, by the time I reached fourth grade, I knew something was different about my family. Grandma never let me go to other kids' houses. I had to come straight home after school or Grandma used a limber maple rod on my legs. But I talked to my friends at school about their homes and families; theirs were happy, loving, nothing like mine. I didn't dare tell them about mine.

I wasn't allowed to go to the library, a movie, or play outside my high-fenced yard. I didn't get to watch TV until my teacher brought one to school to watch a special program on the educational channel. I was fascinated by the pictures. The only reason Grandma sent me to school was because Doc Gilson–and the law– said I had to go. Otherwise, Grandma might have kept me tied and gagged in my room all the time instead of just whenever she got angry. But at least that was when Mama whispered to me softly, comfortingly, told me she'd watch out for me, and I didn't feel so alone.

When I was almost ten, I asked Grandma why our family was so different from other families.

She looked at me with her flint-grey eyes and said, "You..." she emphasized the word, "are different. You were born evil." She paused, then whispered like the north wind through pines, "You killed your mother. You're a murderer."

Her words hit me like an iceberg. "No, no! Mama died in a car accident. That's what Doc Gilson told me. He wouldn't lie to me. Would he?" I looked up at Grandma, but she said nothing, just stared at me with eyes of ice. My lips quivered as I said, "Is that why you hate me so much? Because of Mama?"

"No," she said through gritted teeth. "Because you killed my daughter *and* my husband."

I swallowed past the tight lump in my throat and blinked back tears. Grandpa—yes, I'd forgotten that. He'd been driving Mama to the hospital the night I was born. The winding roads from Grandma's house to City Hospital had been snow-and-ice covered, and Grandpa's car had slid into a ditch. He'd been dead when someone found them. Mama died at the hospital, taking her last breath just after I'd taken my first.

"Bastard!" Grandma said. "You killed them both, but you'll pay for it, oh, yes, every day of your life, you'll pay for it. An eye for an eye, Linda Jean, and eye for an eye."

I ran to my room and sobbed into my pillow, terrified. And Mama whispered softly to me.

I never talked about Mama or Grandpa again. "Silence is golden," and Grandma and I settled int a silence that was heavier than gold, thicker than stone walls, punctuated by the maple rod, nights without supper, and her proverbial comments.

"Waste not, want not," when I pleaded for a new skirt for school, something that didn't come from the Salvation Army, that no one else had worn before. She called me ungrateful, then lengthened one of my old skirts.

"Idle hands are the devil's workshop" when I tried to write a story to enter in a state-wide short story contest for junior high students. She tore up the pages I'd written, then made me burn them in the fireplace.

"Early to bed and early to rise" when I asked to go to a play with my English class. Grandma refused to let me, even though the entire class was required to go.

I stayed home and reread one of my few books. And received an "F" from the teacher and a beating from Grandma for the bad grade.

"Pride goeth before destruction" when I wanted to have my long braided hair cut and curled for high school graduation. Grandma chopped the braid off with pruning shears. I didn't go to graduation.

"A bird in the hand is worth two in the bush" when I had to decide between a definite acceptance to a business school or an uncertain hope of college. Grandma told me I was too stupid to go to college, and I believed her. I didn't dare not believe her. I went to business school, putting away dreams of being a professional writer even though I still wrote. I just hid the notebooks from her.

And always, "An eye for an eye" and the maple rod for every hesitation to act, every failure to meet her demands, every look she didn't like. I deserved the rod. I must have or she wouldn't have beat me.

When I graduated from business school, I was lucky enough to land a secretarial job with Grant Paper Industries, a local company that supplied newsprint to publishers throughout the Midwest. My boss, Mr. Hartley, pleasant and often complimented me on my efforts. I cried the first time he did it, I was so grateful for his approval. I felt worth something, that I was needed and my work was important.

I bought a few new spring outfits for work, simple, yet becoming, and makeup–something Grandma had always forbidden. I almost changed my mind as the cashier was ringing it up, then a tiny spark of rebellion made me go through with it. After I left the store, terror grabbed my throat and I panicked. I'd sinned again, I knew it, and Grandma would beat me if she found the makeup. What could I do with it? The office–I could hide it there, and she'd never know. I could leave it in my desk...and go in early...and put it on there. I trembled, surprised that I'd dared defy Grandma. It was the second time in twenty-one years.

The next morning I told Grandma I had to be at the office early because my boss had given me extra work to do and that I might have to stay a little late to finish it.

She glared at me and said, "Hah. Probably just too stupid to get yesterday's work done on time. You won't keep this job more than a week at this rate."

I hung my head and shuffled out the door, anger swirling with self-doubt in my heart. By the time I reached the office, the warm spring sunlight had brightened my outlook, straightened my back, and made me smile again.

The makeup made me feel wicked, but the excitement warmed me inside, unlike the sun on my skin. I liked the extra color the foundation and blush gave me, the shade of the rose-pink lipstick, the way the mascara made my eyes seem larger. I almost looked...pretty.

Tom Cosgriff noticed something was different right away. He'd often smiled at me when he dropped off memos for my boss. This time he lingered and looked puzzled. "Did you cut your hair?"

I smiled and shook my head.

"New dress?"

"No."

"You look...like you got a promotion or something."

I laughed at that.

"Well, you look really nice today." He turned and went back down to his office.

My heart fluttered, and I savored the feeling. The day went so fast, I was surprised when it was time to go home. I scrubbed the make up off and headed home.

"You're late," Grandma said when I opened the door. "Supper's over, and there's nothing left for you."

I didn't say anything. Whatever I'd have answered, would bring the maple rod across my back. I hurried to my room, hoping she wouldn't come after me. Luckily, she didn't. Mama whispered that everything was all right.

I went to work early every day to put on the makeup and stayed late to take it off. Tom came by my desk even when he didn't have memos to give me. He asked me to have lunch with him, which I did–often. He wasn't the only one to ask. Mike from advertising, John from shipping, Gary from accounting, all stopped to talk to me and ask about lunch. But Tom–Tom's company was more enjoyable than all the others. He made me laugh, and there had been so little laughter in my life.

One day he asked me to dinner. I didn't care where, it didn't make any difference. I just wanted to be with him. But Grandma's shadow loomed before me, holding the maple rod and the ropes she tied me with, her gaze as cold as midwinter's night, he hate hot as hell. Afraid of her, afraid for him, I told him I couldn't.

His smile thinned a bit, and he lowered his deep blue eyes. "Oh," he said and slowly turned away.

It hurt so hear the disappointment in his voice. "Wait!" I touched his arm, startled at my boldness. "Please, ask me another time. I just can't today."

He gazed at me a moment, then smiled again. "All right. Another day."

As he returned to his office, I tried to concentrate on my work. It wasn't easy. He'd asked me for a date! I'd never dated. Grandma hadn't let me. Boys were evil, she said, and I was worse. She'd kept tract of how long I took to get home from school so I wouldn't get into trouble–whatever she meant by that. Tom wasn't evil, I was sure. He was the kindest person I knew. But I couldn't let Grandma find out about him. She might do something, I didn't know what, to drive him away. I wouldn't let that happen. Somehow, I was going to have dinner with him.

It was several weeks before Tom asked me again. This time I said yes, as long as it was right after work. I was afraid to stay out too late, afraid of what Grandma might do to me. Tom smiled and suggested a cozy café two blocks from the office. I nodded, my throat too dry, my heart to full to speak.

"Meet you right here at five," he said.

I nodded again. He winked and went back to his office.

The rest of the afternoon was a blur of shuffled papers, ringing phones, and file folders. My boss discussed something with me, but I had no idea what we talked about. Then Tom stood in front of my desk, holding out his hand.

"Ready?" he said.

I clutched my purse, stood up, and said, "Yes."

The café was warm and dim, filled with the scent of old wood and fresh herbs. I don't remember what I ordered, something with chicken, but I'd never had a better meal. It was hot and savory, and best of all, shared with someone kind.

Tom talked about his hopes to finish his Batchelor degree in business, his plans to start a company of his own someday, his hobbies, the weather, until at last he said, "I don't know anything about you."

Surprised, I dropped my fork. It rang loudly on the heavy stoneware plate, then clattered to the floor. What could I tell him? About Mama? About Grandma? About the rod and ropes and beatings? "I, uh, that is, well, there's really nothing to know."

"You like your job, don't you?"

"Oh, yes, it's simply wonderful!"

We discussed our bosses, the way the company was thriving, and the office gossip. I laughed as Tom did a perfect imitation of the office gigolo. God, it felt good to laugh.

"So what do you do for fun?"

"Well," I hesitated. I'd never told anyone so much about myself. "I write sometimes."

His eyes twinkled deeper blue. "Really? Ever had anything published?"

"Of course not," I said, shaking my head. "They're no good."

"Who says?"

I started to answer, "Grandma," but that would've led to other things I didn't want to talk about. "No one. No one else has seen them."

"Would you let me read them?"

"Maybe. Sometime. I'll have to think about it."

"What about your family?" He leaned his elbow on the table and propped his rounded chin in his hand.

I took a drink of the ice tea. It wasn't nearly as cold as the lump of fear in my stomach. "I, uh, live with my grandmother."

"Your mom and dad?"

"My mom died when I was born."

"And your dad?"

I took another drink. "I don't know."

"Divorced?"

"No," I said, staring at the table, "they were never married." My lips quivered, I swallowed hard, then said what Grandma always said, "I'm a bastard."

There was silence, and when I looked up at him, there was wide-eyed shock on his lean face. I wanted to hide, run away. Then he touched my hand and said, "I'm sorry. I shouldn't pry. And you shouldn't feel ashamed about something you had no control over. It doesn't matter." He gave me a tiny smile. "I like you a lot." He ran his index finger down my cheek, then smoothed the tear away with his thumb. And I fell in love with him.

He drove me home, well almost home. I insisted he let me off at the end of our lane where the transit but usually stopped. I didn't want him anywhere near Grandma. He argued that it was dangerous for me to be walking a mile alone in the dark. I told him I walked it every day and that he shouldn't worry. Finally, he let me go.

Stars popped out of the darkening sky. They didn't shine nearly as bright as Tom's eyes. The breeze was so cool, it raised goosebumps on my arms, but I barely felt it. I was warm inside, as if my heart had been wrapped in a blanket.

When I reached the house, I skipped up the porch steps, pushed open the door, and went inside, still warm and happy.

"Where've you been?" Grandma yelled as she slapped my face. "The last bus came by over an hour ago!"

She clutched my arm and dragged me into the living room where every light and lamp glared like a spotlight in my eyes, and flung me on the couch. I shrank back against the worn upholstery. Grandma had the maple rod in her hand. She started to speak, then her eyes narrowed and her jaw tensed.

"Your face! What—!" She swiped her hand across my mouth, then stared at her palm. "Makeup. Makeup!"

Oh, God, I'd forgotten to take it off! "Grandma, please," I said, cringing.

"You slut!" She slashed at my head. She only hit my arms because I'd crossed them in front of me, but it stung like fire, like acid. "Where were you?" She hit me again. "Where?" she screamed. "You were with a man, weren't you?" Another blow. "Weren't you!"

"Please! Don't!" I begged as I twisted, rolled, tried to block the blows. "I didn't do anything!"

"Evil! Evil!" she said again and again. Each word brought another blow, more agony. Blood began to ooze down my arms, seep through my dress. Bones snapped in my fingers. Ribs cracked. My head spun. My vision has yellow spots, then black spots, then I heard Mama whispering as I sank through a red-grey haze to unconsciousness.

I woke to curtain-filtered light but couldn't focus my eyes. Two glass light fixtures hung from the ceiling overhead where there should've been only one. The ceiling–I was looking up. I had to be on my back. I turned my head. Pain screamed from every muscle in my body. I tried to scream, too, but acid burned up my throat, spilled across my shoulder, and onto the bed.

Grandma had tied me to my bed. I could see welt and clotted blood on my arm, my foot. Blood left rust-brown stains on the sheet. I couldn't be sure how many there were–everything looked doubled–but I knew Grandma had never beaten me so severely before. It hurt to breathe. Each time I did, I heard or maybe felt, a gurgling in my chest. I was cold, so cold, and my stomach convulsed again, leaving my throat raw. I closed my eyes.

When I opened them again, the room was darker. It must've been afternoon. My window only got morning sun.

I heard the phone ring and ring and ring. Finally, it stopped. I heard Grandma's voice cutting though the ringing in my head.

"Yes. No, she won't be in tomorrow. Yes, she's ill. I have no idea. Good bye."

I heard hard shoes on hard wood floors. Grandma hovered over me like a grinning vulture.

"Your office called," she said. "They wanted to know why you weren't at work." She chuckled. "You won't ever go back. I'll see to that."

"No!" I said in hoarse whisper.

She punched my jaw, my eyes rolled back, and I passed out again.

I woke off and on, not knowing if minutes or days had passed. Probably hours. Otherwise, my stomach would've been gnawing me with hunger. I strained at the ropes binding my wrists and ankles to the bed until I was covered with cold sweat from the pain. I tried again, then panted for breath. The rope around my ankle loosened a little or maybe I wanted to believe it was looser. Mama urged me on. God, it hurt so much to move, but I didn't stop trying. I had to get free. If I didn't, Grandma would kill me.

Night came and went while I struggled to free myself, dozing when I was too tired to keep trying. My stomach growled. I felt light-headed. My breathing was raspy, and movement was painful. I had to get free before I became too weak.

Sunlight stumbled through the curtains. My mouth was dry, my lips were cracked, and I hurt all over. It was hopeless. I'd never be free. Grandma was going to watch me die, and there was nothing I could do about it.

The phone rang. "Yes?" Grandma said. "Who? Tom Cosgriff?"

"Tom!" I yelled with all the strength I had left, praying my voice would carry down the hall. "Tom, help me!"

"Shut up, slut!" Grandma yelled back. There was silence for a moment. "Tom, is it? Is he the one you've been whoring with? He is, isn't he?" She chuckled, low and malevolent. "I'm sorry, Tom. Linda's out of her head with fever. I'm not sure she'd know you were here, but if you want to visit, come this evening." She paused. "Of course. See you then."

I heard a click, then Grandma walked down the hall. She stood in my doorway, her smile as kind as a crocodile. "He didn't hear you," she said. "I covered the phone. But your lover will be here after work, about six o'clock. Then, Linda Jean, and eye for an eye."

"No, please," I said. "Don't hurt him. Don't hurt him."

She laughed as she stuffed a rag in my mouth and gagged me.

All day long I twisted and pulled at the ropes, loosening them bit by bit, while I watched the light through the window dim to afternoon, to early evening. Mama told me to hurry, not to give up, to keep trying. *Tom, don't come, don't come,* I prayed.

Shadows filled the room when Grandma opened my door and snapped on the light. "Your friend should be here soon," she said. "Very soon."

I strained at the ropes. Grandma laughed, left and closed the door behind her. I thrashed against the bindings, ignoring the blood oozing from my raw wrists, the rope tearing at my ankles. I had to get free to save Tom.

Wait–the rope around my left ankle broke! I tried to wedge my big toe between my other ankle and the rope around it. Wiggle, push, wiggle, push, I forced my toe under the rope, cringing as I touched the open sores. *Faster, faster,* Mama told me. The rope stretched a bit, a bit more, and still more. Gripping it between my big toe and the next one, I tried to slide it down over my heel. Strain, relax, pull, pant, pull again, inch it down until the rope whipped over my heel to my arch.

Suddenly, I heard a car crunching on the gravel road. *Tom! No, don't come in! Not yet!* I had to get loose, to warn him!

I pulled my foot out and scooted back until I was leaning against the headboard. I tried to roll the gag down with my shoulder, but Grandma had tied it too tight. I pulled my right arm down. The bones in my hand compressed, grinding as I tried to force it through the rope. *Hurry,* Mama said. *Don't stop.*

I heard the front door open. Tom's voice, Grandma's voice. Oh, God, no! I yanked, pulled, squeezed my hand through a bit more. Footsteps coming down the hall. Tom and Grandma talking. The rope was nearly over the first knuckle of my thumb. My hand slipped out. I pulled at the gag as the doorknob turned. The door opened.

Tom stood in the doorway, gaping at me. "What the hell's going on?"

I pulled the rag from my mouth and shouted, "Tom, look out!"

Tom screamed and stumbled into the room. Behind him I saw Grandma with a bloody carving knife in her hand. I yanked at the last rope. I had to get free, had to help Tom!

Grandma leaped at his back and stabbed him over and over, howling, "An eye for an eye!"

Tom twisted and brought up his arm to block the knife. Grandma slashed his upper arm, and when he jerked his arm down, she stabbed him in the throat.

I shrieked pulled with all the strength I had left. The metal headboard creaked, bent. The rope snapped. I scrambled from the bed, grabbed my metal lamp from the night stand, and slammed it down on Grandma's head. She groaned and staggered away from Tom's body toward the door. I hit her again. She turned and stabbed at me, but missed. I bashed her face in. Blood poured from her broken nose, her split lips. She stabbed at me again. Her wrist gave a stomach-wrenching crack as the lamp struck it. She screamed and dropped the knife.

Kill her, Mama said. *Kill her now!*

"An eye for an eye!" I said as I beat her to the ground with the lamp. It felt good to hit her, see fear in her face, hear her cry in pain. Sweat poured down my face. My heart pounded in my chest. And I felt powerful and more alive than I'd ever felt in my life. "An eye for an eye!"

I kept hitting her with the lamp until she was a bloody broken doll twisted on the floor. I wanted to howl in triumph.

You're free, Mama whispered to me.

Yes, I was free of Grandma. I laughed. I cried. I danced around her body. She couldn't hurt me anymore.

I stumbled to Tom's body. Blood still oozed from his arm and throat. His eyes gazed up at me, shiny as sapphires, but there was no life in them. My Tom. She'd killed him, and I hated her for it. Just as she'd hated me for killing Grandpa. And now I understood her hate.

The next day I buried Tom in the woods behind my house–it was *my* house now, not Grandma's. I buried him among the maple and oak trees, and transplanted wild white violets from nearby to cover his grave. I drove his car to an abandoned quarry a few miles away, removed the license plates, and pushed the car into the acid pool. I walked back to the house, destroyed Grandma's will, and forged Grandma's signature on the deed. Mama whispered how resourceful I was.

I tamped dirt firmly around the young plants I bought at the nursery, stood, and wiped my hands on the thighs of my old jeans. The new flower bed in the front yard looked neat and well planned, edged with quartz and limestone rocks. I could almost see the maggots turning Grandma into fertilizer for the marigolds, moss rose, scented geraniums, and irises. No funeral expenses, no coffin, no grave site and expensive upkeep.

"A penny saved is a penny earned." Grandma would have been proud of me.

Grave Blanket

I always see signs for grave blankets and grave pillows at nurseries and florists in late fall, and I couldn't understand who thought up with that idea. Blanket for the dead? Why? I came up with my own reason.

"Excuse me, but aren't you Jenny Roberts?"

The gentle, whispery voice startled me so much, I nearly dropped the flower arrangement I'd just finished. I hadn't heard my shop bell ring as it did when someone opened the door. In spite of my surprise, I recognized the voice. Setting the ceramic bowl on the counter, I turned toward the old woman. "Mrs. Lewis! I haven't seen you since I came back to Whitehall."

I hugged her. She felt thin and fragile, although she'd never been large. She seemed to have shrunk, or perhaps I'd grown taller, because she barely reach my shoulders. Other than that, she seemed the same: white hair wound at the nape of her neck, blue dress with a white handkerchief tucked in the belt at her waist, straw sun hat shading her pale blue eyes.

Mrs. Lewis patted my cheek, and her beige lips formed a thin smile. "I'd heard you'd come home. Since your parents sold their house and moved away, I've missed you."

"I'm sorry," I said with a guilty laugh. "I've been so busy trying to get settled in my new apartment and taking over this flower business, I haven't taken time out for anything else."

"Why don't you come over for supper after work today?" she said, her metal-framed glasses resting on smile-puffed cheeks. "We could have a long talk about what you've been doing since you left town."

"Well..." I thought for a moment. If I went home, I'd probably just throw something in the microwave and eat in front of the TV. It would be nice to share a meal with someone for a change. "Why not? I'd love to."

"Good. I'll see you at seven." She started to leave, then she turned back. "Oh! I nearly forgot. I need a grave blanket."

"A grave blanket?"

She nodded. "For Henry's grave."

"Oh, was he a relative?"

She frowned slightly, and her chin drooped a little. "He was my second husband. Actually, I'm Mrs. Henry Stiles now. I married him four years ago. He died two months ago."

"Oh, I'm so sorry!"

She held up a bony hand. "I'm all right. But I promised him a grave blanket. He always complained his feet were cold. Said when he died, he wanted a blanket to keep him warm." An odd smile pulled lines at the corners of her mouth, and her eyes seemed unfocused. "He believed he'd still be aware of things even after death. Believed in lots of psychic thing." She was silent for a long time, then gave a long deep sigh.

I cleared my throat and asked, "When do you need it?"

She looked startled. "Oh. A few days. Friday would be soon enough."

"No problem."

"We can discuss the details tonight at supper."

I raised an eyebrow. Grave blankets weren't usual table conversation. "Sure, that'll be fine. Seven?"

She nodded. "It certainly is good to see you again, Jenny. I'll be looking for you tonight. I have a whole jar full of oatmeal cookies I just baked this morning." She winked, then shuffled out.

Oatmeal cookies. She'd remembered my favorite kind. Happiness for me always included memories of splashing in the creek during hot Illinois summers, crunching dry autumn leaves beneath tennis shoes, and stuffing my cheeks with oatmeal cookies from Mrs. Lewis' kitchen.

The rest of the day I barely kept my mind on my work: thirty corsages for the Friday night senior prom, flowers for a Saturday wedding, and four "Congratulations on the new baby" arrangements to be sent to the hospital. And just as I was about to lock the shop door, a red-faced man puffed in and begged a dozen roses for a nearly forgotten anniversary. He left, bouquet in hand and thanking me sincerely. I smiled to myself as I turned out the lights and locked the door.

The late May sun was nearly two hours from setting, and the air was pleasantly warm and fragrant. I don't even remember driving to Mrs. Lewis' house–I couldn't think of her as Mrs. Stiles–but soon my rust-red ten-year-old station wagon pulled into her driveway. I guess the way was so much a part of me, I didn't need to concentrate on my driving.

As soon as I stepped out of the car, I realized the house had changed, or rather the yard had changed. There were no flowers anywhere. No roses, iris, hens-and-chicks, no flowers at all. Just grass and two of the ugliest pink plastic flamingos I'd ever seen. I had to glance next door at the house I'd grown up in to be certain I was in the right place.

Mrs. Lewis' flowers had been her pride and obsession. She'd won first prize year after year at the local and state horticultural shows. I remembered helping her with the planting weeding, and cultivating from the time Mama had let me leave my own yard. Mrs. Lewis had given me her love of growing things. Gazing about the neat but barren lawn, I couldn't understand what had happened.

The front door opened, silhouetting the small figure in the shirtwaist dress. "Oh, good. I thought I heard you drive up," Mrs. Lewis said. "Come in. I have some tea ready for us."

Almost numb with surprise, I walked up the stone path to her screened-in porch. I hoped when I entered the house, things would be more familiar, more as I remembered, but I was disappointed. The furniture was the same, but there were no plants anywhere. The ancient philodendron that had formed a living curtain over the double windows behind the couch was missing. The waxy-leaved gardenia no longer perfumed the air. The fuchsias, bromeliads, African violets, gloxinias, begonias, and all her other potted plants were gone, too. The house felt naked, deserted, abandoned.

"What happened?" I said sadly.

Mrs. Lewis gave me a sad smile. "Henry didn't like my tending to the flowers and plants, didn't like plants at all. He insisted I get rid of them when we got married."

I just stared at her incredulously. "But they were yours! He had no right to make you get rid of them!"

Patting my cheek, Mrs Lewis shook her head. "Maybe not, but he gave me a lot in return. Companionship. I wasn't alone anymore. And he was a real joker. Loved to play tricks on me, and I even learned to play jokes on him. We had some good times, Henry and me."

I glanced around the room again. Books lined all the shelves where plants once sat. Books on ghosts, tarot, telepathy, prophesy, Nostradamus, déjà vu, spiritism, life after death–especially life after death. Seemed his obsession. Without even knowing him, I didn't like him. After all, anyone who didn't like plants ...

I realized my mouth was hanging open, so I closed it and swallowed hard. I followed her into the kitchen and sat at the same wooden table where I'd sat all those years ago. Mrs. Lewis had made all my favorite foods. While we ate, we talked about what I'd been doing, where my brother was, all the places Mom and Dad had visited since retiring. Eventually, I asked about the grave blanket.

Mrs. Lewis chewed her lip thoughtfully. "Oh, I suppose whatever is usual."

"Greenery? Flowers?"

"Flowers." Mrs. Lewis paused, eyes sparkling like leprechaun gold. A warm-from-the-oven grin spread across her face. "Make it roses. Lots of red roses."

"But I thought your husband didn't like flowers," I said around a mouthful of beef stroganoff.

Mrs. Lewis tapped the corner of her mouth with her index finger. "Oh, he didn't. But I'm going to give him some anyway."

"Of course, he won't really care now." I choked. How could I be so insensitive? "Oh, I'm sorry! I didn't mean it like that."

Her quiet chuckle surprised me. "Don't worry, Jenny. I know what you meant." She paused and cocked her head. "And you might be surprised."

"About what?"

She shook her head and wouldn't elaborate. Instead, she recalled all the scraped knees and sunburned noses I'd had, all the good times we'd spent together. By the time we'd talked ourselves out, it was nearly one a.m. he gave me a hug at the door and told me to be careful.

"I'll call your Friday when the grave blanket is finished. We can talk about price then."

"Oh, don't forget these." She gave me a plastic container full of the promised oatmeal cookies to take home. "Good night, Jenny."

The next two days were hectic. Orders for thirty corsages and four large flower arrangements came in Wednesday; six more arrangements, two "Get Well" bouquets, and three "Happy Anniversary" planters on Thursday. Friday morning I got a frantic call from a woman who asked if there were any way I could provide flowers for her daughter's wedding–that night! The other florist in town was supposed to make all arrangements and bouquets but had confused the dates and couldn't provide everything on such short notice.

After I'd taken the order for the bridal bouquet and the altar flowers, I suddenly realized I hadn't even begun on the grave blanket. I skipped lunch and worked straight through 'til closing, finished all the orders just as the harried mother of the bride ran into the shop. She was so red-faced and upset, I offered her a glass of lemonade, which she accepted gratefully.

"Look, you take the bouquet with you," I said. "I'll bring the rest to the church in a few minutes. Will someone be there to let me in?"

She smoothed a reddish-brown curl from her glistening forehead. "Yes. And thank you so much! I was just about at my wit's end!"

She paid me, thanked me again for the drink, and left.

Wishing I could afford an assistant, I loaded my station wagon with all the orders, washed up, and changed clothes. I locked up the shop and began deliveries. When only the grave blanket remained, I headed to Mrs. Lewis' house.

She was waiting on the screened porch for me. She was dressed in a pearl grey linen suit and wide-brimmed white hat she'd always worn to church. A blue and white cameo was pinned at the throat of her grey silk blouse. I felt grungy compared to her, even though I was wearing a tailored white cotton blouse and navy skirt.

"Ready?" I asked.

She nodded and slipped on white gloves.

I opened the car door for her. "Which cemetary?"

"Oak Street."

Whitehall had three cemeteries. Oak Street was the smallest and newest of them. When we arrived, we walked through two rows of headstones in a newly opened sections, so new it didn't have trees or shrubs planted around the perimeter. Mrs. Lewis pointed out her husband's grave, a solitary mound of dirt apart from the other graves and with no headstone yet.

It hadn't been easy to get the grave blanket into the station wagon without smashing the flowers. It was even harder to get it out. My hair fell in my eyes, but I managed to get the blanket to the grave. I spread it over the dirt, then stood back as Mrs. Lewis walked to the head of the grave.

"The flowers are beautiful," she said and sighed as she gazed down at the thick carpet of red roses. "I'm going to miss Henry. He was such a practical joker. My life wasn't dull with him. My one regret is that I never was able to pull a truly marvelous joke on him." She smiled, the late afternoon sun blushing her beige skin. "Here it is, Henry, just like I promised. Now your feet won't be cold anymore."

I wondered if Mrs. Lewis was perhaps a little senile.

Suddenly, I heard a sound–almost like a sneeze. Then again, this time stronger. The third time was accompanied by a mist above the grave. I wondered if I were just imagining it, then it happened again.

"Vivien!" A voice, a man's voice, wheezed from the ground. "You know...achoo...I'm allergic...achoo...to roses!"

Mrs. Lewis knelt beside the grave and patted it. With an impish smile, she said, "Yes, Henry. I know."

Human Night at Drek's Place

Many years ago, our writers group tried to put together an anthology of stories of collective nouns of fantasy creatures. We had commitments from numerous well known writers as well as all members of the writing group, and we were going to call it A Phylum of Fantasy. I wrote this story but called it "A Club of Ogres." Unfortunately, we could never sell the anthology, but I still have hopes we will someday.

The lighted sign above the grey-green door read "Drek's Place." Of course, most patrons of the nightclub never looked beyond the pictures below the words: a fanned deck of cards, a joint of blood red meat, and a huge brass tankard. Most ogres didn't read a lot.

It was Friday night, a lousy time to be working. Usually, I went home when the St. Louis County Health Department closed at 5 p.m. Not today.

My boss had called me into his office and said, "Calvin, I'm getting heat from city hall about this food poisoning case so I need you to work overtime tonight."

"Oh, no, not tonight," I said. "I've got plans this weekend."

"Sorry, but if we don't solve this case, we might find our budget cut, and I'd have to lay off someone." My boss just stared at me.

"And that someone would be me."

He shrugged. "I didn't say that."

"You didn't have to." I cursed under my breath. "Fine, I'll check into it."

He gave me his "I-love-my-job" smile. "I knew I could depend on you."

That's why I was sweating in the August heat in downtown St. Louis.

The main door was much taller than me, and I was tall for a human—nearly seven feet if I stretched to my full height. I had to go through the "cat door"; that's what the ogres called the human entrance.

The large main room was crowded, usual for a Friday—human night at Drek's. Bored, rich folks from uptown came to watch from the glassed-in balcony, specially ventilated to keep out the odor of the dining room below. Smelled like a cross between a meat packing plant and a locker room. It'd taken me a while to get used to the aroma myself.

Punk rock music poured from the adjoining dance hall, vibrating through the polished stone floor. I'd only gone in there once, out of curiosity, but never again. Ogres slam dancing is a terrifying sight.

I walked to the bar, climbed up the rungs on the side of the stool, and looked around for Drek. Right next to me, an ogre was eating the last shreds of raw meat from a yellowish bone the size of my arm. I shuddered and turned away.

I couldn't imagine any ogre filing a food poisoning complaint, considering what ogres ate. The longer the meat sat, the better they liked it. I wondered what could make them sick. As for humans, the ones who came here were served wholesome, home-cooked food like Mother never made. Drek hired only first rate cooks, and his place had always surpassed health standards.

Drek came in from the kitchen, face like a dried apple doll: brown and puckered. His eyes were deep-set, as black as sewers at midnight. Sparse bristles on his head and arms were brown-black. He grinned when he saw me, steely teeth gleaming in the track lighting overhead.

"Where you been keepin' yourself, Cal?" He twisted a bottle of Busch beer and poured some in an etched glass mug he kept for me. "Hungry?"

"No, not tonight." I sipped the cold beer. It tasted heavenly, though I shouldn't have been drinking on the job.

"Got a special." Drek rested his forearm on the bar and leaned towards me. "Grilled brook trout, shipped in this morning from out west."

I licked my lips. Brook trout–he knew my weaknesses. Had to eat some place tonight, so why not here? "Potato salad?"

Teeth gleaming, he nodded. "And fresh peach pie."

That was the clincher. On the job or not, I couldn't turn down Drek's peach pie. "You betcha," I said. "Uh, I need to talk with you in private."

"Business or pleasure?"

"Business." I motioned him down where I could whisper in his hairy ear. "Someone registered a complaint against this place. Food poisoning."

"What?" he roared, nearly knocking me off the stool. "What offspring of a degenerate dragon would dare—"

"Drek!" I cut him off. Glancing around the room, I signaled quiet, then whispered, "You don't want everyone here to know about this, do you?"

"No," he growled.

"I'd rather keep it quiet, too. All right?"

"Sure, Cal. Come on back to my quarters."

I walked around the end of the bar and followed Drek to the rooms he called home.

"Sit down. I'll get your meal." Drek disappeared through a door connecting to the kitchen.

I climbed the short spiral stair to the table and chair on a platform he'd built for me. Put me up high enough we could talk face to face.

Ogres were the first genetically engineered, bigger-than-a-bread life form. Monsanto Corporation of St. Louis had been playing with DNA in bones found in several of the thousands of caves in Missouri. The company had patented the new life form, calling it "ogre" because of its size. The Pentagon had contracted for ten, hoping ogres would be the perfect soldiers. Let's just say they fell far short in all categories except size and strength.

Twenty years after the first ogres left the labs for boot camp, the ACLU filed suit on five ogre's behalf. By the time the U. S. Supreme Court ruled that under the 13th Amendment the ogres could not be owned or patented, there were almost one hundred ogres living in the good ol' U. S. A.

Drek and I have been friends since childhood, both outcast. I was also the tallest human in the class. I was clumsy, couldn't play basketball at all, and shunned because I made straight "A"'s.

A fourth generation ogre, Drek's problem had been a lot like mine, smartest ogre on the block, probably in the whole world. But all his siblings were over eighteen feet tall. Drek was only twelve, a midget ogre. He'd continued school long after other ogres quit at age ten. Construction and sanitation work were top of the heap for ambitious ogrelings. Drek had wanted more from life.

I'd wanted to work with people and animals, something in the health field, but not medicine. Drek had wanted to be an investment banker. I got my dream. Drek didn't. He had a Masters in business, but no one trusted him–and ogre–to invest their money. So Drek bought part of an old warehouse and created the most popular ogre club in the city.

I glanced around the room. Drek lived simply, neater than most ogres, and alone. Surprisingly, since ogres usually lived in extended family groups. Sometimes several generations sharing a large apartment. I wondered if Drek wanted to marry and have a family. Of course, there weren't too many midget ogre women around. None that I knew of.

I suppose I should've been cautious about eating at a place accused of food poisoning, but I wasn't. Drek's was actually more sanitary than most of the ritzy human restaurants I inspected regularly. Besides, if I got sick from eating anything

Drek served me, well, let's just say I wouldn't want to be the guy who prepared my meal. Drek would probably break the guy in half.

Drek came back with a table-sized tray loaded with potato salad, savory green beans, and pan-fried trout. A whole peach pie and another bottle of Busch completed the feast. "Now, what's this nonsense about food poisoning?" he asked. "Who in the world would claim I poisoned them?"

"I can't give out the name, sorry." I licked a dab of potato salad from the corner of my mouth. "I think it's more a fluke than anything. A woman filed a complaint after she was admitted to Riverfront Hospital very early Thursday. Blood tests indicated salmonella. She claims she was fine until after she ate here Wednesday night."

"I run a clean place, you know that. I've never had customers get sick. I wouldn't put up with it."

"I know. Strange thing is, there've been no other cases reported. The chances of only one person getting food poisoning are almost nil, so I think you're in the clear no matter what. But I still have to do a complete investigation anyway, for your sake as much as anything else."

Drek sighed. "No problem, I understand. When do you want to start?"

"How about after I finish this fantastic food?" I forked a bite of trout.

"Fine with me."

"After I inspect the kitchen and interview the cooks and servers, I'll need to look at your employee records."

"They're in the office."

"I'll be out of your way quick as I can."

"Take your time. You don't come here as often as you used to." Drek grinned. "Been spending time with that lady cop? What's her name—Sarah, Sonya, Cindy?"

"Sam," I said. "And you know her name as well as you know mine."

"She's such a cute little thing." Drek grinned wider.

Detective Sergeant Samantha Kinnerly might be called cute—never to her face—but "little" wasn't a words anyone but an ogre would apply to her. She was 6' 4", and as strong as an angel-dust addict. I'd been seeing her for about six months, the first serious relationship I'd ever had. Drek had us married already, whether I was ready for it or not.

I took my time with the meal. It was too good to rush through. But eventually, I did get around to doing my job. Drek's kitchen was all stainless steel shine and hospital clean, cleaner in fact, except for a splat of spaghetti sauce on the floor. I startled Jimmy Glauck, an assistant cook, when I walked in with my notebook and inspector's badge, and he'd spilled som sauce as he was ladling it onto hot pasta. Jimmy paled as he looked from me to the red sauce on the floor. Took half a heartbeat before he called for a clean up.

I looked in the usual places, took scrapings and food samples, and checked obvious things. Knives were washed thoroughly between uses. Cutting boards were scrubbed with disinfectant. Hands were washed with antibacterial soap between tasks. Produce was washed and refrigerated promptly. The place used pasteurized eggs, like most restaurants, to eliminate contamination. Chicken and other poultry were cooked completely. I couldn't see how salmonella bacteria could've gotten into any food prepared there, but I'd have to wait for the lab results.

I questioned the staff, much to their annoyance. "We're working!" said Guy Hartley, the head cook. "Can't you come back after we close?"

"No, I'm sorry. I have to do this now. Are there any of the staff who aren't here tonight?"

"No." Guy swirled a skilletful of beef and vegetables. "Everyone works Fridays."

"Who was working Wednesday?"

"Everyone here."

"Has anyone started here, say, in the last week or two?"

"No! Would you please let me do my work?"

"Sorry. I'm not doing this to irritate you. It's for your protection and Drek's. By the way, the trout and peach pie were delicious."

Guy stopped stirring long enough to look pleased, then his masterpiece started to smoke. "Get out! Get out! It's ruined! Ruined!" He began cursing like a sailor.

I left quickly.

Drek was waiting for me in his office, records spread across his desk. Nothing suspicious. Hiring dates, employee references, all normal. Unless the lab tests showed contamination, I was ready to call the complaint unfounded.

"Guess I'd better go," I said and stood up. "Gotto get up early, unlike some people I know."

The phone rang. Drek reached up for it and held up his other hand, signaling me to wait. "Drek's Place."

Drek paused a moment, then bared his teeth slightly. "Yes, this is Mr. Bindanooshlagh." He'd always hated his last name. "What d'ya want?"

Another pause. Drek was frowning now. "Not generous enough. I'm not interested, I don't care how much you offer. Forget it. It's not for sale."

There was a slight pause, then Drek said, "Don't bother. A few days won't make any difference."

Drek stabbed the button to hang up, muttering a graphic ogre curse about the caller's mating habits.

"Who was that," I asked.

"Some lawyer named Thaddeus Rinks."

"He wants to by Drek's Place?"

"No, one of his clients does."

"How much?"

"Too much and not enough."

I blinked. "But how much?"

"Two million."

I whistled, my eyes open wide. "Who's offering?"

"Someone named Giuliano Nakamura. Ever heard of him?"

The name sounded vaguely familiar, but I couldn't put a face or facts to it. I shrugged.

"Well, I'm not selling. This is my place, and it'll stay my place 'til I die." He pounded on his steel desk, bending the top to an obtuse angle.

"Hey, don't get hyper," I said as I held up my hands. "No one can make you sell."

"No one had better try."

I grinned. "Unless they're stupid or suicidal."

Drek looked at me, then grinned back. "Right. D'you have time for a game of chess?"

I shook my head. "I really can't."

"How about Sunday afternoon?"

"You're on."

"I'll have the chess board waiting for you."

"Great." I started to go, then stopped. "Oh, wait. I got plans for Sunday–I hope. Sam and I were supposed to go camping this weekend."

"Well, maybe next week."

"Sure thing. See you later." I headed back to the main room.

On one side of the place a circle of ogres were hunched around a table playing Slap Jack, and Jack didn't look too happy about it. I never could understand how anyone could take a job like that. But with the way economy was going, I guess any job was better than no job at all.

There was a new guy working as Jack tonight. The usual Jack, a jockey-sized guy named Ernie, was laid up in the hospital for a while. Ernie loved dodging the ogres' huge, sharp-nailed hands as they pounded the card table when a jack turned up on the discard pile. But I think he really liked being slapped around. Bit of a masochist, that Ernie.

The designer-dressed humans were watching the action. Sometimes, bets would be made on whether Jack would survive the night. Other times, one of humans would get brave and bet he could go several hands as Jack without getting hurt, and his companions would take him up on it. Rich folks have strange ideas of fun.

I hailed a cab out front and headed back to the Health Department. Took some time to get there 'cause we were caught in the after-the-game rush down by the stadium. From the way the fans were honking their horns, I guessed the Cardinals had won.

I headed down to the basement lab. I could always smell the place as soon as the elevator doors opened. Combination of high school chem lab, eau de barnyard, and Mama Toofee's Midnight Brew.

Bonnie Smith was pulling night shift by herself. "So, what goodies do you have for me tonight?"

I put the samples from Drek's in front of her. "Need these checked for contamination, especially salmonella."

"How soon?"

"Soon as possible."

Her green eyes glittered. "Yesterday?"

"Day before."

She laughed and tousled her copper curls. "Gotcha. Anything else?"

"No. I need to visit the food poisoning case–what's-her-name." I dug the files from my briefcase and ran my finger down to patient's name. "Margaret Jennings-Hanson, Riverfront Hospital, Regent's Tower, room 703."

Bonnie glanced at her watch. "Now? It's getting late. Better wait 'til tomorrow."

"I've got things to do tomorrow."

"On Saturday?"

"Yeah, boss doesn't give time off for good behavior."

"What good behavior?"

I glared at her, but couldn't keep from smiling. "Just get the results as soon as possible. Leave me a message if you can't get me my pager. See y'around."

"Bye. And good luck."

I was dog tired by the time I reached the sidewalk. I decided to wait 'til morning to check out Mrs. J-H. One more thing to do tomorrow. Samantha wasn't going to be happy. I thought about calling her, looked at my watch, and decided one a.m. wasn't the best time to talk to her. I'd called before I'd gone to Drek's, to let her know I couldn't make our movie date. She took it pretty well; she was usually the one who called to cancel because of work. But I didn't know how she'd react when I told her I had to work tomorrow. We were going camping this weekend, had planned it several months ago. This case had put a real kink in that. Why couldn't Mrs. J-H have gotten sick after we'd left?

Took me a while to get another taxi. The whole time I was wishing my car was out of the shop. Third time in five months, darn piece of junk. Taxi dropped me off at my apartment. I trudged up to the second-story three rooms I called home. Big enough for me, and I could afford the rent. I checked my answering machine. Four messages from Sam–each one shorter and sharper than the preceding one–asking why I didn't answer my pager, why I didn't call her back. Maybe I should phone her.

No. Tomorrow morning was soon enough to have my head bitten off. I crawled into bed without showering and whispered a thankful prayer that the guy downstairs wasn't watching wrestling at his usual two hundred decibels.

Hammering woke me. At first I thought it was inside my head, but by the time I massaged my aching eyes open and ran fingers through my hair, I realized the hammering was coming from my front door. Wrapping my sheet around me, I drunk-stumbled from the bedroom to the living room and squinted through the peephole.

Bad mistake. At that moment my visitor pounded again. Ever been poked in the eye by a door? Not my favorite way to start the day. Holding my eye but not my temper, I shouted, "What the heck are you doing? Trying to wake the dead?"

"Since you're up, I guess I succeeded." It was Sam's voice, and she sounded really ticked off.

I fumbled with the deadbolt, unhooked the chain. I barely had time to back away before she flung the door open and stormed in, eyes glinting.

"You were supposed to call me two hours ago," she said, poking me in the chest every few words.

"What time is it?"

She grabbed my wrist and bent it close to my face so I could read my watch. Bright red LED numbers blinked eleven thirty-four a.m.

"Uh-oh. I'm sorry. I didn't get in 'til early this morning and forgot to set the alarm. Really, I'm sorry."

"I beeped you half a dozen times last night. You didn't even bother to phone."

My burning eyes throbbed in time with my headache. "Look, I'm sorry. I'll say it again. I'm sorry, I'm sorry. Okay?"

"Well..." Her glare softened a bit. "We can still make the forest by late afternoon. Where's your stuff? I'll haul it to my car while you're getting dressed."

Crud. Now I wished I'd called her before I'd gone to bed. "Uh, Sam, I can't go camping this weekend. I gotta work overtime."

"Can't go?" Her eyes glinted. "After all our planning? I won't have another weekend off for two months!"

"I said I was sorry."

"Of all the lousy—"

"Sam, I can't help it! If I could, I would! It's a food poisoning case!"

She blinked, stepped back a bit, then asked, "Serious."

I nodded.

"How serious?"

"At the moment, not too, but it involves Drek and a woman who obviously has a bit of money or power or both."

Sam raised an eyebrow, and a smile spread across her face. "Drek? Involved with a woman?"

"No! Not like that. A woman filed a food poisoning complaint against Drek's Place. If there's any proof, I'll have to close down the club, and I don't want to do that unless I have to."

"Is there proof?" Suddenly, she held up her hand. "No, wait. Tell me after you get dressed. I've got some bagels and Danish down in the car. I'll get them and make some coffee." She swiveled me around, aimed me toward the bedroom, and gave me a light shove in that direction.

I smiled to myself as I shuffled to the bathroom in my sheet toga. Sam was one in a million. Make that one in 1.23 million. No one like her in the whole city.

By the time I'd showered and dressed, Sam had coffee brewed. She filled a white ceramic mug and handed it to me. "Now what makes this case so important we can't go camping?"

I didn't answer her right away, but sipped some coffee first. Ah, strong, with a little milk, perfect. "Ever hear of Margaret Jennings-Hanson?"

Sam stared at me over the edge of her own cup. "Why?"

"She's the one who filed the complaint against Drek. Name's familiar but ..." I took another sip.

"She's old money and married older money. Always hosting charity balls, setting up foundations and scholarship funds. Ties to nearly all the prominent families in the city. Widowed about two years ago."

Now I remembered. Young woman married to old man. She'd inherited twice her own worth and had been very generous in setting up clinics in poor neighborhoods. "No hint of scandal, nothing involving the police?"

Sam shook her head. "Not that I know of."

"Well, could you dig a little for me?"

Her mouth scrunched up, and she raised one wispy brow.

"Oh, what about..." I clicked my teeth, trying to remember the names I heard in Drek's office, "Giuliano Nakamura and Thaddeus Rinks?"

Sam almost choked, then stared drop-jawed at me. "Those two are involved?"

"Why?" I leaned toward her. "Who are they?"

"Rinks is probably the dirtiest lawyer still a member of the ABA. The Association tried to disbar him once. Some of the board members had freak accidents; others wouldn't talk. No one could prove a thing. And Nakamura," she paused and shuddered, "he makes Rinks look like a saint. Mr. Mob. The guy's into everything: drugs, prostitution, gambling, political blackmail, killing endangered species. Anything for money. We've been investigating him for ten years. But every time we think we have him, evidence disappears, witnesses take a dive of the McKinley Bridge, a judge rules illegal search and seizure. Something."

I though of Drek and swallowed hard. Why would Nakamura want Drek's Place? Nothing goo, that's for sure.

Sam touched my arm. "What's wrong? What's this got to do with Drek?"

I looked at my coffee. It just wasn't appealing anymore. "Nakamura wants to buy Drek's Place. Rinks called him while I was there last night. Got the impression he'd called before. Drek won't even consider it. My god, what could happen to him if he doesn't give in?

Sam gave me a tenuous smile and my arm a reassuring squeeze. "Drek can take care of himself. I don't think anyone would threaten him. Not if they wanted to live."

"Can you send out feeler about what's happening? Anything strange, rumors about Nakamura or anyone connected with him?"

"Sure. Anything for Drek."

I smiled at her. Well, tried to smile. She knew how much Drek meant to me. I couldn't swear to it, but I suspected she liked him, too. "Thanks, Sam. I owe you for this,"

"I'll remember that." She stood, walked around the table, and planted a kiss on my nose. Then she planted one where a kiss should be. "Want a ride to the hospital?"

Sam drove me to Riverfront–that way I didn't have to call a cab–and went up with me. Mrs. Jennings-Hanson's room was at the end of a hallway, guarded by two guys whose heads missed the ceiling by an inch. Grey silk suits fitted snugly over weightlifter bodies. The two watched me approach but didn't twitch until I reached in my pocket to pull out my ID.

Lightning fast, a hand grabbed me around the neck. The other guy said, "You have no business here. Leave." His voice was quiet, low. His word were pronounced precisely, as if he'd studied with a dialect coach to hide and accent.

"Let him go!" Sam flashed her badge. "The Inspector and I are here on official business. You're looking at assault if you don't!"

"Do you have a search warrant?" the talker said.

Sam leaned forward slightly, eyes like black black diamonds, and said, "I don't need one to arrest you. Assault, assault with intent to do bodily harm, attempted murder, obstructing an officer–I can find lots of others. Release him now!"

The suits hesitated, the hand released me, and they opened the door. The talker went in first, then came back and nodded. My head was pounding with a blood rush. I tried to thank Sam, but all I could do was nod.

Margaret Jennings-Hanson had that society air which said, "I'm important, and I expect to be treated that way." Hair was dark brown with a glint of red. Her face was scalpel perfect. She looked up when we entered and gave us a smile with all the warmth and sincerity of a beauty queen.

"Officer, Inspector, please, come in." Her voice was honeysuckle and mint juleps. She motioned to two chairs, then sat on the edge of her bed. "I must apologize for my body guards. They are zealous for my safety, a comfort in these times." She gave a tiny shudder. I glanced at Sam and shrugged. What could I say to such a marvelous performance?

"You wished to question me about my illness?"

"Yes," I said and took out my notebook and pen. "You said you ate at Drek's Place before you became ill."

"Yes."

"What did you eat?"

She answered with a litany of Drek's finest foods. "Broil lobster, spaghetti primavera, Caesar salad, and strawberry mousse. Oh, and iced mint tea."

"Hm, all possibilities for salmonella except the tea. "Did you eat anywhere else that evening? Anything when you returned home?"

She started to speak, paused, then said, "No, nothing else. I told the doctors all this."

"I know," I said, smiling, "and I appreciate your cooperation. I want to clear up the matter as quickly as possible."

"I certainly wouldn't want this to happen to anyone else." She stared at her forest green robe as she toyed with the velvet belt. "Will the restaurant be closed?"

"I'm sorry, but I'm not at liberty to give you that information. I can tell you I'll take the appropriate action, you may be assured."

"Why, thank you, Inspector. I feel so much safer knowing you are protecting the public." She held out her carefully manicured hand.

I took it and held it just long enough to be gracious. "Good-bye, Mrs. Jennings-Hanson."

Sam and I left, ignoring the suits.

"She's lying," Sam said as we waited for the elevator.

"I know. Maybe not lying, but not telling the whole truth. What I can't figure is why she'd lie."

Sam shook her head. "Where now?"

I checked my watch. Almost two. Too early to check back with Bonnie in the lab–the results wouldn't be ready for hours. Too early for supper, especially since we had breakfast just before noon. I was tempted to file my report without waiting for Bonnie's report. Sam and I could still make the forest and have all Sunday for hiking, bird watching, and swimming. I sighed. No, I'd wait, just to be sure.

"I don't know," I said. "What do you want to do?"

"If we can't go camping, the least you can do is take me down to the Fudge Factory and buy me some maple nut fudge."

"You're on!"

We drove downtown through Saturday traffic to Union Station. As we were parking, I noticed a large crown across the street. A banner was strung across a platform, there were balloons everywhere, and the mayor was giving a speech.

"This project will continue the city's revitalization and bring prosperity," blared the microphone.

I looked at Sam, puzzled.

"Oh, that's where the new cultural center's going to be," she said.

"Oh, yeah." I looked down the side street and grinned. A cultural center right next to Drek's Place.

Sam headed for the Fudge Factory like a wino after booze. Several pounds of fudge and a lot less money later, we got a quick bite at the Key Westg Café, then left Union Station to change clothes for the Muny Opera. Li'l Abner–my favorite musical. I'd been willing to miss it for camping, but since Sam and I were in town, I was going to see the show.

Bonnie Smith had left a message on my machine. No sign of salmonella in the samples I'd brought in the night before. Drek's Place was in the clear as far as she was concerned. Now I could close the case, and maybe camping was still a go for tomorrow. I called in my report, then changed into lightweight shirt and slacks but took a jacket. Even in August, it got chilly in the outdoor theater at night.

Sam arrived, dressed in a brightly flowered cotton dress, delicate shawl of white and gold thread, white evening bag, and matching flats. I just stared at her so long, she frowned and did a quick scan of herself. "A run in my panihose?" she asked as she inspected her calf. "My slip showing? What?"

"Uh, nothing," I said. "I mean, you look fine, great. Really. You're just beautiful."

She smiled, kissed me, then wiped lipstick smudge from my mouth. "Let's go."

The musical was wonderful. As the finale began, my beeper went off. I cursed my boss quietly, then made my way to the aisle and down to the front foyer to find a phone.

"What now?" I said when my boss answered.

"I thought you said Drek's Place was in the clear?" He was almost yelling.

"It is."

"Oh, really? Well, maybe you'd like to tell that to about two dozen people who showed up at the Riverfront Hospital in the last hour or two!"

"Two dozen!" I glanced at Sam, who's followed me.

"Yes, and a couple of them are ogres. All suspected salmonella cases, one critical, and all ate at Drek's today!"

I winced. "I'll get right on it."

"You better. This time someone might die. I want this solved tonight, even if it means closing Drek's permanently!"

His slamming receiver nearly popped my eardrum.

"Bad?" Sam said.

"Worse." I nudged her toward the car, explaining as we went. At least we'd avoid most traffic, leaving the Muny before the show was over.

It was nearly eleven when we arrived at the hospital. I went straight to ER. Bonnie Smith was there, taking blood from several patients, newly admitted and suffering all the symptoms of food poisoning. Bonnie saw Sam and me, gave us a grim look, and motioned us to a quiet corner.

"This makes thirty people since nine o'clock," Bonnie said. "All of them ate at Drek's."

"What did they eat?" I said.

Bonnie grabbed several charts from the admitting desk and scanned them. "Fish, chicken, no meat, fish, salad, various vegetables, beef, pork, alcohol, no alcohol, mousse, pie, pie, mousse, cake, melon, melon, melon...wait." She checked the charts still at the desk. "All have one thing in common: melon. I'll bet the people admitted already had melon, too."

"Melon?" I said, surprised. "Even the ogres? Can you find out for sure?"

She dialed up third floor and asked the supervisor to look at the charts. After a few minutes, Bonnie hung up. "Melon, every one of them. Better get over to Drek's and shut it down for now."

I nodded, grabbed Sam, and headed for the parking lot.

We made it to Drek's in record time. I ran down the stairs to the bar. "I gotta close you down," I said to Drek. "Thirty people who ate here today are sick."

"Damn." Drek's dark eyes wavered between grief and anger. "All right." He turned to the remaining patrons, all ogres, and shouted, "Closing up! Go home!"

The crowd commented on Drek's choice of mating partners and refused to leave. Drek called for his two ogre bouncers, Crusher and Fifi, who threw a few patrons out the door before the rest shuffled up the stairs and outside.

Drek turned back to me. "Anyone really bad sick?"

"One's critical."

Drek swore again. "Do you know the cause?"

"Everyone ate melon."

Drek motioned us to follow him to the kitchen.

Guy, the head cook, bristled when he saw me. "What do you want this time?" he snapped.

"Where's the melon you served today?" I said.

"Gone. Very popular during the summer." He started to turn away, but halted. "Wait, here is one." He picked up a large pale orange cantaloupe. "The last one, too."

"I need a plastic sack," I said. One of the assistant cooks grabbed a small trash bag from a box. "Now, put the melon in the bag along with any knives used to cut the others, and rinds, seeds, and leftovers. Wash your hands thoroughly, and scrub every counter with disinfectant. Sterilize all the dishes. Then all of you, take a two-day vacation. This place is closed until I say so. Got it?"

Guy muttered something I couldn't make out, but I'm sure it wasn't kind.

"Everyone who worked here today stil here?" I said.

Guy looked around. "No. Jimmy Glauck went home about an hour ago. He said he was sick."

"Maybe he ate some of the melon, too." I turned to Drek. "Can I use your phone?"

"Sure."

I called Riverfront and asked if Jimmy Glauck had been admitted. No, the receptionist said. I hung up. If Jimmy hadn't gone to the hospital, he might be home, too ill to get help. Food poisoning can be deadly even in perfectly healthy people. "Where does he live?" I said.

"I'll check," Drek said and started to leave.

Guy stopped him. "1647 Union, apartment 5F."

Bad section of town. "Sam, let's go. He might be really sick."

Swam headed west on Market, then turned north on Union. We arrived in front of Jimmy's dilapidated apartment building just in time to see him strapping two ratty suitcases to the biggest Harley I'd ever seen. Sam and I got out of the car. Jimmy took one look at us and ran.

"Police officer!" Sam said. She was after him like a missile, radared in and following every move he made. I followed quick as I could, but I couldn't match her speed. Neither could Jimmy. Halfway down the block, she snagged his leather jacket and tackled him beside a street light. He wriggled and squirmed, but she had an arm lock on him and a knee in his back. She patted him down for weapons.

"Let go o' me!" he said. Dark blond bangs fell over his eyes. He tossed his head to flip the hair back. "I didn't do anything!"

Sam pulled out her badge. "Why'd you run?"

I squatted beside him. "We thought you might be sick from tainted melon."

"I'm not sick," he said. "But I will be if she doesn't get her knee outta my back!"

"Sam, come on. Let him up."

She stood up but kept a grip on his arm. Jimmy got up slowly.

"So why'd you run from us?" I said.

"Hah!" he said glaring at us. "You show up in this neighborhood with a cop, late night, and you ask why I ran? You're dumber than I thought!"

Sam glared at him. "You ran before you knew I was a cop."

"Someone told you about the food poisoning?" I said.

"What?" Jimmy jerked his head toward Sam, then back at me. "No! I mean, yes! I mean, I don't know anything."

"You're awfully eager to get away from us," Sam said.

Jimmy's eyes grew wide, but he didn't say anything.

"Kinda hot for a leather jacket, isn't it?" I said.

"No, I...I'm going on vacation up north, around Minneapolis. Ridin' my Harley." He glanced at Sam again. "Look, I gotta get rolling now."

"Guess you're not sick," I said. "You can go."

"Thanks."

"Not so fast," Sam said, tightening her grip on his jacket. "There's something you're not telling us."

Suddenly, a car bolted from the darkness, coming straight up Union. The driver must have slammed the pedal to the floor because the car squealed up the street. As Sam and I stared at the car, Jimmy twisted from Sam's grasp and bolted for his Harley. We started after him.

An arm stuck out the passenger's window. A small black gun spat yellow-orange sparks and explosions like a string of firecrackers.

Sam dropped to the sidewalk and dragged me with her. "Drop! Get down!" she yelled at Jimmy as she snapped open her purse and pulled out her snub nose 38.

Instead, Jimmy froze, like a frightened rabbit. Bullets shattered against building, smashed windows in Sam's car, and hit Jimmy square in the chest, slamming him against the brick wall. His head snapped back, then he slid to the concrete, unconscious. A parting shot or two, and the car fled into the darkness. Sam fired at the tires but missed.

Sam jumped up and ran to Jimmy. I was right behind her.

"Is he dead?" I said, swallowing hard.

Sam put her fingers on his neck. "Got a pulse, but he's not breathing and he's going into shock."

Sam started mouth-to-mouth while I checked for wounds. Jimmy's head was bleeding. There was a ragged-edged hole in his jacket, nearly eight inches in diameter, but no blood. I unzipped the ruined jacket, pulled back the torn shirt, and found a bruise that covered his entire chest.

"What kind of bullet does something like that?" I said.

Sam paused between breaths, glanced at Jimmy's chest, gave another breath, then said, "Don't know yet. Take over while I call an ambulance from my car phone."

I started the breathing. Sam was back in a few minutes, bringing a blanket she'd packed for our trip, and covered Jimmy to slow the trauma symptoms. The rescue squad arrived not long after that, along with another squad car. Jimmy's head wound had clotted, but he was still unconscious. While Sam gave a statement to the officers, the paramedics gave Jimmy oxygen, hooked up an IV, and slid him inside the ambulance.

I started to get into Sam's car when I noticed she was running her fingers over the bricks, the sidewalk where Jimmy fell, and the remains of his jacket. The paramedics had cut it off. "Aren't we going to follow the ambulance?" I said.

"In a minute." She rubbed the front of the shredded jacket between her fingertips.

"What's so interesting?"

"Oil, on this, the bricks," she studied the sidewalk, "no bullets anywhere, only plastic fragments and BBs."

"So?"

"Glazer safety slugs: plastic-cased bullets filled withBBs and oil, shatters on impact, blows big holes in people."

"But..." I halted, "he was just bruised all over."

"He's be dead if he hadn't been wearing this." She held up the tattered black leather. "Someone wanted him dead, someone who didn't expect him to wear this jacket on a hot August night."

"Come on." I grabbed her hand. "I want to be there when he wakes up."

We brushed the broken glass from the front seat, climbed in, and headed for Barnes Hospital, where the ambulance had taken Jimmy. He was in the ER when we arrived so we couldn't see him. A nurse said she'd let us know when he was conscious.

"I'm phoning for guards," Sam said. She called her precinct to report in, then hung up. "Police protection on its way. I'll stand guard until someone else arrives."

I leaned against the wall. "Why would some gang want to kill Jimmy?"

"Gangs don't use Glazer safety slugs," Sam said. "We're talking professional hit here."

"The mob?" I said, astonished. "The mob tried to kill a nobody cook?"

"A nobody cook who works at Drek's. And Nakamura has tried to buy Drek's."

"But why kill Jimmy?"

Sam chewed her lip. "I don't know. But I will."

It was five a.m. and no sleep when the nurse finally told us Jimmy was awake. He was black and blue, mummy-wrapped around his head and chest, and anxious to talk to us.

"They tried to kill me," he said in a frong-croaking voice.

"Who?' Sam said.

"Rinks' goons."

"Why?"

"I don't know! I did what they wanted. And I was leaving town. They didn't have anything to worry about. I wasn't going to tell."

"Tell what?" I said. "What's this got to do with Drek and the food poisoning?"

Jimmy cringed and turned his face from us. "I had gambling debts I couldn't pay. Rinks told me he'd take care of them if I did him a favor. All I had to do was put some liquid in a certain person's food. I refused so Rinks threatened to hurt my parents if I didn't do it." Jimmy shuddered, then continued. "I didn't want to. But what could I do?"

"That's when Mrs. Jennings-Hanson got sick," I said.

Jimmy nodded. "Rinks said she knew about the food poisoning, she was part of the whole thing, but I got the impression she was going along for the same reason I was–blackmail, something about furs and stolen artifacts. When you came to inspect Drek's Place, I thought it was over. Then I got a call from Rinks early this morning saying I had to do another job. This time a lot of people had to get sick. One person wasn't enough for what Rinks wanted. I told him now way. He told me he had people watching my parents, and if I didn't do what I was told, Mom and Dad would have an accident. So...I did what he told me. He had the melons delivered to Drek's Place, and...I didn't say anything."

"Would you testify to all this in court?" Sam asked.

Jimmy looked from her to me, then back again. "What about my family?"

"I'll see what I can do."

He swallowed hard and nodded. "All right. I'll testify."

Sam smiled and touched his arm. "Good. I'll have an officer take your statement. You should have a lawyer present."

Jimmy gave her a feeble smile. "Know any good ones?"

Sam nodded and winked.

I left the room and headed for a phone. First, I called the office, filed a report with a promise to put it in writing in a few days. Next, I called Drek.

"Hi, Cal. Is Jimmy all right?"

"No food poisoning, but someone tried to kill him."

"Jimmy?" I heard Drek's steely teeth grinding. That was always a sign someone was going to get crushed. "Who would dare?"

Should I tell him? Department regulations said no. Legally, he had no right to the information. But I'd bet my Uncle Bill's twenty-dollar gold piece that Rinks and Nakamura would beat the system and get off scot-free. On the other hand, telling Drek might cost me my job.

I took a deep breath. "Rinks blackmailed Jimmy into putting salmonella in the food, then tried to kill him to shut him up permanently. I'd bet Rinks and Nakamura were trying to pressure you into selling. If they owned Drek's Place, they'd be in the very heart of the new cultural center. Lots of money to be made there. Who knows what else they might do? I hope Jimmy's testimony will convict them, but I've a feeling those two have connections in city hall and probably the courts."

Drek was silent for a moment, then a chuckle rumbled from deep in his throat. "Don't worry, they won't escape. Me and my family'll see they don't."

"Don't do anything stupid. Promise me, please. Drek?" No answer. "Drek!" The phone went dead.

"Cal," Sam tugged on my coat. "Quit yelling. This is a hospital. What's wrong with Drek?"

"Nothing," I said softly. "Nothing at all."

Dumb, Cal, real dumb, I thought. *If Drek gets into trouble, it'll be your fault.*

"Jimmy's giving a statement, and we're trying for warrants for Rinks and Nakamura," Sam said. "Ready for some breakfast?"

"Breakfast? What time is it?"

She twisted my wrist so I could see my watch. Why did I keep forgetting I had one? Nine-thirty on a Sunday morning. Yeah, breakfast sounded good, breakfast then sleep. "Cafeteria?"

"My place." Sam's smile brightened to a grin.

We drove through the sapphire morning to her condo in the West End, left to her by a well-to-do aunt. I loved that area, close to Forest Park, bygone luxury faded to comfortable affluence. Wished I could afford to live there.

Sam fixed toast, juice, and coffee while I made omelets and fried bacon. Filled the hole in my ribs. I slid into the self-satisfied lethargy of Sam's reclining chair and settled in for a nap. Sam turned on the radio for some quiet music, then climbed onto my lap and wrapped her arms around my neck.

"Good job, Cal." She kissed me.

I kissed her back, smiled up at her, then closed my eyes. She hugged me; I hugged her back. She was teddy-bear comfort in my arms. I could get use to this. I felt her ruffle my hair a couple of times before I fell asleep.

"Cal. Wake up."

Someone shook my shoulder. I clung to sleep by my fingernails, but finally I had to let go and open my eyes. Sam bent over me, her eyes wide, her mouth quivering with a suppress smile.

I stretched the cramps out of my shoulders and legs. "What's up?"

"Want to go for a ride?"

"Where?" I said around a yawn.

"West county."

Gazing out her window, I saw yellow streaks of sunset against darkening blue. "Kinda late for a ride, isn't it?"

Her eyes glittered with delight. "I've been waiting for this ride for years. We got warrants for Rinks and Nakamura. County police are working with the city on this one. We're going knocking on Nakamura's door, and I thought you'd like to be there, too."

"You bet," I said and scrambled out of the chair.

Sam drove me to county headquarters where we joined eight county sheriffs, five city detectives, and a couple of agents from the state Anti-crime and

Racketeering Bureau. I figured they'd be enough. I'd barely stepped out of the car when I heard a call on the police band–trouble out at Nakamura's place. Everyone piled into their cars and headed into the magenta-blue evening, lights flashing, sirens shrilling.

We reached the entrance through the ten-foot high stone fence twenty minutes later. One side of the wrought iron gate was twisted like licorice. The other side lay on a flower bed between the driveway and trees that bordered the wall and shadowed the road.

It took ten minutes up the winding drive through thick woods until we reached the mansion. What was left of it, that is. The place looked like a shattered house of cards: granite blocks tossed everywhere, some snapped in half, some smashes; glass littered the ground like crushed diamonds. Splintered doors, broken furniture, torn fabrics–I doubted there was anything salvageable.

"What the hell could've done this?" said one of the county cops.

"How the hell should I know?" said an ARB agent.a

"Looks like someone's been at this for hours with a wrecking ball or an army of ogres."

The ARB agent shook his head. "A bomb maybe?"

"Better send for the sniffers, see if anyone's in there."

Glancing at the rubble, I spotted a slight movement from the corner of my eye. I jerked my head toward the movement and saw several pairs of eyes in the woods–eyes about treetop level–and the glint of steely teeth in the last light that peeks between clouds and horizon. Suddenly, the eyes disappeared into the woods, soundlessly. It always amazed me how fast and quiet ogres could be when they wanted to be.

"Cal?" Sam's voice made me jump. "Are you all right? Did you see something, Nakamura maybe?"

"No," I said slowly, a shiver creeping down my back all the way to my toes. "Nothing, nothing at all."

Sam scanned the area. "Well, we can't see much tonight, especially with the clouds moving in so fast, but I've called for an investigative team. Forensics, too, just in case."

"Um, yeah, good idea."

"You don't have to stay. Why don't you take my car back to your place? I can catch a ride with the guys. Besides, I'll probably be working most of the night. And I'll have to remember to call tomorrow about getting my window fixed."

No reason for me to hang around. I doubted they'd find anything, and if they did, I didn't want to see it. And I had to go to work tomorrow. "Okay. I'll bring the car back in the morning."

"Hope it doesn't rain tonight."

"I'll put a tarp over it so the seat doesn't get wet."

She handed me the keys, her fingers lingering on mine, then she turned back to the other cops.

I walked back to the car, climbed in, backed around, and headed down the long lane.

The distance from Nakamura's to Drek's Place was forty miles as the crow flies, and I nearly flew getting there. No one came when I pounded on the cat door. I tried the alley door to the kitchen. Nothing. If Drek was home, he wasn't answering.

I took my time driving back to my apartment, maily because I was alert enough to know I was too tired to be driving. Faint thunder rumbled in the west as clouds slithered across the late evening sky. I stopped at a twenty-four hour super store and bought a tarp and some rope. A few block from my apartment, rain speckled the windshield just enough to smear under the wipers. I parked the car and tied the tarp over it. Felt like forever climbing the steps to the fifth floor. When I got inside, I stripped down, climbed into bed, and turned out the light.

That's when I noticed the red blinking light on my answering machine. Fumbling in the dark until I pushed the play button, I rolled over and listened.

"Hi, Cal," said Drek's voice. "Sorry I missed you. I'd like to invite you to come over tomorrow night–yes, I know, that's Monday, "Ogres Only Night"–but we're going to have a special game of Slap Jack. Two Jacks instead of one. You won't want to miss it. I promise it will be very entertaining." He chuckled. "See you then."

I lay there a few moments, the drizzle outside turning to a downpour, and wondered who were going to be the Jacks. I smiled in the dark and thought, no, I knew who they would be.

Threefold to You

Sometimes people don't consider the consequences of their actions. Even in a good cause, consequences can be terrible.

Koleesa first learned about the invasion of Visali when a handful of soldiers slammed open her cottage door. Startled, she dropped her willow wand into the bubbling potion, then cursed.

"Silence, witch!" said an officer wearing the green and gold of Visali. "Bind her," he told two soldiers, the turned to Koleesa. "Our lord king wishes to speak with you."

Soldiers tied her wrists with thongs.

"K-king?" She was unused to speakingVisalian: she hadn't spoken to anyone but Magda her cat in years. Magda! She sent a warning thought, hoping the cat was close enough to hear. "King?" She narrowed her midnight eyes. "Why?"

The officer hesitated, his thick brown brows pulling together over his crooked nose, then said, "Reff and the Maleze horde have invaded out land."

"Ah." Her voice crackled like fur.

"You must stop them," the officer said.

She shrugged back her tangled mess of gray hair. "One king, other king, all same. No help.

The officer leaned over her until they were nearly nose to nose. "You will help my lord," he said, steel soft. "Gag her."

The officer turned and walked outside. Two soldiers gripped her arms, another tied a cloth around her mouth, then the two pulled Koleesa from her cottage.

They walked through briars, brush, trees, and vines the vibrant green of the early spring morning. Koleesa shivered as fingers of chilly air crept through her often patched robe; the damp cold crept into her bones, aching worse than in winter. Even her anger didn't warm her. She couldn't escape; the soldiers were too strong, and she was too old.

Nearly an hour later the woods ahead thinned out, became brighter, golden. The officer called like a bobwhite, listened for a reply, then walked out of the woods to a green-brown plain covered by a tent city.

The king's green and gold tent was pitched beside the road that led to the pass through the southern mountains. Scores of other tents stood on both sides of the road. Soldiers barely glanced up as Koleesa and her captors passed them. They were too intent on huddling beside fires, rubbing hands to keep warm, and blowing steamy breath on them.

The officer strode to the king's tent, saluted the door wards who swept back the heavy flap, and entered. Koleesa hesitated, but her guards dragged her inside.

King Athelain loomed like a black bear behind a heavy table spread with a map. He stared steadily at his officer and soldiers, but Athelain's face was statue calm. "Remove her gag."

One of her guards untied the cloth.

"This is the witch?" Athelain asked.

"Yes, my lord," the officer said as he clapped his fist to his chest, then snapped his fingers. A soldier entered the tent, carrying a large bag that yowled and hissed and danced. "And her familiar."

"Magda!" Terror twisted in Koleesa's throat: she'd hoped Magda had escaped. She strained toward the sack, but two soldiers held her back. Sending a calming thought to Magda, she asked if the cat were unharmed. The cat sent back images of anger and claws scratching legs and arms.

"The cat's your familiar, isn't it," the officer said; it wasn't a question. "Your power."

"No hurt Magda! No hurt, no hurt!" Her shoulders drooped, and she whispered, "What king want?"

Athelain shifted his gaze to the rough sack that pitched back and forth as the cat tried to claw free. The soldier tied the sack to a tripod of spears set beside the table, to the king's right. Athelain looked at Koleesa. "The Maleze have invaded Visali. I need your power to stop them."

His voice surprised Koleesa. It was mellow, almost musical, and seemed powerful enough to project for miles. But the tone–that surprised her most of all. It had authority, but no demand, no threat, a simple statement of fact.

"How?" she asked.

"Come." He motioned toward the table.

She glanced at the officer, who ordered the soldiers to release her arms. Pausing only a moment, she shuffled forward and gazed at the crinkled yellow map. Visali was outlined in black. Cities were circles; villages, dots. Rivers and the vast Lake Erlyn in the north were blue.

"Here," Athelain said, pointing at the southern pass, "here is where Reff is, according to last reports. You must stop him before he enters Visali."

Koleesa frowned, puzzled. "Big army, many men. You fight, you win."

"No," Athelain said. "We cannot reach him before he enters Visali, not even if all my soldiers were mounted. You must stop him while he is still in the pass or he will spill over my kingdom like a killing flood. You must use your power to save my kingdom and my people."

Koleesa creaked her head from side to side. "Too many men. Not enough me. No spell big enough."

His eyes fixed on her like a snake mesmerizing a bird. "Find one."

There was no threat in his tone, but Koleesa shuddered, her throat dry, her heart fluttering wildly in her bony chest. She'd known other kings, other lords, when she was young and had traveled the lands. Petty tyrants who'd threatened, powerful men who'd tried to frighten, but she'd never feared them. She feared Athelain because he didn't threaten. He didn't need to. He had Magda, her cat, her familiar, her very life.

"How?" she cried. "How?"

"Trap them, bury them, destroy them anyway you can."

"Bury?" She thought for a few moments. "Rock?"

"No, that would block the road. We need the trade it brings."

"Bury," she repeated, her pinched face looking even more gaunt as she searched her memory for possibilities.

"There must be something you can do." For the first time, Koleesa heard a hint of desperation in his voice.

"'S no spell."

"There is no spell?" he asked, as if uncertain what she'd said.

"'S no spell."

Suddenly, his eyes widened. "Snow spell? Can you conjure snow? A snowstorm? One as great as an entire winter's snow in one huge storm?"

"No!" Koleesa shrank back. "No ask. Not understand."

His voice hardened. "Can you conjure a snowstorm?"

"No. Can't. Threefold...threefold."

"Threefold? What do you mean?"

"Big rule. Learn magic, learn rule."

"What rule?" Anger joined Athelain's desperation.

She swallowed hard and tried to stop shaking. "Rule rhyme." Closing her eyes, she said the catechism she'd learned from her teacher.

> "Good or evil that you do,
> Will come threefold back to you."

She opened her eyes. "Understand? You do. Something happens."

"You mean consequences. There are consequences for what you do."

"Yes!" She nodded vigorously. "Consequences. Bif consequences for big spell. No do."

"Everything has consequences." He pointed to the pass. "If you do not stop Reff here, he will march across Visali, killing, burning, raping, destroying my people and my land. My army might be able to hold him back for a while, but he has five times as many men and stronger weapons." He leaned forward and gazed at her with eyes deep as a well and just as dark. "Whatever the consequences, I'll pay them. I, myself." He touched his chest. "I'll pay the price. I have sons to rule after me; I do not fear death. My people, my lands, are worth the risk."

"No, no," Koleesa said, dismay bubbling in her throat. "Consequences. Consequences!"

"What consequences?" he shouted.

She couldn't tell him; she didn't know. There was only dread in her heart. Then the answer came to her, like a voice in her ear, whispering in Visali the words of a riddle.

> "Land to sky to land below
> Cold death to defeat the foe
> Gone, gone, it then will be
> Until the threefold time you see."

Koleesa gazed at Athelain, waiting, hoping he could decipher it.

Athelain frowned. "What does it mean?"

"Meaning for you to find."

"Tell me!"

"Can't tell, can't tell! Spell no work if tell." She shook her head sadly. "Poor king," she whispered. "Not understand. Not understand."

"And *you* do not understand that I will do anything, everything I can to protect my people." His voice became cold as snow. "And know this, witch: if you fail, your blood will be the second to spill on the ground." He glanced at the struggling sack. "Do you understand?"

"Yes," she hissed. "Understand."

"Then make the snowstorm."

"Magic borrow, not make." She paused, but when Athelain said nothing, she continued. "Snow is cold water. Can make water cold, but not make water. Must borrow much water, much water for much snow." She paused again, then pleaded, "Think, think. Understand?"

"Yes," he said, impatient. "I want a snowstorm."

She closed her eyes and moaned softly. "Need things."

Opening her eyes, she said, "Kettle, fresh water, fire for heating water, salt, clean sand. Willow wand, silver ring, bat dung, knife. Cup and cloth and blood–fresh blood, your blood, king."

"How dare you, witch!" The officer drew back his hand as if to slap her.

"Hold!" Athelain said. "She will have all that she needs, even my blood, if it saves my people. Gather all she has asked for."

The officer stiffened, the saluted. Glaring at Koleesa, he turned sharply and left the tent.

"A chair for her," Athelain said. A servant stepped from the shadows, startling Koleesa, and set a chair facing Athelain. "Sit. If you wish."

Koleesa sank into the wooden chair. Her knees protested as she bent them, but her feet were grateful for the rest. She closed her eyes, sent a reassuring image to Magda, and though she tried to saty awake, fell asleep.

Athelain touched her shoulder. "Awaken. All is ready."

A blanket had been wrapped around her, and her wrists were untied. She groaned as her back popped, and she rubbed the kinks out of her neck. "Please," she whispered as she looked up at Athelain, "no do. Please. Threefold to you."

"It must be done. Come."

He offered her his hand. Everyone else in the tent gasped. Koleesa was surprised by his courtesy. Slowly, she wrapped her gnarled fingers around his large but gentle hand. He eased her to her feet, released her hand, and walked out of the tent. She followed him, still surprised.

The sun shone nearly overhead as Koleesa stepped outside. The bright light made her squint and shade her eyes. A large black kettle–her kettle–hung by a chain from an iron tripod. A crackling fire had heated the water in the kettle to boiling.

The officer handed her the willow wand she'd dropped when the soldiers had taken her. "We have everything you asked for." He waved at two soldiers holding bags, a bottle, and a silver cup. He drew a dagger from his belt. "And here is the knife, but I will hold it, I will draw the king's blood."

"No." She pointed to herself. "Me draw blood. Only me or spell no good."

The officer's hand tightened around the hilt. "Never."

Athelain turned on him. "*She* will take my blood. I will do what she asks. As will you."

The officer clenched his jaw but said no more.

Koleesa turned to the soldiers holding the ingredients for the spell. "Give what ask for. Quick. Understand?"

They nodded.

"Salt." She the bag from the soldier, grabbed a handful of salt, and sprinkled it into the kettle. "For salt draws water."

"Sand, for sand hides water." She scattered the sparkling grains in the kettle.

"Silver ring." She looked at the soldiers, but Athelain took a silver ring from his finger and handed it to her. "For silver freezes water."

"Bat dung." A soldier handed her a bottle from her cottage. "For bat dung causes water to fall."

She turned to the officer and held out her hand. "Knife."

Anger darkened his face, fear flickered in his eyes, but he handed the hilt to her.

She took it and turned to Athelain. "Sword arm." He held out his right. "Other," she said. He held out his left. "Bare wrist."

He unlaced the sleeve and gazed steadily at her.

"Cup," she said. "A soldier offered her the silver cup, but she shook her head. "Hold under wrist. Catch blood."

The soldier's hand shook so much, he had to grip the cup with both hands to hold it beneath Athelain's wrist.

Koleesa looked at Athelain. He nodded, his face calm, his eyes full of trust. She gripped his forearm, pressed the tip of the knife to his wrist, and made a shallow cut across the skin. Blood welled from the wound, oozing down its length and into the cup–ten crimson drops.

"Bind cut, stop bleeding," she told the officer as she handed him the knife. Relief had replaced part of the fear she'd read in his eyes.

She took the cup and held it over her head. "Fresh blood king's blood, given, not taken. Blood that is life, hot and red." She poured the steaming red liquid into the kettle and stirred it with the wand. "Blood, to bring death."

She closed her eyes, felt for Magda's presence, and joined their minds. In the magic tongue she'd learned so long ago, she chanted, "Salt and sand, ring and dung, blood for death, be it now done. Water and clouds, now snow become. Let it be done, let it be done."

Power flowed into her lungs, out of her heart, coursing through her to Magda and back again, building like fire, hardening like steel. Hands tingled; skin prickled. Light bloomed behind her eyes until all she could see was dazzling white, like sunlight on snow. Suddenly, the power fled, taking the white light with it.

Her eyes snapped open and stared at the kettle. Over the potion hovered a tiny whirlwind, white and glittering, swirling, swirling. It rose into the air, growing, widening, building until Koleesa could barely see the top. The force of the wind knocked everyone to the ground, flattened the tents. The whirlwind roared like a wild beast and charged northward. In moments it had vanished.

"What happened?" the officer sputtered as he sat up and wiped dirt from his mouth. "Did it work?"

"Yes," Koleesa gasped, too drained to move.

"How soon?" Athelain asked.

She looked up at him and whispered, "Before supper."

Athelain smiled, yet there was more sadness than joy in his smile. "Help her," he told his servants. "Let her rest in my tent. Give her whatever she asks for." He knelt and took her hand. "She has saved us all. All will be well now."

A tear trickled down beside her stubby nose. "Listen. Listen. Good or evil that you do, will come threefold back to you. Understand?"

He nodded and smiled and patted her hand. "Rest now. We will talk later."

Koleesa hobbled through the woods, away from her cottage. Magda prowled beside her. The sack tied to Koleesa's back held all her possessions–an ancient book, a few bottles and vials, a dish and cup, and five gold coins which Athelain had given her. She hadn't wanted to travel again, but she had no choice. She couldn't stay now.

The snow had come with racing black clouds. Such a storm even the oldest campaigners had never seen. Snow had begun falling just before supper, all through the night, and all the next day. Even the king's camp received a dusting of snow, but the pass through the southern mountains was so deep that the lower peaks nearly disappeared.

The Maleze army was buried beneath the snow. The handful who escaped were quickly tracked down by Visalian soldiers. Athelain's kingdom was safe from invasion. He was deeply grateful. He'd released Magda, offered Koleesa a place at his court, and given her gold when she'd refused. As she walked east, Koleesa gazed at the green plains of Visali and mourned for them. "King not understand," she whispered to herself. She'd borrowed water from Lake Erlyn for the spell, the great lake that fed the Visali rivers, that irrigated fields, provided water for cities, animals, and the Visalians. Precious water, more precious than they knew. Three years without rain, three years of the lake shrinking to little more than a pond, three years of dry riverbeds, of empty fields, of death–she shuttered. She'd tried to warn Athelain; he'd been too desperate to hear her, to understand the riddle. "Threefold to you," she whispered as tears clouded her eyes. "Threefold to you."

How I Ended the War

Most fantasy stories are about kings and queens, princes and princesses, nobles and knights. I prefer stories about ordinary people in extraordinary situations, especially if they make me laugh.

I was a born cook. I was not a born sorceress, but I wanted to be one. I worked at an inn for ten years and saved every coin I could so I could buy an apprenticeship with someone who could teach me. All I could afford was a local third-rate wizard named Barkins, who agreed to take me on as long as I cooked and cleaned for him. It was a fair deal so I jumped at the chance.

I picked up on herbal magic right away since I used herbs in my cooking. I could make a potion to heal warts from comfrey and silver walsma. I made sleeping draughts from chamomile, valerian, and hypolia. And I made powders that could settle the stomach from peppermint and ginger. But when it came to the higher magics, I didn't do so well.

I have to admit, Barkins tried. He really did. And eventually, I learned enough basic magic that he didn't throw me out. Actually, I think he liked my cooking so much, he would have kept me even if I hadn't learned magic.

The only spell I was really good at was enlarging things. Once I was baking a cake when Barkins dropped a heavy kettle as he was carrying it from a storage closet to his conjuring room. Why he had to come through my kitchen, I have no idea. The cake fell flat, and I opened the oven door and just stared at it sorrowfully.

An idea flashed in my mind. Why not try the enlarging spell I'd just learned? So I let the cake finish baking as well as it could, took it out of the oven, and set it on the counter to cool. I gathered my herbs, a bullfrog, a pinch of yeast sponge, some charcoal, sulfur, and bat guano. The frog kept trying to jump off the table until I finally put him in a small cage.

I mixed all the items–except the frog—in a marble mortar until it was grey-green-tan-black-yellow powder. Fetching an elm twig, I took the frog from the cage, held him over the mortar, touched the elm twig to the frog's head, then lit the other end of the twig from the candle on the table and started to chant the spell. When I touched the burning elm twig to the powder, there was a loud bang, and smoke filled the air. I fell on my backside, dropped the frog, and started choking from the smoke. The frog escaped, and I never saw it again.

Barkins came running to the kitchen just as the cake started to expand. "What are you doing?" he yelled as the cake climbed over the edge of the table.

"The enlarging spell," I said as I backed toward the kitchen door.

"You used enough to turn a chick into a roc! There's enough cake here to feed the entire town! Get rid of it! All of it! Now!!!" He grabbed a handful of cake, looked at me and stuffed it in his mouth as he ran for the door.

The cake continued to grow until it filled the entire kitchen. I used a sickle to cut it into pieces. I put a cloth-covered table outside the front door.

"Free cake!" I called as I hauled out chunks of cake. I gave it away to neighbors, passersby, beggars, anyone I could talk into taking some. It actually tasted quite delicious, but too much of a good thing is not a good thing.

After the cake was nearly gone, I wrapped the rest up and put it in a tight-lidded wooden box. It took me a while to clean the kitchen. Even though I was tired, I decided to try the spell again, but just used a tiny pinch of everything. I had to go catch another bullfrog from the pond just west of town.

What should I try to enlarge? I thought. *Maybe I should try the spell on a chick, like Barkins said.*

I traded a neighbor a piece of cake and some strawberry jam for a fuzzy little yellow chick. Being very careful, I tried the spell again, and the chick grew to the size of a large goose. I danced around the table, I was so excited.

Barkins was a bit surprised that I'd managed to perform the spell so well, especially after he'd eaten the roasted giant chick. "Maybe you're ready for the counter spell—shrinking," he said as he chewed on a chick leg. "You'll need a dried plum, some dried apple slices, dried dandelion root, a dried earthworm, wood ashes, some unwashed wool, and sulfur."

I began gathering the items.

"And a willow wand," Barkins said, his mouth still full. "And the mortar and pestle."

I set everything on the table. "Now what?"

"Put the plum, apples, dandelion, earthworm, ashes, and sulfur in the mortar and grind them up. Add the wool. Wave the willow wand over the mortar three times and point the wand at the target of the spell. Take an ember from the hearth and drop it in."

I ground the dried items and sulfur, and added the wool. "But what should I shrink?"

"Whatever you want," Barkins said as he grabbed the other chick leg and left the room.

So what should I try to shrink, I thought. *Something big that would be better if it were little.*

At that moment I heard the honking of the neighbor's goose. That creature was the bane of my life. Whether I was gardening, hanging out clothes, or just walking to the market, that bird would sneak up on me and nip my legs.

I gathered some lettuce, cabbage, and few handfuls of grass. After scanning the back yard, I placed the food on the ground in a line leading up to a cage, then put a large amount of lettuce inside. I hid just inside the back entry, holding the rope attached to the cage door. Soon that evil bird took the bait, and I had the subject for my spell. I grabbed the cage and hurried inside before the squawking drew the neighbor's attention.

I set the cage on the table, waved the willow wand around the mortar three times, and pointed it at the goose. Fetching an ember from the hearth, I dropped it in. White smoke shot up and surrounded the goose, who squawked louder. He started to shrink, smaller and smaller, until he was no bigger than my little finger. I picked the tiny goose up by the neck and stared it in the face.

"Nip me again," I said, "and I'll make you even smaller next time."

I did an enlarging spell and returned the goose to its normal size and let it go. He never bothered me again.

So I learned slowly, but added a number of spells to my memory: Growth, Purify, Antidote, Truth Tell, and a few others. I was well on my way of achieving my dream.

I'd been with Barkins for five years when the war started. People fleeing from the army of George the Humongous told tales of burned villages and towns plundered. Things didn't look so good.

Scared by the stories the refugees told, townsfolk kept pounding on Barkins' door, begging him to save them. Barkins nodded and stroked his scraggly beard and said, "Not to worry. Barkins the Magnificent will take care of this."

Right. Two days later, George the Humongous was almost on our doorstep, and Barkins had done a vanishing act, leaving me to deal with the townsfolk and face George all by myself.

Now the town of West Morningdale had a stone wall around it, and there was a small squad of guards, but not enough to repel George and his horde. So the town mayor came to me and said it was my duty to defend the town.

"But how can *I* fight a huge army?" I demanded. "I'm just an apprentice!"

"Surely you know something that would save us," he said, glaring intently at me. "After all, you've been with Barkins long enough to learn lots of spells and whatever it is you wizard types do. Remember, if you fail, you'll die with the rest of us." He turned, his fur-trimmed velvet coat flaring out, and strode quickly away.

So here I sit on the roof of Barkins' house, staring across the fields outside the town walls. I see what looks like a black tide creeping toward the town, just like locusts. Army like that would eat everything in sight.

Eating. Something clicks in my head, and I start to grin. I scurry down from the roof, run to the mayor's house, and quickly lay out my plans. The mayor looks skeptical at first, then he starts to smile, too. He calls his chief guard and gives him orders. I run back home and start to mix up a bunch of potions and gather items for spells.

We have maybe a day to be ready. The mayor enlists everyone in town to help prepare a feast for George and his horde. No one sleeps that night. I visit every house and inn, even the mayor's kitchen, and added my own magical touch to every dish–a sleeping potion. I enlarge piglets, ducklings, chicks, and calves, and direct the men to butcher and roast them, using my own special basting sauce with more sleeping potion in it. I send boys to gather every table in the town and carry them outside the town gates.

"And wine," I tell the young men. "Barrels of wine, but bring them to me before you take them out."

Then I tell several young girls, "I need cloths, sheets, anything to cover the tables. And plates. And cups, mugs, glasses. Anything to drink from." They take off running.

By the time the sun rises the next morning, I am exhausted, but everything is ready.

I wear my best dress–which means the one with the fewest holes and stains–and a clean apron. I walk outside the town gates and cringe just a bit when they clang shut behind me. Before me is a long row of tables loaded with roasted meats and fowl, roasted carrots and turnips, fresh baked bread, meat pies, stuffed cabbage leaves and grape leaves, pickled onions and beets as well as regular pickles, berry pies, hazelnut tortes, baked apple dumplings, and bowls of cherries and early berries. And at one end there are ten barrels of wine.

I hope there's enough for George's army, I think. I glance up at the parapet. The mayor is there as well as lots of townsfolk with buckets of flower petals and waving pennants. Several men play drums and flutes, and everyone cheers.

We've done everything we can, I think.

George the Humongous rides up on a sleek, black horse. Only thing about him that is humongous is his nose. And maybe his ego. I can't tell what color his hair is because he's wearing a slightly dented helmet, but his rounded beard is black with a few stray white hairs in it. His chainmail has several rents in it, and his pants and boots are covered with dirt.

Bowing, I say, "Welcome, mighty lord!" Never hurts to flatter someone who can do you harm. "You and your men must be tired and hungry. We prepared a feast for you, but our town square isn't big enough for all the tables. So we brought them out here."

George scowls at the tables. "I suspect the food is poisoned."

I do my best to look shocked and annoyed. "Of course not! If you want proof, I'll sample everything before you eat or drink."

"Then do so," he says.

I smile and start with a piece of chicken, a boiled carrot, a bit of this, a morsel of that until I have tasted everything, even a sip of the wine we set out.

"See," I say, "everything is quite good and poison free."

George stares at me—I guess to be sure if the poison takes a while to affect me. "Very well," he says. He turns to the man riding beside him. "Feed half the men, but keep the other half on alert."

The soldier salutes, turns his horse, and calls out to the soldiers on the right side. The army descends on the food like the locusts they are. I watch them wolf down the food while the other half of the troops glare at their compatriots but don't move.

After the half that got to eat first have satisfied their hunger, George allows the other half to eat as well. Good thing we made heaps of food. George dismounts and walks toward me. That's when I notice that he's wearing high-heeled boots, and his eyes are at the same height as my chin. Definitely not humongous. He walks the entire length of the tables, tasting the roast pork, nibbling at the fresh cherries, munching on a chicken leg, and guzzling a large tankard of red wine.

"We're going to conquer this town, you know," he says, wine dribbling down his chin, "in spite of this feast."

"Why, there's no need to conquer this town," I say, smiling coyly. "We welcome you and all your men. I promise, you'll never forget us."

He snorts and continues to eat the drumstick and drink and drink and drink. Maybe his capacity for wine is why he's called humongous.

The sun is nearly overhead when some of the soldiers start to sit down and yawn. More and more yawn and shake their heads. Even George is having trouble walking and is rubbing his eyes.

"You must be exhausted from your travels," I say, suppressing a slight yawn. "Let's sit down for a while."

I spread out a white cloth for us. He staggers a bit.

"Let me help," I say and ease him to the ground. I'm starting to feel a bit drowsy myself, but I fight to keep my eyes open. "It's such a lovely day," I say, "too lovely for a battle, especially when we won't fight."

"But we want to fight," George says. "That's what we do." His eyes seem to cross, and he blinks several times. "But maybe not now."

He yawns so wide, I can see his cracked and yellowed teeth. He starts to slump. I catch him and lower him to the cloth. I take off his helmet and begin stroking his forehead. He smiles, but his eyes are glassy. Soon his eyes close, and he starts snoring, just like all his men. I wait a short while, then get up slowly and go to check on the soldiers to make sure they are asleep, too. Yawning and rubbing my eyes, I turn and signal the guards on the wall before I slip to the ground and fall asleep as well.

When I wake up, I am in my own bed, still in the clothes I wore for George's approach. The sun is shining through my tiny window, and I'm surprised the potions have worn off so quickly. What if the soldiers wake up too soon? What if they can still attack the town? I crawl out of bed and stagger toward the stairs. Gripping the railing tightly, I descend the stairs cautiously and holding my head. I still feel groggy, but I need to know what happened, so I hurry out into the streets.

The sun is still overhead, so I'm sure this isn't the same day. In the streets people are laughing and dancing. Some lead horses, including George's black one, from outside the gate. Some townsfolk carry tables and barrels. A few wagons lumber by, loaded with armor, weapons, and various items. I stumble toward the town gates and carefully climb the stairs to the top of the wall.

The mayor is there, and he smiles at me. "I'm surprised to see you awake so soon. The horde is still sleeping."

I peek around one of the crenellations and gaze across the fields. All the tables that had held the feast are nowhere in sight. George the Humongous and his army lay on the grass, snoring away. They are stripped of their armor, weapons, even their shoes and boots. The remains of two catapults smoke and burn.

"We brought in everything," the mayor says as we gaze at the sleeping army. "Horses, wagons, supplies, even coins and jewelry we found." Then he frowns for a moment. "But what's to stop him from attacking other towns and eventually coming back here?"

I consider this. How can I insure George can't cause more destruction? What can I do?

I smile at the mayor. "I have an idea."

Running back to my house, I grab a large cloth bag. Dried plums, dried apple slices, dried dandelion roots, dried earthworms, a container of sulfur, a bagful of wood ashes, a fistful of wool, and the willow wand go into the bag as well as the largest mortar and pestle I can find. I scoop a glowing ember into a small kettle, take the bag and kettle, and run back to the wall.

George is stirring. A few soldiers begin to groan and open their eyes.

"Close the gates," the mayor calls down to the gate wards.

The gates creak as the guards close them and set the huge brace in place.

I place the mortar on the stone walkway and begin grinding the ingredients, then add the wool and wait.

George rolls over, slowly pushes up on his hands and knees, and gazes at the walls. Anger clenches his teeth and narrows his eyes. He reaches to his right side and clutches at his hip as if reaching for a weapon. He jerks his head toward his side and stares at where his sword isn't. He sits back on his heels and runs his hands over his long-tailed shirt. Pushing to his feet, he sways unsteadily. Some of his men crawl forward and manage to stand up.

George glares up at me. "You damned witch!" he calls. "I will kill you with my bare hands!"

"Considering all you have is your bare hands, that might be difficult," I say, shielding my eyes.

"A sword!" he shouts. "Someone give me a sword! Archers, let fly!"

His second in command trudges unsteadily to George's side and says something too soft for me to hear. He whirls around toward his army and has to grasp his second's arm to keep from falling. George's head swivels from side to side as his men gradually creep to their feet, and his shoulders sag. Slowly, he turns back toward me, his face a pasty yellow like winter egg yolks. His mouth opens and closes like a fish out of water.

"My catapults," he says, his fists clenched. "My ballista, my siege towers, my sword, my armor!" His face turns red, and his eyes looked as if they would pop out of his face. "You–you –" He looks as if he is strangling.

The second leans in close and says something in George's ear. They seem to argue for a bit, then George nods and slowly turns to look at me.

"We'll be back," he says, "and we'll destroy this town and you with it."

"I don't think so," I say.

I lift the mortar and set it on the ledge of one of the crenellations. Waving the willow wand over the mortar three times and pointing at the army, I dump the ember into the mortar. White smoke billows from the mortar and surrounds the invaders. When the smoke clears, George and his men are barely half as tall as they had been. Their shirt hems drag the ground.

George starts sputtering, and he looks enraged. His second tries to pull him away, but George fights him.

"I'll kill her!" George screams. "I'll kill her!" He runs toward the gates and kicks the heavy wooden doors, then shrieks in pain and hops on one foot.

"If you come back again," I say, "I'll make you so small, you'll disappear completely."

Slowly, George turns from the town and begins limping away. The second calls out orders, and the soldiers begin shuffling back the way they had come, arms across their chests as if cold.

George looks back at me several times, appearing to mutter something as he limps away. I can't help but smile at the sight of him and his great army slinking away wearing their oversized clothes. It's an hour or two before the horde has diminished to a brown cluster of dwarves, like ants scattering after someone has disturbed their hill.

As the last soldier disappears over the rise, the mayor turns to me. "You saved us all," he says. "You are amazing."

I smile as I gaze at the empty field in front of the gates. "Not really. I just remembered something my mum told me."

"And what was that?"

"The way to a man's heart is through his stomach."

Jayco's Song

I've often thought sirens must be the loneliest creatures in the realm of fantasy. Never a friend, a companion, no one to share their lives with. Would it even be possible?

The midmorning sun hid behind cotton boll clouds as Jayco flung his net out into the calm sea. *Good,* he thought as he glanced at the sky. *No shadow to scare the fish.* He waited a few moments, then began to drag the heavy net into the boat. All the while he paced his work to the song, his song, that hummed through his thoughts.

Jayco never thought of himself as cursed even though the villagers said he was. He hadn't heard a word since he was fifteen years old, almost thirty years ago. Sometimes he missed the sounds that had almost faced from his memory, but it didn't matter. Hearing wasn't necessary to a fisherman. He could smell the tang of salt water, the tar and wood of his boat, his food as it cooked. He saw the seasonal ocean currents, the clouds blowing across the sky, the sea gulls wheeling above schools of fish. And he felt the sun on his back, the rhythm of waves, the tug of a full net. What did he need to hear except the words his own mind whispered as he patiently waited for a good day's catch? But sometimes...sometimes he wished...

Suddenly, the net jerked in his hands, nearly pulling him into the water. *Dellazu's horns! Probably a shark.*

Lacing leathery fingers through the net, he strained until the cording cut into his skin. Hand over hand, he inched the net into the boat, then had to brace his feet to keep from being pulled in as his catch fought back. His jaws ached from gritting his teeth. His arm and back muscles began to cramp. Suddenly, he fell backwards against the side, empty net flopping on top of him.

Jayco sat up slowly, wincing as the salt water stung his raw hands and the welts the net left on his face. He pushed and pulled the water-heavy net until he found the rent, a yard long and half as wide. It was early in the day, too early to go back to shore empty-handed. He had his net shuttle and extra cording in the boat. All he needed was a place to spread out the net to repair it.

Shading aqua eyes, he scanned the horizon. Yes, there it was to the northwest– Edolin Island. None of the other villagers sailed within a league of the rocky land with few trees and patchy vegetation, jutting from the sea. He didn't believe the old sailors' stories of a demon who lived there, nor of the shipwrecks and drowned men.

Raising his single sail, he caught the gentle breeze in the rough cloth and steered the tiller toward the island. As he drew closer, he noticed slight ripples where the sea hid reefs and rocks just below the surface. Tacking the sail and steering north, he found a sheltered cove. The boat thudded against the sandy bottom. He lowered the sail, hopped into the shallow water, and pulled the boat onto the shore.

The soaked net was unwieldy, but Jayco spread it on the warm sand to dry. He wound cording around the net shuttle until it was full, the surveyed the damage. *Not too bad,* he thought as he smoothed the torn edges together. *Take less than an hour. Be easier if I could hang the net up, but I'll make do.*

He pulled a piece of drift wood from the beach, sat down on it, and began weaving and knotting the net whole again. Sweat trickled down his lean face, baked by sun and weathered by sea. In his mind he hummed his song, the only song he remembered, a haunting lament, though he didn't remember when he'd learned it.

He was working on the last tear when he sensed a presence, someone near. Before he could look around, a soft hand touched his stubbly cheek. Startled, he leaped to his feet and spun around. The sun, just climbing above the barren peek, blinded him for a moment. When his eyes adjusted, he could see a female figure, slender. The wind teased waist-length hair.

Then...he saw her face. He froze, held captive by eyes as green and deep as the sea. No flower from heaven's fields could've been as perfectly formed as her face; no snowflake, as fair and delicate as her skin. Her hair glowed like the sun itself. And her lips–cherries, rubies were pale by comparison. If Jayco could've moved, he'd have knelt before her.

The woman's lips moved, but he didn't understand her. He cupped his hands to his ears and shook his head, hoping she'd understand he was deaf.

She looked surprised, then smiled. "You did not hear me singing?"

Jayco froze. He'd understood her, heard her words in his head, just like his song! Fear made him shiver, though sweat trickled down his back. His throat felt desert-dry; his breath came in muffled gulps. *Dreaming,* he thought. *Must be dreaming. Or dead.*

Her smile was warmer than sunlight, but her lips never moved. "No, you are not dreaming nor dead."

I hear her! he thought, amazed. *I really hear her!*

"And I hear you. I hear your thoughts, and you hear mine."

Jayco stared at her, frightened yet excited. His separation and loneliness, loneliness he hadn't really admitted until that moment, crashed down on him like breakers in high seas. *It's been...so long since I spoke with someone.*

She took a step closer to him. "How did you avoid the reefs?"

Jayco swallowed to wet his dry throat. *Saw them.*

Green eyes widened. "You saw them?"

No, eddies in water.

Her lips parted slowly. "Ah-h-h. You see what other do not. What is your name?"

Jayco's tongue felt thick, slow, as if he'd drunk too much beer. *Jayco. Name's Jayco.*

"Jayco." Her smile was springtime warm. "I like that."

His vision wavered as grateful tears filled his eyes. *Your name?*

She smoothed away the wetness on his cheek. "Cerisse."

Cerisse. The name caressed his thoughts like a prayer.

She motioned to him. "Come with me. I know a cool place by a clear stream. Are you thirsty?"

Wariness needled his mind, and a wordless warning crept down his spine. He started to turn away but decided not to. *Yes. Yes, I am.*

She led him like an unresisting child to a shady glen in the trees. Glittering water tumbled down stairs of worn rock to a small pool. Cupping her hands to capture the icy liquid, she offered it to Jayco. Instead, he caught his own handfuls of water and soothed his dry throat, but his gaze never left her. Swaying like a willow in the wind, she walked a short distance, sat beside the pool, and waved for him to sit next to her.

Are you...a goddess? he asked, trembling.

She shook her head.

He splashed cold water on the back of his neck and on his chest to cool the fire that surged through him. Slowly, he walked toward her and sank to the grass.

Her hand, cool as silk and soft as velvet, caressed his jaw down to the pulsing hollow of his throat. "Jayco, would...would you lie with me?"

Jayco's breath caught in his chest. She'd asked him—old, deaf Jayco—to lie with her, touch her, know her as man knows woman! He hadn't touched a woman like that since his first hesitant explorations as a boy. No woman had wanted him after the accident had taken his hearing, an accident he didn't even remember. Why now? Why not ask him when he was young, before his skin became leather hard, before his body was scarred and his hands were calloused? What perverse god had sent beauty incarnate to remind him how the years were carved on his face?

He watched as she lay back against the grass and held her arms out to him.

"Please, Jayco, no man has ever set foot on this island. No one has ever touched me."

Jayco wanted to touch her, hold her softness in his arms so badly, his chest knotted with a sweet but painful ache. Since his accident, he'd had little joy in his life. The sea claimed his days, drink blurred his evenings, but loneliness filled his nights. Touching her would be touching perfection...no, he couldn't. Perfection touched was perfection marred. Squelching his desire, he shook his head.

Cerisse...His hand inched toward her cheek, then drew back. He sighed as if every regret in his life had condensed into one empty, silent moment. *Too old. I'm just too old.*

Her hands beckoned him as a starstone beckons steel. "No, you're not too old."

He closed his eyes, shutting out her emerald eyes. Tears squeezed from the corners of his eyes, and his mournful song whispered in his head.

A sharp-nailed hand gripped his chin like a barnacle grips hulls. His eyes flew open, his gaze reflected in her lupine stare.

"My song." Cerisse's mouth was tight with anger. "You know my song."

Jayco gaped at her. *Your song?*

"Yes! You were singing my song in your thoughts! Where did you hear it? How can a deaf man know my song?"

Jayco was old, but net fishing had built hard muscles and a lean body. Prying her fingers from his chin, he dove across the pool, rolled, and scrambled to his feet. A quick glance over his shoulder showed Cerisse pushing to her feet. He started to run until he saw her reflection in the pool. Her hair was the color of pine needles; her skin was palest green. Although her eyes were still deep emerald, there was a predatory gleam in them.

He dragged his gutting knife from its sheath. *What are you? What do you want?*

She stalked the opposite side, her hands curled like claws. "How do you know my song?"

Don't know! He watched her cautiously. *Heard it in my head after the accident!*
"What accident?" She shifted directions.

Afraid to turn his back to her and run, he paralleled her every step. *Don't remember! Only what they say! My boat wrecked! Fell in, hit my head! Woke up deaf with the song in my head!*

She stumbled, then stared at him, wide-eyed and open-mouthed. "Where? Where was the wreck?"

He flung his empty hand toward the sea. *There! On the reefs! Villagers found me clinging on wood and took me back to shore!*

Cerisse's eyes filled with fear, and she became pale as death. She whirled away from him.

Jayco cocked his arm back. *Stay or I'll throw!*

She stood paralyzed for a few moments, as if wondering if he meant it.

He saw her foot start to move again. *Don't! Best aim in the village!*

Cerisse faced him, the look of a cornered animal in her eyes. "You survived, the only one in all the eons I have loved! That's why I have no power over you!"

Anger and fear made Jayco's throat raw. *What are you?*

Her head drooped like a wilted flower. "I was a maegd of the Sae Cynnraeden– a mermaid. Fair enough to draw the attention of the Lord of the Deep, but I did not want him. I spurned him, and he cursed me for it. He transformed me into a siren, then banished me from the sea to this island. A thousand changes of the seasons have I been here, utterly alone, forbidden to return to the sea, unable to leave the land."

She sank to the ground as if she had no strength to stand. "Once, I would sing to my people, and they would weep from the song's beauty. Now, because of the Lord's curse, my song drives men to madness, lures them to rocks and reefs and wild currents swirling around this island. No one can hear me and live. I'm compelled to sing, to kill. He left me no choice." Slowly, she lifted her chin and met Jayco's eyes. "What will you do, now that you know what I am, what I've done to you?"

Jayco stood still, his thumb rubbing the bone hilt of his knife. He studied her reflection, alien yet beautiful. Knife gripped firmly, he sprang across the pool.

Cerisse cowered as he moved within inches of her. "Will you destroy me?" she asked.

His rough, scarred hand enfolded her smooth, flawless one, raised it, and kissed her palm. *Destroy the only beauty I've ever known? No. I couldn't.*

Tears streaked her pale cheeks. "What...what would you have me do?"

He sheathed his knife. *Let me stay with you.* He touched her soft hair.

"But why? I'm cursed to sing, to lure men to their deaths. I have no choice!" She dove into the pool, submerging in the water. Moments later, she bubbled to the surface, choking.

Jayco leaped in, grasped her arms, and dragged her to shore. He slapped her back until she stopped coughing. *What happened?* he asked as he cradled her head against his chest.

"The curse," she sobbed. "The water won't accept me, won't let me die. The Lord of the Deep's curse still exiles me from my home."

Jayco held her gently, compassion bringing tears to his eyes. *Sing to me. Sing to me now.*

"Why? My singing brings only death."

Not to me. I can hear you singing without danger to me or guilt for you. Sing, Cerisse.

She stared up at him incredulously, a scintilla of hope shining in her eyes.

Jayco cradled her chin in his hands, gently smoothed away her tears with his thumbs, then smiled. *Don't you understand, Cerisse? Neither of us has to be alone anymore.*

She sang to him, only him, for the rest of their days.

Harts Gambol

I love dragons. I have shelves filled with figurines and statues. I even have half a dozen stuffed dragon toys. Dragons, whatever their size, are delightful and devious and dangerous. But I still love them.

Sunlight hit Lindan's blue-grey eyes like a fist, sudden and painful, after a week of travel through the shadowy forest of Aldigon with light filtered through dense branches. Shielding her eyes against the glare, she squinted at the wide clearing, then choked, horrified.

She stared at a heap of crumbling stone and a weed-choked garden. "That's Harts Gambol? My luxurious castle with formal gardens, scenic view, and impregnable walls? My retreat after years of wandering? It's no more than a small keep! No wonder Redolan was so willing to gamble with it! I should've known better than to trust a Black Wizard!"

Thistles and wild roses pulled at her forest green cloak as she picked her way toward the keep. Muttering to herself, she reached a limestone arch in a waist-high rock fence. As she scanned the building, she realized it looked a little better up close than it had from a distance. Granite blocks had fallen from the merlons, one corner tower had nearly crumbled, but at least part of the masonry looked sound.

Only one area of the grounds showed half-hearted attempts to keep the weeds at bay: a large garden surrounded by marble statues of deer. Rows of herbs – culinary, medicinal, and magical–thrived in the southern side of the courtyard. The statues gave Lindan the uneasy feeling that they were alive, as if deer had been wandering about the garden when they'd been changed to stone.

Looking around, she shook her head, disgusted. "Redolan cheated me!"

"Why should you worry about the master's ethics? You seem unconcerned about trespassing on another's property."

Lindan wheeled around, trying to locate the speaker. No one was behind her; no one was anywhere in sight. "Who are you? Where...what are you?"

"Why should I answer you?" the tiny voice asked. "I insist that you leave here at once."

Lindan held herself straight and regal. "I don't have to leave. I own this keep."

A giggle came from behind here. "No sane person would buy Harts Gambol."

"I didn't buy it!" Lindan jerked the rolled and tied deed from her rucksack. "I won it in a card game!"

Laughter flitted across the garden. "And that proves my point."

"What point?"

"You are not sane."

Angry, Lindan's eyes narrowed, and her jaw tightened. Holding the deed high above her head and stretching her other hand, palm out, in front of her, she said, "I, Laurellindanis, wizard of the seventh tier, command you to leave my keep!"

"I will not!"

Lindan's jaw dropped. Never had her magic failed. Clearing her throat, she tried again. "By the powers of Light and Good, I banish you from this place. Be gone for time and eternity."

A breath of wind touched her cheek, and something small but pointed poked her chest. "This is *my* home, and I am not leaving it! I was here before Harts Gambol was built, and I will still be here long after it is dust. If you own this keep, you may stay, but I am not leaving."

Lindan tried to think of other spells that might work, but nothing came to mind. She stood, gaping, until her shoulder started to cramp from holding her arm up. Lowering it and rubbing her muscles, she said, "Well, I guess you could stay, but...just who or what are you?"

The voice sniffed. "Butterfly."

"You're a butterfly?"

"Of course not! Butterfly is my name."

"Oh." Lindan slipped the deed back in her sack. "What are you? And where are you?"

"Must you ask so many questions? I am directly before you. And what am I?" Wind chime laughter tinkled in the air.

The first things Lindan saw were stained glass wings that reminded her of a swallowtail butterfly. Next, a semicircle of pointed teeth hanging level with the end of her nose. Both were attached to a tiny reptilian body that barely measured from Lindan's fingertips to her elbow. The creature's scales were iridescent blue-green.

"Why, you're adorable!" Lindan said.

"Adorable?" Butterfly sniffed and fluttered his wings. "I am extraordinary! Amazing! Magnificent!"

Lindan smothered a grin. "You left out conceited."

Butterfly did on a lazy midair loop. "Conceit implies unjustified pride. I have every reason to be proud, as any casual observer can see. Therefore I am not conceited."

No wonder Redolan wanted to get rid of this place, Lindan thought. "I've never heard of a creature like you before, a miniature dragon with butterfly wings. Exactly what are you?"

"Lepidoptera derkesthai lutel."

"Meaning?"

Butterfly's grin was like sunshine on snow. "Scaly winged little seer."

Lindan sighed and shook her head. "I'll stick with Butterfly. I think I'll explore the inside of my keep."

"Very well," he said with the waived for the garden door, "but do not go up to the roof."

"Why?"

"That is my perch, and I own it."

Lindan stared at him confused. "But I own the keep."

"You do not own the roof."

She shook her head. "That's ridiculous. The roof is part of the keep, and I own the keep. You can use the roof if you like."

"How magnanimous of you," Butterfly said sourly. "If you read the deed carefully, you will note that I most certainly own the roof."

Lindan took out the deed, untied the thong, and scanned the writing. Yes, the clause was there; she owned everything but the roof. "I don't believe this," she said. "Why do you own the roof?"

"That was the price I demanded from Hertiphimus for building Harts Gambol in my meadow."

"Wonderful," she said. She started to roll up the deed when tiny scrawls at the bottom of it caught her attention, scrawls she hadn't noticed before. Squinting, she deciphered the words. "Possession of this deed constitutes ownership of Harts Gambol, with all rights, privileges, and curses pertaining to said property." She looked up at Butterfly. "Curses? What curses?"

"Each owner has a different curse, some mild, some severe. Hertiphimus could not eat any meat or fish. The very smell made him ill. But Redolan," Butterfly gave her a coy smile, "could be away from Harts Gambol for two weeks at most before his magic strength started to wane. He was forced to teleport back and remain for several weeks. On one occasion he did not return until he had lost his

magic, then his health. He almost died before another wizard brought him home."
Butterfly preened his wings. "Redolan craved cities and women and gambling.
Staying here infuriated him, even though he drew his power from here."

Lindan hugged herself, smiling. She'd always wanted a home, a place she could
come back to. "Is the curse always different?"

"No, Winslow and Vandalor both were unable to sleep at night."

Lindan grinned. "Well, I can always hope."

Suddenly, Butterfly dove straight at her. Lindan ducked and started to run for
the keep when his claws clutched her shoulder.

"Will you *please* stand still?" Butterfly said, holding on. "My wings are tired!"

Pushing her graying hair from her thin face, Lindan stood up slowly and
frowned at him. "Warn me next time."

Folding his wings, he wrapped his tail around her neck like a turquoise necklace.
"Shall we inspect the keep?"

Lindan walked toward the garden door, which opened as soon as her hand
touched it. Yellow light appeared inside a glass globe ensconced to her left,
revealing a narrow stone corridor that retreated into darkness. The ceiling was
low, just a couple inches above Lindan's head. She turned enough to look at
Butterfly. "You know your way around here. Why don't you give me a guided
tour?"

"I suppose I can spare the time, Lindie."

"Lindan," she said firmly, glaring at him.

"I prefer Lindie."

"I don't."

He frowned petulantly. "Oh, very well! Lindan. Straight ahead is the main
hall." He pointed up the corridor as Lindan started forward. "The kitchen is to
your right. To the left is the front door. Spiral stairs there..." with his tail he
motioned beyond the open hearth in the center of the room, "lead to the second
and third floors."

Surveying the hall, Lindan noted it wasn't spotlessly clean, but it wasn't as
messy as it might have been. "A little sweeping and washing and this place'll be
fine."

Butterfly sighed. "Redolan did not care for it properly. Unforgivable. This was
a popular spot when Hertiphimus lived here. He was the one who built Harts
Gambol, you know."

"No, I didn't," Lindan said as she spotted a few strands of dirty spider web hanging from the ceiling.

"He followed the ley lines to a node of magic power right here. That is why he wanted to build Harts Gambol."

Lindan closed her eyes and searched for the taste of magic. Yes, there it was–strong, stronger than anything she'd ever felt, more potent and intoxicating than fine brandy. No wonder Hertiphimus had wanted the meadow!

Butterfly's tail twitched around Lindan's neck, tickling her. "A kindly old wizard he was, once we finally became acquainted. I did not wish to share my meadow with anyone else. It was sometime before he and I reached an understanding." He grinned at her.

Lindan was sure Butterfly had made life miserable for Hertiphimus until the little reptile had gotten exactly what he wanted. "I think I'll check out the kitchen. Did Redolan keep any wine here?"

Butterfly laughed. "Yes, but it seldom lasted long. He relished wine almost as much as he did women."

"Well, I'd love something besides water."

She walked into a wide room that smelled of mold and decay, and she grimaced. Broken bottles lay on the floor. Unwashed crockery and dishes were stacked haphazardly on the table. "What a mess," she said in disgust.

She picked her way through remains of spilled food and searched until she found one unopened cask. It took her awhile to pound in the tap, but soon she held a cup of dark red wine with a strong, fruity bouquet. The fragrance made her thirstier. She took a drink...then doubled over and vomited. Pain twisted her stomach, pierced her head, and clawed her spine.

"You do not drink wine very often, do you?" Butterfly asked as he stared at her.

"But...I do," she whispered between gasps. "All...the time. A little too often, my friends say."

The ridges over Butterfly's eyes rose, and he cocked his head. "But have you imbibed wine since becoming owner of Harts Gambol?"

Confused, Lindan said, "No."

Butterfly grinned. "I believe we have discovered your curse: abstinence from wine." When she gave him the sour look, he said, "It could have been much worse."

Struggling into her feet, Lindan wiped her mouth. "Let's go upstairs. Maybe I'll find a bed."

Butterfly clung to her shoulder as she climbed the steps. The second floor was divided into two rooms: the library to her right, a bedroom to her left. Clothes carpeted the bedroom floor. Blankets were wadded on the bed. One corner of the room had almost fallen away.

"Redolan was a slob," she muttered.

Butterfly leaned an elbow on her head and propped his chin on his claw. "That was his best quality. He had little respect for others. I am delighted he is gone."

The library was an unexpected surprise. Ceiling-high shelves were filled with books, scrolls, and maps, all ancient and scrupulously dusted. Lindan picked up one volume and glanced through it.

"Tovaine's seventh eye!" she said, astonishment smoothing wrinkles from her face. "I've never even heard of some of these spells! This is...astounding!"

Butterfly hopped over to a shelf ladder. "It has taken many years to accumulate all this knowledge."

"This library is as valuable as the magic node!" Lindan scanned the hundreds of books in awe. "Why in the world would Redolan get rid of Harts Gambol without taking some or all of these with him?"

"He did not."

"He didn't what?" Lindan asked, puzzled.

"He did not leave without taking many of the books with him." Butterfly flew up to the next shelves and perched beside a black leather-bound book. "This one, for instance."

"He took one like this?"

"No." He sounded exasperated. "He took this one."

"I'm surprised he brought it back."

"He did not. It returned by itself. Anything that belongs to the keep always returns to the keep. That is Hertiphimus' own spell book. Redolan took it with him on his last trip, but when he transferred ownership of the keep to you, the book returned here." Butterfly folded his wings and tongue-washed his fore claws like a cat.

A nervous quivering settled in Lindan's stomach. "Anything that people own always stays at the keep? Even my spell book?"

"Anything that is already here will remain at the keep. You brought your spell book with you, so you may take it with you if you leave. However, if you die while you still retain ownership of Harts Gambol, your book becomes the property of the keep."

She felt a little relieved. "But didn't Redolan know about this, too?"

Butterfly shook his head. "He was the apprentice of Pylaides, the former owner of Harts Gambol. Redolan inherited the keep when Pylaides died unexpectedly, but the old wizard never divulged that particular information."

Lindan thought about it for a moment, then gasped. "Oh, gods!" She flopped down into the only chair in the room and slouched deep into the velvety cushion. "I'll bet Redolan knows now, and I'll bet he's not too happy about it, either."

Butterfly frowned and tapped a tiny claw against his jaw. Knowing Redolan, he will not accept the situation. If I were you, I would prepare to defend your right of ownership or surrender the deed to him."

Chin in hand, Lindan crunched up her mouth. For years she had wanted a home, a place she could rest and spend her last years, no more wandering. At last, she had one. "I won fair and square. I won't give it up without a fight."

Butterfly settled on her shoulder again. "That is a certainty."

Lindan chewed on the nail of her little finger and wondered how much time she had before Redolan decided to reclaim Harts Gambol. He probably wouldn't notice he was missing anything for a few days since he'd been having a really good time at the wizards' conclave and mystical fair. Redolan had seemed especially fond of women and Dragon's Blood, a potent brandy favored by many wizards at the fair. "Maybe it'll be a week before he misses anything." She sighed. "But I can't count on that. Better to be prepared, just in case."

"Redolan has an abominable temper. He injured his toe getting out of bed one morning. Enraged, he slammed a Storm Wind through the wall. If he returns to reclaim Harts Gambol, he will not be restrained by rules of combat. You will need to use all means to defeat him, even unethical ones."

Lindan gasped, shocked at the thought.

Butterfly pointed out to the next floor. "The workshop is upstairs. Also, another bedroom. Beyond that is the roof. Each of the turrets contains an observatory. You might consider repairing the broken one to keep Redolan from entering that way."

Lindan winced. "And I thought I'd finally found a peaceful place to rest."

After she'd checked out the rest of the keep, Lindan began mending the broken walls. That evening she spent pouring through books in the library. There was enough reading to keep her busy every evening for the rest of her life. One spell caught her attention: Stone Spell. It transformed any living material to stone. Remembering the deer in the garden, Lindan shivered. Had they been alive? Had Redolan turn them to stone? She wasn't sure she wanted to know.

It took two days for her to seal all the cracks and clean all the rooms. Setting traps in the keep and wards around the perimeter took another two. She spent the next day weeding and cultivating the herb garden. Butterfly perched on her shoulder and talked ceaselessly. By sunset, Lindan was aching, tired, but pleased with the improved appearance of her home.

Lindan was still sleeping the next morning when the alarm ward she placed around the meadow sounded like distant thunder, tingling on her skin like rubbing cat fur. Leaping from bed, she ran to the window and peered out. Redolan stood halfway between the woods and the stone fence, frowning, his hands clenched.

"He attempted to teleport inside the keep," Butterfly said, appearing beside Lindan so suddenly, she jumped. "It is fortunate that you conjured a barrier or he would be here now."

Heart hammering against her ribs and barely able to breathe, Lindan slumped against the stone wall. A cold sweat coated her skin, and she shivered. "I hope I'm ready for him."

"I hope so as well," Butterfly said softly, his brow ridges drawn together in a frown. "You could allow him to buy the keep or gamble for it. The only other way he can acquire Harts Gambol is if you are dead."

Lindan shivered. "Let's hope it won't come to that."

She slipped on shoes and a deep green robe, tied her hair back with a thong, and took a deep breath before she went down to face Redolan.

He flashed a smile as she walked toward him, making Lindan's stomach jiggle uneasily and her skin prickle. The morning sun brought out white streaks in his black hair. His eyes were dark opals. The robe hugging his lean form seemed to shimmer ebony and violet.

"Good morning, my dear Lindan," he said, soft as snowflakes. "I hope I didn't awaken you."

Lindan tried to appear relaxed and unconcerned although her whole body was tense. "What do you want?" she asked, already knowing the answer.

"I thought I would see if you'd settled in comfortably. Harts Gambol has certain...quirks." He paused, and his smile faltered. "No, truthfully, I came to tell you how you won that card game." He lowered his chin, but his dark eyes were fixed on her. "I cheated. I rigged the game so I could be free of this crumbling pile of rocks."

"That's what Butterfly said."

"I'm certain he did." Redolan sighed and shook his head. "I can only imagine what else he told you. He would do or say anything to be rid of me. I refused to let him control me as he did Pylaides and the others who owned Harts Gambol. Butterfly looks harmless, but he's powerful enough to resist being controlled even by a wizard as great as Hertiphimus. Who knows what the creature's capable of?"

Doubt prodded Lindan. Why shouldn't she believe Redolan? She only had Butterfly's word for the wizard's intent, and Butterfly had a personal interest in this situation. She frowned slightly. Suppose...suppose Butterfly had lied to her, had wanted her to keep Harts Gambol because he could manipulate her but not Redolan. Confused, chewing her lip, she glanced away.

"Look out!" Butterfly shouted, although she couldn't see him.

Lindan dropped to a crouch just in time to avoid the fiery dart Redolan aimed at her. The barrier was gone! Grabbing a handful of dirt, she tossed it at his face. A simple strategy, but it worked. Redolan yelled as he tried to rub the dirt from his eyes. Lindan leaped up, drew power from the magic ley lines, and called a Storm Wind.

Circling his palms in front of him, Redolan formed a Force Wall. The Storm Wind crashed against it. The wall held firm. Lindan pushed the wind forward. Redolan pushed back. Lindan's head began to ache from the tension as she poured her strength into the wind, but the wall wouldn't budge. Finally, the wind shattered against it and vanished.

Lindan cupped her hands and called light—bright as sun, white as moon, pure and blinding, as sudden and painful as when she'd first come to Harts Gambol --then hurled it at Redolan. He screamed as the light blotted out everything else, but somehow he held the wall intact.

Gasping with his eyes closed, he stamped his foot. The ground trembled. The tremble grew to rolling waves like a stormy sea. Lindan barely kept her balance.

Redolan wiped a hand across his eyes and blinked them clear. Holding the wall intact with one hand, he reached inside his belt pouch and pulled out a black powder, which he threw at Lindan.

Darkness surrounded her, so thick she could almost touch it. She turned and ran, but the darkness seemed endless. Dropping back to the ground, she shape-changed into a black leopard. Darkness became shades of gray to her eyes.

Bounding for the lighter areas, she reached the edge of darkness and stumbled into blinding light.

Redolan was waiting for her, hands raised to cast another spell, but her cat form seemed to startle him. He hesitated long enough for her to lunge at him. Her claws had almost reached him when lightning flew from his fingertips. Lindan screamed as white-hot pain slashed her left side from shoulder to haunch. Redolan screamed, too, as Lindan's claws raked deep, bloody gashes down his arm.

Lindan tumbled several times before she lay in a heap, back in her human shape. The burn down her side was as black and crisp as the edges of her singed robe. Breath came in ragged gasps, and her body twitched compulsively. Although yellow-edged black spots dotted her vision, she could see Redolan approaching her. He stood over her and smiled, but his eyes were dark granite, cold and hard.

"You should've surrendered the keep to me," he said, his laugh like a river in winter. "Now I'll inherit it a second time. Harts Gambol is *mine*."

His hand reached toward her like a deadly spider. Lindan tried to move away from it, but her body wouldn't respond. She stared at his eyes, unable to look away.

Glowing with Death's Touch, Redolan's hand was only inches away when he yelled and jerked it back. Butterfly appeared, his jaws clamped around the wizard's forearm. Redolan flung his arm up, down, side to side, trying to loosen the dragon's hold. Finally, Butterfly let go, then whipped his tail across Redolan's eyes. The wizard yelled, buried his face against his arm, and stumbled back.

Lindan blinked her eyes, freed from the wizard's gaze.

"Attack him!" Butterfly shouted. "Now, Lindan, now!"

"You damned nuisance!" Redolan cried and aimed a streak of lightning at Butterfly. The little creature shrieked and dropped to the ground, his wing ragged like shattered glass.

"That's enough!" Lindan said as she struggled to her feet. She clutched the air in front of her and squeezed.

Redolan's face turned pink, then red. His mouth opened, and he gasped for air.

"How dare you hurt Butterfly!" Lindan said. "I didn't want to harm you. It's against my code. But you need a lesson in humility, courtesy, and respect. I'm going to give you time to think. Maybe after a few decades you'll have learned kindness and how to control your temper."

She touched his arm, reached out to the magic node in the earth, and with the last of her strength drew the power into her. Her voice a whisper, she said, "Stone."

Lindan thought she heard a hopeless wail as she felt Redolan's flesh turn hard and cold under her hand, then she lost consciousness.

The scent of wintergreen and aloe filled Lindan's nose as she took a slow, deep breath before opening her eyes. She was lying in her bed, covered with a white sheet and blanket but wearing nothing. Late afternoon sunlight brightened the room as she sat up gradually. Checking her side, she found a reddish-white scar where the lightning had burned her.

"How long have I been out?" she wondered aloud.

"Almost a week," said Butterfly as he appeared at the foot of the bed. "I have nearly worn myself to a frazzle taking care of you. Look at my wings!" He turned slightly and held out a damaged wing. "Tattered, dull, limp–I will have to rest at least a week to restore their sheen."

"How did I get here?"

"I carried you."

Lindan stared at him skeptically. "I know I'm light, but not that light."

Butterfly fluttered his wings and smoothed them gently. "Do not be silly! I had to shapechange."

"You?" Lindan's jaw dropped. "You shape-changed? To what?"

"A man," Butterfly said with a disdainful sniff. "It is not easy for me, but if necessary, I am capable of it. And it was necessary, to bring you here and to care for you. The previous owners kept a large supply of medicines. The ointment I used healed that burn quickly. Only a little scar remains." The corner of his mouth twitched with a smile. "You are well-formed — for a woman."

Lindan gave him a grim smile. "Thanks." She lay back down and stared at the ceiling. "He's still out there, isn't he?"

Butterfly rolled his eyes. "Of course. Statues do not move by themselves."

Lindan closed her eyes and shuddered. She'd never use dark magic before.

As if reading her thoughts, Butterfly curled up on the pillow, rested his head on her shoulder, and patted her arm. "You had no choice. He intended to kill you. Truly, there was nothing else you could have done."

"I know," she said with a deep sigh. "I know, but--"

"No!" Butterfly interrupted. "Do not punish yourself with unwarranted recriminations. Redolan attacked you first. He gave you no choice. And he is not dead."

Lindan sat up suddenly. "Tovaine's third eye! I forgot to check. Is there a spell to turn him back?"

Butterfly look startled, then grinned, his sharp little teeth gleaming. "I do not know, but we have the library." He chuckled. "And we have ample time to find out."

Do Virgins Taste Better?

This story was one of the group's exercises. We were all to write a story that started with, "And then the dragon came." I went home from our meeting, wrote this story, revised it the next day, and sent it out to the group. They loved it and insisted I send it out. Marion Zimmer Bradley liked it, too, and bought it for the dragon issue of her magazine. I've never had a story come to me so quickly again.

And then the dragon came. As if I didn't have enough problems.

It landed about fifty feet away from me, with all the grace of a sack of mud. The dry autumn breeze brought the faint sounds of cheering from the watchers on the castle walls. After the dust cleared and I stopped choking, I stared at the scaly horror. I'd never seen a dragon up close and since this was likely to be my one and only chance, I figured I'd satisfy my curiosity. I shifted slightly in the manacles to ease my aching wrists, and studied the monster.

The dragon looked like a wizard's idea of a practical joke: take a small brown lizard, attach bat wings and antelope horns, mix grated horseradish with mustard seed, black peppercorns, onion, and garlic, and shove it all down his throat for the world's worse case of heartburn, then nearly drown him in a growth potion. What do you have? One absolute nightmare for virgins. Oh, well, curiosity satisfied.

The dragon didn't change shape as some dragons do. He waddled towards me, wings folded and tongue flicking in and out, until he was only a few yards from me.

"You finally got here," I grumbled, as I rubbed the top of one bare foot with the other. "Certainly took your time, didn't you?"

The dragon stopped, one of its front claws hanging in midair. Rearing its head as high as its neck would stretch, he gazed at me for a moment, then dove toward me like an eagle about to snatch a fish from water.

I knew I was about to be dragon food, and tensed for death.

Iridescent eyes as big as my head stopped, inches away. "Am I to understand that you have anxiously anticipated my arrival, that you actually welcome my presence?"

I rattled the chains that bound me to the two posts. "Do you think I'm standin' here in these because I like it? So let's get on with it. Go ahead. Eat me. See if I care. I'll be better off."

The dragon pulled back a bit. "This is not the usual attitude of those who have been left to satisfy my appetite."

"Really? I suppose you always ask permission before you eat someone."

"That is not my usual procedure."

"Didn't think so. Well?"

The dragon cocked its enormous head and pulled its brow ridges together. "I do not understand."

"I want to die. Life's nothing but one mess after another. So be a sweet ol' dragon and eat me."

I closed my eyes and waited...and waited...and waited. Nothing. No bad breath, no tearing teeth, no clutching claws, nothing. Finally, I opened one eye, just the tiniest slit.

The dragon was sitting on its haunches like a trained dog, its eyes swirling like oil rainbows on a water puddle.

"Please eat me. I can't take one more day."

That sorry excuse for a menacing monster just stared at me. "What's the matter? Think I'm not good enough to eat? I swear I'm virgin pure, and cursed to stay that way."

"Cursed?" An eye ridge went up, and just a wisp of smoke trickled from the dragon's nose. "Do you mean that literally, or are you merely employing a figure of speech?"

"If you mean am I really cursed, you bet. Say, do all your kind talk like scholars?"

The dragon's mouth opened and closed several times before any sound came out. "In what way are you cursed and by whom?"

"First, how hungry are you? This might take a while."

"I consumed a score of sheep two days ago. My hunger will not become unbearable for another day."

"Lucky sheep," I muttered to myself. "Well, dragon, relax and get comfortable, and I'll tell you all about my curse and why I want you to eat me."

My scaly companion lay down, crossed its front legs, and poised its head in front of me. I could smell his brimstone breath and almost gagged.

"Well, dragon–by the way, do you have a name? I'd really like to know who's eating me?"

The dragon jerked back a little, and I saw his wings tense. "May I ask why you wish to know my name?"

"Yes, you may ask."

If a dragon could look puzzled, this one sure did.

"It's a joke."

The dragon wasn't laughing. Dragons aren't known for their sense of humor. Oh, well, nice try.

I shifted in my chains again, to ease the chafing of my wrists. "I really don't want to keep calling you 'dragon' all the time."

He gave me a smile that looked like miles of teeth.

"You may call me Antedamitos. Of course, that is not my real name, but it will be acceptable."

"And a mouthful!" I said. "Why don't I call you Antee or Dammit, uh, no, not that. Antee then?"

Antee nodded. "And whom do I have the pleasure ...?" He smacked his lips, which made my stomach real shaky. "Of addressing?"

"Covaris."

"I am honored, Covaris."

Somehow, I doubted that. "And I'm not stupid. I know a dragon never gives his true name. After all, I learned some magic from Mike and Pat."

"I assume that Mike and Pat are wizards."

"Were. Dead now. That's part of the problem. But things were bad from when I was born. You see, my mum was a witch."

I don't remember when I first knew I was different from other people, because I didn't see many while I was growing up. My mum and dad and me, we lived in Monger Woods, in a pile of rocks my dad built and roofed with branches, reeds, hides, anything he found lying around. Usually in someone else's yard. Dad wasn't the most reliable sort of man. I don't think he did one honest day's work in his life. But he always put meat on our table. We just never asked where he got it.

Mum provided everything else we needed. She traded her skills with medicines and potions for clothes, grain, chickens, or whatever. She'd studied magic with two wizards before Dad married her.

"The two wizards you mentioned previously?" Antee asked, as he scratched designs in the dirt.

"Same ones," I said, then continued my story.

Mum knew all kinds of things, like how to make love potions and headache cures, and lots of tricks and things. She delivered babies, treated sick children, brought rain, and chased off grain-eating insects. You'd think folks would be thankful for all her help.

The year I was ten, a plague struck the land. As usual, everyone from miles around came begging Mum for help. She worked day and night for weeks, treating hundreds of people and curing them. All but one, that is. An old man, who must've been older that the hills; but that didn't make any difference. He'd been the king's huntsman, before he got too old to see his hand in front of his face.

When the old man died, the king decided Mum had poisoned his old friend, or used evil magic on him. So good ol' king had Mum dragged away and burned as a witch.

Dad took to drinking too much and starting fights. About a year after Mum's death, he picked a fight with one of the king's guards, a man named Smiley. Dad ended up with a hole in his gut just the size of Smiley's sword.

There I was, just eleven years old and an orphan, with no place to live, because Smiley and some of his friends knocked down our house. So what was I supposed to do? Only thing I could: find those two wizards Mum always told me about. She'd warned me long ago somethin' might happen to her and Dad. She told me if it did, I was to go to Mike an' Pat, they'd take care of me. So I set off for their tower. Didn't take me long to get there, just three days, but I was so hungry and worn out, I passed out on their doorstep.

Next thing I remember was waking up in a bed, a real bed, and I was warm. The air smelled like marsh gas mixed with sour wine and something worse. An old man, who had more hair on his chin than on his head, was feeling my forehead.

"Are you Mike?" I asked.

He raised his droopy eyebrows and said, "My name is Mikastinal."

"And my name is Patrinadikos," said another man, who stood behind the first.

"Yeah. Mike and Pat."

The two looked at each other, then back at me.

"Only one person ever called us by those names," said the first man.

I smiled. "My mum."

"Is she well?" asked Pat.

"No, she's been dead for a year. My dad's dead, too. That's why I'm here. Mum said if I was ever in trouble, I was to come to you."

Pat and Mike looked at each other again with dropped jaws.

I settled into a nice, comfortable life with them. Their last apprentice had just died–I didn't want to know how or why–so I took over his duties. The two wizards did teach me more about potions and medicines than Mum had, and I earned a little money on the side from what I learned.

Things were going well until I was almost fifteen. That's when Mike and Pat noticed I wasn't a little girl anymore. Do you have any idea what it's like running from two old men?

"I have never had any reason to run from humans," Antee said, with a haughty toss of his head.

"You're lucky," I mumbled.

Things really got difficult. Mike would chase me around the kitchen. Pat would corner me in the library. Finally, they had it out with each other, a battle of magic. There are supposed to be rules for that. Pat stuck to the rules. Mike didn't. He had a spell ready and waiting in case the battle went against him.

You wouldn't believe the ruckus those two caused: lightning flashing everywhere, balls of blue and red fire flying in and out of windows, floor shaking, trees cracking. I doubt anyone within two hundred miles slept that night. Mike an' Pat did a few spells I didn't know they knew. If I hadn't been the prize in the fight, I would've enjoyed the show.

It came to a point where Pat had forced Mike to his knees. I figured the battle was about over. Was I wrong! Mike looked up at Pat, grinned, then used his reserve spell. Mike mumble some words I didn't know—though by the look on Pat's face, *he* did—and pointed at me. I felt as if he'd knocked the breath out of me. I hit the floor and threw up.

Mike glared at Pat. "Now she's mine."

Pat looked as if he were ready to explode. "How could you do that to her!"

"Do what?" I gasped.

"He has put a curse on you. Any man who touches you..."

"Except me," Mike interrupted.

I thought Pat was going to kill Mike with a look.

"Except him," Pat continued, "will instantly burst into flames and burn to death."

"She belongs to me, or to no one."

I wanted to ram my fist down his throat until he choked.

Pat grabbed Mike, and blue lightning started crawling all over them. Mike fought back with red lightning. With an explosion that nearly dropped the ceiling on my head, the two wizards turned into a little heap of black ash.

"How dreadful!" Antee said sympathetically.

"Yes, and the smell was worse than...a two-week-old fish." I almost said 'than dragon's breath,' but I'm not that stupid.

The tower started creaking, and the stones started to fall. I made a dash for the door, just in time to keep from being squashed.

Now I was in worse trouble than before. No home, no family, and cursed besides. I had to eat, so I just started my own business of selling potions and medicines, following in Mum's footsteps.

"I am slightly confused," Antee said, propping his chin up with one of his foreclaws. "Since Mike was killed in the battle, why are you still suffering from the curse?"

"Don't you know anything about magic?" I asked sarcastically. "Regular spells end at the maker's death, but not curses. Mike made the curse, so he's the only one who could dispel it."

Antee's eyes swirled brightly. "Ah, I see. Mike is dead and cannot remove the curse."

"Now you understand."

Things went pretty well, until one night I was sleeping in a village where I'd just delivered a set of twins. A young man decided he'd share my bed whether I wanted him or not. He had a surprise coming. No sooner did he grab me than he looked like someone had dipped him in oil and put a torch to him. He creamed so loud, he woke up the whole village. The hut burned down with him in it.

I fled before the villagers reached the hut, but rumors about what might have happened started spreading. Every once in a while, a man would try to force himself on me, but he never got farther that one touch.

After that, people weren't quite as friendly as before. I made enough to live on, just barely, but I didn't have any friends. A really miserable way to live.

One day, I was near the palace when I was stopped by some guards, out collecting taxes. The king liked to squeeze everything he could out of his subjects. A bad-tempered guy, the king. I guess any man would be, if he hadn't ever had a woman.

Anyway, these guards really loved their work, and took everything they could from the peasants. And who do you suppose was in charge? Smiley. The same guard who'd killed my dad.

"Where's your man, slut?" Smiley asked, with a leer that told me I was in trouble again.

I wanted to kill him, but I'm not a fool. "I don't have a man. I'm a healer."

"Really? I'll wager you have the cure for what ails me." He started loosening his belt.

"Don't touch me, if you want to live."

He grinned, undid his pants–I suppose he thought I'd be impressed–and slammed me up against him.

He couldn't say I didn't warn him.

While Smiley was still blazing like a bonfire, two other guards tried to grab me, and joined him in his fire dance. At that point, someone must have hit me on the head.

I woke up in a room as black, cold, and damp as the bottom of a well at midnight. The place stank worse than any stable I'd ever slept in. My head felt like someone was still pounding on it. I was hanging by a rope around my wrists, my feet barely dragging the floor. I tried to yell, but I could barely breathe, hanging like that.

I don't know how long I was there before someone opened a door and walked in. After the torchlight stopped tearing at my eyes, I stared at my visitor. Had to be the king. No one else would wear those silks, furs, jewels, and lace.

"You are responsible for murdering three of my guards," he said in a tone colder than the dungeon.

"Wasn't my fault. I'm cursed. I told them not to touch me, but they wouldn't listen."

"Cursed? How so?"

I didn't answer right away, which was a dumb mistake.

He gave a nod to someone I couldn't see behind me. The rope went slack, and I landed in a heap on the muddy floor. My arms hurt like hundreds of thorns were poking the skin. My legs were jelly, and my body felt like I'd been massaged by a rock slide.

Suddenly, I was jerked up in the air again, and my brain and stomach changed places.

"Answer my questions," the king said softly, threateningly.

My throat was so raw, when I tried to talk, I could barely make a squeak. "Any man who touches me burns up."

"Really. Rather unusual. Why were you cursed?"

Eventually, I told him the whole story; but not before he'd had me dropped and pulled back up again a few more times, used heated irons on my belly, and a cat-o-nine tails on my back. The king thought Mike's curse was real funny. If I could've touched him with my foot, it would've been worth dying, just to see him burn.

That's where you come in, Antee. The king decided to do what's always done when dragons come to the neighborhood: bribe them with a virgin, to leave as quickly as possible. See, the king figure he'd be rid of two problems at once. He'd punish me for killing his guards, and convince you to leave his territory. A very cunning man, the king.

He got four women, who looked as if they could take on a legion barehanded and win, to drag me out here and chain me to these posts. And he even came out to gloat for a while, before he went back to the castle. He's probably watching right now.

So here I am, just waiting for you to end my misery.

Steamy tears formed at the corners of Antee's eyes, which glowed with the sunset. "I have never heard such a tale a woe."

"Yeah, my life's been hard. So could you do what you came here for?"

"It grieves me greatly that I must do so, but you are a virgin and I do crave untainted flesh. I hope that you will find it in your heart to forgive me."

"Just be quick, please." I stared at the ground, feeling the heat of his breath. Suddenly, a thought hit me like cold water on a hot day. "Wait! You're a dragon, right?"

"I would think that is obvious."

"And you've got all the powers dragons usually have?"

Antee gave a smoky sniff of disdain, making my eyes water.

"Including the power to change shape?"

He shot me his puzzled look again. "Of course, but I do not see of what benefit that particular ability will be to you."

"So how about you turn yourself into a man and take my virginity?"

It was hard to read his expression. I imagined it was a cross between disgust at the thought of rutting with a two-legged creature, and amusement that I'd had the gall to suggest such a thing.

"Hey, for a human, I'm not that bad looking," I said, my pride wounded.

Antee swung his head around the stakes I was chained to so he could look me over real good. After all, my torn, singed dress didn't hide much. "You are indeed well formed for a human."

"Don't strain yourself giving me compliments. So, would you like to be the first to take me?"

He stood on his haunches again, put his claw over his heart, and bowed his head slightly. "I know that you intend to honor me, but I must decline your offer."

"But why?"

"Any man who touches you bursts into flames. I have no desire to immolate myself."

"Antee, think. You wouldn't really be a man. You're a dragon, no matter what shape you take. And dragons aren't hurt by fire."

He scratched his bony jaw thoughtfully. "That is quite true."

"If you took me, I wouldn't be a virgin anymore, and the curse would be broken. You could find another virgin to eat."

"Indeed!" His eyes glittered with interest. "Do you have someone specific in mind?"

"Well, do you only eat females?"

"It is not essential that the virgin is female."

I grinned and felt warm all over. "Did you know the king isn't married yet? As a matter of fact, he hasn't been with a woman at all."

The gleam from Antee's teeth nearly blinded me. "Truly? A virgin of royal blood?"

"You bet. Why? Do royal virgins taste better?"

His tongue flicked in and out, his eyes bulged, and his voice sounded like a greedy little kid. "Oh my dear sweet soon-to-be former virgin, royal virgins are an absolute delicacy!"

I grinned and said, "I think you and I are going to be good friends."

Antee broke my chains, and gently grasped my in his front claw. Even though it was twilight, the guards on the walls must have seen what was happening, because I heard them cheering the dragon. Antee launched himself into the cool night air and flew away from the castle.

When he'd spotted a cave that suited him, he landed and let go of me. I sat on the ground for a moment, stunned from my first ride in the sky. While I recovered, Antee turned himself into a dark-haired man, tall and lean and handsome enough to make my heart ache. He picked me up, carried me into the cave, and ended my curse. That's a night I'll never forget. Wouldn't want to!

Afterward, we flew to the palace, where I introduced the king to Antee. The dragon was delighted; the king wasn't. I almost felt sorry for him–almost, but not quite.

I've been with Antee for over a year now and have loved every minute. I've traveled to new places, places I'd only dreamed of seeing, and my nighttime activities have been, well, let's just say I wouldn't trade Antee for all the ordinary men in the world.

Just one thing's been bothering me for the last few months.

What do you think a dragon-human half-breed will look like?

About the Author

 Deborah Millitello wrote her first SF story, her first poem, and her first play when she was in fourth grade, and she's been writing ever since. She loves gardening, growing herbs, berries, and orchard fruits, making jams and marmalades, baking, knitting, crocheting, good music, hot tea, and of course, reading. She lives with her husband Carl, who has put up with her writing obsession for almost forty-five years. She lives in a small town in Southern Illinois and works at a doctors' answering service.

Her first book, *Thief's Luck*, was published in 2006. Her second book, *The Water Girl*, was published in 2015.

.

Word Posse Fun Fact

Marion Zimmer Bradley was one of the most mentoring writers in the field of SF & F. There are scores of writers who sold their first stories to her, including me. She offered guidance and criticism that helped me and many others become better writers. I was fortunate enough to meet her once at her home in the Bay area. I am so grateful for what I learned from her.